The Regent's Daughter

JEAN PLAIDY HAS ALSO WRITTEN

BEYOND THE BLUE MOUNTAINS
(A novel about early settlers in Australia)

DAUGHTER OF SATAN
(A novel about the persecution of witches and Puritans in the 16th and 17th centuries)

THE SCARLET CLOAK
(A novel of 16th century Spain, France and England

Stories of Victorian England
IT BEGAN IN VAUXHALL GARDENS
LILITH

THE GOLDSMITH'S WIFE
(The story of Jane Shore)

EVERGREEN GALLANT
(The story of Henri of Navarre)

The Medici Trilogy
Catherine de' Medici
MADAME SERPENT
THE ITALIAN WOMAN } Also available in one volume
QUEEN JEZEBEL

The Lucrezia Borgia Series
MADONNA OF THE SEVEN HILLS } Also available in one volume
LIGHT ON LUCREZIA

The Ferdinand and Isabella Trilogy
CASTILLE FOR ISABELLA
SPAIN FOR THE SOVEREIGNS } Also available in one volume
DAUGHTERS OF SPAIN

The French Revolution Series
LOUIS THE WELL-BELOVED
THE ROAD TO COMPIÈGNE
FLAUNTING, EXTRAVAGANT QUEEN

The Tudor Novels
Katharine of Aragon
KATHARINE, THE VIRGIN WIDOW
THE SHADOW OF THE POMEGRANATE } Also available in one volume
THE KING'S SECRET MATTER

MURDER MOST ROYAL
(Anne Boleyn and Catharine Howard)

THE SIXTH WIFE
(Katharine Parr)

ST THOMAS'S EVE
(Sir Thomas More)

THE SPANISH BRIDEGROOM
(Philip II and his first three wives)

GAY LORD ROBERT
(Elizabeth and Leicester)

THE THISTLE AND THE ROSE
(Margaret Tudor and James IV)

MARY, QUEEN OF FRANCE
(Queen of Louis XII)

The Mary Queen of Scots Series
ROYAL ROAD TO FOTHERINGAY
THE CAPTIVE QUEEN OF SCOTS

The Regent's Daughter

JEAN PLAIDY

G. P. PUTNAM'S SONS   NEW YORK

G. P. Putnam's Sons
Publishers Since 1838
200 Madison Avenue
New York, NY 10016

First American Edition 1989

Library of Congress Cataloging-in-Publication Data

Plaidy, Jean, date.
The regent's daughter.

Bibliography: p.
1. Charlotte Augusta, Princess of Great Britain,
1796–1817—Fiction.   2. Great Britain—History—1789–
1820—Fiction.   I. Title.
PR6015.I3R43   1989   823′.914   88-32199
ISBN 0-399-13428-X

Printed in the United States of America
1   2   3   4   5   6   7   8   9   10

CONTENTS

Father and Daughter   9
Charlotte's Household   24
Minney, Prinney and Mrs. Fitzherbert   43
The Old Girls and the Begum   68
The Will of the People   88
Oatlands   101
Summer by the Sea   109
The Arrival of Mercer   125
The Rival Dukes and Mary Anne   141
Maria Triumphant   161
Mystery in St. James's   173
Death of an Old Girl   178
The Gallant Captain Hesse   189
Charlotte in Revolt   210
The Battle for Miss Knight   236
A Letter to the *Morning Chronicle*   248
Encounter of Two Carriages   259
Slender Billy   271
The Hasty Betrothal   287
Enter and Exit Leopold   298
The Dismissal of Orange   316
Night Flight   331
The Reconciliation   344
Charlotte in Love   355
Married Bliss   366
The End   377
Bibliography   382

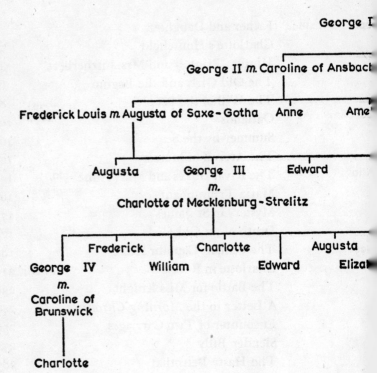

George I

George II *m.* Caroline of Ansbach

Frederick Louis *m.* Augusta of Saxe-Gotha   Anne   Ame

Augusta   George III   Edward
m.
Charlotte of Mecklenburg-Strelitz

Frederick   Charlotte   Augusta

George IV   William   Edward   Eliza
m.
Caroline of
Brunswick

Charlotte

ophia Dorothea of Celle

Sophia Dorothea

Caroline   George   William,   Mary   Louisa
                                  Duke of Cumberland

lliam   Henry   Frederick   Caroline Matilda,
                                                  Queen of Denmark

iest   Adolphus   Sophia   Alfred
      Augustus   Mary   Octavius   Amelia

Father and Daughter

'THERE are worse people in the world than your snuffy old grandmother,' said the Princess Charlotte, giving George Keppel a push with her elbow.

George said nothing. He was never quite sure of Charlotte. If he agreed with her too readily she would be angry. 'You have no opinions of your own,' she would say. 'You think you have to a ... agree with me.' And when she stammered he knew she was really angry. 'How shall I ever know what people are thinking if they always agree with me? Eh, George Keppel?' And when she did not have her own way she would kick the furniture in a sudden rage; but these moods were often worth while because they were over quickly and then she would laugh and be anxious to make up for what she would call 'a most regrettable display of my ill temper'. 'Why don't you tell me I'm an ill-tempered beast, George Keppel?'

Pretty Minney Seymour was a far more comfortable person, thought George Keppel.

The fact was that Charlotte was older than either of them; three years older than he was and about two older than Minney; and Charlotte was not only ten years old but the daughter of the Prince of Wales.

'Never forget,' said his grandmother, Lady de Clifford, the snuffy one to whom Charlotte had referred, 'that Her Royal Highness could one day be your queen.'

It was difficult to imagine Charlotte a queen, though she could be rather an arrogant little girl. She was not dainty like Minney; she leaped about rather awkwardly; she had pale blue eyes, hardly any eyebrows and lashes, and a very white skin. If she had had some colour in her face she would have been pretty, for she was very animated. But she had a way of leaning to one side which was not very graceful. She certainly was not his idea of a queen.

George and Charlotte had called with Lady de Clifford at Tilney Street, for Lady de Clifford was a friend and near neighbour of Mrs. Fitzherbert and it was only a short distance from Lady de Clifford's house in South Audley Street to Mrs. Fitzherbert's in Tilney Street and how pleasant for Minney to have children of her own age—or near enough—to play with while the two ladies enjoyed a *tête-à-tête* in Mrs. Fitzherbert's drawing room.

The three children were at the window looking out on the street when Charlotte had made her remark; it was obvious the other two knew that this was a preliminary to some revelation. Charlotte had a deep sense of the dramatic.

She turned from the window and gave each of them a little push. This was a sign that window gazing was over and Charlotte was ready to talk.

'Something is going to happen . . . soon,' she said dramatically, and as Minney looked alarmed, went on impatiently: 'It has nothing to do with you. I have heard nothing about *your* affair.'

'I'm going to stay with dear Mamma?' asked Minney fearfully.

'She is not your Mamma, however much you wish she were,' declared Charlotte. 'So let us have truth, Minney, *please.*'

'Yes,' said Minney meekly, 'but I do want to go on living here with Mamma . . . I mean Mrs. Fitzherbert. But I know I shall. Prinney says I shall and he won't let anything stop it.'

There was silence. Minney knew she should not have mentioned Prinney, who was Charlotte's father but behaved more as though he were Minney's. The complicated ways of adults were very difficult to understand and often caused misgivings to the young. Charlotte, who was always a little sad when Prinney was mentioned, was thinking of her father, that great and glittering personage of whom everyone whispered and for whose approval she longed. She remembered how when she was younger she had been received by him while he was at breakfast. There she had stood watching him, never failing to marvel at the wonder of his person: the colours of his cravat which lay in such elegant folds high about his neck so that she had the impression that his chin was trying to escape from it and that it would not let it; the pinkness of his face verging on red; and his pale blue eyes smiling at her kindly although they would rest only fleetingly on her. Her aim was to claim their attention and have them smile at her with love. He had a slightly turned-up nose which made her want to laugh and gave her pleasure because in some way it detracted from his great dignity and made him human; his tight buckskin breeches were so smooth and white and his legs in their fine stockings enormous, but most wonderful of all were the masses of curling hair from which came a faint but exquisite perfume; a few diamonds glittered on the whitest and most elegant of hands; this was the Prince of Wales, Charlotte's Papa and Minney's Prinney.

'It is the law which will decide,' said Charlotte quickly. 'And that is right and how it should be.'

Minney looked hurt and George Keppel said reassuringly: 'It's going to be all right, Minney. No one's going to take you from your Mamma.'

Charlotte shrugged her shoulders impatiently.

'*I* was going to tell you something,' she reminded them. 'I have not been allowed to see *my* Mamma. Oh, it is all very well for them to say she is indisposed, but I know that not to be so. Why must I not go to Blackheath? Why must she not visit me? There must be a reason.'

Minney and George waited for Charlotte to give it.

'It is because something is going on. Do you know what, Minney?'

Minney declared her innocence and one thing about Minney was that she *was* so innocent that one had to believe her.

'You should keep your ears open,' said Charlotte. 'It must be discussed with Mrs. F . . . Fitzherbert.'

She hesitated to say Mrs. Fitzherbert's name because she knew that that lady was deeply concerned in the troubles of her family. She believed that she ought to dislike her. But how could one dislike Mrs. Fitzherbert—that affectionate, comfortably shaped woman who was one of the few people in Charlotte's world who knew how to mingle affection and authority in a manner acceptable to young people. There were times, thought Charlotte, when she envied Minney Seymour, that was if she were allowed to stay with Mamma Fitzherbert which, Charlotte was fully aware, was not certain; and if Minney had to leave that loving guardianship she would be the most unhappy little girl in the world. Poor Minney! Charlotte was immediately touched by the sorrows of others. She could not pass a poor man, woman or child on the road without wanting to give them something. 'My dear Princess, restrain yourself,' was Lady de Clifford's constant warning.

She *must* restrain herself; there was so much she must learn; she was going to be Queen of England one day because it was certain that Papa and Mamma would have no more children. How could they, when they hated each other and never saw each other? She, young Charlotte, aged ten years, knew that the most important factor in her life was the relationship between her parents.

That was why she was so disturbed by what she had overheard.

It was true that she kept her eyes and ears open. Lady de Clifford would have a shock if she knew what her charge had discovered. She had found a means of reading the newspapers —and one could learn a great deal from them. When she visited Mamma at Blackheath she had a most unusual time; but then Mamma was a most unusual woman. There she was allowed to read the papers and see the cartoons, the lampoons, the prints which could be bought in the shops and the subject of these was very often the affairs of the Prince and Princess of Wales. Dignified Mrs. Fitzherbert was not exempt. Charlotte considered that it was not everyone whose father had two wives.

She had adjusted herself to her life: Carlton House where she was the Princess destined for a throne, where she had to be plagued by a bevy of tutors and never forget her great destiny; and Blackheath where life was conducted in the most eccentric manner, where she met strange people and for a brief hour or so every week tasted freedom. There she had enjoyed the passionate devotion of her wild mother ('Charlotte, my angel my love, my little baby. Why should they take you away from me?'), and they would weep together, but they mostly laughed and Mamma taught her to be most disrespectful to Grandmamma, whom she hated in any case (and she was one who was more snuffy than Lady de Clifford) and to the spinster aunts who alternately cooed over 'darling Charlotte' and criticized her manners, her stammer and the way she leaned to one side.

She looked forward to visits to Blackheath; and at the same time she longed for the approval of that glittering personality who was undoubtedly her father, for people were constantly remarking how alike they were and her own looking glass told her this was true.

Now she wanted to talk to her companions about the change in her life which she was fully aware was due to some development in the relationship between her mother and father; she wanted to learn whether George Keppel had discovered anything, or more likely Minney. For Minney lived here in Tilney Street where the Prince of Wales was the most constant visitor and it was certain that if something were happening he would discuss it with Mrs. Fitzherbert.

'There are a lot of wicked people in the world,' said Charlotte, 'and they are trying to make a mischief.'

Minney's pretty face was solemn, George's intent.

'Yes, and they are trying to punish my Mamma.'

'Why?' asked George.

'Why? Because she is the Princess of Wales, that's why. And they don't like her because she is a German and different . . . and she laughs a lot. Oh, you should come to Montague House. There is no place like Montague House, but because my Mamma is not like other people they hate her and want to harm her.'

'How will they harm her?' asked George.

'That's what I want to know, silly. I have to find out and save her from them.'

Minney's face puckered; she hated trouble.

Charlotte turned on her suddenly. Minney was everything that Charlotte was not—pretty, small, dainty and protected by the affection of her dear Mamma who was not her Mamma at all, but Mrs. Fitzherbert who had adopted her and might not be able to go on doing so.

'You might have discovered if you had not been so *deaf*. They must talk about it.'

'Charlotte, I haven't heard a word.'

'No, you silly little thing. You don't see anything. All you do is listen to your dear Mamma telling you not to worry because she won't let you go.'

Charlotte glowered and her long light brown hair fell about her face; she was really worried.

'Minney is not silly, Charlotte,' said George indignantly.

There! Even George, whom she always made do her bidding, was taking Minney's side. She felt a sudden anger against the pretty little girl and, seizing her ear, pinched it hard, at which Minney cried out and Charlotte was immediately contrite. 'It didn't hurt! Or d . . . did it? Poor little Minney, that was wicked of me. I'm talking about wicked people and I'm as b . . . bad.' She kissed Minney. 'Oh, I'm a beast, dear dear Minney. Let me look at your ear. Oh, it's red. I'll give you my . . . my . . . what shall I give you, Minney? What would you like best? Dear Minney, I did not mean to pinch your ear, but you should try to discover what's going on around you. It's important.'

'It's nothing, Charlotte,' said Minney, for the repentant

Charlotte was always irresistible, and a moment's discomfort
was worth while to bring the young Princess to this mood. 'It
doesn't hurt now and I will try to listen . . . I will really.'

George was looking on in some indignation. He loves
Minney, thought Charlotte, faintly jealous. Everybody loves
Minney. I suppose because she is good and so pretty.

'I want to know what is happening, why I am not allowed
to go to Montague House now, and what the Prince of Wales
says about it.'

'He wouldn't tell Minney.'

'No, stupid. But Minney is *there* and *they* will talk. All she
has to *do* is listen and pretend she is not.'

'That's deceitful.'

'Oh, don't be such a prig, Saint George Keppel.'

The door had opened and two ladies came into the room:
Lady de Clifford and Mrs. Fitzherbert.

Lady de Clifford's hazel eyes went at once to her charge and
she frowned slightly. I must be looking untidy again, thought
Charlotte. Poor Lady de Clifford was a dragon, but a
frightened dragon. So must it be when people wait on the
future Queen, thought the Princess. She must teach me discipline and at the same time not offend me mortally, or I
might remember it against her or her family when I come to
power.

Poor Lady de Clifford. Her turban was slightly awry. Why
did she wear the ugly old thing? There was too much rouge
on her ageing cheeks; it showed up the wrinkles; and she was
carrying the all important snuffbox in her hand. Snuffy old
thing! She was almost as fond of her snuff as that old ogre
Charlotte's grandmamma and namesake, the old Begum, as
Mamma called her. Only Mamma, whose English was not of
the best said 'de old Begum'. 'Old Begum,' Charlotte would
mutter to herself when she was face to face with that old
woman whom she supposed she hated more than any other
human being.

Charlotte always felt a strange emotion when she was in
Mrs. Fitzherbert's company. Mrs. Fitzherbert moved regally
like a Queen. In Charlotte's eyes she was beautiful . . . perhaps
the most beautiful woman in the world. The Prince of Wales
thought so and he was a connoisseur of beauty and elegance.
Her clothes were never flamboyant but always becoming;
she wore no rouge, but then she had the most perfect natural
complexion, that pink and white which no artificial adjuncts
could quite produce; and her hair was lovely, a mass of gold-
coloured waves, unpowdered and completely natural, not

puffed out with false pieces. And although she was beautiful she had a look of what Charlotte thought of as a mother. She was comfortably plump with a magnificent bosom—soft and pillowy, thought Charlotte, to cry against, which was perhaps one of the reasons why the Prince of Wales loved her so much; he was always weeping, in the most elegant way of course. Even she had watched his performance occasionally with the utmost admiration. Mrs. Fitzherbert was the complete opposite of the Princess of Wales. There could not have been two women less alike—and how strange that they should both be her father's wives. But were they? Nobody seemed absolutely sure ... except Mrs. Fitzherbert, of course, who would never have received the Prince so intimately in her house if she did not believe it.

What a strange family I have! thought Charlotte.

Now Mrs. Fitzherbert's eyes had gone to Minney and they were soft and maternal. Charlotte would have liked them to look at her in that way. She had her own mother, but in spite of the fact that the Princess of Wales covered her with kisses, fed her with her favourite sweetmeats, declared that she lived for her darling Charlotte's visits, she was not as motherly as dignified Mrs. Fitzherbert was towards Minney.

There was a change in Minney too. She was no longer the meek one, the one who had to take the most humble part in any game, who was subjected to the bullying of Charlotte and patronizing protection of George Keppel. She was the loved one now.

Mrs. Fitzherbert, her eyes still on Minney, said: 'His Royal Highness will soon be here. You should be ready if he wishes to see you.'

Minney expressed delight, but the main emotion of Charlotte and George was apprehension.

Lady de Clifford's anxious eyes were on her charge.

'Your hair is very untidy, Princess Charlotte. And may I see your hands.'

Charlotte held them out and Lady de Clifford tut-tutted in exasperation.

'The Princess is so energetic,' said Mrs. Fitzherbert with a smile. 'They should be washed. His Highness would most certainly notice. He is *so* fastidious.'

Charlotte forgot that she had been about to protest—a gesture of defiance to show George and Minney that she did not care. Because Mrs. Fitzherbert had spoken one had to obey. She thought fleetingly how different it would have been if Mrs. Fitzherbert had been her father's only wife and she

had been that lady's daughter. To wish this were so would be
disloyal to dear Mamma who loved her so violently, yet how
much happier—how much more *tidy*—it would have been.
But, thought Charlotte, immediately ashamed of disloyalty to
Mamma, not so exciting. And Charlotte liked excitement.

'I should go at once, dear, and then you will be ready when
His Highness comes.'

So Charlotte was led away by Lady de Clifford, leaving
Minney and George—those little paragons who had managed
to keep clean—alone with Mrs. Fitzherbert.

Charlotte washed her hands in the water which was
brought and Lady de Clifford began a long monologue to
which Charlotte did not listen entirely, just enough to know
that it consisted of the usual entreaties to remember this and
not forget that when in the presence of His Royal Highness so
that she did not shame herself or her governess.

The long light brown hair had to be combed and made
tidy. 'Princess Charlotte, do stand straight. His Highness has
noticed . . .' 'Princess Charlotte, when you begin to stutter
speak slowly. It should help to correct the fault.'

Lady de Clifford took an extra pinch of snuff—always
so useful in moments of tension. Charlotte's gown was a little
grubby. His Highness, that arbiter of elegance, would notice.
He would be reminded of the distressing fact that although
the Princess Charlotte looked like him she had inherited the
habits of her mother. It was to be hoped that any unfortunate
characteristics she had inherited from the Princess of Wales
would be suppressed.

She looked critically at her charge. A pity the Princess had
not remembered that visits to Tilney Street could often mean
that she might meet her father, and that on those occasions
she should not indulge in the rough horseplay for which she
seemed to have such a fancy. But there was nothing further to
be done. At least Her Highness was clean.

'We should now go to Mrs. Fitzherbert's drawing room,' said
Lady de Clifford. 'Come, Your Highness.'

When he comes, thought Charlotte, I will sweep such a
curtsey that will astonish him. Not like last time when I
almost fell over doing it. She giggled at the thought, but it
was a nervous giggle; it had been most shaming. She knew
why she so often caught a certain expression in his eyes when
they were on her; it was as though he had to force himself to
look, force himself to speak affectionately. It was because she
was reminding him of someone whose existence he preferred
to forget: her mother.

She walked sedately to Mrs. Fitzherbert's drawing room with Lady de Clifford and told herself: This time I will try to please him.

Lady de Clifford opened the door and stood aside for the Princess to enter. Charlotte took a step into the room and then stopped. The scene which faced her was unexpected. Minney's high-pitched laughter was mingled with deep chuckles of pleasure and the occupants of the room were so absorbed in each other that they had not heard the opening of the door.

Seated on an ornate chair which Charlotte knew was kept for one person only was a large figure, sparkling, handsome, elegant, scented. The Prince of Wales had arrived while Lady de Clifford was tidying her charge. On his knee was seated Minney, one arm about his neck, her face close to his, far more at ease than she was in the company of his daughter. She was pulling the curls of his wig and saying in a very loud voice: 'Why, you are a very *curly* Prinney today.' How dared timid Minney whom *she* could reduce to terror by a sharp word or a pinch of the ear, behave so . . . so familiarly towards the Prince of Wales! And there was that bold George Keppel leaning against the Prince of Wales with his hand resting on one elegant white buckskinned thigh and laughing as though the great figure in the chair was of no more importance than his snuffy old grandmother.

Charlotte's impulse was to stride towards them, send George Keppel flying and pull Minney off her father's knee. Surely if that were anyone's place it was Charlotte's? But when had she ever sat on his knee? Vague memories came back of days long, long ago when she was a baby and had been taken to see Grandpapa and her father had been there and had set himself out to amuse her. But the memories were so vague that she might have dreamed them.

She did not move; she knew she dared not. And a great pride came to her. If he preferred silly Minney Seymour to his own daughter, let him.

Mrs. Fitzherbert, aware of her standing there, came over to her and laid a hand on her shoulder. Charlotte wanted to turn and bury her face against that delicately perfumed plumply elegant figure.

'And here is the Princess Charlotte herself.' As though, thought Charlotte, she was the one he had come to see. But it was not true. Mrs. Fitzherbert was merely pretending because she understood.

Charlotte came forward and curtsied clumsily. George

Keppel moved away from the Prince's chair; Minney remained clinging to him.

There was a change in Mrs. Fitzherbert's drawing room.

The Prince held out his hand and Charlotte approached him. Minney slid off his knee then and went to stand beside Mrs. Fitzherbert.

'I trust you are well,' said the Prince. 'There is no need to ask. Your looks answer for you.'

'I am well, Y . . . Your Highness.'

How gauche, he thought. And that stutter!

He could not help the cold note which crept into his voice when he spoke to her. She brought back such unpleasant memories. That woman they had forced him to marry. His first sight of her. Coarse and over-rouged, her eyebrows crudely blackened; her hideous white gown; and the immediate knowledge that she was not personally clean. His nose twitched at the memory. How could they have done that to him! He had known it had to be a German Princess but why had Caroline of Brunswick had to fall to his lot? He would never forgive Lord Malmesbury, his father's ambassador, for not warning him. And the wedding—which he had almost refused to continue with and the wedding night! God preserve me from memory of it! he thought. In fact he could remember little of it for the only way he could face it had been by reducing himself to a state of intoxication. *She* said he had spent the greater part of his wedding night under the grate. She may have been right for he was certain that he would have preferred the grate to a bed shared with her. But by exerting tremendous will power and subduing his finer feelings he had managed to consummate the marriage and had actually lived with the creature until she became pregnant.

And the result was this gangling girl, this hoyden; who looked so like himself yet reminded him whenever he was in her company of that woman.

He could not take to her for that reason. Normally he loved children. He would play with dearest Minney when he came to Tilney Street; and he would look for her, flattening her nose against the glass when she was watching out for *him*. With Maria and Minney and himself it was a family circle— the sort of home, he told himself, he had always longed for, so different from the dreary atmosphere in his father's royal palaces—or even the ceremonies he could not escape at Carlton House.

And now here was Charlotte spoiling the illusion that he

was in the heart of his family—a reminder of her mother, the last person in the world of whom he wished to think.

'The children have all been playing together,' said Mrs. Fitzherbert, sensing his discomfiture and doing her best to dispel it. She was reminding him that he must not blame Charlotte for her mother's conduct; and she was right.

They would play a game together—the sort of game he played with Minney. Oh no, he could not play games with Charlotte. She would be whooping round the drawing room irritating him and he might let her know it.

So he could only ask Charlotte how she was proceeding with her studies and her riding. He talked about horses for some time, but Charlotte noticed how he avoided looking at her. Mrs. Fitzherbert noticed too.

And after a while the Prince rose and said he would leave. He kissed Charlotte coldly on the cheek; he tweaked George Keppel's hair when the boy bowed to him, to show that he need not stand on the ceremony his grandmother had warned him he must show; he picked Minney up and held her over his head while she giggled and screamed: 'Put me down, Prinney. You're dropping me.'

And then he went out with Mrs. Fitzherbert, slipping his arm through hers and calling her 'dear love'.

And Charlotte, watching, felt a black anger rise in her that was half sorrow, because here was a family circle from which she was shut out.

* * *

George Keppel was with his grandmother waiting for Charlotte to join them; she had imperiously dismissed them, implying that she had something to say to Mrs. Fitzherbert.

Charlotte stood in the drawing room with the blue ruched satin on the walls and the gilded furniture which seemed royal in the most comfortable way, just like Mrs. Fitzherbert herself.

Charlotte knew that the Prince had curtailed his visit because she was there and she wondered whether he had implied to Mrs. Fitzherbert that he was displeased to find her entertaining his daughter.

Charlotte believed in saying what she meant. The niceties of diplomacy were not for her. It was not honest, she had long ago decided, to say one thing and mean another; and she would not be dishonest if she could help it.

'He left because I was here,' she burst out.

'He had only called in for a short time,' Mrs. Fitzherbert assured her. 'He did mention that.'

'Yes, when he knew I was here.'

'My dear Princess, surely a father would be pleased to see his own daughter.'

'Not this father; not this daughter.' She laughed. 'We don't want to pretend, do we, Madam.'

Mrs. Fitzherbert did not answer, but she looked sad.

'Because,' went on Charlotte, 'if we did, it would be no use, would it? The truth remains however much we try to hide it.'

She lifted her head defiantly. Mrs. Fitzherbert had taken a step towards her, her beautiful face softly maternal, her hand a little unsteady as she laid it on Charlotte's arm. Charlotte's defiance suddenly deserted her; she flung herself against Mrs. Fitzherbert and hid her face. She needed every bit of restraint to prevent herself bursting into tears.

'I'm his daughter,' she said in a muffled voice, 'and he doesn't *like* me. It's the truth. No one can deny it.'

Mrs. Fitzherbert placed a hand tenderly on Charlotte's head and held her against her. She did not deny Charlotte's words; she was mutely telling her that it was so and that she was offering her sympathy.

'Why,' cried Charlotte. 'Why . . . *why?*'

Mrs. Fitzherbert did not answer. What need was there for an answer? Charlotte knew it already and was not so much asking a question as expressing indignation at such injustice.

Charlotte gave herself up to the luxury of this sympathetic embrace.

Then she said: 'You . . . you could perhaps speak to him.'

She looked up into Mrs. Fitzherbert's face and saw there were tears in the lady's eyes; this was too much. Charlotte began to cry in a quiet, sorrowful and resigned way

Then they were sitting side by side on Mrs. Fitzherbert's blue satin couch, Mrs. Fitzherbert's arm about her while they both wiped their eyes.

'You . . . you will speak to him?'

Mrs. Fitzherbert nodded.

'If anyone could make him like me, you could.'

'I will do my best,' promised Mrs. Fitzherbert.

Charlotte smiled wryly and thought: People should not have to be persuaded to love their children.

After a while she took her leave of Mrs. Fitzherbert and went and joined George and Lady de Clifford in the carriage.

*   *   *

She was silent during the journey back to South Audley

Street. George noticed the traces of tears on her face and was apprehensive. Charlotte rarely wept except in sudden anger and then the mood was over almost as soon as it had begun. But it was unusual for her to be so quiet. Clearly this mood was due to her encounter with her father.

Lady de Clifford did the talking. Her turban shook with dismay. The Princess had not been a credit to her governesses. Upon her word, it would not surprise her to receive a summons from His Highness to be told that she was not considered suitable to have the charge of his daughter. Oh, no, that would certainly not surprise her, for by the manner in which the Princess Charlotte had behaved, he would most certainly be right.

'Perhaps,' said Lady de Clifford, 'I should resign. Perhaps I should admit my unworthiness before it is pointed out to me.'

'Perhaps you should,' snapped Charlotte suddenly.

George looked from his grandmother to the Princess. In a moment Charlotte would leap up and fling her arms round Lady de Clifford's neck, kiss her rouged cheeks and beg forgiveness. That was Charlotte's way. Her dear, dear Cliffy must not talk of leaving her. Charlotte would be desolate without her.

Charlotte did no such thing, but she allowed the drive to proceed in silence.

Oh dear, thought George, she *is* put out. And he longed for Minney's comfortable society.

In his grandmother's house he was aware of the seriousness of the occasion.

When they were alone together, she said, 'I'm angry, George Keppel. I'm boiling over with anger.'

'With whom are you angry?' George asked fearfully.

'With fate,' she said mysteriously.

'That's a funny thing to be angry with,' said George with a giggle.

'It's not funny in the least. It's t ... tragic. You have to soothe your feelings; and that is what we are going to do now.'

'How do you soothe feelings?'

'I'll show you.' She was mysterious. 'I'm glad,' she went on, 'that we haven't got that silly little Minney Seymour under our feet.'

'Oh,' protested George mildly.

'I know you think she's pretty and you want to protect her and all that, which is just what you would do. *She* doesn't need protecting. She has Mrs. Fitzherbert to do that, and I can tell you this, George Keppel, she's the best p ... protector anyone could have.'

'All right,' said George. 'Where are we going?'

'Follow me,' said Charlotte.

'Where?'

'You don't ask questions. You obey your future Sovereign.'

She laughed suddenly, her resentment momentarily forgotten. She could always make George do what she wished by referring to herself as his future Sovereign.

She herself was not certain where she was going. All she knew was that she wanted to soothe her hurt feelings. She wanted some sort of revenge.

Her steps led her to the kitchen—always an attractive place. The servants at South Audley Street were in awe of her and at the same time they were delighted when she came down and ate fresh cakes as they came from the oven.

She pushed open the door of the kitchen and looked inside. There was no one there. But on a baking tin lay two juicy looking lamb chops.

'Those,' she said, 'will be for your Grandmamma's supper, I'll swear. There's nothing she likes so well.'

She began to imitate Lady de Clifford which she could do very well. Mimicry was a gift she had inherited from her father and he would have been amused to see how good she was; but she could never bring it off in his company. Now her voice was exactly that of Lady de Clifford as she whined that the Prince of Wales would dismiss her for failing in her duty.

'And she has, George Keppel, because I am rather w ... wicked, you know.'

'You are not wicked at heart,' George told her.

'You will see,' she said. 'Go and fetch the pepper pot. It is in the cupboard. I have seen them put it there. And be quick, George Keppel. This is a secret mission.'

He stared at her and he saw that she was growing really angry. Oh dear, why could they not play sensible games? But she liked rough ones with forfeits and she invented the most difficult tasks which had to be performed to her satisfaction.

He came back with the pepper pot.

'Sprinkle it over the chops,' she commanded.

He did so lightly. 'Again,' she cried. And then: 'Again.'

'It will spoil the chops,' he warned.

'George Keppel, will you disobey your future Queen?'

'No,' said George, 'but it will spoil the chops.'

'There are worse things spoilt in this world than chops.

Here, give it to me.' She took it and with an almost demoni-
acal delight, showered pepper over Lady de Clifford's supper.

'Someone is coming,' said George.

She dashed to the cupboard, put the pot out of sight and
made for the door.

Outside they started to laugh.

George sneezed and Charlotte rolled about with delight.
She pushed him roughly and he sneezed again.

Someone was coming; they ran up the stairs gasping and
laughing.

'Poor Grandmamma . . .' began George.

Charlotte frowned. 'They will taste horrible. They will be
spoilt. But she will order some more to be cooked.'

It was a wicked thing to have done, she reasoned, but in
some way it soothed her. It made her think of something besides the cold look in her father's eyes when they rested on her
and the sound of Lady de Clifford's voice droning on about
her inadequacies.

Charlotte's Household

AT Lower Lodge Windsor there was less freedom than in
Carlton House where one could pay visits to South Audley
Street, Mrs. Fitzherbert's house in Tilney Street and Montague House at Blackheath. The last though, had been out
of bounds for some time and that was due to the mystery
which Charlotte was determined to solve. There was some
reason why they would not allow her to visit her mother.

They had never liked her going; she knew that. Grandmamma would have stopped it if she dared but Grandpapa,
dear old Grandpapa, who mumbled and sometimes talked so
fast that he was impossible to follow, and could behave in such
a strange manner, had put his foot down and said she and her
mother were not to be separated. And Grandpapa was after
all the King. But now even he must be agreeing that she
should be kept from her mother.

Why?

Here at Windsor she was in the heart of the family and had
to remember constantly that she was the Princess Charlotte,
one day destined to be the Queen. She had to learn how to be
an example to her subjects.

'Are kings and queens examples then?' she asked the Bishop,
Dr. Fisher, who was in charge of her education. Secretly
she called him Bish-Up—with the accent on the last syllable;
and she could not enjoy his company for he preached con-
tinuously and he was never satisfied with her progress and, as
she told Mrs. Campbell, her favourite of the ladies who
worked under the directorship of Lady de Clifford, one would
think he were training her to be the abbess of a convent
rather than a queen of England.

'My dear Princess Charlotte,' he had intoned in what she called his very reverend voice, 'it is indeed the duty of all rulers to be a shining example to their subjects.'

'It is to be hoped that they were not always so, for some were very wicked.' She laughed mischievously, there was nothing she liked so much as an argument with some of her pompous mentors and if she could prove them wrong—which was often the case—she would chuckle over her triumph for days. 'There was George I who imprisoned his wife for thirty years for doing once that which was a habit with him . . .'

Oh delightful! The poor man was surely about to blush. She hurried on: 'And George II who was ruled by his wife and didn't know it. And . . .' Well, she must not mention poor Grandpapa who behaved so oddly and kind as he was, such strange behaviour could scarcely be used as an example.

'We have had great monarchs,' he reminded her, 'and you would do well to consider them.'

'There was Queen Elizabeth. Oh, I think of her often. I read of her. But you must admit, dear Bish-Up, that she could be a little wicked sometimes. Perhaps it is necessary to be a little wicked sometimes. I do hope so. Being good all the time is a little dull. Although it is nice to come back and be good after one has been a little wicked.'

The Bishop frowned and turned her attention to theology.

I disconcert them, thought Charlotte. They do wonder what sort of woman I shall be when I grow up. I suspect that they would like to punish me very severely, but they do remember that I will one day be the Queen.

The fact was that one did not really want to mould oneself on anyone. One should be oneself. But what am I? wondered Charlotte, apart from a Royal Highness one day to be a Majesty? It is hard to separate oneself from that.

She really preferred Dr. Nott to Dr. Fisher because he was more humble, less sure of himself, and he really cared that she should improve; and he it was who had pointed out to her that she had a tendency to disguise the truth. It was difficult, of course, because when she was with her mother she had to pretend not to care for her father; she had to listen to disparaging remarks about him and pretend to be amused by them; and when she was with her father she must never betray the fact that she had seen her mother; and this tended to embarrass her, for she was so anxious not to refer to her mother that she sometimes found herself led into the indiscretion of doing so. Then she would try to extricate herself by telling some barefaced lie such as: 'But I have not seen the

Princess of Wales for weeks'—when she had seen her but a few days before. Dr. Nott took her to task for this habit; she must overcome it; to lie was a sin.

'Yes, yes, dear Notty,' she would cry, 'but the Prince does not want to hear that I have seen my mother. I was thinking of his comfort, and should one not think of the comfort of one's parents? One must honour one's father and mother, but you must admit, Notty, that when they don't honour each other that puts their offspring in a delicate situation.'

He was not going to be involved, dear Notty, who was far too meek to teach the Princess Charlotte; and because she was fond of him even though she liked to disconcert him now— she was always quick to come to his rescue and would add: 'But I will try to be truthful. I do realize that one should be.'

Oh dear, she thought, how shut in I am at Windsor. And what is happening at Montague House?

She smiled, thinking of it—her mother's home. The Princess of Wales embracing her when she arrived. 'My angel, my pet, let me look at you. Why you are lovely ... lovely ... though the image of your father! Ha, ha, he could not disown you if he tried. And he'd like to ... just to put me out. But he can't, not with those eyes of yours. You're one of *them*, my precious darling.'

Hot, rather suffocating embraces, not always very fragrant. Mamma did not like bathing and her women found it very difficult to make her change her clothes. 'Come along in, my sweetest.' Arms entwined into the drawing room, which was not really like a royal drawing room.

'We are having a special entertainment for you, my darling. Oh, not a silly children's party. You would not like that. And no ceremonies, eh? Enough of them with de old Begum, and de bulls and cows.' Mamma laughed wildly. 'Bulls and cows' was Charlotte's own name for her numerous uncles and aunts which, in a careless moment, she had whispered to her mother. The Princess of Wales loved laughing at the family into which she had married. And it was not surprising, for they all hated her and had been most unkind to her, with the exception of the King, of course. Dear Grandpapa would never be unkind to anyone. And there was another secret. She had long been aware of how everyone watched him as though expecting him to do something odd. She often wondered what. Perhaps it was to die—but that was not so very odd. Dear Grandpapa, she wanted him to go on living for a long, long time. She would tell him so. Oh no, she would not, because then he wondered whether anyone had discussed his death before her.

How careful one has to be in a family like ours, thought Charlotte.

She was shut in by people who watched her all the time because she was an heir to the throne. The only thing that could prevent her attaining it as far as she could see would be the birth of a brother to her parents. And that was most unlikely.

She did love some of these people who surrounded her— Dr. Nott, for one. Well, hardly loved, but she was fond of him. Perhaps the two she loved most were her dressers Mrs. Gagarin and Miss Louisa Lewis. They were comforting as one imagined mothers might be. They scolded in a tender way which pleased her so much that she often behaved in such a way as to provoke their reproaches.

But she did not talk to them of what happened at her mother's house. She was aware when they accompanied her there of their silent disapproval. Mamma never gave them a thought. She never altered anything because they were there. At the entertainments she gave she laughed wildly as she ran about playing Blind Man's Buff, her eyes bandaged, her arms outstretched, and she always caught one of the gentlemen and the forfeit for being caught was a kiss. There was always a great deal of kissing going on at Mamma's parties and there were always plenty of bluff hearty gentlemen living in the house, it seemed. They were very courteous to Charlotte although they did not kiss her—only when there was a forfeit in the games in which she joined.

Her mother's house was quite different from anything she had ever known—or was likely to.

There was a sailor whom everyone called Sir Sydney—and wherever he was there was lots of gaiety; he was constantly chasing and kissing the ladies; but he could tell a good adventure story of how brave he was. Charlotte particularly liked the one in which he defended Saint Jean d'Acre.

Mamma used to listen, her eyes alight with pleasure.

'One of these days,' she said, 'I shall sail round the world. Will you come with me, my precious?'

Charlotte had replied that she would like to but she thought that, since she would one day be Queen of England, her place would be at home.

That made her mother screech with laughter. 'You see, Sydney, they are making a queen of her already.'

Strange Montague House, where everything was so different

from what it was at Windsor or Carlton House. But perhaps it
was Mamma who was so strange that she would transform any
place where she was and even Kew would become strange if
she lived there.

She had not realized how interested she was in the manner
in which life was lived at Montague House until she was not
able to go there.

It is excuses all the time. Well, I am going to find out, she
promised herself.

Who would tell her? Mrs. Gagarin and Louisa Lewis she
had hoped, but however much she tried to worm it out of
them they would not tell her. They had such a stern sense of
their own duty.

Her thoughts went to Mrs. Udney, who, with Mrs. Campbell, was attached to the household as assistant governess.
Charlotte was quite fond of Mrs. Campbell, though she was
rather a colourless woman always talking about her family
connection with the de Cliffords—and it was no doubt due to
this that she had been given the post. Mrs. Udney was of a
different nature. There was something about Mrs. Udney
which Charlotte did not like. She was rather good looking
with charming manners, so that one took to her at first and
then began to wonder. Charlotte had seen her fly into a
sudden temper, which was something with which Charlotte
could sympathize, but then *she* did not pretend to be so calm
and gentle. She had heard Mrs. Udney sniggering with Mrs.
Campbell, and when she was aware of the Princess's attention
she would smother her sniggers. Charlotte could not help
wondering what it was that brought that expression to her
face until one day she discovered that it was the affairs of the
Princess of Wales.

There were, of course, many rumours; and she did hear of
them at her mother's house where one could read the papers
and see the cartoons. But she believed that even her mother
might keep some from her; and these would probably be the
ones she most wanted to see.

Mrs. Udney would be in the Princess's bedchamber at this
time putting her clothes away and setting out what she would
wear for her audience with her grandmother and aunts. So to
her bedchamber went Charlotte and there as she had expected she found Mrs. Udney alone.

'I thought you'd be here, Mrs. Udney,' said Charlotte, coming straight to the point. She sat down on the bed and
bounced up and down on it while Mrs. Udney put her head
on one side and regarded her with amusement.

'I want to know why I do not go to Montague House,' said Charlotte bluntly.

'Because Your Highness is at Windsor.'

'As I am not a child, Mrs. Udney, I would prefer you did not treat me as such.'

Mrs. Udney inclined her head by way of apology. Oh yes, thought Charlotte, there is something about her which I do not like.

'I command you to answer my questions,' she said imperiously. 'Do you know why I am not allowed to go to Montague House? A plain yes or no, please.'

'Why . . . yes, Your Highness.'

'Then pray tell me.'

'Your Highness, I might be exceeding my duty.'

'Your duty to whom?'

'Those who place me in my responsible position.'

Charlotte coaxed: 'Oh come now, please tell me. I do want to know. And why shouldn't I? It concerns me, does it not?'

'It does, Your Highness.' Mrs. Udney's little pink tongue licked her lips and she really looked as though she found this rather to her taste. 'Your Highness would not tell tales of me.'

'Tales of you? Whatever for?'

'If I were to talk of this matter it might be frowned on.'

'I have told you *I* will frown if you do not.'

Mrs. Udney came close to the bed and said: 'You know all is not well between the Prince and Princess. You know they do not . . . live together.'

'Of course I know this. The Prince lives at Carlton House and Brighton; and my mother is at Montague House; and if she comes to London she stays at Kensington Palace.'

'I meant they do not live . . . as husband and wife. Your Highness understands?'

'I understand p . . . perfectly,' declared Charlotte, stammering a little because it was one of those lies which Dr. Nott deplored.

'But that does not prevent their having other . . . friends.' Mrs. Udney's smile was sly; Charlotte felt that it was distasteful in some way but she was not sure why.

'Friends. Of course they have friends. Everyone has friends . . . I hope.'

'Rather special friends, Your Highness. And with special friends there are sometimes . . . results.'

'Results? What results?'

'Your Highness always disliked the boy. Your Highness said more than once that he was a vulgar little brat.'

'You mean . . . my mother's adopted boy?'

'I did mean William Austin, Your Highness.'

'What has he to do with this?'

'Everything.'

Charlotte was puzzled.

Mrs. Udney put her face close to Charlotte's and all her fine manners had suddenly gone. 'Some are saying that the Princess of Wales did not *adopt* the boy. They are saying that he is her own.'

'That he is my father's son! How silly. If he were . . .' The enormity of the possibility overwhelmed her.

Mrs. Udney went on: 'Oh, no, not the son of the Prince of Wales. There were plenty of other gentlemen ready to be the . . . friend of Her Highness.'

Charlotte did not fully understand but she knew that was some fearful slander against her mother. How dared this . . . this creature stand there looking so sly and knowing . . . yes, and *pleased*.

The ungovernable temper of which Dr. Nott and Lady de Clifford despaired was in the ascendant.

Charlotte brought up her right hand sharply and gave Mrs. Udney a stinging blow across the cheek.

Then appalled by what she had done and what she had heard, she ran out of the room.

*   *   *

Mrs. Udney could not allow such treatment to pass and immediately reported it to Lady de Clifford.

'Why, Mrs. Udney,' cried her ladyship, 'what on earth has happened.'

Mrs. Udney's eyes were blazing with fury and there was a red mark on her cheek.

'Her Royal Highness has just seen fit to slap my face.'

Lady de Clifford put her hand to her eyes. 'Oh, no, no! How could this have happened?'

'Madam came into my bedchamber in a *mood*. She fired a few questions at me, was not pleased by my answers; then she rose and slapped my face like a vulgar fishwife.'

'Where does she learn such manners?'

'Where could she but at Montague House?'

'I greatly fear she is growing like her mother. Oh dear, if only she were a little more like the dear Prince.'

'I pray she does not behave as her mother does.' Mrs.

Udney's fury was diminished slightly by a certain gleeful pleasure at the prospect. 'Then there would be ructions at Carlton House and Windsor as well.'

'I beg of you, Mrs. Udney, do not even suggest such a thing.'

'I believe she has heard something of what is happening.'

'Do you think she could?'

'Everyone is talking about the Investigation and the general belief is that William Austin is the Princess's little bastard by Sir Sidney Smith or Captain Manby or Lawrence the painter. Young Willikins cannot be said to lack a father, although his actual identity is unknown.'

'Mrs. Udney, I beg of you. But I shall have to tell the Bishop of the Princess's behaviour. I really cannot have her actually laying hands on those who serve her.'

'I sincerely hope she has discovered nothing,' said Mrs. Udney piously, 'for who knows how she might romance about the affair. She does not always keep to the truth. Do you not think it is better to refrain from mentioning anything that might remind her of her mother and the life she leads at Montague House?'

'I do indeed,' sighed Lady de Clifford.

At least, thought Mrs. Udney, they would not broach the subject, and if Charlotte were reprimanded for slapping the face of one of her attendants she would not tell the reason why since it concerned her mother.

Mrs. Udney was sure that she could explain what had happened and do no harm to herself.

She went back to Mrs. Campbell and told her that the Princess was becoming unmanageable and this was her mother coming out in her.

*   *   *

Dr. Fisher, Bishop of Salisbury, was pacing up and down the room waiting for his pupil to arrive.

When she came he was immediately aware of her defiant looks. So she guessed that news of her misdemeanour had reached him.

Smug, pompous, looking self-righteous, he suggested that they should pray together for humility.

'Humility?' demanded Charlotte. 'Is that a good quality for a princess to have?'

'It is a good quality for us all to have, Your Highness. And particularly princesses.'

'Bishops too, Bish-Up?'

'For us all,' replied the Bishop. 'Those of us who are in
positions of authority—or who are being trained for such—
must remember it especially. Pride is one of the greatest of
sins. One of the seven most deadly.'

'So humility must be one of the virtues—or do they not go
in opposites? Perhaps it is possible to have humility *and*
pride. One changes, you know, Bish-Up. I do. I am sure that
sometimes I am very, very humble. Yet I can be proud.'

He put the palms of his hands together and raised his eyes
to the ceiling. His most pious attitude! thought Charlotte.
This means he is very shocked about something and of course
it is my slapping Udney's face. Serve her right.

'Proud, overbearing, hot-tempered and behaving in an unseemly manner. Lady de Clifford is alarmed at your inability
to control your temper.'

'It's true, Bish-Up. It flares up and flies out . . . and then it is
all gone. Almost as soon as I have done something quite
dreadful I begin to feel sorry. That must be the old humility
creeping in. I told you, did I not, that one can have the
deadliest of sin side by side with a lovely virtue.'

'Being sorry afterwards is not enough.'

'Oh, I know one is supposed to *suffer* for one's sins. I never
liked the thought of that very much. If anyone did me a
wrong and then was very sorry I should want to say "Forget
it" and make it as though it has never been.'

'That might not be God's way.'

'I didn't say it was. I said it was *my* way. And I happen to
think it's a good way.'

The Bishop sighed. 'I despair,' he murmured.

'Now you should never despair, Bish-Up. That's bad. It's
almost as bad as losing your temper. You should always hope.
You should be like Queen Elizabeth. Think of all that time
when she was in prison and never knew from one day to
another whether she was going to lose her head. But she went
on hoping and in the end the crown was hers. I should wish to
be like her in a way . . . when she was good. But she could be
very wicked.' Charlotte laughed. 'Perhaps that's what I like
about her. Bish-Up, do you think she had a hand in the
murder of Amy Robsart?'

'We are not discussing the conduct of Queen Elizabeth but
that of the Princess Charlotte.'

'Oh, we are discussing *my* conduct. I thought we were discussing sins and virtues. And I thought we all had those.'

'You acted violently towards one of your servants, I am
told.'

'Hardly violently. She said something I did not like so I slapped her face.'

'And do you think that was becoming conduct for a princess?'

'It was most unbecoming not only for a princess but for anyone. It would even have been so with a bishop.'

'We are discussing an act which you have performed, not the suppositious conduct of others.'

'Well, to tell the truth, Bish-Up, I lost my temper. You know what my temper is like. She displeased me . . . violently, so I slapped her . . . far less violently than she displeased me, I do assure you.'

'You did not stop to think. I have had to reprove you on other occasions for the quickness of your temper.'

'It's true, Bish-Up.'

'And have I not told you what you should do when you feel one of those uncontrollable fits of rage? How many times have I told you to repeat the Lord's Prayer to yourself when these occasions arise. "Forgive us our trespasses as we forgive those that trespass against us." '

'I did in fact, Bish-Up. The first bit anyway.'

'And you are telling me that even that could not prevent this unfortunate outburst?'

'It did much good, my lord Bish-Up. If I hadn't said those first lines, I should doubtless have killed her.'

She was laughing at his discomfiture.

What could one do with the Princess Charlotte? It was, he told Lady de Clifford afterwards, enough to send him to her father to beg to be released from the almost impossible task of controlling her.

* * *

'Oh dear, oh dear!' sighed Charlotte, romping into the sitting room which Louisa Lewis shared with Mrs. Gagarin while they mended a gown which she had torn. 'The Very Reverend Bish-Up has been on at me again. How I wish he were not such a *good* man—or did not think he was such a good man. Perhaps that is it. It makes him so shocked by the sins of others. What are you doing? Mending that old dress? Did I tear it again?'

Louisa threw an adoring glance at Charlotte and said: 'Yes, Your dearest Highness did.'

'That was a nice way of saying it. As though you loved me for all my faults.'

She thew herself against Louisa and putting her arms about

her neck kissed her. Louisa pricked her finger and her part of the dress fell to the floor, but she did not complain. Charlotte was always boisterous.

'You were always the one for tearing things,' said Mrs. Gagarin indulgently.

So Mrs. Gagarin must have a hearty kiss too.

'I was always a great tearer,' she cried laughing. 'Miss Hayman is always telling me how I used to tear my caps showing her how Mr. Canning raised his hat and bowed to me. She used to hold me up at the window to see him pass. I think I remember it ... or perhaps that is due to hearing Miss Hayman mention it so many times. She was very sad when my father dismissed her and she couldn't look after me any more. Well, she became my mother's friend and went to Montague House and I am sure she finds it very lively there.'

She was inviting them to talk of Montague House and what she thought of as That Matter, but they were more cautious than Mrs. Udney and said nothing, though she fancied they exchanged glances over her head.

She sighed. 'My Lord Bish-Up is most displeased with me. I have to do a sort of penance. Guess what. But you never will. I am to wear the uniform of a Charity School Girl. This is very plain and it is to be hoped that after having worn it for a whole week I may have learned a little humility.'

'A Charity School girl!' cried Louisa. 'The Princess a Charity School girl!'

'It is not the clothes that are important, dear Louisa. It is the soul within. I shall be the same Charlotte inside my Charity School girl's costume as the one you see before you now. And I daresay I shall soon be tearing that as I do all my clothes. But perhaps I do need to learn humility. I slapped Mrs. Udney's face, you know.'

'I've no doubt she deserved it,' said the loyal Louisa.

'Oh, she did, but I shouldn't have done it. I should have folded my hands together thus, raised my eyes to the ceiling so and have said as the dear Bish-Up would: "Madam, you have committed a grave error. Pray mend your ways ... saying the Lord's prayer before you utter. Wear a Charity School girl's gown." Oh there are lots of things I should have done, but what I did was slap her face.'

They were laughing. Dear Gagy! Dear Louisa! She could always rely on them.

'Now let's talk.'

'What about, Your Highness?'

'Me, of course. Talk about the things I used to do.'

It was one of those cosy chats when they all laughed together about the antics, comic and tragic, good and wicked, which had been recorded of Charlotte. They would never admit to the wickedness—that was why they were so much more comforting than the Bishop—they said the worst were natural childish mischief and high spirits.

'Always so good,' said Mrs. Gagarin. 'Do you remember the boy in the ditch?'

They all remembered it; they had heard it many times before, but that was no reason why they should not hear it again.

'There he was lying in the ditch—a poor starving boy—and Your Highness would not leave him there. "What ails you?" Your Highness wanted to know. He was cold and hungry and he had hurt his hand. It was sore and bleeding. And what did Your Highness do but bind it yourself. Of course they did not like that. They reprimanded Your Highness. You might have caught some disease. And what did Your Highness say?'

Charlotte supplied the answer: '"Jesus was not afraid to heal the leper, so why should I be to bind this poor boy's hand?" Why, that might have been my Lord Bish-Up himself talking. But at least I did it. And I gave him food and money and he was very grateful to me, that boy. I was not always such a paragon, was I?'

'You had your naughty moments.'

'Quite a number of them.'

'I remember when Her Highness sang in the royal drawing room,' said Louisa, giggling a little.

'Such a little thing. The Princess Mary made her stand on a stool and sing for the company.'

'She was wearing a pink silk dress with a white satin sash, looking lovely.'

'And I sang the wrong notes I remember. They all clapped and said I was wonderful . . . and they only did that because I was the Princess.'

'It was a pretty sight. The King wept openly.'

'He weeps very easily.'

'And the Prince was so proud.'

'I don't think he could have been really proud for he sings so well himself. He probably pretended to be proud because it was good manners to do so. He thinks so much about manners.'

'And all the Princesses applauded and the Queen was pleased.'

'She is not often pleased with me.'

'Oh, she was very pleased. It was a beautiful occasion.'

Charlotte was pensive suddenly. 'But something bad came out of it. Oh dear, I'm afraid I *am* very wicked. The next day I asked my music master how I had sung and he said, "Perfectly." I was in a sudden rage because it wasn't true. I was angry with myself really for standing up there and not singing perfectly. So I turned my anger on him and I said he was a fool and I would not be taught by a fool who was afraid to correct his pupil because she was a princess.'

'Well, that was good. It shows how right you were not to accept flattery.'

'But I refused to allow him to teach me and he was dismissed and although afterwards I asked my father to bring him back to teach me, he did not. So you see that was pride in a way ... pride in a sort of virtue which ended in that poor music master's dismissal. I hope he has forgiven me. Oh let's not talk of me. Let's talk of you. Tell me about Mr. Gagarin, do please. I love to hear of him, I wonder where he is now. In Russia do you think? But perhaps it pains you, dear Gagy. Does it?'

'It's all too long ago.'

'Then tell us again.'

So Mrs. Gagarin told the story of her love for Mr. Gagarin ... only he wasn't plain Mr. Gagarin; he was a great nobleman in Russia who had come to the English Court on some mission.

'No sooner had he set eyes on you,' said Charlotte, 'than he fell violently in love.'

'It's true,' said Mrs. Gagarin, her eyes momentarily soft.

'And you ought to be the lady of a great mansion in Russia, dear Gagy, instead of mending my old dresses. Do you wish you were there with ... him?'

'It's all so long ago, Your Highness.'

'And what happened? What happened?'

'You know.'

'Yes, but I want to hear it again. And then you received a letter. Go on from there.'

'It was from his wife, for he was married already.'

'And so you were not his wife at all. Oh, my poor, poor Gagy. Your heart was broken.'

'Yes, my dear Charlotte. I thought so.'

'But it was mended again. *I* mended it, didn't I! Oh, say it. You used to say it. You said that when you came to look after your dearest Charlotte. You did.'

'Yes, as soon as I came to look after my dearest Charlotte, it began to mend.'

Charlotte was delighted. It was the reason why she wished to hear the story so often.

'Then,' she said solemnly, 'I cannot be so bad, can I? In spite of my Lord Bish-Up's terrible warnings of what will become of me if I continue in my ways.'

She rocked back and forth in her chair.

'You'll break it one day, dearest Princess, if you jerk it back so sharply.'

She did not care. What was a broken chair when she had mended a broken heart?

* * *

They dressed her in the Charity School girl's gown with much clicking of tongues. Indeed, what if His Highness the Prince of Wales saw fit to call? What would he say to see his daughter so attired?

Well, it was the Bishop's order and the Bishop would have to answer for it.

And how did Her Highness feel to be so humiliated? She gave no sign that she was distressed. She was smirking at her reflection in the mirror. And no Charity School girl's gown could disguise the royal features. In fact she looked more than ever like her father.

'I hope,' said Louisa Lewis, as angry as it was possible for one of her mild nature to be, 'that my Lord Bishop will be satisfied.'

Charlotte smiled at her dressers—her dear good faithful Louisa and Gagy of the mended heart. She loved them both dearly. She embraced them fervently, disturbing the coiffure of one and almost tearing the sleeve in the dress of the other; but they were accustomed to her rough caresses and would not have had them changed one bit.

Into the room she went where the Bishop was waiting for her. If he expected to see her enter shamefacedly he was disappointed.

'Good morning, my lord Bish-Up,' she cried. 'It's a very bright morning. And look at my new gown. It's a good fit. Do you not agree? It might have been made for me.'

She beamed at him and pirouetted so that he might see the back as well as the front.

He was disconcerted. He had expected some shame.

But what could one do with such a pupil? he plaintively asked Lady de Clifford later. He feared the worst.

* * *

In an effort to make her conscious of the evil of her ways the Bishop had warned her to repent.

'How can you know,' he had asked, 'when your last moment will come? What if you were to die with all your sins upon you?'

That made Charlotte think a great deal not so much about her own fate but of that of her possessions which she would leave behind her.

What of her darling dogs, her precious birds? She loved them so much. What a tragedy for them if she should die.

Then there were her books. And what of her jewels? As the daughter of the Prince of Wales she had some very valuable jewels; she had even been allowed to wear some of them when she had attended her grandmother's Drawing Room. She must really look into her affairs.

'I will make a Will,' she told Mrs. Campbell.

'At your age?' demanded that lady.

'My dear Mrs. Campbell, who of us knows when our last hour shall come?'

Mrs. Campbell grew pale. She was constantly talking about her mysterious illnesses. Charlotte listened when she was sorry for some bout of ill temper because she knew how much Mrs. Campbell liked talking about the terrible state of her inside. Charlotte was very fond of Mrs. Campbell because it was always possible to discuss any topic with her and fond as she was of illnesses—and she seemed positively to dote on death—she liked to argue about everything and could always be relied upon to take the opposite point of view for the sake of the argument.

So this was one subject on which she was in agreement with the Princess.

'That's true,' she said. 'Sometimes by the way my heart beats . . . unevenly and thump, thump, thump . . . I could certainly believe my last hour is close at hand.'

'Exactly,' said Charlotte. 'I am young yet but who knows Old Death may be waiting round the corner for me. So, dear Camby. I must make my will.

'You do that. It'll keep Your Highness amused for quite a while I shouldn't wonder.'

And it did.

What fun to think of all one possessed and how pleased people would be when they received their legacies. But perhaps they would be a little sorry. Dear Charlotte, they would say, she was always such a hoyden but she had a good heart. And although she plagued the Bish-Up she mended Mrs.

Gagarin's heart and she and Louisa Lewis loved her dearly.

Charlotte was almost in tears thinking of her own funeral. The drums would roll; and all over London the bells would toll. Her rooms would be hung with black and the Prince of Wales would weep such tears as even he had never wept before. The Princess of Wales would be in a frenzy of grief. She might say to the Prince: 'Let us be together. Let us have another child. It is what Charlotte would have wished.'

But I wouldn't wish it. Because they hate each other and I don't want them to have another child. I want to be the only one so that I shall one day be a great Queen like Queen Elizabeth. But what would it matter, if I were dead? But I don't really want to be dead.

One only made a will *in case* one died. That was what one had to remember. It was just in case she should die suddenly and no one would know what to do with her possessions.

'The Last Will and Testament of Her Royal Highness the Princess Charlotte.' How important it looked. And what were the most valuable things she had? Her dogs and her birds— her most cherished possessions. Dear Mrs. Gagarin was so good with them and they were almost as fond of her as they were of Charlotte herself. She would leave dear Gagy her dogs and birds. There would be no need to tell her to take care of them. She would be a good mistress to them.

Charlotte felt sad to think of her darling dogs looking in vain for their mistress; they would sit at the door of the death chamber and howl and refuse to be comforted. Perhaps like the little dog which had belonged to Mary Queen of Scots they would refuse to eat and pine away in spite of all Gagy's efforts to comfort them.

But it was only in case she died. It did not mean that she had to because she made a will.

There were her jewels. People would say that they were the most valuable things she possessed. They were jewels which belonged to an heir to the throne. They did not really belong to her; when she married they would be passed on to her son's wife or perhaps her daughter. They were not really hers to leave. She sighed. What fun it would have been to have given dear Campbell a pearl necklace worth a fortune. But no, Princesses had their duties.

Her jewels then to the Prince and Princess of Wales. But not all of them . . . only those very valuable state jewels. She could do something with the lesser trinkets, so Mrs. Campbell should have some of them and Lady de Clifford some. They would be delighted. All her books she would leave to Dr.

Nott. 'With my papers,' she wrote, 'some of which it will be necesary for him to burn.' He was so much more pleasant than the Bishop so she expressed the wish that the King would look after him and make him a Bishop. That would put the Bish-Up's nose out of joint and she would leave him merely her Bible and Prayer Book—he, being such a good man, would think these the greatest gifts anyone could bestow.

And dear Louisa. She hoped the King would reward her and dear Mrs. Gagarin for their services most handsomely and give them a house to live in and look after them.

And Mrs. Udney. That made her laugh.

'To Mrs. Udney,' she wrote, *'nothing,* for reasons.'

* * *

Everything she did seemed to raise a storm, thought Charlotte. Who would have believed that the mere act of making a will could have caused such trouble.

She had omitted to put the will away and 'someone' had read it and reported to Lady de Clifford.

That Mrs. Udney, I'll swear, thought Charlotte, and chuckled to picture the woman reading what had been written about her.

'Of course,' said Mrs. Udney to Lady de Clifford, 'you see what has happened. Mrs. Campbell dictated the will. Sharing her jewellery with you! Do you think Charlotte would have thought of that.'

'It would not surprise me what Charlotte thought of.'

'Campbell always hated me and so does Dr. Nott. That man is quite a menace. It's time someone spoke to the Bishop about him.'

Mrs. Campbell was red-eyed and Charlotte wanted to know why.

'They are saying I dictated your will. They are making the most hideous slanders. My health won't stand it.'

'They are wicked,' said Charlotte. 'I will go to Cliffy and tell her that I am quite capable of making a will without being dictated to.'

'It's no good,' sighed Mrs. Campbell. 'I feel so faint. I really think I ought to resign from Your Highness's service.'

'No, no, dear Camby. I won't allow it.'

'Dearest Princess, if only everyone was as sweet as you!'

'Sweet,' cried Charlotte. 'I do not like that word. Are you going to eat me then? Sweet! I think it is such a silly word for a person.'

'My dear good Princess.'

'Good! Good for what? What am I *good* for?'

Mrs. Campbell sighed. Her Highness was in a cantankerous mood doubtless because of all this fuss about the will for which she blamed herself.

She had almost made up her mind to retire. She looked forward to a quiet life in which she could devote herself to her ailments.

* * *

Dr. Nott was in a quandary. This was most embarrassing. The Princess Charlotte had suggested that he should be made a Bishop and that much should be done for him. Had this been put into the mind of the Princess, everyone was asking. And who would have put it there but Dr. Nott?

With downcast eyes Dr. Nott gave her her Latin lesson. She was not listening; she was thinking of poor Campbell who had been so wrongfully accused and who had really seemed as if she wanted to go away and be ill in comfort.

'Your Highness is not attending this morning.'

She sighed. 'No, dear Doctor. I have a great deal on my mind.'

'It was good of Your Highness to have mentioned me for a bishopric in your will.'

'Good again,' she said. 'Good for what? as I said to dear Campbell. It was not good at all. It was being *just*. You deserve a bishopric and I trust the King will grant my request.'

Dr. Nott smiled in his meek way and said that if it meant he must wait for the Princess to die that he might receive the bishopric it would be a great tragedy for him ever to have it offered to him, so he trusted Her Highness would outlive him by many years—which he thought was most likely—and he would be happy to serve her for as long as she needed him.

'That was a pleasant speech, dear Doctor,' she said, 'and it moves me so much that I am in no mood for Latin this morning. Therefore let us put an end to the lesson.'

She rose, but unfortunately he had put his foot on the train of her gown and as she leaped up and moved away there was the sound of tearing material and she saw that the train was almost torn from her skirt.

Poor Dr. Nott, he was the sort of man, she reflected, who would often find himself in embarrassing situations.

'Your Highness's pardon ... I fear I have ruined your gown. How unfortunate. It would only have been a little tear if it had not run as it did.'

Charlotte examined the damage.

Then she burst into loud laughter.

'Well, we can hardly blame you because it ran, Doctor. You most surely held it!'

Then rolling the torn train about her arm she ran out of the room, leaving the saddened Dr. Nott shaking his head sadly over this most difficult, unaccountable and wild young pupil, who could at times be lovable.

*   *   *

The result of the writing of that will was certainly felt throughout the household.

Mrs. Campbell resigned. Her ill health made it essential, she said, but everyone knew it was due to the horrible things that were being whispered of how she was trying to win benefits from the Princess by flattery.

Dr. Nott was suspected of the same fault. He did not leave but he too pleaded ill health. He needed a rest from his duties, he declared, which with such an important pupil were indeed arduous.

Charlotte was in despair. She had lost Mrs. Campbell and now Dr. Nott was talking of going. And she was left with the Bish-Up and Mrs. Udney. They were the ones who should have gone.

She went to Lady de Clifford and told her how she enjoyed her studies with Dr. Nott, how she felt it would be impossible to work without him. He must go away for a little rest because he was ill, but he must promise to come back.

At length it was arranged that this should be the case and Charlotte took a tearful farewell of Mrs. Campbell.

Meanwhile there was the Bishop, whose visits were more frequent during the temporary departure of Dr. Nott.

And Mrs. Udney remained, sly and calculating, with a temper—carefully concealed—which rivalled Charlotte's.

How strange the things that can happen to a Princess and those who serve her, thought Charlotte—the Bish-Up who had his bible and prayer book and Mrs. Udney who had nothing seem more content than dear Campbell with her promised jewels and Dr. Nott with his future bishopric.

There was a lesson in it, she was sure.

But then, was there not a lesson in everything?

Minney, Prinney and Mrs. Fitzherbert

MRS. FITZHERBERT sat on her balcony looking over the Steyne and watched the scene below. Brighton—the place she loved best in the whole world because she had known such happiness there. Now that the Prince had made such extensive alterations at the Pavilion she had moved from the little house she had occupied close by, but this one suited her perfectly. It was to her the home she shared with her husband and her dearest daughter.

It was a strange irony of fate that many would say that the man she called her husband was not, and her daughter was adopted.

She shivered a little in the bright May air, for an awareness of the uncertainty of life had come to her. All was happy at the moment, but she knew it could change within a few weeks.

The Prince would always have an eye for women and although he assured her at every meeting that she was his dear love, his soul, the wife of his heart, that did not prevent his indulging in minor love affairs now and then. He always returned to her penitent and contrite but because she had a hot temper she could not always restrain her comments. There could be a little rift and although the reconciliations which followed were pleasing to them both, there were moments of uneasiness when she felt that she wished to imprison every bright moment and keep it for ever—just in case in the future there was change.

And then Minney—darling Minney—her comfort and solace, her beloved child could be snatched away from her by her relatives who were at times trying to take her. Life was full of alarming possibilities.

Miss Pigot, her faithful friend and companion who had been with her when she had first set up house after her marriage to the Prince, came on to the balcony, fussing a little. The sun was bright but there was a keen wind. Wouldn't Maria like a silk wrap about her shoulders?

'Oh, Pig, you treat me like an old woman,' she said, 'or a child perhaps.'

'People who sit in draughts behave like children,' retorted Miss Pigot.

'Sit down a moment and talk to me. Where's Minney?'

'At her lessons. She's having difficulty with her essay. That's why she's been kept.'

'Dear child. What a good little thing she is! Oh, Pig, how lucky I am to have her.'

'And lucky she is to be with you.'

'Sometimes I'm afraid of too much happiness.'

'Nonsense, Maria. What's happened to you? Everything will be all right.'

'But this case. It drags on and on.'

'Cases always do.'

'But what if they should win and take her from me?'

'His Highness will see they don't do that.'

Maria smiled. 'You look upon him as a god, I think.'

'Well, he is the Prince of Wales. God bless him. Now don't you fret. Would you like me to bring a dish of tea?'

'Wait until Minney joins me.'

'That shouldn't be long if I know Miss Minney. And it wouldn't surprise me if His Highness was here at any minute. He'll be putting in an appearance at the usual place, I'll be bound.' Miss Pigot laughed. 'It always amuses me. The way he appears and no one sees him coming. Well, that's our little secret.'

'Such things are a constant delight to him. He's a boy at heart—and always will be, I think.'

'And what's wrong with that? I must say when we heard you were to lose that nice little house right in his garden so to speak, I was a bit put out. But this you might say is even closer to the Pavilion even though it's farther away. It makes it like part of the place and that's how I reckon it should be. And what amazes me is how all the time it was being made there was no talk about it.'

'He took Minney to the Pavilion the other day by means of the passage. She was delighted.'

'How he loves that child!'

'And she him.'

'Well, who could help it?'

'Pig, you're a besotted old fool.' Maria looked at Miss Pigot fondly. 'And so am I,' she added.

But why worry on a lovely May morning when everything seemed well, and below, the Steine was gay with the colours of the promenaders' fashionable clothes and every now and then one of them would look up and bow to the regal figure seated on the balcony. Maria Fitzherbert was 'Mrs. Prince' to some who took the epithet from old Smoker the man who dipped the Prince in the sea each morning, and to many others she was the Queen of Brighton, the true Princess of Wales although the Prince had married for reasons of State and the scandalous Princess of Wales was living apart from him at Montague House, and there was young Princess Charlotte to prove that Mrs. Fitzherbert was not his legal wife, for how could he have married a foreign princess and produced a child who was heiress to the throne if that were so?

But these were matters which had been the cause of too much controversy and Maria was ready to take Miss Pigot's advice and forget them.

And here was Minney—pretty dainty Minney come to the balcony having escaped from the schoolroom for her hour with dear Mamma, as she called Maria; and, she thought fiercely, no one was going to stop her doing so.

'Minney, my love, Piggy is going to bring us a dish of tea.'

'That will be lovely, Mamma. What a glorious day, but shouldn't you have a shawl?'

'Piggy has just been scolding me for the same reason. Between you you will make an old woman of me.'

Minney ran inside and came back with a grey silk shawl which she placed about Maria's shoulders.

'Darling child, what should I do without you?'

There were lights of fear now in Minney's eyes. 'But you are not going to do without me.'

'We shall do everything in our power.'

'No one will dare go against Prinney's wish.'

'This is matter of law, dearest, and your aunt could claim that she is nearer to you than a woman like myself who am no relation.'

'But my mother *gave* me to you.'

'Don't distress yourself, dear. We shall have to await the verdict and abide by it.'

'If they take me away from you, I shall never abide by it.'

'We should see each other now and then.'

'But this is my home. I couldn't imagine any other. You are my dearest Mamma. I never knew another and I will never accept another.'

'My darling Minney, you are my great comfort.'

Minney looked alarmed. Oh dear, was Prinney being bad again. She knew a great deal about the wickedness of Prinney. When she sat on his knee and they laughed together he was such a jolly man, and he seemed so happy; he always looked at Maria in a melting way which was very affecting and tears came into his eyes when he talked of how happy they all were together. And yet there were whispers about him and she couldn't help knowing that he did make dearest Mamma unhappy at times. And then when she played with Charlotte that very knowledgeable young person would tell her secrets which she had picked up through keeping her eyes open which, she was always pointing out, was a talent Minney seemed sadly to lack. All was not as well as it often seemed. There were undercurrents which Minney did not understand; and that was why dearest Mamma was often a little sad and Piggy went around clicking her teeth.

But when he came large and glittering, when he laughed and wept and said how happy he was to be home with his dearest ones, how pleasant life was, Minney could always be deluded then into thinking that that was how it was going to be forever. There he would sit with his elegantly arranged neckcloth which always seemed to be trying to keep his chin from escaping ('My *chin*, Minney,' he had said when she told him so. 'I'll tell you a secret. I have more than one.'), the beautiful cloth of his coat so smooth to the touch, fitting his large torso so neatly, the great diamond star, which she never failed to find fascinating—he was indeed a fairytale Prince and next to Maria she loved him best in the world with Miss Pigot a very close third. It was their home—the three of them were in a magic circle. And if Maria was Mamma, Prinney was Papa, although it was difficult to think of Prinney in such a role, particularly as he was in fact Charlotte's father.

Well, thought Minney, he is my Prinney, and our names even rhyme.

Maria, looking at the child, thought: Should I prepare her? It would be a terrible shock to her if she had to go. I am sure her Aunt Waldegrave would do everything to make her happy, but Minney is such a loyal little soul and she has already given her allegiance to me.

Miss Pigot arrived with the tea and Minney poured gracefully and charmingly. How can I ever bear to part with her?

thought Maria, and watching her Miss Pigot knew what was in her mind.

I pray God the case goes our way, thought Miss Pigot.

* * *

While she sipped her tea Maria was thinking of the first time she had seen Minney. That was at the period of her greatest despair when the Prince of Wales had married Princess Caroline of Brunswick. It had happened more than ten years ago and she would never forget the day when Orlando Bridgeman, Lord Bradford, had brought her the news that the ceremony had taken place. She had fainted, for that had seemed like the end of everything.

But she had been so sorry for him when she had heard how he loathed the marriage, how his bride was repulsive to him, and how as soon as she was with child and he had done his duty he left her. And when little Princess Charlotte was born he had declared that he would never live with his wife again. She knew that he hated the woman, that he could not bear to hear her spoken of, and that nothing would please him more than to be rid of her. And now that this investigation was going on, who knew what would come out of it?

But it was not the end. He had tired of Lady Jersey, who had influenced him so strongly at the time of his wedding, and he had sought every opportunity of returning to Maria. With his usual abandon he had begged her, implored her, gone to all the lengths which she had experienced before. The most telling of course was his imminent death. So it had been when he had attempted suicide for her sake. Some denied he had really done this and that it was a piece of play-acting on his part, but she liked to believe it was true. She had stood out against him, telling him that in marrying Caroline of Brunswick he had denied his marriage to her and since he denied it she had no wish to remind him of it.

It had all been a mistake, a terrible mistake, he had declared. He had wept; he had knelt. She was his true wife; he demanded she do her duty and return to him; if she did not he would publish the truth. The whole of England should know that she was his true wife and that creature ... that coarse vulgar German *hausfrau* ... could go back to Brunswick. Maria had been shocked, for she saw the purpose in his eye and she knew him capable of the most impulsive actions.

'And your little daughter, the Princess Charlotte?'

'She can take the child with her, for if I am not married to her mother what is her position here?'

Maria was shocked. 'That innocent child! Your own daughter!'

'I have no room in my heart for anyone but you.'

'What a pity you did not remember that before you allowed them to bring the Princess Caroline to England.'

But what was the use? He was determined; and because she loved him, she knew she would give in in the end. But she had insisted on being treated with the dignity of a wife; and had sent to Rome for the Pope's verdict on whether or not that ceremony which had taken place in her house at Park Street was valid. The answer had come back from Rome that it was; she had returned to the Prince and for a time they had been idyllically happy.

But knowing it was not in his nature to be faithful to one woman she was always aware that such happiness could not last. He was the lover of all women, as Sheridan had said, so how could he be the lover of one? Maria was however sure that she was supreme in his affections, and however much he might stray, he wanted her there all the time. She was his 'dear love', his 'soul's wife', as he was fond of telling her.

Yet she could not rely on him. Was that why she clung to Minney? Did she believe deep in her heart that if ever the Prince left her she would turn to this lovely child whom she looked on as her own? But now they were threatening to take Minney from her. It was one of the greatest sorrows of her life that she had had three husbands and no children.

The Seymours had been Maria's particular friends and in fact Lord Hugh had expressed his disapproval of the Prince's public marriage to Caroline of Brunswick so strongly that the Prince had been annoyed by his criticism and had cut him ever since. But the friendship between Maria and Lady Horatia was very deep and it had been a cause of great grief to Maria to see Horatia growing weaker and weaker and to know that her friend was suffering from galloping consumption and had no hope of recovery. Lord Hugh had arranged to take his wife to Madeira for the winter as soon as their child was born.

Little Mary Seymour (Minney) was born on a bleak November day at Brompton. Maria arrived soon afterwards to see her friend and the new baby, and as soon as she took little Mary into her arms she loved her, but like her parents she was alarmed by the child's frailty.

What a momentous day that was in her life—and although she was so anxious on account of Horatia, how could she be anything but grateful for the turn of fate which brought her Minney.

Horatia had already borne seven children, two of whom
were girls, and Maria had often envied her her large family; so
when it was discovered that the new baby was not strong, it
was decided that she must certainly not undertake the journey which was essential to her mother's health, but must be
left behind with someone who would care for her.

The first person Horatia had thought of was her friend
Maria Fitzherbert; she wrote to her telling her of her
dilemma and Maria's response had been immediate. Her dear
Horatia must not think of postponing her trip; Maria would
take any of the children into her house and they should be
cared for until Horatia's return.

Maria had been in Bath at the time but had set out at once
for Portsmouth where the Seymours were staying. There she
saw the frail little Mary and took her tenderly into her
arms.

'This is my child until your return, Horatia,' she had
said.

'I know you, Maria. You will worry yourself to death over
her. Perhaps it would be better for her to go with some of my
relations who have several children. They won't be alarmed at
any little ailment—and I believe she will have many.'

'Horatia you are not going to take her from me now.'

Horatia smiled. 'You know there is no one with whom I
should rather leave my child. I am thinking of you.'

'Then the matter is settled. Little Mary is my baby until
your return.'

Of course Horatia was relieved; and so was Hugh.

'God bless you, Maria,' he said. 'I know we shall sleep more
peacefully now we know that the baby is in your hands.'

So Maria took little Mary and in a very short time loved her
as tenderly as though she were her own child.

For two years Horatia remained in Madeira and her health
improved a little so that she made up her mind that she would
return to England as she was eager to have all her children
with her. Maria, glad as she was to see her friend, was desolate
at the thought of parting with Mary who had now christened
herself Minney; but before Horatia could put her plan into
action she died; and a few weeks later Lord Hugh, who had
remained in Madeira, also died, leaving little Minney an
orphan.

When Lord Hugh's will was read, it was found that pro-
vision had been made for the guardianship of all the children
except Minney who had been born after he had made the
will. It was however ruled that Lord Hugh had intended the

same arrangement to apply to his youngest child and Lady
Waldegrave, Horatia's sister, immediately offered to take
Minney.

Maria, horrified at losing the child, begged to be allowed to
keep her a little longer. She pointed out that Minney was too
young to be taken from one whom she had come to regard as
her mother, and the executors, headed by Lord Henry Seymour, agreed that Minney should stay with Maria for a
further year before she was passed on to Lady Waldegrave.

Maria's great hope during that year's respite was to win the
consent of Minney's family to keep the child. The Prince of
Wales, who, since Maria regarded Minney as her daughter,
sentimentally wished to share in the parentage, petted the
child, played games with her and in every way possible took
on the role of affectionate father.

'If,' Maria used to say to Miss Pigot, 'I could only be assured
that I was not going to lose Minney, I should be perfectly
happy.'

If this and if that! thought Miss Pigot. Why did there
always have to be an If.

But she put her faith in the Prince of Wales. He clearly
wished the child to remain with Maria, so surely her family
would not go against him.

But Lord Henry Seymour was a very determined man.
Lady Waldegrave wanted the child and she was her aunt.
Maria for all her dignity and respectability was after all in the
eyes of the State the mistress of the Prince of Wales. Lord
Henry was going to insist on justice being done. The year was
drawing to a close; little Mary should go to her aunt.

Minney, realizing the controversy which was raging about
her and having some inkling that it was to separate her from
Maria, was frightened. She followed Maria wherever she went
and could not bear her to be out of her sight. This seemed
particularly pathetic to Maria and she was determined to
fight.

When she told the Prince of her fear he went into battle on
her behalf like the chivalrous knight he liked to believe himself to be.

'You shall not lose Minney, my dearest love. I shall see to
that.'

His chamberlain wrote to Lord Henry that His Royal
Highness had decided to settle £10,000 on Miss Mary Seymour provided she was left in the care of Mrs. Fitzherbert.

With great delight he took a copy of the letter to show
Maria. And what joy it gave him to witness her pleasure. 'My

dearest love, what is £10,000? I would give the whole world
for your happiness and that of our dear Minney.'

But Lord Henry was not to be lured by money. He wanted
justice. Mary belonged to the Seymours and the Seymours
would take over the care for her. Mary, he pointed out, would
have enough money of her own; she did not need His Highness's generous gift.

Maria was now in despair. She had never liked Lady Waldegrave, for the woman was one of those who had refused to
accept her as the Prince's wife; she knew what would happen
if Minney went to her; it would be final separation.

Seeing her unhappiness, the Prince declared that he would
not allow this to happen. Minney was Maria's child; Maria
had looked after her since her birth; to take her away now
would be a tragedy, not only for Maria but for Minney. He
would not stand by and see this done.

'But what can we do?' asked Maria. 'It is true they are her
legal guardians. Oh, why did I not foresee this? If Hugh and
Horatia had known what would happen they would have
taken steps to make Minney *my* child.'

The Prince disliked being frustrated and such an issue as
this was one which strongly appealed to him. Now he would
show Maria how she could rely on him. He was going to win
Minney for her; he was going to show her his devotion to his
little family.

He consulted Samuel Romilly, a brilliant young lawyer
who suggested that there could be a way out of the difficulty
since the will was made before Mary was born, but shortly
afterwards the obstinate Sir Henry had employed a lawyer to
work for him and the tiresome case of Fitzherbert against
Seymour had begun.

Maria could think of nothing else as with the custom of
such affairs the case dragged on.

One point which had been brought out was the fact that
Maria was a Catholic and the Seymours were Protestants. Was
their child, given into the care of an undoubted Catholic, to
be brought up in that religion? Maria had retorted that she
firmly believed that a child should be brought up in the
religion of its parents. Mary Seymour had had no instruction
in the Catholic Faith from her and the child should be
brought up in the Church of England until she was able to
decide for herself.

This matter of religion was undoubtedly one of the main
reasons why the Master in Chancery came to the decision that
the rightful guardians of Mary Seymour were her own family

and although Maria Fitzherbert had brought her up from babyhood, since the child's own family were demanding her, justice insisted that to them she should go.

When this news was brought to Maria she was desolate. The Prince arrived at the house in Tilney Street to find Minney in tears, clutching Maria and sobbing, declaring that she was never going to leave her.

This was more than he could endure.

'I tell you they have not won yet. Do you think I am going to allow them to. Henry Seymour is an arrogant dog. He wants to show me that he can flout me. By God, he knows my feelings on this matter. I've already seen Romilly. We're going to take this to the House of Lords.'

Maria lifted her grateful eyes to his. She was fearful because there was justice in the verdict though it ignored human feelings, but she loved Minney as a daughter and Minney loved her as a mother; it was cruel—though perhaps just—to tear them apart. But could the Prince of Wales divert justice?

He believed he could. He was astonished that the Seymours should have gone against his wishes. He would not forget that.

And now while she sipped tea on the balcony of her house on the Steine and Minney sat with her she was asking herself what hope there was that the case would go her way and that her dearest wish would be granted.

If I lost Minney, she thought, I should never be happy again. Even the Prince's love and devotion—and when she thought of that she was a little uneasy although he had shown himself assiduous in his care for her since the case started—could not make up for that.

I want them both, she thought, with me forever.

And at that moment he appeared on the balcony. He must have stood there for some seconds before they had been aware of him.

She turned and gave a cry of joy. The sight of him never failed to delight her. He was indeed a sparkling figure exquisitely dressed, glittering and scented. He bowed to Maria, his eyes twinkling with love and pleasure. It was the bow for which he was noted and which never failed to impress all who beheld it. It was the essence of grace and charm and it always implied that the pleasure he found in the company of the person to whom he was making it was the reason for its grace.

'My dearest love . . .' His voice was soft and musical.

'Such a great pleasure, my dearest.'

Minney cried: 'Prinney!' And there was no ceremony then. She flew at him and gave a little jump at which he lifted her and she put her arms about his neck. 'You smell so lovely this morning, Prinney. And this is a beautiful new neckcloth.'

'I designed it with help from Brummell.'

'Oh, it *is* soft!' She buried her face in it. Maria watched them affectionately. If only Minney were their own child; if only there did not have to be this fearful battle, this tragic uncertainty.

He put Minney down and she brought his chair forward and when he sat placed herself between him and Maria. She took his hand and examined the rings.

'Such lovely things he always has, does he not, Mamma? I could look at him for ever even if he were not my dear Prinney.'

He sat back in his chair, eyes glazed with sentiment. 'Dearest Minney, so you are a little fond of your old Prinney then?'

'Old?' said Minney. 'I had never thought that you could be old ... or young ... or anything.'

'So you see, Maria, Minney has placed me among the immortals. I cannot grow old although it seems I have never been young.'

'Are you going to sing for us?' asked Minney.

'Here on your Mamma's balcony? Do you want to collect a crowd?'

'Yes, I do. No I don't, because then you will have to be on duty and bowing and smiling to them, instead of talking to me. We'll sing when we are in the drawing room.'

'Minney has spoken,' said the Prince.

Why, Maria asked herself, could he not be on those easy terms with his own daughter? Poor Charlotte! She was sorry for the child; and she was a charming creature, too. Perhaps in the presence of the Prince she was gauche and uncertain. Who could wonder at that, considering the state of affairs between their parents?

What ironic problems life presented! Charlotte—an heiress to the throne—separated from her mother and with a father who could not love her because she reminded him of her mother. And her own sad problem—dear Minney who was her child and not her child.

Minney left them after a while as she always did, knowing that the Prince had come to see Maria and would no doubt wish to talk to her.

'Minney grows more enchanting every day,' he said when the child had gone.

'Which makes it all the harder if ...'

'We are going to win, never fear,' he replied lightheartedly.
'Oh, if only I could believe that.'

'My dearest, I have sworn we shall have Minney. Do you
think that I would not keep my word?'

She smiled at him fondly, but his words scarcely comforted
her. How many times had he betrayed her trust in him. She
thought of the infidelities; it was not marriage with Charlotte's mother which had brought about their painful separation but his infatuation for Lady Jersey. He had once been
completely under the spell of that woman whom he now
could not bear, sufficiently involved with her to desert Maria.
True, he had come back to her, but after such a shock, how
could one help wondering when the next would come? So she
could only smile at him when he asked her if she could not
trust his word.

'Lord Henry seems so determined. And I know Lady
Waldegrave has never been a friend of mine. They are going
to do everything they can to take Minney away from me.'

'Don't despair. I shall think of something.'

'I have thought of something,' said Maria. 'Lord Henry
gives himself airs, but he is not the head of the family. Lord
Hertford is that, and he has so far kept out of the affair. I
wonder if I called on Lady Hertford and asked her to speak to
her husband it would help.'

'An excellent idea. And I will let them know my wishes. I
fancy you have hit on the solution, Maria, my love. We'll go
over that insolent fellow's head and speak to Hertford.'

Maria's spirits rose at the prospect; she wondered why she
had not thought of it before.

'I shall call on her tomorrow,' she said.

'And when you have called, I will send for Hertford to
come and see me. I am sure of success now, my love.'

He was smiling, wishing to talk of pleasant things. How
well she knew him. He never wanted to discuss that which
was unpleasant. He began to tell her about Brummell's new
invention to the trouser leg.

'It is cut at the sides, Maria, and closed by the most exquisite buttons and buttonholes you ever saw. As Brummell
says, this gives great scope and he has many ideas for buttons.'

Maria had never liked Brummell; she considered him arrogant and he presumed on the Prince's friendship she believed; and what had the fellow ever done but become the
dandy to outdo all other dandies? But the Prince's interest in
clothes had drawn them together and he was often in Brummell's company.

He went on to talk of the way in which Brooks's Club had deteriorated.

'It's since Fox went.' His eyes filled with tears. Fox had had more influence on him than any other man. He had died only recently and since his death the Prince had become even more devoted to him. 'The wit is not there ... how could it be without the incomparable Fox? Sherry is getting old, too. Stab me, that son of his, Tom Sheridan, has the most lovely wife I ever saw—apart from you, Maria. I said when I saw her: "By God, there's only one woman who excels Tom Sheridan's wife and that's my own Fitzherbert." '

'You see me with the eyes of affection.'

He was delighted with the remark, his comfort restored.

'Well, I admit to it, but you are still the most beautiful woman in London to me.' He sighed. 'You still look the same as when I first saw you along the river bank. Do you remember, Maria? That was long ago. There have been changes since. Poor Fox gone. Brooks's is not the same without him. The conversation is dull and so is the food. Beefsteaks and leg of lamb, boiled fowls with oyster sauce. I've asked my chef Watier to found a new club and that is exactly what he is going to do.'

'You think the *ton* will let it take the place of Brooks's?'

'By all means, when they know that it is under the management of my chef. Brummell and my brother Fred will give it their support and in a week or so there won't be a vacant place at any of the tables.'

He was beaming with joy at the certain success of the venture and Maria thought it was the moment to introduce a subject which might not please him so much but of which she was determined to speak.

'How devoted Minney is to you. She speaks of you continually. I can tell you that nothing is done in the right manner unless it is done as Prinney does it.'

He smiled indulgently.

'It is Prinney this and Prinney that, all the day through. And Pig is the same. In this house you are not so much His Royal as His Holy Highness.'

'They are a dear pair and I am devoted to them both.'

'Dearest, I wish that you could show the same affection for Charlotte that you show to Minney.'

'Charlotte!' The mention of his daughter had jerked him out of his pleasant reverie. 'How lacking in grace that girl is.' He shuddered. 'She is so *gauche*.'

'She is overawed in your presence. Believe me, she can be so charming.'

'To others, but not to her father?'

'It is because she is so much in awe of you . . . so anxious to please.'

'My dearest Maria is apt to believe the best of everyone. I always feel that the child is proclaiming her indifference to me, her desire to flout me.'

'Oh, no no. That's not so.'

He was mildly astonished. He was not used to being contradicted, although Maria did it now and then.

'So I do not know my own daughter?'

'Please understand me. Charlotte is so anxious to win your approval that she becomes over-anxious. She admires you greatly.'

'How can you be sure of that?'

'It would be impossible for her not to.'

His good humour was momentarily restored and she hurried on: 'If to please me . . .'

'Anything in the world to please my dear love.' His hand was on his heart as it was when he bowed to the people's cheers—a not very frequent blessing these days except in Brighton.

'If you would smile at her, show her a little affection, indicate that you are pleased to see her, I think you would make her very happy.'

He sighed. 'Every time I look at her, Maria, I think of that creature.'

'Why should you? Charlotte is very like you.'

'She may have my family's looks but her manners . . . that awkwardness . . .' He shivered. 'That is her mother and anything that reminds me of that woman puts me into an ill temper. By God, Maria, this affair at Montague House! This child she has! If it can be proved that it is her own then I can surely be rid of her. She can be sent back to Brunswick. I should feel a great deal more at ease if she were out of the country.'

'And you think it is possible to prove this?'

'These matters are difficult to prove, but I am sure. And if only I could get the help I need, I would divorce her. You cannot imagine what peace of mind that would bring. The most unfortunate day of my life was when I allowed myself to go through that ceremony with her.'

Maria was silent and he was unhappy, for he was deep in a subject which he would have preferred to forget. There were

tears in his eyes, tears of self pity. That he, the most elegant of
Princes, the First Gentleman of Europe, should have been
married to that coarsest and most vulgar of German Princesses! Now he was on the subject he could not stop talking of
it.

'To think of her there ... living that degraded life at
Blackheath, receiving those men and living on intimate terms
with them ... as I am convinced she did. The sailors, Smith
and Manby, the artist Lawrence ... any one of them might be
the father of that boy, and do you realize, Maria, that that boy
could have been presented to the nation as a future King of
England. She has actually said that she would foist him on me
if need be. She has said that before he was born she had spent
a night or two at Carlton House and that as I was under the
influence of brandy most of the time I could not deny it. It's
treason. Oh, God, Maria, do I deserve this?'

'The Princess of Wales is certainly a very strange woman.'

'Strange! She's half mad. She behaves like a maniac. These
Douglases have done the right thing in bringing this to public
notice. Before this investigation is through I hope—by God,
how I hope—to prove that this so-called wife of mine is an
immoral creature unworthy in every way to bear any title that
has come to her since she arrived in England. I am going to
prove this, Maria. I am determined.'

'You upset yourself. We can only wait for the verdict, as
with Minney. Let us pray that it will be the right one in both
cases. But because you have such a kind heart you will, I
know, not blame that poor child for her mother's shortcom-
ings. You will be kind to her and make her love you. I am sure
that she longs for a little kindness from you. Will you try it ...
to please me.'

His good humour was coming back. He saw himself as the
kindly parent who would not allow the child to suffer for her
parent's wrongdoing. He would win her allegiance from her
mother. And at the same time he would please his dearest
love.

He took her hand and kissed it.

'You may rely on me to do what you ask of me ... at all
times,' he said.

The people on the Steine looked up and saw him.

They were delighted with him and Maria, who had always
been a favourite. It was one of the sights of Brighton to see
him sitting there on her balcony, tender and affectionate. In
Brighton Mrs. Fitzherbert was the Princess of Wales, not that
other woman who was now causing such a scandal through

what was being revealed in this case they called the Delicate
Investigation.

The royal lovers, how charming they were—two large not
very young figures up there, but a reminder to all who were
not so young that youth was not necessary to romance.

And no one saw him leave the Pavilion; he just appeared
on the balcony. They said there was a secret passage from the
Pavilion to Mrs. Fitzherbert's house which he had had made
so that he could visit her at all times unseen.

How romantic! How charming! Trust the Prince of Wales
to provide them with some excitement.

So they passed to and fro below and occasionally they
caught his eyes when he would nod or smile and on some
occasions rise and give them the chance to witness the most
graceful bow in the world.

*   *   *

Maria took an early opportunity of calling on Lady Hertford, who received her graciously. Lady Hertford was by no
means a beauty but married to one of the richest Tory peers
in the country, she had a very high opinion of herself. She was
always elegantly dressed, her only frivolity being her interest
in clothes; this was instinctive and she was reckoned to be the
best-dressed woman in England.

She had been friendly towards Maria in spite of the fact
that she was an ardent Protestant; it was true Maria—as far as
she was concerned with politics—had Tory tendencies and
Lady Hertford was an ardent Tory and as the two reigning
passions in her life were maintaining Toryism and achieving
elegance this gave them something in common. At the same
time Maria's position with the Prince of Wales was rather
dubious and although Maria lived as respectably as one could
wish, Lady Hertford was extremely frigid by nature and
averse to the slightest scandal. Still, she looked on Maria, if
not as a friend, as a worthy acquaintance.

So now she took her hand with as much warmth as she was
capable and bade her welcome.

'My dear Isabella,' said Maria, 'I have come to speak to you
of a matter which causes me a great deal of concern, and I am
going to ask you if you can help me. The Prince will join his
supplication to mine.'

'The Prince?' said Lady Hertford.

'Oh, yes, he is almost as involved as I am over this because
he loves the child dearly. I refer to your relative Mary Seymour.'

'Ah, yes,' said Lady Hertford, 'this pitiful case. The family seems determined to take Mary away from you.'

'And I—and the Prince—will do all we can to prevent it. You see, Isabella, Minney—our name for her—is like my own child. I have had her since she was a baby. It will break her heart and mine if they separate us.'

'I understand that the child's Aunt Waldegrave wants to take her.'

'Why?' demanded Maria. 'If she loved the child she would want to make her happy and Minney is happy with me.'

'Mary regards you as her mother,' said Lady Hertford with the air of Solomon. 'It is certainly wrong to take her from you.'

Maria was delighted for it appeared that Lady Hertford was on her side.

'You say the Prince will be displeased if they win this case?'

'I don't think he will ever forgive them. You see he is very fond of Minney . . . and she of him. You should see her climb on his knee and inspect his clothes. She calls him her Prinney. Oh, Isabella, if you could see those two together! I know he will be desolate if she is taken from us . . . for her sake as well as mine.'

Lady Hertford was thoughtful. The Prince supported the Whigs. What a triumph if she could be the means of bringing him over to the Tories! The old King was ailing. In fact there were rumours that he was often incoherent. He had had one unfortunate bout when there had almost been a Regency. The Prince of today could be the King of tomorrow.

She said: 'I think, Maria, that I might speak to my husband about this. He is after all the head of the family and if anyone should decide this child's future it is he . . . and not some band of lawyers.'

'Oh, Isabella, that is exactly what I think.'

'I could speak to him.'

'If you would you would earn my eternal gratitude . . . and the Prince's.'

'Leave this to me, Maria. I will see what can be done. Now, could you drink a dish of tea?'

*   *   *

Lady Hertford lost no time in telling her husband about Maria's visit.

Francis Seymour, second Marquis of Hertford, was a man of great political ambition. He had spent some forty years in the House of Commons and had been Lord of the Treasury in

Lord North's administration. When his father was created
Marquis of Hertford he had become Earl of Yarmouth and
taken his place in the Lords.

Isabella was his second wife; she was rich in her own right
and her husband respected her opinions; therefore he listened
intently to what she had to tell him.

She folded her beautiful hands in her lap and said somewhat primly: 'The child's place is clearly with Maria Fitzherbert. It would be cruel to take her from her. She is happy
there. Besides, it would displease the Prince.'

'Yet,' pointed out Lord Hertford, 'it might be better for her
to be brought up with her own family. It is not as though she
is alone in the world.'

'My dear Francis, Mary has been well looked after with
Mrs. Fitzherbert all these years. I am sure it would be most
harmful to remove her now. I think the Prince will never
forgive Henry for being so insistent.'

'He'll fare none the worse with the King for suffering the
Prince's displeasure.'

'The Prince is but the Prince . . . as yet. Should we not look
to the future?'

'One should always look to the future.'

'Maria Fitzherbert says that His Royal Highness will be
speaking to you soon on this matter. I think you should shake
your head and say that it is very difficult but that you will do
your best to please him. Let him think that you wish to work
for him, to please him. And then perhaps in due course let
Maria Fitzherbert have the child.'

'But if the law says her aunt Waldegrave is to have her . . .'

'My dear Francis, are you the head of the family or not? Let
the case proceed. Let them, if they will, give the custody of
Mary to Lord Henry. Then you step in as head of the family
and declare that the best guardian for Mary Seymour is Maria
Fitzherbert. That, my dear Francis, will bring you the
Prince's eternal gratitude . . . or as lasting as is possible with
His Highness.'

Lord Hertford smiled at his cool, elegant wife. 'You are
right, as usual, Isabella,' he said.

*   *   *

The Prince kept his word. He intimated that he would like
to visit the Hertfords and was cordially welcomed at their
house. He discussed at great length his desire to see Mary
Seymour happily settled with Maria and the Hertfords both
pledged their support.

'Your Highness realizes the difficulty,' Lady Hertford said. 'For myself and my husband there is no question of what is best, but Henry is stubborn I fear and having started this case he is determined to go on with it. We must try to find a way of outwitting him.'

The Prince looked at this elegant woman and thought her enchanting. There was something about her which was so graceful. What a figure! And so well did she carry herself that it was a joy to see her walk across a room. Her gown was exquisite. She reminded him of a china ornament—a collector's piece—cool, aloof, unattainable . . . almost. It was a long time since he had seen a woman who attracted him in a certain way as yet indefinable.

He was glad that this affair had sent him to the Hertfords.

They must discuss the matter in detail, said Lady Hertford, because if they did so they might discover some way out of the difficulty.

She gave the Prince her gracious smile that was completely without warmth. 'I have no doubt,' she said, 'that this court will award the child's guardianship to her family. So we shall have to work out a way from there.'

The Prince was completely fascinated.

'I am sure we can,' she added, 'if we but set our minds to it, and both my husband and I feel strongly that the best solution is for Mary to remain with Mrs. Fitzherbert.'

The Prince would have seized her hand and kissed it, but without seeming to do so she managed to evade him.

'How can I thank you for showing such kindness to me?' he asked fervently.

'Your Highness has no need to be grateful to me,' she told him. 'I am thinking of what is best for the child.'

He was impressed. What an unusual woman. He admired her remoteness almost as much as her elegance.

'May I call on you tomorrow so that we may discuss this matter further?'

'Lord Hertford and I are at Your Highness's command.'

'No,' he told her fervently. 'It is I who am at yours.'

*　　*　　*

After that he was a constant visitor. He sometimes called when Lord Hertford was not at home, for Lady Hertford could discuss the matter of Mary Seymour as well as her husband, and this she did.

He would sit watching her glacial features, her gracious movements and marvel at their excellence. But she remained as remote as the moon and never seemed to be aware of his admiration.

Sometimes the tears would come into his eyes when he tried to tell her that he could almost be glad of this controversy over the child because it had brought him the friendship of herself and her husband; to which she replied that if it brought also the happiness of the child it would then be a double blessing.

He went to Maria and told her that although the case seemed to be going against them he had great faith in the Hertfords, particularly Lady Hertford who seemed to possess such fine feelings with regard to Minney's happiness.

'We are going to win,' he cried.

'If we do,' Maria told him, 'it will be due to your efforts.'

'My dearest, you know I would not spare myself in my desire to bring you and Minney together for I am convinced that the place of two such special people is under the same roof.'

She embraced him and wept; and he, ever ready with the tears, wept with her.

'My dearest love, the three of us shall be together, never fear.'

Miss Pigot said that as the dear Prince was determined they were bound to win. He summoned several of his friends among the peers who would be giving their vote and told them why they must vote for the child's being left with Maria. It was hard for them to refuse him; but there remained a contingent of those who would be only too ready to work against him.

And when the case was nearing its end he called on the Hertfords and was received by them both—a little to his disappointment—for he had been hoping for a *tête-à-tête* with Isabella.

'We have had an idea,' she told him, 'and I trust Your Highness will think it a good one. Francis believes that it means certain victory.' She inclined her head to her husband. 'Pray explain it, Francis.'

Lord Hertford said: 'I propose to make a statement in the Lords during which I will explain that this matter is distasteful to me. It is a family matter; and as there is some dispute as to who should be the guardian of little Mary Seymour, I believe that I, as the head of the house, should take over that duty myself. *I* shall be the child's guardian. Henry cannot object to that. He dare not. Justice would most certainly be with me.'

'You will take the child?' asked the Prince.

'I will, Your Highness. And when she is given into my care I shall appoint the one whom I think most suitable to care for her, who, Your Highness can have no doubt, will be Mrs. Fitzherbert.'

The Prince had risen, tears springing to his eyes. He grasped Lord Hertford's hand, and gripped it for a moment; then he turned to Lady Hertford. He would have embraced her but she must have realized his intention for with skilful grace she had somehow placed herself behind her husband.

'How can I thank you good people for all you have done?' demanded the Prince.

'It has been our duty and our pleasure,' said Lady Hertford.

'It cannot fail,' added Lord Hertford.

'My thanks ... my warmest thanks!' The Prince looked momentarily melancholy. 'One thing occurs to me. This matter has brought us close together. We have discovered friendship. I hope that now it is over that friendship will continue.'

He was looking at Lord Hertford but he was thinking of his wife.

'We are honoured,' said Lord Hertford.

'Honoured indeed,' echoed Lady Hertford.

The Prince was delighted. He took his leave and went at once to Maria.

'Maria, my dearest love, I have the best news in the world. But perhaps I won't give it to you yet. Or shall I? Let me say this. Minney is ours ... for ever.'

'The case is not over.'

'That's the secret part, but I promise you that Minney is yours. You need never have another qualm. I have settled this matter.'

'But they are meeting tomorrow.'

'Let them. You will see.'

'You have made some arrangement?'

He was nodding delightedly. It was at such moments when her love for him was almost unbearable. He was like a boy who has provided some rich treat which he is going to enjoy as much as those for whom it was intended, and if he meant that the anxiety about losing Minney was over then she was the happiest woman in the world.

'You must tell me, please,' she cried. 'I cannot endure the suspense. I must feel sure before I can be completely at ease.'

So he put his arm through hers and they walked up and

down her drawing room while he told her. 'As head of the
family, Hertford is going to claim Minney and he has sworn
to me that as soon as he has done that he will proclaim you her
guardian.'

She clasped her hands together. It was rarely she wept but
she did so then. These were tears of joy.

'You have done this . . . *you* . . . my darling.'

He admitted it. 'Have I not told you that I would do anything in the world for you?'

For a moment those unpleasant thoughts came into her
mind. Anything? Had he not betrayed her . . . once when he
had let Fox deny his marriage to her in the House of Commons and a second time when he had left her for Lady Jersey?
Had he not been guilty of many infidelities. But the present
dilemma had appealed to his chivalry; he loved Minney even
as she did, and the loss of the child whom she regarded as her
own would have been a greater tragedy than anything that
could have befallen her then or now. She was sure of that.
With such an unaccountable lover perhaps a woman turned
naturally to her children—and Minney was her child.

But he had done this for her. He had thrown himself into
the fight for Minney with all that youthful sentiment of
which he was capable, and at such times he was at his most
lovable.

This must be the happiest time of her life; she had him and
Minney as well.

'We should tell them,' she said. 'Minney and Pigot. They
are as anxious as we are.'

'We will tell them now,' he said. 'Send for them.'

And so they came and he embraced them both. He always
laughed at his dear Pig who wanted to curtsey and grew fiery
red when he seized her as she was about to do so. Of course he
loved that sort of adoration; and there was Minney. 'Prinney,
darling, what are you doing here now? This is not your
time.'

And he, with his sense of the dramatic, took the little girl
by the hand and led her to Maria.

'Here is your mother, Minney. I give you to her. Love each
other always.'

Minney looked from one to the other and understood what
he meant for her days had been haunted by the fears that one
day a carriage would draw up and a wicked aunt would
come to take her away; at night sometimes she would awake
crying because she thought they had come by stealth to take
her. But there he was, looking like a plump benevolent god.

Their fears were over. He—being a god—had worked the miracle.

Minney threw herself into Maria's arms and clung to her for some seconds; then she turned to him. He was her dear, dear Prinney, the best Prinney in the world.

And they were all laughing and weeping together with Miss Pigot standing by crying and laughing too.

*   *   *

The weeks that followed were indeed happy ones for Maria, for everything worked out as the Hertfords had said it would. Lord Hertford made his announcement in the Lords and as a result was, by a unanimous vote, granted the guardianship of his brother's daughter which he would share with his wife. No sooner was this given him than he declared that he appointed Mrs. Maria Fitzherbert to continue to act as a mother to his niece.

It was wonderful. After three years of uncertainty they were safe.

Miss Pigot was continually pointing out how His Highness had worked to give Maria her heart's desire; and Maria agreed with her. As for the Prince, he went about beaming his pleasure, playing games with Minney and being very gracious to young George Keppel. Even his manner towards his daughter had changed and although he could not feel at ease with her as he did with Minney and George, there was a new warmth in his manner. Maria noticed this and was delighted that he had listened to her.

She intended to add Charlotte to her little family circle and since she was the Prince's daughter to try and be a mother to her and bring a little security into her life.

Minney would be eight years old in November of the year and Maria planned to give a very special party to celebrate this event.

When she discussed this with the Prince he cried: 'Certainly. Let it be ball and a supper. It shall take place in the Pavilion. You must start arrangements at once, my dearest love.'

Minney was delighted at the prospect of such a ball and she and Maria set about making the plans.

The Prince meanwhile went to London. There he called on the Hertfords and was entertained by them. It was beginning to be noticed that he was a constant visitor there; and if Lady Hertford had not been known to be a lady of great frigidity and one whose concern for her reputation was known to be greater than her desire for royal patronage, there would have been a new scandal and people would have been asking each other whether Maria Fitzherbert was not heading for more troublous times.

*   *   *

Minney, planning for her ball, believed now that they were all going to live happily ever after. The bogey had been removed for wicked Aunt Waldegrave had been defeated by the all-powerful Prince.

Prinney had said her birthday should be celebrated at the Pavilion—that exciting Palace which never failed to enchant her. She was to make up her lists of young guests and she would receive them in the gallery among the dragons and pagodas and the lanterns. It was like a fantastic dream of fairyland. Mamma would dress her in her first ball gown of blue silk with a wide white sash; and then she would go through the secret passage—always a delight—from Mamma's house on the Steyne to the Pavilion.

When her guests were assembled she would take them into the banqueting hall—the most elaborate of all the rooms. She had always been fascinated by the banqueting hall since she first remembered seeing it, when she had gazed up in amazement at the great palm tree painted on the ceiling and the fearsome dragon from whose claws appeared to swing the massive chandelier.

Minney loved Brighton especially in the summer when the streets were crowded with fashionable people strolling for the benefit of the sea air, or riding in their carriages. She liked to sit on Mamma's balcony and look over the Steyne; and it was pleasant when they rode together in the carriage. There was always gaiety round the Pavilion. The Prince's band played in the mornings in the gardens there and people came just to listen to it—perhaps hoping to get a glimpse of the Prince and Mamma, and herself too, because since the case she had become quite notorious.

It was a great treat—although a frequent one—to visit the Pavilion and to sit on the lawns and watch Prinney playing cricket which he liked to do; and when he scored she always applauded more loudly than for anyone else which made Mamma laugh. There were musical evenings which were held in the music room which was dominated by those fascinating gold and green dragons, for Prinney loved music, but of course Minney did not attend these. She supposed she would when she was a little older.

And now she was to have her first birthday ball and this was an indication that she was growing up.

*   *   *

In the gallery she received her guests—all the young people of Mamma's circle whose parents had been very eager to get them invitations.

Minney had become an important little person since the Prince treated her as though she were his daughter.

Gravely she received her guests as she had seen Maria do and the party was a great success. George Keppel and George Fitzclarence were at her side all the time, both determined to look after her. Everyone, thought Minney, wants to look after me. I'm different from Charlotte, who always seems to be so capable of looking after herself.

Then she sighed and said: 'I wish Charlotte could have been here.'

'She's at Windsor,' said George Keppel. He shuddered. 'I hate Windsor. London's more fun.'

'Poor Charlotte!' sighed Minney. 'I don't suppose she likes it there at all.'

George Fitzclarence who was the eldest son of the Duke of Clarence—Charlotte's Uncle William—and the actress Dorothy Jordan, said that Charlotte would have to stay there he believed for a long time, because it was hardly likely that they would let her see her mother.

Minney's expression clouded. She had forgotten that although her troubles were over, those of others might persist.

'Poor Charlotte,' she repeated.

The two Georges laughed.

'She wouldn't like to hear you call her that.'

Minney joined in the laughter. 'No. She would pinch my ear . . . hard.'

And thinking of Charlotte in a bellicose mood made it impossible to be sorry for her. So they gave themselves up to enjoying Minney's party.

The Old Girls and the Begum

'NOBODY ever had a stranger set of relations than I,' Charlotte told Louisa Lewis and Mrs. Gagarin. 'Really, they do the oddest things. Do you think they are all a little mad? Grandpapa is, I know. Pray don't look so shocked, dear Louisa, because you know it to be so. Did he not have to live in retirement not so long ago? My father was then hoping for the Regency but the old Begum put a stop to that. Oh, you poor dears, I am in a mood to shock you today.'

The two women exchanged glances which Charlotte intercepted. 'Pray don't make secret signs,' she cried imperiously. 'I know you talk about them when I'm not there. Don't deny it. I don't blame you. Everybody talks and why should they not? Conversation is one of the most amusing pastimes I know. And who could help talking about such a family as ours? There is my father with his affairs; there is Uncle Augustus who once made such a fuss about marrying his Goosey and now has left her. There is Uncle William who lives with that actress Dorothy Jordan as though she is his wife and there are all those little Fitzclarences to prove it. George Fitz is rather fond of Minney Seymour. I do declare everyone is fond of Minney Seymour. She is such a good little girl . . . not like wicked Princess Charlotte.'

'My dear Princess, you should not say such things. There are many who are fond of you.'

She turned to them and gave them each one of her rough embraces.

'You two, of course,' she said. 'But you are rather f . . . foolish to think so highly of me. I'm not a very pleasant character sometimes, I fear. Although I am not bad at others. I have my moments. Oh dear, and I have to attend my grandmother's Drawing Room. I think I shall go for a walk instead and then when it is time I shall not be found and Grandmamma will say what an ill-mannered creature I am—just like my mother, and she will think up some new and exquisite torture for me.'

'You know Her Majesty would never dream of torturing you.'

'But sometimes I think she would like to. She watches me with that big mouth of hers shut so tightly . . .' Charlotte had transformed herself into the Queen; she seemed to grow small and malevolent.

'Oh, do give over, dear Princess Charlotte, do,' said Mrs. Gagarin.

'I shall go for a walk first and then I shall come back and be prepared in good time to present myself to the Begum and the Old Girls.'

She grinned with delight to see the shocked horror these names always aroused when she used them. Perhaps that was why she did. It was a sort of revenge.

She snatched up her cloak and ran out. She heard Louisa calling her but she paid no heed. She was not supposed to walk out unaccompanied. What nonsense! Anyone would think she was as fragile as Minney Seymour. 'And I'm not . . .' she said. 'Nor as precious.'

She was saddened for a while. He was kinder now, so Mrs. Fitzherbert had spoken to him. She sensed that he was trying to make an effort, but there was always a barrier between them. It was her mother, of course. And what was happening about her mother? What was the Delicate Investigation going to reveal?

She knew now more than they thought. They were trying to prove her mother immoral; they were trying to show that that frightful infant Willie Austin was her mother's own baby and that her mother had performed an act of treason, for if Willie were indeed her mother's child and her mother insisted that the Prince was his father . . .

Impossible, for then she, Princess Charlotte, would not long be an heiress to the throne. At least she would have to take a step backwards.

Willie Austin—that horrid, vulgar little brat! She had always hated him—in common with everyone else except her mother. Perhaps she had been a little jealous to see her mother petting him, kissing him, making the great fuss of him she always did.

Indeed she had a very strange family.

The castle loomed before her. Why did she hate living at
Windsor when it was such a wonderful place? So much had
happened here in the past—the home of her ancestors.

When I am queen, she thought, there shall be feasting here.
It will be quite different then. I shall give balls and there will
be fun and laughter. It will not be the grim old place Grandpapa and the Begum have made it.

The terraces had been built by Queen Elizabeth and the
gallery was called Queen Elizabeth's Gallery. My favourite
part of the castle, thought Charlotte. I suppose because she
made it.

It was not surprising that she thought so often of Elizabeth.
There was so much here to remind her and at Hampton,
Greenwich and Richmond. How thrilling to have been so
often in fear of her life when she was young—and what
triumph for her when at last she was proclaimed Queen of
England. And those men who danced attendance on her and
whom she would not accept as her lovers!

Charlotte laughed aloud. I will be like her, I think, if I am
ever queen.

If! Why should she say that? She *would* be queen one day
for her father and mother would never have a son—and no
one could ever believe that that horrible child her mother
doted on at Montague House could possibly have been sired
by the Prince of Wales. So why should she say If? Because she
had made a will recently? Because there was something eerie
about the castle and the great forest. Because strange things
happened to members of her family?

'I *shall* be queen,' she said aloud. And then looked about
her almost defiantly. It was rather a wicked thing to have said
because not only Grandpapa but her father would have to die
first.

No one had heard. There was no one near. She looked towards the forest and thought of Herne the Hunter. He would
not be abroad by day—if he ever was. She did not believe in
such legends . . . not by day at any rate.

There was no Herne the Hunter; no one had ever seen
him. But she did know that people were afraid to be alone in
the forest by night lest they should come face to face with the
ghost of Herne with the stag horns on his head. It was death to
see him. She shivered. What dreadful things had Herne the
Hunter done which had made him hang himself on an oak
tree and haunt the forest for ever more?

There was so much romance at Windsor and yet living here

was so dull ... made so since she was not allowed to see her mother, because she was under the constant supervision of the Queen.

And now if she did not go in and allow them to prepare her for the Drawing Room she would be late and in disgrace—and not only herself but her attendants.

She grimaced. Who would be a princess? And yet ... how angry she had been at the thought of that horrid little Willie Austin robbing her of her inheritance!

No, she would be a queen ... as shrewd and clever ... and perhaps as wicked as Elizabeth.

I wished they'd named me after her instead of after the old Begum, she thought.

*　*　*

The King was seated at his table turning over some State papers. He could not keep his mind on them; he could not keep his mind on anything. And it is getting worse, he admitted. What's happening to me, eh, what? Perhaps I ought to abdicate. Give it over to George, eh?

He frowned; his face was scarlet and that made his white brows look whiter; they jutted out ferociously above his protuberant eyes. He was not in the least fierce; he was the mildest of men; he only wanted to live in peace—but events would not let him; and there was his family to plague him.

His sight was failing him; he could not read the papers without holding them closer to his eyes and then his mind would not concentrate on what was written there.

A poor fellow, he thought. And there's no respect for me ... not with my ministers, my people nor my family.

Yet there were some members of his family ... his daughters for instance. Amelia most of all. Blessed Amelia, the delight of his life, who gave him so much pleasure and so much anxiety. Yet as long as he had Amelia he could find life worth living. The others too he was fond of ... Augusta, Elizabeth, Mary and Sophia. Charlotte, his eldest, was living happily with her husband, which was more than he had hoped for, in Wurtemberg with her Prince, once the husband of Caroline's sister Charlotte who had died mysteriously ... at least they hoped she was dead, poor girl, for if she were not then that other Charlotte, Princess Royal of England and his eldest daughter, was not married at all. But the first Charlotte had disappeared mysteriously in Russia. She must have been rather like Caroline ... the sort of eccentric young woman to whom dramatic things happen.

Caroline was another source of anxiety. All this scandal.
Those men she entertained at Montague House and behaved
so wantonly with by all accounts. The terrible scandals that
happened in this family! His sons seemed to have no moral
standards at all. And he had always been such a virtuous man.

And what was coming out of this Investigation he could not
imagine. He knew what his son, the Prince of Wales, wanted.
He wanted the case proved against his wife. He wanted a
divorce.

'Shocking, eh, what?' said the King aloud.

And there was the child, Young Charlotte—all ears. She
was a sharp one. His mouth curved into a smile. Little minx,
that was Charlotte. But he was glad to have her here under his
care. She was his granddaughter. None of them must forget
that, and although he was ill and his sight was failing—and
his reason too some said—he was still the King.

The Queen had come into the room. She came unannounced as she would never have done before his illness.
He had been the master then; but now, he was too old, too
feeble.

'Your Majesty, I have come to accompany you to the Drawing Room.'

'Oh, yes,' he said, but he continued to sit at the table.

She was looking at him anxiously. She was always watching
for the signs. When he began to speak rapidly, when he was
incoherent, when the veins stood out at his temples and his
face was puce colour she really began to be frightened. It
was not that she had a great deal of affection for him. She had
never loved him. That had not been possible. When she had
come to England he had been kind to her and had successfully
hidden his disappointment to find a plain and gauche young
German girl was to be his wife when he had dreamed of lovely
Sarah Lennox with whom he was in love; he had at least not
blamed her, but had meekly accepted his fate while at the
same time he made it clear that she should have no power
outside her own household; she had come to England to bear
children and that was what she had done for twenty years—
fifteen children and that didn't leave much time in between
pregnancies.

But when he had lost his reason and she had made her
alliance with Mr. Pitt against the Prince of Wales and Mr.
Fox, Queen Charlotte had become quite a power at Court;
and when the King had recovered—though not fully—he had
been too weak, too ill to oust her from the position she had
made for herself.

'Is there any news?' he asked.

'You mean of the Investigation. There is nothing fresh.'

The King shook his head. 'I thought she was a pleasant woman. Not without good looks . . . ready to be a good wife . . .'

The Queen's mouth shut like a trap; it was thin and wide and even had she possessed perfect features apart from it— which she certainly did not—it would have prevented any claim to beauty.

'I knew it was wrong right from the beginning. And so did George.'

The King shook his head and tears came into his eyes. There were almost always tears in his eyes. The Queen was not certain whether they were due to ophthalmic weakness or emotion.

'I thought he was going to refuse . . .' he began.

'Better if he had,' retorted the Queen. She felt a grim satisfaction because the marriage had gone wrong. She had had a niece, beautiful, accomplished Louise of Mecklenburg-Strelitz who had needed a husband at the time—and the Prince, to plague her, had chosen his father's niece, Caroline of Brunswick, rather than his mother's.

'Perhaps it will come right between them,' said the King.

The Queen gave a snort of laughter. 'After this Investigation that is hardly likely. She's a coarse and vulgar creature and George is the most fastidious prince in Europe.'

'Too much time spent on prancing about in fancy dress. This fellow Brummell . . .'

'Oh, you know what George is. He's always been the same.' Her expression was one of mingling pride and anger. She had loved her first-born as she loved nothing else on earth—or ever would. She had craved his affection. And when he had scorned her she had deliberately sought to soothe her feelings by turning that love into a fierce hatred. They would be surprised, she often thought, all these people who surrounded her and regarded her as cold Queen Charlotte, incapable of emotion. There could never have been fiercer emotion than that she felt towards her eldest son. When he had been born she had believed that to be the happiest moment of her life; she had not been able to bear him out of her sight; she had a wax image made of him which she kept on her dressing table. Her beautiful George, her clever precocious son who had charmed everyone with his brilliance and arrogant manners and his fastidious ways as a boy. And when he had flouted her, shown so clearly that there was no place for his dowdy old mother in his life, love had turned to hate—but the love was still there smouldering. This doddering old man meant nothing to her compared with her brilliant magnificent son.

And the idea of marrying him to that dreadful creature! Thank God, she had had no hand in that and had in fact done all in her power to prevent it. Now perhaps they were sorry they had not taken her advice ... and none more so than George himself.

'The child's mother swears that this ... Willie ... is hers. She gives details of the hospital where he was born. That makes a clear case for Caroline. They can't accuse her of being his mother. How I wish ... What's the use. These scandals. They're no good for the family, eh, what?'

'The sooner she is sent back to Brunswick the better.'

'We can't do that.'

'Well, if she is not found to be the mother of this boy there are many other things she can be accused of. It's quite shocking. The Princess of Wales living apart from her husband and entertaining men!'

'It was he who refused to live with her, you know. I spoke to them both. "Never," he said. "I'd rather die." And as for her, she said if he didn't want her he could stay away. But I could see she would have had him back if he would go.'

'Nothing can be done until the Investigation is completed. But I do think that woman should be kept away from Charlotte.'

'The little minx,' said the King fondly.

'Indeed so and in need of correction which she shall have. There is an improvement since she has been here at Windsor.'

'Good fellow, Fisher. Nott too ... She's bright, eh, what?'

'Far from brilliant but by no means foolish. I do not like the stammer though; and she is too impulsive and most ungraceful. I have seen her father shudder when he looks at her.'

The King's face grew a shade more puce. 'His conduct has not always been so ... so good ... that he can afford to be critical of others, eh, what?'

The Queen said: 'I was speaking of deportment. Charlotte is gauche and clumsy. It must be rectified.'

'She dances prettily.'

Fond and foolish where the young were concerned, thought the Queen.

She said: 'She must spend more time with her aunts.'

Her aunts. His daughters. His darling love Amelia—kind and gentle, always affectionate to her own father, and yet he could not think of her without alarm, because of all the family she was the invalid.

'Amelia's cough . . .'

'Is better,' said the Queen.

They always told him it was better. But was it?

'And that pain in her knee?'

'It is nothing. The doctors say it will improve.'

He couldn't really believe them. They had to soothe the poor mad old king.

'It is time we went,' said the Queen. 'We shall be late for the Drawing Room.'

*   *   *

Ugh! thought Charlotte. What a family!

Lady de Clifford was close to her, praying she would do nothing to bring disgrace on herself and her governess. There seated on her chair was the Queen and beside her the King. No one need be frightened of him. He was simply poor old Grandpapa who was always kind and liked to be told one loved him. The old Begum was a different matter.

Lady de Clifford had made her practise her curtsey at least twenty times.

'But Cliffy, I know how to curtsey.'

'This is the Queen, my dear Princess.'

Indeed it was the Queen. How ugly she was! When she had been a little girl Charlotte had said: 'The two things I hate most are apple pie and my grandmother.' Someone had repeated that. They thought it funny. And on another occasion when they gave her the most horrid boiled mutton she had compared the Queen with that. 'There are two things I hate most in the world, boiled mutton and my grandmother.' The dish had changed but the grandmother remained. That was significant.

She must advance across the room which seemed enormous. Her hair hung in long ringlets and she was wearing a pink silk dress. There were a few pearl decorations on it. She felt stupid in it and would have been much happier in a riding habit. But of course one did not attend the Queen's Drawing Room in a riding habit.

She almost tripped and righted herself in time. She was aware of the sudden silence. All the Old Girls ranged round Grandmamma's chair were watching her. Mary would be sorry. Mary was the prettiest of the aunts and she was always charming to Charlotte, but she had begun to wonder whether Mary repeated to the Queen some of the things she said.

She was close to the Queen; she made her curtsey. Yes, it was a clumsy one and the Queen had snake's eyes; you almost expected a long darting poison tipped fang to come out of that ugly mouth.

The thought so amused Charlotte that she began to smile unconsciously.

She turned to the King. She should of course have greeted him first. He would not notice though and perhaps the Queen would be pleased even though it was a breach of etiquette. He put out his hand and she grasped it.

'Dear Grandpapa,' she said with great affection because he was not like the Queen.

Oh dear, he's going to cry, she thought. He looked awful when he cried; his great eyes looked as though they were going to pop out of his head. She did not curtsey—the one she had done would do for them both. That would show that it had really been meant for the King. She went and stood close to him and kissed his cheek. It was wrong of course but he did not care. He put an arm about her and said: 'Well, and how's my granddaughter, eh, what? Getting on with all those lessons, eh? Leading Fisher a dance? And Nott, eh, what?'

'As well as can be expected, Grandpapa.'

Amelia laughed and when Amelia laughed the King was very happy. In fact, thought Charlotte, they wouldn't be such a bad old family if it were not for the Begum.

The Queen said: 'Stay by me, Charlotte. I have some questions to ask you.'

'Thank you, Your Majesty,' she said demurely.

The questions were about her household, about her lessons. How was she getting on with her religious instruction? The Queen had not always been pleased by good Dr. Fisher's reports.

'But he is so good, Madam. We cannot all be as good as he is.'

'It should be our earnest endeavour to try.'

'Oh yes, Your Majesty.'

'I am asking Dr. Nott to let me see some of your work.'

Charlotte smiled, she hoped blandly, to disguise the apprehension in her heart. Would this give rise to longer hours of study? Oh, why could she not go to live at Montague House and become a part of that strange but merry household? Her mother would never have expected her to curtsey at this and that and address her by her title every now and then. Why could not her grandmother be a grandmother as well as a queen?

'He tells me that you do not seem to be able to master the rules of grammar. Why is that?'

Charlotte thought for a second. 'It's because the rules of grammar master me, I expect.'

'You are too frivolous, Charlotte. Try to be more serious.'

Charlotte lowered her eyes. 'I fear it is in my nature, Madam.'

'That is no excuse. It must be suppressed. I hear you are fond of writing letters to everyone you can think of . . . full of idle observations, and that you write pages of irrelevant nonsense when you should be more profitably engaged.'

'George was the same, so I've heard,' said gentle Amelia. 'He loved to write. It is a gift in a way.'

'What's that, eh?' demanded the King, eager to hear what his darling had said.

Amelia went to her father and put her hand on his arm.

'I was saying, Papa, that Charlotte is like her father. She loves to write. I always remember hearing that.'

Tears again, thought Charlotte. What a watery old Grandpapa! But Amelia did look very affecting leaning against him—she was so slight and slender, like a fairy; she really did look as though she were made of some light and airy substance which a puff of wind would carry off. Perhaps Grandpapa thought this and that was why he was always so frightened of losing her.

'It is a most *un*satisfactory habit and quite useless,' said the Queen.

Oh dear! sighed Charlotte to herself. How I wish that I were far away. At Montague House? For a while. But there was no security at Montague House. Mamma was affectionate in as much as she kept embracing and kissing and calling one her love and angel. But there were times when she seemed to forget and perhaps she was more devoted to Willie Austin than her own daughter.

No, she would have liked to be in Tilney Street with calm and dignified Mrs. Fitzherbert, whose affection would never be over-demonstrative but steady, so that one would know it was always there.

Tilney Street—or the house on the Steine—and the Prince of Wales arriving and taking his place as though it were his home.

'And where is my little Charlotte?' he would say; and she would run out and climb on his knee and call him Prinney.

But this was what Minney Seymour did. Minney who was not his daughter at all.

It was unfair. She should have been there. How different that would have been.

'Charlotte, you are not attending to what I am saying,' said the Queen.

*   *   *

It was less of an ordeal to be with the aunts. They tried to pamper her a little; after all she was their only legitimate niece and they all adored her father, although they were afraid to say so openly.

So she was Darling Charlotte to them; but they kept a close watch on everything she did and said, and she did suspect that to curry favour with the Queen they reported these to her.

They are a nest of spies! thought Charlotte dramatically. Aunt Augusta was the oldest of the Old Girls although she had an elder sister who was now married and living abroad. That was Charlotte, the Princess Royal, who used to write long letters to Eggy—Lady Elgin—who had been Charlotte's governess before Lady de Clifford's time. Eggy used to read the letters to Charlotte sometimes to show what a good aunt she had and to teach her to count her blessings, of which Good Aunt Charlotte was supposed to be one. She used to send presents from abroad which were always unusual and welcome. There were dolls dressed like German peasants and once a miniature set of teacups and saucers. These presents however were usually accompanied by some homily. 'Pray tell Charlotte that I am sending her a fan and when I go to Stuttgart I shall not fail to bespeak some silver toys *if* she continues to be a good girl.'

Dear old Eggy always read these letters in a voice of deep solemnity, impressing on Charlotte the need to improve herself. Eggy had been far more of a martinet than Lady de Clifford because Charlotte had quickly discovered that the latter was a little afraid of her—afraid perhaps of losing her position, of displeasing the Prince of Wales, of proving to them all that she was quite incapable of controlling the Princess Charlotte. Aunt Charlotte on the Continent must have received long letters about her progress not only from Eggy but from the Old Girls. Fragments of the letters came back to her now: 'As she has once found that she is clever, nothing but being with older children will ever get the better of this unfortunate vanity, which is a little in her blood as you know full well. I approve very much of your trying to get the better of her covetousness.'

Such a little monster I must have been! mused Charlotte.

And her aunt had suggested that when she went to the country after being inoculated—for she could not be

allowed to go near the cottage people until she had been—she
might be taken among the very poor so that pity might be
aroused in her. She should be encouraged to give freely of her
pocket money to the poor.

And Eggy had seen that she had. Charlotte had found one
of those account books only recently with the amounts she had
given set down in her childish handwriting: It was all 'To a
poor blind man 2s;' 'To a lame woman 1s' and so on—
columns and columns of it.

Perhaps, Charlotte reflected, it was better that Aunt Charlotte was in Germany for she seemed to be of a critical
nature: 'As for Charlotte's being much on one side you could
easily make her get the better of it by making her wear a
weight in her pocket on the opposite side.' (She remembered
those weights.) 'As for her stutter, she must try and overcome
that. She must calm herself before she speaks.' 'We must watch
these little shadows on her character. If she behaves ill to
others she should be punished severely. For lies or violent
passions I believe the rod is necessary.' 'I always feared the
child's cleverness would lead her to be cunning to gain her
points.' 'I hear that she is good at music and repeats French
well and prettily. Though all this sounds very well I was a
little hurt that she displayed these accomplishments without
showing any timidity. Were she my daughter I should prefer a
little modesty.'

Charlotte could see that there would have been no pleasing
that aunt who bore the same name as herself and rejoiced in
the distance which separated them.

That left Augusta, Elizabeth, Mary, Sophia and Amelia.

She studied them now as they bent over their embroidery;
and she, of course, was supposed to be doing the same. Why
did her threads always seem to get knotted? Why did she
suddenly find that one stitch—some way back—was too big
and in the wrong place? I was not meant to be a seamstress,
she thought. Did Queen Elizabeth have to sit over her needlework stitching away like some little needlewoman? How foolish it all was. She did not want to learn to sew but to be a
queen.

Aunt Augusta was sketching. She was the artistic one of the
family; she could also compose music which was very clever
indeed. Grandpapa sometimes listened to it and sat nodding
his head and afterwards he would say: 'That was very good,
Augusta my dear,' as though she were of Charlotte's age and
had just mastered some difficult piece on the harpsichord.
Then there was Aunt Elizabeth who was always affectionate

and liked to be called Aunt Libby which was what Charlotte
had called her as a child; she thought it showed what great
friends they were, but Charlotte did not trust her. Aunt Elizabeth was always looking for drama. She would have liked to
play a big part in state affairs and be involved in some terrific
plot, Charlotte was sure. Mary was still pretty although she
was getting old—she must be nearly thirty now. Poor Mary
who had been the best looking of all the princesses and was
hoping to marry her cousin the Duke of Gloucester one day.
He was very fond of her and was always at her side, and when
he was there she glowed very prettily and looked nearer
twenty than thirty; but then he would go away and she would
be upset and grumble about how they were kept sheltered
from life and then her face would pucker and she would look
discontented and quite old. Poor Mary! Poor all of them!
They were not very happy, and who could wonder at it, for
Grandpapa, much as he loved them, could not bear to hear
that any man wanted to marry them and he went on trying to
make himself believe that they were really very young girls
who had to be protected from the world. Theirs was not
exactly an enviable lot considering this and the fact that they
were in constant attendance on the old Begum whose temper
was very sharp, particularly in the winter when she was
troubled with rheumatic pains.

Then there was Sophia—a bit of mystery, Sophia; there
were secrets in Sophia's eyes, and Charlotte had seen her
whispering with General Garth in corners. General Garth
was often in attendance because he was one of Grandpapa's
favourite equerries; but, Charlote ruminated, he seemed to
like Sophia even better than the King.

And then Amelia—dear fragile Amelia, whose health gave
her family so much anxiety; and who was sweet and kind to
everybody particularly poor Grandpapa, and who did not
worry as the others did about not being allowed to marry because she knew that she was far too fragile to be a wife.

These were the aunts then—the Old Girls—whose company
must be borne. They were always kind to her and she would
have liked them if only she could have trusted them.

Now Aunt Elizabeth had taken up Charlotte's piece of
embroidery and was clucking over it in an amused sort of way.

'Why, dearest Charlotte, this would never do. What would
your Papa say if he saw a piece of work like that?'

'He wouldn't know that there was anything wrong with it.
He's an authority on women, art and fashion—and that does
not I believe include embroidery.'

Aunt Elizabeth gave a little gasp of dismay; Aunt Mary chuckled.

'One thing we can always say of our dear little Charlotte,' said Amelia, 'is that she says what's in her mind.'

'How could one speak of what was *not* in one's mind?' asked Charlotte gravely.

'I meant, dear, that so many people dissemble. They say one thing and mean another.'

'And is it a fault to be outspoken?'

'Far from it.'

'Then at least I have one virtue.'

'You have many, dearest child,' said Amelia.

'But,' said Elizabeth, 'they do not include embroidering.'

The sisters all laughed.

'Put it right for me, dear Aunt Libby, before the old . . . before anyone sees it.'

Covert smiles. They knew she was going to say the old Begum. Perhaps they thought of their mother as that. Perhaps they did not like her any more than Charlotte did, but because they were old and were expected to behave with decorum they had to pretend. I shall never be like that, thought Charlotte. But then when I'm old I shall be the Queen.

She watched Aunt Elizabeth's deft fingers unpicking her clumsy stitches.

'I should like to know,' she said boldly, 'when I am to see my mother.'

Hushed silence! But she was not going to let them pretend. 'I have heard, of course, about this Delicate Investigation. What a strange way of describing an investigation!'

The Princesses looked at each other in dismay and Mary said: 'It describes it exactly. It is a very delicate matter.'

'You mean one that is not to be discussed.'

'I mean one, dear, which it is better to forget.'

'But how can I forget it when I don't see her? It's weeks and weeks . . . months and months . . .'

'His Majesty thinks it best,' said Aunt Elizabeth as though that solved the matter.

But everything His Majesty thought best was not necessarily so—for instance, refusing to allow his daughters to marry and making them live this life of frustration until they were ready to do almost everything to escape it.

'A child should surely be allowed to see its own mother,' said Charlotte primly.

'It would depend,' replied Augusta mysteriously.

'On what?'

'On circumstances.'

'What circumstances?'

'Oh, dear Charlotte, you must not speak in that er ... peremptory manner. It is not really very becoming.'

'But I want to know.'

'You will understand,' said Amelia gently. 'All in good time.'

'But Willie Austin is *not* my brother.'

Augusta said: 'Where does the child hear these things?' No one answered.

Charlotte knew that they were thinking she was far too precocious. Perhaps having parents who hated each other and created public scandals made one precocious.

'Everyone whispers about them,' she said scornfully. She was about to mention the cartoon she had seen but thought better of that. They might find some way of stopping her seeing them.

'I think,' she said, 'that I should be allowed to see my mother.'

Augusta, as the eldest, thinking it behoved her to speak said: 'I will speak to the Queen about this. And tell her what you have said.'

'Not the Queen,' cried Charlotte in alarm. 'Tell Grandpapa instead.'

'I fear it would upset him.'

Charlotte turned to Amelia. 'If you could tell him ... not specially ... but one day when you are talking to him. Say I asked about my mother and that a child ought not to be separated from her own mother.'

Amelia smiled. She was accustomed to having to make requests to the King.

'I'll see how he is and if I can introduce the subject without upsetting him.'

Charlotte was about to say more when Amelia hurried on: 'Augusta, do play that latest piece of yours. I am sure Charlotte would like to hear it.'

She would discover little from the aunts, that was certain.

While the music was being played the Duke of York came in. This was Uncle Fred—her favourite among her Uncles. He greeted her exuberantly. He was not one to stand on any ceremony.

'And how is my little niece today?'

'Very well, Uncle.'

He kissed her warmly; he was very fond of women, as were the rest of the uncles and her father as well, of course. But their trouble was that they could not be faithful for long. The Duke of York had now become quite friendly with his wife although at one time they had hated each other. Aunt Frederica of York interested Charlotte far more than any of the Old Girls; but Uncle Fred was not often at Oatlands where she lived; he was always deep in some love affair with a woman other than his wife.

But she liked him; he was jolly, gay, kind and carefree. A very pleasant sort of uncle to have. She liked him even better than Uncle Augustus, Duke of Sussex, for he had disappointed her when he had left dear Aunt Goosey for another woman.

We are a strange family and no mistake, thought Charlotte. Here are the Old Girls living like nuns in a convent and scarcely allowed out of the old Begum's pocket while the Old Boys live the most scandalous lives. Uncle Augustus had not been considered to be married to Goosey although he had declared he was at one time and there had been a case to prove he wasn't. He had married her it was true, but this was in defiance of the Royal Marriage Act which Grandpapa had made law and which said that no member of the royal family under the age of twenty-five could marry without his consent. Uncle Augustus had married Goosey—she was going to have a child—and then the State had said No, they were not married, and Goosey's baby was a bastard, which had infuriated Uncle Augustus at the time; but perhaps he did not care now since he and Goosey had parted.

As for Uncle Fred, he had disliked his wife and refused to live with her almost from the first; Charlotte was glad they were good friends now though, for she liked them both; in fact she thought they were her favourite uncle and aunt.

Fred was clearly not clever like the Prince of Wales; he just wanted to enjoy life and to see everyone about him enjoying it too. He had been her father's greatest friend at one time and they still were devoted to each other. In fact all the brothers were friends, which was one of the pleasantest aspects of the family, and unusual too. For, thought Charlotte, we are a quarrelling family as a rule.

'What's the music?' asked Uncle Fred.

'One of Augusta's own,' Amelia put in.

'It's good. Makes you want to dance, eh, Charlotte?'

Charlotte agreed that it did.

'Play it in waltz time, Gussy,' said Uncle Fred; and Augusta complied.

'Come, Charlotte,' said Uncle Fred, 'we'll waltz together.'

'Oh, Uncle, I don't know how.'

'Time you did then. Don't you agree, girls?'

Aunt Elizabeth thought that when the time came for Charlotte to learn to waltz her father would decide that she should have lessons.

'I'll take the blame for introducing them prematurely,' said Uncle Fred. He was on his feet and holding out his hands to Charlotte.

This was better than sitting stitching or trying to prise information out of aunts who were determined not to give it.

'Now, Charlotte, hold your head up, take my hand . . . thus. Off we go.'

She was awkward, she knew, but this was only Uncle Fred who was never critical.

'Capital! Capital!' he kept saying. 'That's our clever Charlotte.'

She smiled up at him gratefully. His protuberant blue eyes—such a feature of the family—were alight with kindness, and his cheeks were scarlet with exertion, but he was clearly enjoying this.

'Come Mary,' he said. 'And you too, Elizabeth.'

They rose and waltzed round the room. Sophia who was not very strong and Amelia, who of course would become quite breathless if she attempted to dance, were the spectators.

'That was good,' cried Uncle Fred, when the music stopped. 'I'll tell your father he ought to be proud of his daughter. You'll soon be gracing his ballroom, Madam Charlotte.'

Charlotte standing there flushed, slightly breathless, was happy. She pictured herself at Carlton House. She could see clearly the room with the tall pier-glasses which gave the impression that the room went on and on. She thought of the glittering chandeliers which threw down a rosy light on all the company and the crimson velvet hangings with their gold fringe and tassels.

In the midst of all this splendour she would dance and the Prince of Wales would notice her and be proud of her. He would stand before her and make that bow at which everyone marvelled and say: 'I think my daughter should dance with me.'

And seated nearby, looking exactly as a queen should look —and that was as different as it was possible for anyone to be from the old Begum—would be Mrs. Fitzherbert, smiling, well pleased, because everything was well between the Prince of Wales and his daughter.

How often all her dreams came back to this happy ending; and it was only in reality that it seemed as far away as ever.

* * *

Seated at her table in Lower Lodge, her books about her, Charlotte heard the sound of carriage wheels. She ran to the window and looking out saw her mother alighting.

She has come to see me! thought Charlotte excitedly. At last we shall be together. She must have ridden all this way from Blackheath to see me.

As she ran from the schoolroom she collided with Dr. Nott who was about to enter and nearly knocked him over.

'My gracious me,' he murmured; but she had run past him. She would put on a clean dress, for the one she was wearing was a little grubby. Not that her mother would notice.

Lady de Clifford came running from her room crying: 'Princess Charlotte, what has happened. Where are you going?'

'My lady, my mother has come.'

'It's impossible,' cried Lady de Clifford, turning pale.

'I tell you I have seen her with my own eyes.'

Lady de Clifford knew that the King's orders were that the Princess of Wales was not to visit her daughter. If Charlotte had indeed seen her mother then the Princess had come to Windsor in defiance of that order.

Flustered and trembling she decided she must delay Charlotte. 'You should be ready when you are sent for,' she said, although she did not believe that Charlotte would be sent for. Oh dear, what a dreadful task this was! She would die of palpitations one day. Trying to keep Charlotte in order was enough, but to have these unfortunate situations thrust upon her by her eccentric relations was more than a woman could endure.

'You should put on a clean dress . . . and comb your hair and then . . . you will be in readiness,' she babbled.

'Help me then. I must be ready. I daresay they will give us only an hour together or something silly.'

Charlotte hastily put on a clean dress and allowed Lady de Clifford to comb her hair.

'I should return to the schoolroom,' she said, 'for they will expect me to be there and that is where they will look for me.'

Lady de Clifford agreed and returned to the schoolroom with her.

They had not been there very long when they heard the commotion from without.

The Princess of Wales had come out to her carriage. Oh dear, thought Lady de Clifford, she does not look in the least like a princess. No wonder the dear Prince . . .

Caroline's black wig was a little awry; her heavily rouged cheeks were startling beside the white lead with which the rest of her face was covered apart from those very black brows which had been painted on.

She was talking loudly in her atrocious English. She was trembling with rage clenching and unclenching her fists and even turned to shake one at the windows.

It was clear to Lady de Clifford that the Princess of Wales was being turned away from Windsor.

'Cliffy,' whispered Charlotte, 'what does it mean?'

She wanted to run down to the carriage to tell her mother that if no one else wanted her she did.

Lady de Clifford had laid a hand on her shoulder; she was saying: 'I doubt not the Princess has come without an invitation.'

'Without an invitation! To see me . . . her own daughter!'

The coachman had whipped up the horses, Lady de Clifford noticed with relief, and the carriage had started to move.

'They have driven my mother away,' cried the Princess Charlotte.

*　　*　　*

Gentle Amelia tried to comfort Charlotte.

'You see, Charlotte dear, His Majesty cannot visit the Princess nor allow her to visit us until this little matter is settled.'

'What little matter?'

'The Princess of Wales has been entertaining people at Montague House who are not quite the sort of people who—who should be the friends of royal people, do you understand?'

'How is that? I met Sir Sidney Smith there. He is a great Admiral and he fought for his country. You should hear how he defended Saint Jean d'Acre. He told me about this. He could tell wonderful tales. And he used to carry me round on his shoulders.'

'He could have been a very brave and daring sailor but still unfit to mix with a royal princess. You are too young to understand.'

'I am not too young,' said Charlotte rudely. 'I liked Sir Sydney. And there was Thomas Lawrence too. He is a very great painter. It is a good thing to paint well, I suppose you'll agree.'

'It is very good, but to be able to paint does not mean that one is fit ...'

'And my mother is not allowed to see me because she knows these people?'

'One day you will understand.'

'One day!' cried Charlotte scornfully. 'What's the good of one day when this is *Now*. Why is it that learning some things is so good for one and others have to wait till "one day"! I should have thought all knowledge was good. Don't you think that's true, Aunt Amelia?'

Aunt Amelia said that when she was older she would understand; and she then began to cough; and as, when Aunt Amelia coughed, everyone had to try to stop her doing so because it so upset the King, Charlotte had to run and get her soothing syrup and that was the end of that little conversation.

But, determined Charlotte, they are not going to keep me from my mother. I love her, and she loves me. She wouldn't have come to Windsor to be insulted by Them if she did not.

She thought constantly of her mother and longed to see her again.

Augusta told her that there was to be a party for young people at Windsor and she could ask anyone she wished.

'I thought,' said Aunt Augusta, 'that you might like to ask Lady de Clifford's grandson, young George Keppel, and perhaps little Sophia Keppel as well. You may invite them both if you wish.'

'You said that I might ask anyone I wished?'

'Yes, that is so.'

'Then I ask my mother,' she said boldly.

Aunt Augusta looked as though she were going to have a fit of the vapours. Really, she confided to Elizabeth afterwards, Charlotte could be most embarrassing.

The Will of the People

CHARLOTTE was glad to be back in Carlton House for that meant visits to Lady de Clifford's house in South Audley Street and to Mrs. Fitzherbert's in Tilney Street.

Here she could play with George and Minney and she constantly plagued Lady de Clifford to take her and George to Tilney Street.

These were the most exciting expeditions because she never knew when her father would call. What fun to ride in the carriage sitting beside George while Lady de Clifford sat smiling opposite them pleased because she was going to enjoy a tête-à-tête with dear Maria Fitzherbert and Charlotte always seemed to behave more decorously in her house than anywhere else.

It was a small house, compared with Carlton House, but Charlotte loved it. On the first floor french windows opened on to a balcony and from this one could look out on Park Lane, for the house was on a corner. Charlotte loved to open those french windows, stand on the balcony and pretend that there were crowds below cheering her because she was to be their queen. She often thought as the carriage rolled along and people took little notice: Oh, you do not know that in this carriage is one who will one day be your queen.

Mrs. Fitzherbert received her as though she were really pleased she had come, and she whispered to her that she had a promise from the Prince of Wales that he would look in that day.

Charlotte returned the pressure of Mrs. Fitzherbert's hand and it was though they shared a secret.

'Do you think he will be pleased to see me here?' whispered Charlotte so that neither George nor Minney could hear.

'He will be delighted. He has told me so.'

That was wonderful news. Now when he came she would not be nervous; perhaps she would not stutter and be able to seem as bright as she did in her own schoolroom.

She would feel safe while the plump figure of Mrs. Fitzherbert presided over the scene like a benevolent fairy.

*   *   *

The Prince of Wales left Carlton House for Tilney Street with mingled feelings. He had to face the fact that since the Seymour case, during which his friendship with the Hertfords had become a very close one, he had fallen in love.

Falling in love had, of course, been the major preoccupation of his life, but when he had returned to Maria he had believed that as long as he had Maria he would never seriously hanker after another woman.

How wrong he had been! But then how could he have guessed there would have been such perfection in the world as that possessed by Isabella Hertford?

He had already confessed his devotion to her, but she remained aloof.

'Your Highness's kindness is appreciated, and I trust that my husband and I will always remain your very good friends.'

'It is more than friendship I need.'

She smiled at him. 'Your Highness will remember that I am a married woman and you are a married man . . . some say doubly so.'

Her fresh coolness delighted him; in his heart he wondered whether he really wanted her to surrender. When he thought of the sexuality of Lady Jersey he was nauseated. How different was Isabella. She would not surrender, she implied, on any terms. And what could he do? There was nothing he could offer her that she should possibly want. She was as rich as he was—richer possibly—and her great passion was politics —Tory politics at that. When the Prince considered all that lay between them—his politics, her frigidity, virtue she called it—it seemed a hopeless case. And yet it was the hopelessness which he had always found so attractive; and while she held no hope of surrender, she implied that she was not displeased by his attempts to seduce her.

At the same time she made certain demands; she wanted assurances that he really was as infatuated as he declared himself to be.

'Could she doubt it?' he demanded.

'Yes,' she replied. 'You are so frequently in the company of that very virtuous lady who—rumour has it—would never so compromise herself if she did not consider you to be her husband.'

'Maria Fitzherbert has been my very good friend for many years.'

'Then, Sir, since you are so satisfied with *that* friendship, why do you seek mine?'

Because, he told her, she was the most beautiful, elegant and fascinating creature he had ever met, and he could only be truly happy in her company. He wished to give a banquet for her at Carlton House. Would she allow him to do this?

She was thoughtful for a while. She was not very anxious to appear in public with him. She cherished her reputation which had never been touched by scandal, and she had no intention of becoming one of the women with whom it would be said he was having a light love affair. She had no doubt that while these were progressing he made ardent protestations to the ladies concerned, as he was doing to her now. He was merely the Prince of Wales; he had very little political power, nor would he have while the King ruled; but as she pointed out to her husband, the King was a very sick man and at any moment there could be a new sovereign—or at least a Regent. Then the Hertfords should have that King or Regent at their command. They had to remember that. But in the meantime she must keep him dangling. Even so neither of them must forget that while he believed himself to be Maria Fitzherbert's husband no one was going to get very far with him. That woman had a very firm hold; and if the Prince was to be of any use to the Hertfords it had to be broken. It had been broken before by Frances Jersey; and what Lady Jersey could do Lady Hertford was certain that she could do better.

So her task at the moment was to keep the Prince at bay while slacking Maria Fitzherbert's hold on him.

Maria had considered herself a friend of Lady Hertford; it was for this reason that the entire affair had begun, for Maria had sought Isabella Hertford's help in the Seymour case. Friendship? thought Lady Hertford. That had little place in her life. She loved politics and very little else—except her own person of course; it was a great delight to dress herself and know that she was the most elegant woman present when she entered a ballroom and everyone turned to look at her. The Snow Queen, they called her. Well, why not present a different kind of beauty to the Court? And in any case her cool elegance was the complete opposite of the blowsy appearance presented

by the Princess of Wales. The very contrast in them was
enough to make the Prince admire her.

But she was not concerned with the Princess of Wales but
with Maria Fitzherbert. She was going to amuse herself by the
manner in which she ousted Maria. Outwardly they would
continue to be friends, while slowly she undermined Maria's
influence.

Her first move was typical of her.

She would be delighted to attend the banquet at Carlton
House, but did the Prince know that people were beginning
to whisper about them? 'About myself and Your Highness!
That is something which has never happened to me before.
My reputation is at stake. I am a married woman; Your Highness is a married man. I could not dream of attending the
banquet at Carlton House unless Mrs. Fitzherbert was present
also.'

She was adamant. Those were her terms. It was not as he
had visualized it. He had pictured Isabella beside him while
they dined so that he could pay court to her. And how could
he with Maria present? The banquet, he explained, was to be
given in honour of Lady Hertford. He had not counted on
Maria's being there.

'Your Highness must see that only if Mrs. Fitzherbert is
present could I attend.'

So now, driving to Tilney Street the uncomfortable task lay
before him of requesting Maria's presence at a banquet at
which Lady Hertford was to be the guest of honour.

Maria should please him in this, he told himself. He had
done so much to please her. In fact he was on his way to Tilney Street now, because she had specially requested it.

'To please me,' she had pleaded, 'be as attentive to Charlotte as to Minney. Will you do this . . . for me?'

He had hesitated. Charlotte was so *gauche*. God knew he
had tried hard with the girl, but she was so like her mother.
She reminded him of her all the time and because of this he
longed always to get away from her. But since it was his dear
Maria's special wish, he would come.

As he rode through the streets he was recognized, but the
crowds were silent. There were no cheers now; he was no
longer the darling of the people. They even preferred his mad
old father. They were blaming him now because of the Delicate Investigation. They said he persecuted his wife. He had
tried to bring a case against her and had failed, although during the course of that case surely everyone had realized the
sort of woman Caroline was. Perhaps William Austin was not

her own child, but that did not mean that she had not behaved in an extremely immoral fashion with the men who
visited her house. He preferred to believe the maid Mary
Wilson who had told another servant that she had gone into a
room at Montague House and actually found the Princess
Caroline and Sir Sidney Smith engaged as she put it 'in the
fact'. This they had heard and yet they still believed Caroline
to be the wronged wife. They blamed him for the failure of
the marriage; and in addition they suspected that he might
have previously married Maria Fitzherbert, which was in a
way the truth. Maria *was* his wife, if not in the eyes of the
State in those of the Church, and for Maria he had risked his
crown and sacrificed much. It was because of Maria that he
was greeted with sullen silence as he rode through the streets,
for it was Maria's staunch Catholicism that the people would
not endure.

What I sacrificed for her! he thought. Is it asking too much
that she do this little thing for me?

She was waiting to greet him in the hall; he embraced her
fervently.

'My dearest love!'

'I am so happy to see you. Charlotte is with Minney and
George Keppel.'

'Oh, yes . . .' This was something else he was doing for her.

'They will have seen your carriage arrive. I'll swear they
were watching from a window. They will be so excited.'

He wasn't listening. 'I should like to be with you for a little
while first, my dearest.'

Arm in arm they went into her drawing room.

'And how is dear Minney?' he asked.

'In excellent health. In fact since the case has been over she
has been in high spirits. Poor lamb, she was far more worried
than I realized.'

'I shall never forget what we owe the Hertfords,' said the
Prince.

'It was a brilliant idea. I have told Lord Hertford so often
how grateful I am that I believe he is getting a little weary of
my gratitude.'

'We should do more I suppose than offer them words of
thanks.'

'What could we do? I think, in fact, that Minney's happiness is enough reward for us all.'

'Even so I thought of giving a banquet at Carlton House.
Lady Hertford should be the guest of honour. I would be
obliged to devote myself to her for the whole of the evening.'

Maria suffered more than a twinge of uneasiness. She had heard the rumours. It could not be true. Isabella Hertford was such a frigid creature. A fashion-plate it was true and that appealed to him, but she would never indulge in a liaison outside her marriage—not even with the Prince of Wales.

'Should they not both be guests of honour?'

'Why . . . yes . . . of course. Perhaps you could devote yourself to Hertford.' He was beaming with pleasure. That would be it. 'There could be two tables . . . one at one end of the room with you at the head and Hertford on your right and at the other end my table with Lady Hertford.'

Oh, no, thought Maria. The Prince's table was the only table at which it would be an honour to sit and her place was at that table. She always had a place there—next to the Prince of Wales. It was his way of saying to the world that he regarded her as the Princess of Wales and expected everyone else to do the same.

'I think that both Hertfords should be with us at your table,' said Maria firmly.

But that would not suit him. How could he make verbal love to Isabella under Maria's nose?

'No,' he said coolly, suddenly becoming very regal and the Prince of Wales in place of Maria's 'dear love'. 'I prefer it my way.'

Maria felt indignant. She wanted to tell him that she had already heard the rumours about his growing passion for Lady Hertford. She controlled herself with an effort and said coolly: 'Lady Hertford herself might not care for the arrangement.'

'I have already spoken to her.'

'Without consulting me,' she said; and immediately cursed her hot temper which Miss Pigot had informed her had been her downfall during the Jersey affair.

'Did you expect me to consult you about my Carlton House arrangements?'

Oh dear, she thought, we are going to quarrel. And Charlotte is waiting upstairs for him. In a moment he would walk out of the house and Charlotte would believe it was because she was there. Poor child, how dared he treat his wife—for she was that, whatever anyone said—in this way; and how dared he refuse his daughter that affection which she so obviously craved.

She said quickly: 'Of course I did not. Charlotte is eagerly awaiting you. Please . . .'

'And you will agree?' he asked eagerly. 'You will come to the banquet as I ask?'

She thought: We are bargaining. Be nice to your daughter and I will be present so that the woman whom you hope to make your mistress is not compromised.

No, she thought. I won't do it. Then she thought of that young girl who was eagerly waiting now, listening for his footstep on the stair.

What does it matter? she thought. He has been unfaithful before. But that was what she had told herself when Lady Jersey had appeared on the scene and had brought about their parting. But he had come back to her. He knew he needed her. Very well, let him have his flirtations, his infatuations, his light love affairs. He would always come back to Maria.

She said: 'I agree. And now come and show your daughter that world famous charm.'

* * *

How impressive he was! Charlotte was proud of him. No one else had a father like him. George Keppel had Lord Albemarle, who was all right; poor Minney had no father at all, though she had Mrs. Fitzherbert, who was perhaps a great deal more comforting—but Charlotte had the Prince of Wales.

He looked enormous—tall and fat; his eyes were laughing; he looked as though something had pleased him; he had somewhat pouting lips which gave him a petulant air and his slightly tilted nose made one want to kiss him. His clothes were magnificent; they made Charlotte feel awkward just to look at them, because they fitted him so perfectly. His coat of very fine dark green cloth was single breasted and he wore it buttoned right up to the chin; his breeches were of leather and his boots Hessian; his neckcloth was of white silk with tiny gold embroidered stars on it; it had many folds and came right up to his chin. He wore a wig which was a profusion of honey-coloured curls. A truly magnificent figure.

He sat down on the chair and Minney ran to him. George remained decorously in the background and he said: 'And Charlotte? Come and tell me what *you* have been doing.'

Mrs. Fitzherbert smiled and nodded to her as though to say: Don't be nervous. And she felt that with that good fairy standing there nothing could go wrong.

So she spoke up and told him about the Bish-Up and Dr. Nott, imitating them—and some of the amusing things that happened in the schoolroom.

To her delight he thought them funny too, and so did Mrs. Fitzherbert, who started everyone laughing a great deal, and when Mrs. Fitzherbert laughed so did the Prince.

'Why not a game?' said Mrs. Fitzherbert. 'A guessing game.'

All the children were delighted at the prospect, and Mrs. Fitzherbert suggested one at which Charlotte always shone.

So they played and Charlotte won a great many points at which the Prince was surprised and pleased; and Charlotte thought on more than one occasion that Mrs. Fitzherbert chose questions to which Charlotte knew the answer. And looking across the room at her seated on the chair—serene and plump but with her lovely figure and her skin as fresh as a young girl's and her masses of golden hair untouched by powder, Charlotte loved her; and a wish came to her. If this were my home . . . if these were my parents . . . But she would not go on with it because it was unfair to her own mother, who had come down to Windsor especially to see her. It was not her fault if she had been turned away.

When the Prince took his leave he was affectionate to his daughter and Charlotte's eyes were shining with pleasure. It had been such a happy afternoon—she rarely remembered enjoying herself so much.

The carriage came to take her with George and Lady de Clifford back to Carlton House, and when she took her leave she threw her arms about Mrs. Fitzherbert and buried her face in that magnificent bosom.

Maria held her tightly for a few seconds in a special grip which meant that she understood. Charlotte was saying 'Thank you' and Maria was implying that this was a beginning. She was going to make everything right between Charlotte and her father.

Out into the street they went—Lady de Clifford leading. A little crowd had gathered about the carriage. Someone said: 'That's her. That's the Princess Charlotte.'

She inclined her head and smiled graciously—like a queen she hoped.

'It's a shame. Bringing her up to be a Papist.'

What did they mean? Lady de Clifford had grasped her arm and was hurrying her into the carriage. George leaped in beside her, and the horses started forward.

'No popery!' shouted a voice, and the cry was taken up by the crowd.

'What is the matter with them?' said Charlotte; and as no one answered she forgot the silly people and went over every incident of the afternoon, dwelling on those delicious moments when she had scored points and startled her father by her intelligence.

It was a lovely cosy feeling to think that she and Mrs. Fitzherbert were in league together.

* * *

George Keppel said: 'I shall never do my French and Latin in time. I expect I shall be punished in the morning.'

'Do it now,' she commanded.

'I can't. I need lots of time.'

'Here. Give it to me.'

She was in such a benevolent mood that she wanted everyone to feel as happy as she did. George had not done very well in the game. She supposed the Prince had thought what a silly little boy he was and how different from Charlotte. Of course he was younger—but perhaps the Prince did not know that. She hoped he didn't—and then was ashamed of herself.

'I'll do the Latin exercise for you,' she said, 'while you do your French. There. Come on, we'll start now.'

They worked in silence at the table. She was very happy. She loved all the world. She finished the Latin in a very short time and watched George frowning over the French. She would give him a watch. He had no watch. It would teach him to be more aware of the time and then he would not be behind with his Latin and French lessons. She would give him a horse, too.

She would speak about all this to Lady de Clifford at the first opportunity. And in time she would be on such terms with her father that she would implore him to take back her mother; and they would all live together like a happy family —her mother, her father and dearest Mrs. Fitzherbert.

George had finished his French and picked up the Latin.

'There are lots of mistakes in it,' he said.

'Be thankful it's done,' retorted Charlotte severely.

He would like a watch, she thought fondly. And he shall have it.

* * *

Mrs. Udney was secretly amused.

'Pray, Mrs. Udney, what do you find so funny?' demanded Charlotte.

She saw then that Mrs. Udney was holding a paper behind her back.

'Something in the paper is it?' said Charlotte. 'Let me see it.'

'I don't think it would be my duty to allow Your Highness to see it.'

'Mrs. Udney, I command you to show me that paper.'

Mrs. Udney raised her eyebrows and continued to hold the paper behind her back, but with a quick movement Charlotte snatched it and ran to the window with it.

'Your Highness!'

'You may report to Lady de Clifford that I have no manners if you wish. *I* shall report that you are most ... d ... disobedient.'

'I am only concerned for Your Highness's good and I am not sure whether it is good for you to see that paper. I beg of you ... most humbly ... to give it back to me.'

'I shall see first what it is you are trying to hide from me.'

'It is on the second page, Your Highness.'

'Oh,' said Charlotte, 'and it is about my mother I daresay.'

'Oh no, Your Highness. It is you this time.'

There was no doubt that Mrs. Udney was pleased ... the horrid creature.

'Would Your Highness like me to find it for you?'

Charlotte looked at her through narrowed eyes. Perhaps it was as well to let her do so. There might often be pieces in the paper which she ought to see and therefore if she made it clear that she expected Mrs. Udney to show her, the woman might do so—for clearly she enjoyed these pieces.

Charlotte handed her the paper and Mrs. Udney opened it and laid it on the table.

'There, Your Highness.'

'But what is it supposed to be? That's meant for Mrs. Fitzherbert I suppose. It is not much like her.'

'Yet Your Highness recognized her.'

'It's Mrs. Fitzherbert all right, but it makes her nose longer and it is just not beautiful enough.'

'The object of these cartoons is not to show off beauty but to make the point.'

'Point? What point? And who is the child she is carrying in her arms? Minney Seymour, I suppose.'

'Oh, no no. See, the diadem she is wearing. That proclaims her to be royal.'

'You ... you mean ... my ... myself?'

'Who else, Your Highness? You *have* been visiting the lady a great deal lately and the point is that the people don't like it.'

'The ... p ... people! What has it to do with the people?'

'Everything the royal family does is the concern of the people.'

'But . . .'

'You see, Your Highness, she has been given a pair of wings and she is flying up to Heaven with you in her arms. Look what you are holding. A rosary . . . and images of the saints. You see, it means that she is making a Catholic of you.'

'But it's nonsense.'

'She *is* a Catholic and she does seem to be a very special friend.'

'She has never talked to me about religion.'

'The people won't believe that.'

'It's just n . . . nonsense,' said Charlotte angrily and picking up the paper she threw it on to the floor before walking haughtily out of the room.

*   *   *

Lady de Clifford never took her to Tilney Street now; this meant that not only was she cut off from Mrs. Fitzherbert but from the Prince of Wales.

'Why do I never go with you to see Mrs. Fitzherbert and Minney nowadays?' she demanded in her forthright way.

Lady de Clifford looked embarrassed.

'My dear Princess, it is really better not.'

'Why not? I liked visiting Mrs. Fitzherbert. She is my good friend.'

'In view of the circumstances . . .'

'What circumstances?'

'You don't understand these things.'

'Nothing makes me more angry than to be told I don't understand. If I don't understand, then explain.'

'Mrs. Fitzherbert is . . . scarcely a lady you should visit.'

'Why not? Nobody could be kinder. She is like a queen. I often think Queen Elizabeth must have been a little like her only not so kind. Come along, my lady, do not try to change the subject. Why must I not visit Mrs. Fitzherbert?'

'Your mother . . .'

'My mother always spoke most kindly of her—and in any case I am not allowed to see *her* either.'

Oh dear, thought Lady de Clifford, I shall be saying something most indiscreet soon. I really think the task of looking after such a princess is too much for me. It was better to tell the truth otherwise she might say something more shocking.

'You know that Mrs. Fitzherbert is a Catholic and that you may well one day be Queen of England.'

'I *shall* be Queen of England one day, my lady.'

'Therefore the people do not wish you to become a Catholic.'

Charlotte stamped her foot. 'Am I not receiving my religious instruction from the Bish-Up and do you think he would make a Catholic of me?'

Lady de Clifford put her fingers to her ears and begged Charlotte not to utter such heresy.

'Then tell me how I am in danger of becoming a Catholic.'

'You are in no danger of course, but the people remember that Mrs. Fitzherbert is a Catholic and it is possible that, if you see her very often, she might persuade you to become one.'

'It's nonsense . . . nonsense.'

'The people are often mistaken, but princes and princesses have to behave in a way which pleases them.'

'So the people have decided that I am not to see my dear Mrs. Fitzherbert.'

'They have made this quite clear.'

'I suppose the old Begum has given her orders.'

'Her Majesty has said nothing as yet, but she will as soon as she reads the spate of comments in the newspapers.'

Charlotte felt an impulse to cry—loudly and angrily. But she did not. There was too much weeping in the family and it had made it a rather ridiculous habit. Real tears should be for real tragedy; and this was one she felt; but she must not cry.

'Cliffy,' she said, 'dear Cliffy, could I see Mrs. Fitzherbert once . . . just once more? Could we ride there . . . with me dressed like an ordinary young lady . . . just once . . . so that I could talk to her? I promise it would be just that once.'

'It would be very unwise,' said Lady de Clifford.

But Charlotte knew how to wheedle her governess.

* * *

She did allow herself the luxury of tears when she was alone with Mrs. Fitzherbert.

She lay against the sweet smelling bosom and told Maria how unhappy she was that they were not to meet.

'I shall have news of you,' soothed Maria. 'And perhaps later on this nonsense will be forgotten.'

'You see,' Charlotte explained, 'it had started to change. You changed it. But it won't go on now.'

'It can. I will talk to the Prince about you. I will make him interested in what you are doing.'

'Yes? But it won't be the same. I loved it here. This little house is so different from Carlton House and Windsor and Kew and the rest of them. It's different from Montague House. It's like a home . . . the sort of home I should like to live in sometimes. Perhaps I'd like to come to it when I felt sad. I have to learn to be a queen and so I suppose I need a palace for that. But I want to come and see you sometimes.'

'Well, perhaps you will one day. These things happen and then after a while they are forgotten. You'll come again perhaps and play with Minney.'

'Minney is lucky . . . does she know it?'

'I think she does.'

Charlotte stood up straight and said almost regally: 'Goodbye, Mrs. Fitzherbert.'

'Let us say *au revoir* instead of goodbye.'

Charlotte held up her face to be kissed.

'You are still my friend?' she asked.

'I'll always be your friend,' said Mrs. Fitzherbert.

Oatlands

THE Princess Charlotte was not exactly ill but she was now and then listless; her appetite was not so good as it had been; suddenly she would fly into a rage and although it was quickly over, Lady de Clifford thought she should report to the Queen that the Princess Charlotte's health was not as good as it had been and it might well be that she needed a change of air.

The Queen consulted the King, who immediately began to worry.

'The child should see her mother. It's this she's fretting for. Not natural, eh?'

'I do not see what good her mother could do her. We cannot allow them to meet until this affair is settled. George said he was going to look through the evidence again. There is no doubt about it that that woman is leading a very immoral life at Montague House. It's no place for the Princess.'

'There was nothing proved against her. I think those people ... those Douglases, or whatever their names are, were rogues.'

'The sort of people with whom one would expect Caroline to be on friendly terms. No, the child cannot see her mother ... not yet at any rate. That would be tantamount to receiving her at Court and that we cannot do. George would be very much against it.'

'I'm not so sure,' said the King with unusual firmness, 'that *I* should be against it. I'm sure the woman means well. She's all right. Not bad looking. I can't see why George can't live with her. It's what's expected of us, eh, what?'

'She is impossible. I can scarcely believe that she is a princess. She behaves like some low serving girl. No, with Charlotte's temperament—which I fear she has inherited from her mother—it would be folly to bring them together.'

'Something will have to be done about it soon. She's got friends in the House. Canning's one ... Perceval's another. They'll be bringing the matter up, depend upon it. And then what are we going to do, eh, what?'

'At least do our duty by the child until we are forced to do otherwise. The sea air would be good for her. I believe Bognor to be an excellent spot. I think I shall have enquiries made.'

'There could be no harm in that, eh, what?' said the King; and he was thinking of the Princess of Wales with her ready laughter and low-cut gowns, and free ways with all those men who had visited Montague House.

Nowadays, he thought, these young people! They don't think of doing their duty. All they want is pleasure.

Then he thought of Sarah Lennox making hay in the gardens of Holland House as he rode past and how pretty she was, and how he had thought of nothing but Sarah Lennox for weeks, until he married a plain German Princess and had turned from Sarah to do his duty.

We were different, he thought. Not like the young people nowadays. My sons for instance ...

He must not think of them. When he did, he heard voices in his head and he thought he was going mad.

Let the Queen arrange what should be done about Charlotte. But he was not going to let her and George treat that poor woman too badly. A nice woman ... in her way. If she had been sent over as *his* bride ...

He looked at Charlotte's plain face and her cold eyes and ugly mouth. He had never loved her, but she had done her duty and so had he.

Why couldn't people be like they used to be?

*	*	*

It was decided that while plans were being made for Charlotte to spend a period by the sea she should go and stay with the Duke and Duchess of York at Oatlands.

Charlotte was not displeased. Uncle Fred was her favourite Uncle and his Duchess, being eccentric in the extreme, interested her.

Life was certainly odd at Oatlands and Charlotte was far from bored; she shared to some extent the Duchess's love of animals though she was not as fanatical about them. Still, a short stay at Oatlands could be a pleasure.

Merry Uncle Fred, having escorted Charlotte to his home, left her there with his wife while he went off to be with his latest mistress which Aunt Frederica did not mind in the least.

'We live our own lives,' she told Charlotte, treating her as an adult, which delighted the Princess. 'It is a way wise people come to in time.'

The Duchess was as good as her word for she allowed Charlotte to follow her own inclination, too. To live at Oatlands was more like living in a zoo than in a royal palace; and as long as her animals were happy Frederica cared about little else. It was not unusual for Charlotte to awake in the morning to find a monkey swinging on her bedcurtains. The dogs were innumerable for there were many strays who had found their way into Frederica's haven. There were also rabbits, hares and birds; for if she found any animal that was unable to fend for itself it was brought to Oatlands to be healed by her and then allowed to go free or make its home there. No animal was ever turned away; cats, dogs, monkeys, rabbits and squirrels lived in the park or the house whichever they preferred.

And because her animals liked Charlotte, and Charlotte liked them, Frederica was fond of Charlotte.

It was a solace therefore to be here—far away from Grandmamma's ill temper and constant criticism, from the people who had spoilt her friendship with Mrs. Fitzherbert, and she knew that her father would not call at Oatlands; he disliked his sister-in-law and the smell of the animals would have offended his delicate nostrils. So there was no danger of any startling controversy. One could live the quiet country life: a few lessons with docile Dr. Nott, walking with the dogs, riding with the horses and talking to the Duchess.

Charlotte found that she enjoyed talking to the Duchess as much as playing with the animals. She may have been looking for someone to take the place of Mrs. Fitzherbert, and if Aunt Frederica was an odd substitute and Charlotte could not imagine her ever pleading for her with the Prince of Wales, she was sympathetic and seemed to understand that what Charlotte wanted was to live simply for a while.

Oatlands itself was an interesting place. Situated at Walton, it was close to the river Thames and Henry VIII had built it as a pleasure house. Queen Elizabeth had lived here. That made it very exciting for Charlotte—only it was not the same building, for that had been burned down more than ten years before. The Duchess had told her about the night of the fire.

'The Duke, your uncle, was fighting in Flanders, and my servants woke me. I smelt the smoke . . . and then I heard the crackle of fire. It was a wonder we were not all burned in our beds.'

Charlotte listened and thought of the gatehouse and battlemented towers ablaze. She had seen a picture of Oatlands as it had been when Queen Elizabeth had lived there. There had been two quadrangle courts, the principal of which had a machicolated gatehouse at each end; there were magnificent bay windows and turrets; and in the paddock Queen Elizabeth used to shoot with her crossbow. What a pity that it had all been burned down, and Uncle Fred had had to build the present Oatlands in its place!

'But,' sighed Charlotte, 'it is not the same.'

'I saved most of the animals,' replied the Duchess. 'How frightened the darlings were!'

And Charlotte smiled, knowing that on that terrible night her first thought would have been not for her jewels, nor her servants, but for all the dogs and cats and monkeys.

It was a pleasant household and a friendship quickly grew up between them. The Duchess liked to live by routine which was comforting because one always knew where she would be at a certain time. The greater part of the day was spent looking after the animals but she liked needlework too and would sit out of doors when the weather was suitable and give orders to her servants while she sewed. She was greatly concerned about the poor of the district; and the care of them, with her needlework and animals, made up her life.

She told Charlotte that one of the main duties in life was to look after the poor. It was all very well to pray for them and this must be done, but practical assistance was sometimes of greater help and Charlotte should give part of her money to the poor and make sure that she never heard of a deserving case without doing what she could for the sufferers.

The Duchess had had cottages built on the estate and here she housed certain people who took care of the puppies which were constantly being born.

Charlotte would sit with her and lure her to talk of her life for she always enjoyed hearing of the fate of princesses. The most terrible thing in the world she had always thought was to be taken from one's home and not only married to a strange man but sent to a new country.

'I am fortunate,' she remarked. 'I shall always live in England because I am to be the Queen. And because I am the Queen I shall choose my own husband.'

'Fortunate indeed,' agreed Frederica in her odd German accent, which might have been difficult to understand if Charlotte had not grown accustomed to it during her conversations with her own mother. And Grandmamma had a slight German accent too.

'Ah, I remember the day I heard I was to marry the Duke of York.'

'Were you disappointed because it was not the Prince of Wales?'

'Naturally as the daughter of the King of Prussia I wished to marry a king, or a prince who would one day be a king.'

'Uncle Fred is very nice.'

Frederica looked sad, and no wonder, thought Charlotte. He was not a very good husband—but a little better than her father was to her mother.

Charlotte studied her aunt. She was not very beautiful. She was far too small; she had the blue eyes and fair hair of the German royal houses, but her skin was pitted with smallpox and her teeth were bad.

She started to speak in rapid French and Charlotte had to concentrate to follow her—but it was no worse than her atrocious English. She told how she had married the Duke and set out for England with him.

'It was the year 1791 and you know what was happening in France at that time. Ah, the terrible things those people did to their king and queen! The mob can be terrifying.'

Charlotte nodded, thinking of those people surrounding her carriage and shouting 'No popery!' And because of them she had been forbidden friendship with Mrs. Fitzherbert!

'They gathered about our carriage and I thought they would murder us. But the Duke was not afraid. He stood there and faced them and assured them that although we were royal we were not French. His courage disarmed them and they let us go on our way, but I thought for a time that my end was at hand. The Duke himself drove our carriage to show them that he was not behaving like a royal person.'

'And then when you came to England what did you think of it?'

She smiled. 'Things are never what one imagines them to be, my dear. The King's Levee. Shall I ever forget it! My hair was dressed high ... high ... up here, and decorated with crêpe and feathers which were a great burden. I was in white and silver and my satin sleeves were edged with diamonds. Oh, it was so hot and heavy. I was all white and silver and

there were diamonds on my stomacher. I thought I should
faint with the heat of it.'

'Poor Aunt Frederica! But you liked it, did you not?'

'It is freer here than in Prussia. But there were troubles.'

'You met my father.'

'Oh, yes . . .'

'And . . .'

But she did not wish to speak of the encounter. She had
refused to accept Maria Fitzherbert as Princess of Wales and
so had offended the Prince. She had been hurt and unhappy
because of her husband's infidelities; he had hated her
animals; she had hated his mistresses. It was soon clear that
she was not going to give him the heirs for which he had
married. Oh, no, she had not been happy in those early years
in England.

And then—because he was Commander-in-Chief of the
Army he had gone to Flanders, and Oatlands had been
burned and rebuilt and he had bought the manors of Brook-
lands and Byfleet to enlarge the property and she had decided
that this should be her home. Here she would reign—some
way from the Court; her animals would give her all the affection and excitement she needed; and she did not care what
her husband did.

She had wanted children but when she found that she was
to be barren she turned more and more to her animals. As for
Frederick, as the years passed her animosity towards the man
who had so bitterly disappointed her began to fade. He no
longer expressed his disdain for her animals and his annoy-
ance because she filled the place with them; she never uttered
a complaint about his numerous love affairs. Sometimes he
came to Oatlands see her and they talked amicably together.

They had become friends.

She knew that the dear kind half-crazy King deplored the
situation. The marriage was as much a failure as that of the
Prince of Wales—perhaps more so because in spite of all the
scandal attaching itself to that union, at least it had been
fruitful. This pleasant eager young girl was the result of it. At
least they had provided the heir; so that the family could
breathe a sigh of relief and with a good conscience go on living
their own lives as they wanted to.

And that was what Frederica and Frederick were doing,
and it was proving not unsatisfactory.

So the days passed for Charlotte and her friendship with
odd Aunt Frederica helped to soothe her for the loss of Mrs.

Fitzherbert, which was strange, for there could not have been women more unlike.

One day Lady de Clifford told her that news had come from Her Majesty that they were to return to Carlton House and there make preparations to visit Bognor, where they would stay for the summer months. The Queen thought that sea breezes would be good for the Princess.

'I should have liked to go to Brighton,' sighed Charlotte; and thought of her father in his magnificent Pavilion perhaps giving a ball to welcome his daughter.

'Her Majesty suggests Bognor.'

Charlotte grimaced and went out into the park there to walk round and say goodbye to all that had become so familiar in the last weeks.

She picked some flowers from the garden and took them to that plot shut in by yews which was the cemetery. She walked between the grey tombstones and laid the flowers on the grave of Rex—one of Aunt Frederica's favourite fox hounds. Not that she ever hunted; she loathed any such activities. She could never understand people who made much of some animals and were cruel to others. Her love extended to the whole of the animal kingdom. And when her darlings died, they were brought here and ceremoniously buried and prayers were said over them. Aunt Frederica believed they all went to Heaven because animals were not like human beings and did no wrong; they only acted according to instincts. Charlotte had replied that Heaven must be overcrowded with animals and sparsely inhabited by human beings—a statement with which Aunt Frederica agreed. And that, I suppose, thought Charlotte, was why she was eager to go there.

Sitting on the edge of the grave Charlotte thought of death —other people's, not her own. Sometimes she believed that she was immortal and would never die; and at others she felt that death was close. It had been one of the latter moods which had set her making her will. That made her laugh when she remembered the fuss; and then she was sad thinking of Poor Mrs. Campbell who had gone because of it.

How carefully one must behave if one were a princess. Perhaps people like Aunt Frederica were lucky. They had come through the difficult part of life and had made a niche for themselves. Aunt Frederica living here aloof from the family, on mildly friendly terms with her husband, making no demands on him, busy with her charities, her needlework and her beloved animals, was perhaps the most contented member of the royal family.

Charlotte rose and left the animals' cemetery.

In her rooms Lady de Clifford was preparing for their departure. She was looking very pleased. She did not care for Oatlands. She was sure that the animals carried disease which might harm the Princess Charlotte and she wondered whether she should report this to the Queen. But Charlotte did enjoy staying with her aunt and her spirits had improved. So perhaps the visit had had something to recommend it.

That night Charlotte was awakened by the sound of dogs' barking in the grounds. She rose from her window and stood there for a while looking out on the strange scene. There was a woman in flowing robes, her hair about her shoulders, striding across the park, and around her were some twenty dogs, some of which had awakened Charlotte with their barks.

Charlotte smiled. She looked like a supernatural being; but of course it was only Aunt Frederica taking one of her nightly strolls. She slept very little and often walked about the Park during the night. She was perfectly safe, for several of those great slavering hounds would have torn anyone apart who had attempted to attack her.

Charlotte went back to bed. She would miss this strange household when she went back to the life considered suitable for the heiress to the throne. But it would always be pleasant to think of Oatlands and strange yet reliable Aunt Frederica who had made it quite clear that she was Charlotte's friend.

Yes, in a way, she had found a substitute for Mrs. Fitzherbert.

Summer by the Sea

BOGNOR delighted the Princess, for there she insisted on more freedom than she could possibly enjoy in the royal palaces. A mansion belonging to a certain Mr. Wilson had been put at her disposal and here she came with some members of her staff headed by Lady de Clifford.

It was pleasant to wake up every morning and to stand at an open window and smell the sea. She bathed three or four times a week and she would shriek with delight when she was immersed into the water; she loved to wander along the shore running in the face of the boisterous wind, sometimes pausing to pick up oddly-shaped stones which caught her fancy. She insisted that her attendants kept their distance and Lady de Clifford said that as long as they had her in view all the time she might enjoy this freedom.

This was delightful because it enabled her to meet people and talk to them, often without their being aware of who she was. In her green riding habit and little straw hat she looked like any young lady of a noble house; no one would have guessed by her clothes and manner that she was an heiress to the throne.

She discovered that a baker named Richardson made the most delicious buns she had ever tasted; the aroma of his bakehouse would float out into the street and when she smelt it she could never resist going into the shop.

She had talked to Mr. Richardson for a long time before her attendants came bursting in to make sure that she was all right and he realized who she was.

She was amused by his confusion. 'But, Mr. Richardson,' she told him, 'the fact that I am the daughter of the Prince of

Wales makes no difference to the fact that you make the b . . . best buns in England.'

Mr. Richardson rubbed his floury hands through his hair and put smudges of white over his face, which Charlotte found very endearing. And after that she took to calling in at the shop at the time when the buns were taken out of the oven and she would sit on a high stool eating them and commenting to Mr. Richardson on the quality of the day's batch. It was one of the happiest occasions in her new life—as it was in Mr. Richardson's.

Lady de Clifford shook her head and did not approve of these free and easy manners, but there was nothing she could do about it. She had to have the Princess in good health and she seemed to wilt when she lacked freedom.

'Just for a while,' Lady de Clifford promised herself. 'And now she is getting older, I really think she needs someone firmer than I.'

Poor snuffy old Lady de Clifford! thought Charlotte, and tried not to worry her more than she could help.

Four beautiful grey ponies arrived at Bognor and with them a little market cart. She was almost wild with delight when she saw them.

'But they're so beautiful, Cliffy. Do you not think so?'

The messenger who had brought them gave her a note accompanying the gift. It was written by the Prince of Wales. He hoped that she would find this little conveyance useful. He had at an early age derived great pleasure from riding and driving; he hoped that she would find the same in this gift from her affectionate father.

She leaped about with delight, treading on poor Lady de Clifford's toes, she embraced Mrs. Gagarin and she even felt kindly towards Mrs. Udney.

Her father had given her a present! He had remembered her existence!

In a more sober moment she asked herself whether Mrs. Fitzherbert had persuaded him to give her such a magnificent gift.

But what did it matter? She had her cart and her four lovely greys; and she was going to perfect her riding. She was going to surprise him when she saw him next.

* * *

Perhaps it was too good to last. Why did something always have to happen when she was most happy! She had seen the old men in the lanes and they had touched their forelocks to her; she did not see how they could harm her.

But Lady de Clifford had thought it her duty to report to the Queen that there was a home in the neighbourhood for old soldiers who suffered from ophthalmia; she did not know whether the disease was infectious, but she believed that Her Majesty should know.

The Princess Charlotte must not run the slightest risk. None of the King's sons had produced another heir to the throne and Charlotte was on that account very precious. She should leave Bognor at once for Worthing; and there she should be joined by the Queen and her aunts.

Charlotte wailed in fury. What would become of her freedom under the eyes of the Begum and the Old Girls? What of Mr. Richardson's buns?

There was no help for it. The party left for Worthing.

*   *   *

How different was Warwick House from Mr. Wilson's Bognor mansion. But perhaps that was because royal etiquette had been introduced into it. It was like Windsor or Kew. There were the Queen's Drawing Rooms where one must sew and read and Charlotte had to undergo catechism at the side of her grandmother. She had to see that her snuffbox was at hand when she needed it; she had to endure the alternate affection and scolding of the Old Girls.

Even the sea could not make up for that.

Warwick House was at the end of a narrow lane; and there was nothing about the place to suggest that all this royal ceremony was going on inside. It was true two sentries were always posted at the gate; but for them it might have been any gloomy old country house.

'Charlotte, you are too boisterous. I think you often forget your position.' This was the constant complaint of her grandmother. 'Stop fidgeting, child. How awkward you are! I do declare you have the manners of a cottage child.'

Nothing pleased her. Even her daughters talked of her illtemper.

'It's her rheumatics, poor Mamma,' said Amelia, who was always ill herself and could pity others who were.

It was from the aunts that she heard some news of her mother.

'I doubt not that before long you will be able to see her,' whispered Aunt Mary. 'I believe the King is going to receive her.'

'Why have they been so unkind to her?' demanded Charlotte.

'Hush! There are things you cannot understand. You will one day.'

It was exasperating, but if one protested it might stem the flow of information; so the only thing to do was to curb one's impatience and try to be calm. It would make her very happy to see her mother again.

It was Mary who told her that her grandfather, the Duke of Brunswick, had been killed at Jena.

'This terrible Napoleon Bonaparte,' sighed Aunt Elizabeth. 'He is dominating the whole of Europe. And to think that he thought of invading England too. Dear Lord Nelson put a stop to that.'

Charlotte was well aware of Napoleon's activities. This was the kind of lesson which she assimilated with ease. She knew full well what the country owed to Lord Nelson and what sorrowing there had been when he fell only a few years ago at Trafalgar.

And now that wicked man had killed her grandfather—or at least his soldiers had. Poor Mamma, she would be very upset for she had loved her father. She had once told Charlotte that she had loved him better than any man she ever knew. But one could never be sure; she expressed her feelings with such extravagance. One day she loved Charlotte better than anyone in the world and the next it was Willie Austin—or her Willikins as she called him. Still, she would be very unhappy because of the death of her father.

'And,' went on Elizabeth, 'your Grandmamma Brunswick is in England.'

'Shall I see her?'

'You certainly will. Your Mother is allowing her to live at Montague House and she is in her apartments at Kensington Palace.'

At Kensington Palace! Then that surely meant that Mamma was received at Court. She was no longer in disgrace.

*   *   *

There was a further surprise. The Prince of Wales sent his own carriage to Worthing to pick up his daughter and Lady de Clifford and bring them over to Brighton where they might visit the Pavilion and see a parade of the Prince's own regiment.

Charlotte was delighted. First the little cart and the four greys—and now he was sending his carriage for her! Mrs.

Fitzherbert might well be behind this but what did that matter? She was at last to be given the chance to know her own father. And if when she returned to Carlton House she might visit her mother she could be loved by them both; and perhaps one day their differences would be forgotten because they would both have one great interest in common: their own daughter.

Perhaps that was a dream, but it was a very pleasant one and riding along those country roads often beside the sea, in *his* magnificently upholstered carriage, with *his* coachman very grand in his scarlet and green livery, Charlotte felt she had every reason to believe that her most cherished desire would be fulfilled. Her white muslin dress was very pretty; she had argued with Mrs. Gagarin that it would be dirty before the day was over, but Mrs. Gagarin had said they should take a chance on that. The Prince would expect his daughter to look her best. And, declared Louisa fondly, Charlotte looked a real picture with those lovely white frills and flounces and her straw hat with the blue ribbons to match her eyes.

'Do I look nice?' Charlotte had pirouetted before the glass and pictured her father's approval. 'By God,' he would say, 'I have a damned pretty daughter.'

They came into Brighton at a jog trot. There was no place quite like Brighton; here was an exhilaration in the air which was nowhere else. This was the town where the Prince of Wales reigned supreme; he had turned it from a humble fishing village to the most elegant place in England—next to London, perhaps. But it was so different from the capital that it need not regard even that as a rival. Here everyone seemed happy; the ladies were fashionable; and the costumes of the gentlemen made one gasp in admiration. The influence of Beau Brummell and the Prince of Wales was evident everywhere.

It was the Prince's birthday and therefore a great day in Brighton. He was forty-five years old and that was something the people were determined to celebrate. The streets were hung with banners; the children carried posies; and everywhere there were loyal shouts.

As soon as the carriage appeared they cried: 'God bless the little Princess.'

'Wave,' whispered Lady de Clifford. 'Incline your head. Smile. Show that you appreciate them.'

Charlotte was waving frantically, beaming on everyone.

'Oh dear,' sighed Lady de Clifford. 'Not so violently. Pray remember that you are a Princess.'

'Princes and Princesses, Kings and Queens, they must always please their people,' said Charlotte in the tones of the Bishop; which made Lady de Clifford sigh even more deeply.

And now here they were at the magnificent Pavilion itself and the band was playing on the lawn. The carriage drew up and Charlotte jumped out. How often had Lady de Clifford warned her that she should wait to be helped and then step daintily down. But Charlotte was far too excited to remember these admonitions.

She had seen her father. He was in the uniform of her own regiment and about his waist was a belt decorated with diamonds. He was clearly very happy as he always was on occasions like this and because it was his birthday and the people of Brighton had determined to honour him, and in any case had always been loyal to him however unpopular he was in London or any other part of the country, he was prepared to shower his charm on everyone and that included his daughter. He embraced her with emotion—tears in his eyes—but was that for the benefit of the spectators?

Now she was being greeted by her uncle William, Duke of Clarence. Uncle Fred was not here today, she was sorry to see.

Uncle William's greeting was not as affectionate as it might have been. She had overheard it once said that some of her uncles did not like the idea of a girl's inheriting the crown. Well, thought Charlotte, they would have to put up with it, for they could have twenty sons and not one of them could oust her from her position. Not that Uncle William showed any signs of having any legitimate sons. He had several children by the lovely actress Dorothy Jordan—young George Fitzclarence, whom she bullied when she met him was one of them—but they could never inherit the throne, so there was no reason why Uncle William should dislike her for being the legitimate daughter of the Prince of Wales. She thought Uncle William rather stupid anyway and much preferred what she had seen of Dorothy Jordan, who was lovely and had the same warm motherly quality which she had discovered in Mrs. Fitzherbert. She wondered whether Dorothy Jordan was here today; if so she would not be far off because although she was merely the mistress of the Duke of Clarence she was accepted everywhere. The Prince of Wales was fond of her and, unlike his parents, he did not consider the absence of marriage lines a reason for banning a beautiful and interesting woman from society.

Now here was Uncle Augustus, Duke of Sussex, who was, next to Uncle Fred, her favourite uncle. He was tall like the Prince of Wales and his complexion was decidedly florid. He seemed pleased to see Charlotte and he had made it clear on more than one occasion that he was her friend and would help to bring about a better understanding between her and her father, but he could behave rather oddly; he was not so simple and straightforward as Uncle Fred in whom she felt she could put greater trust. She was saddened too about his break with dear Goosey, because he had gone through so much for her sake—marrying her against his father's wishes and having a court case and when it went against them, with the support of his brothers, setting up residence with her all the same.

The nicest thing about the uncles was that they always supported each other and if any of them were in any difficulties the first person they thought of going to was the Prince of Wales.

And after greeting Uncle Augustus it was the turn of Uncle Adolphus, Duke of Cambridge. She never felt she knew Uncle Adolphus who, in his Hanoverian military uniform, was like a foreigner.

Delightedly she thought how much more elegant, dazzling and brilliant was her own father.

The Prince was smiling as he watched. At least, she thought, he's pleased with me today. 'Now,' he said, 'we are going on to the lawn. The crowds will expect to see us together.'

Walking beside her father, Charlotte was happy. Brighton was the most beautiful place on Earth on a hot August day with the sea sparkling and glittering before her and the wonderful Pavilion behind her and the dear people cheering them all—especially her, she thought; and she peeped slyly at her father, wondering how he felt about this. Oh, yes, there were more shouts of 'Long live the little Princess' than there were of 'God save the Prince of Wales'.

This was her day, in spite of the fact that it was the Prince's birthday. She beamed and waved at the people—forgetting all instructions to be decorous. Why should she be, when the people liked her as she was? The band was playing; the sun was shining and the people cheering. What a happy day!

Then she thought of her mother who was not here. How strange that was. Her father's birthday and her mother not here! The three of them should have been together. Wasn't it a family occasion? But of course the Princess of Wales never went anywhere that the Prince might be.

On such a day one should not dwell on these controversies so she gave herself up to pleasure.

The picnic was delightful. The footmen served champagne to all the guests who took it in their carriages which were all lined up in order of precedence. Mrs. Fitzherbert should have been in the carriage next to the one Charlotte occupied with the Prince and her uncles. But she was not; instead there was the very cold—though she admitted elegant—Lady Hertford, looking remarkably pleased with herself.

The champagne made Charlotte feel lightheaded. What a glorious day! She trusted she was not displeasing her father by her rather loud laughter. Fortunately Lady de Clifford was not close enough to hear.

She did see Mrs. Fitzherbert on that day; she was in her carriage with Minney not far from Mrs. Jordan's carriage in which the lovely actress sat with several of the Fitzclarence children.

Mrs. Fitzherbert inclined her head graciously but the Princess leaped into the carriage and kissed her.

'My dearest Mrs. Fitzherbert, I feared you were not here.'

'Oh, yes, I still attend functions like this.'

She was obviously a little sad and Charlotte wondered how anyone could be on a day like this.

'I hope,' she said, 'that soon this silly notion will be forgotten and we shall be visiting you again.'

'God bless you,' said Mrs. Fitzherbert tenderly.

'When I am old enough to please myself no one shall tell me where I may and may not go.'

'I am sure that will be so,' said Mrs. Fitzherbert with a warm smile, and she added: 'Minney has missed your visits, haven't you, Minney?'

'Very much,' replied Minney. 'Mamma and I were saying so only this morning.'

Charlotte was pleased that they had talked of her.

'One day it will be different,' she said; and because she noticed that she was attracting attention, she said goodbye and left them.

And after the picnic there followed the review which she witnessed from her father's carriage. How proud he was of his own regiment, the 10th Hussars, and he seemed to grow more and more magnificent in his own splendid Hussar's uniform as he took the salute.

When it was over they went to the Pavilion. What a magic palace it was, what an Aladdin's cave! Although it was her father's home it was unfamiliar to her. It was true she had once had a children's ball here. She had stood in this vestibule with its odd but splendid decorations and received her guests. They had gathered in the ornate banqueting hall where now the Prince would entertain the chosen guests; and in the music room she had listened to an occasional concert.

She wished that she might live with her father and mother in this house which he so loved and for which he was always planning alterations; it was beginning to look like an oriental palace and everywere was his love of Chinese art evident.

In those little paragraphs in the newspapers which gave her so much pleasure—partly because she knew that her Grandmother would have given orders that they were to be kept from her if she was aware that she saw them—she heard a great deal about the Pavilion. Mrs. Udney was constantly chuckling over the papers and Charlotte's curiosity, which her Grandmother would, she was sure, have called prying, made a bond between them. She did not dislike Mrs. Udney half as much as she had once; and Mrs. Udney's way of calling attention to these paragraphs with a little chuckle or giggle or a clicking of the tongue was the sign for Charlotte to demand—imperiously so that Mrs. Udney could not refuse—to see the paragraph.

There were references to Mrs. Fitzherbert which she did not always understand but she did guess that Mrs. Fitzherbert was not as happy as she had once been. Perhaps dear little Minney was not climbing on *his* knee so often. But quite a lot of the references concerned the Pavilion and since Charlotte had read of it she longed to see her father's new bathroom. She slipped away from the throng of people—not easy for a Princess, but Charlotte was nothing if not resourceful—and made her way to her father's apartments.

This was his bedroom. His bed was as she would have expected it to be—elegant in the extreme. It had been made for him in France and was unexpectedly simple, but she could recognize the graceful lines. She climbed the bedsteps, sat on it and bounced up and down laughing, sticking out her legs and looking at her long lacetrimmed drawers. They were not quite as clean round the lace edges as they had been when they set out from Worthing.

All the furniture was beautiful and everywhere was the Chinese influence. She looked round admiring the ormolu clock and the candelabra. Dismounting the bedsteps she took a closer look and saw the clock was in the form of a cupid driving in a beautiful chariot, which was drawn by butterflies.

It was lovely, and Cupid was represented in the candelabra also.

My father is very much attached to Cupid, she thought. But I suppose he would be.

But she had come to see the bathroom and there it was; its walls were of white marble and its bath of which she had read was sixteen feet long, ten feet wide and six feet deep. It was a miracle of a bath because it could be supplied with sea water.

What an exciting man my father is! thought Charlotte. If only . . .

Then she remembered that she had read somewhere that one of the reasons why her father disliked her mother was because he loved bathing and she did not.

It is a very sad thing, she thought, that a girl has to learn all the important things about her parents from the newspapers.

She dared not linger for fear she would be missed; so she rejoined the guests and hoped no one had noticed her absence.

And after that memorable day Worthing seemed less desirable than ever.

*   *   *

Charlotte had a piece of good luck. The Queen had noticed that she had not maintained the good health she was enjoying when she arrived at Worthing and decided that the place did not agree with her as well as Bognor. She had made enquiries about the danger of living near a hospital for those suffering from ophthalmia and had learned that the disease was only contagious when people were in immediate contact and for instance slept on the same pillow. There was no evidence of anyone in Bognor having caught the disease.

The Queen summoned Lady de Clifford and said that in the circumstances she believed that the Princess Charlotte might go back to Bognor for the rest of the summer while she herself and the Princesses, her daughters, would return to Windsor.

What joy! Bognor again and freedom! No more lectures from the Begum! No more boring sessions with the Old Girls! Instead long rambles on the sea shore and conversation with Mr. Richardson while she munched his buns.

'Now,' said Lady de Clifford, 'you must get plenty of fresh air. There is nothing like fresh air, Your Highness.'

'Nothing like fresh *Bognor* air, my lady,' cried Charlotte hilariously.

Her health began to improve and there was no doubt in

anyone's mind that Bognor was the spot best suited to the Princess.

The days were full of interest for her. She liked to mingle with people, to talk to them, to discover how they lived. For this, she told Lady de Clifford, is the duty of one who is to be their Sovereign.

Lady de Clifford was always nervous of such talk. It was in any case bad taste and she was not sure that it was not treason. But Charlotte always laughed at her. Her familiarity with the ordinary people was alarming but her father could behave in the same way and like her father she could at a moment's notice become imperious.

On one occasion she was driving her four greys along a country road with Lady de Clifford beside her when she saw a woman, poorly dressed, with nine children trailing behind her.

Charlotte pulled up with a jerk which almost sent Lady de Clifford out of her seat.

'What a large family!' cried Charlotte. 'Are they all your own?'

'Yes, sweet lady, they are all my own and a terrible task I have to try to feed them!'

'So many!' cried Charlotte.

'But all the children of my own wedded husband,' the woman assured her.

Charlotte studied the children and said: 'How did you manage to have so many of an age. Now, come, I want the truth. I always want to hear the truth and I cannot abide lies. I will give you a shilling if you tell me the truth.'

Charlotte felt in her purse which she always carried with her in case she met any deserving poor person whom she thought she should help.

The woman looked at the shilling. 'I have lied to you, my lady. Two of these children are mine. One by my husband and the other by another man. The rest of them are borrowed.'

'To arouse pity, I daresay,' said Princess severely. 'I was going to give you a guinea if you had told me the truth at first. But you lied and although you have told a plausible tale now which I accept as truth, you only told it because I offered you a shilling. You shall have two shillings because I believe at last you told me the truth.'

The woman accepted the two shillings with many thanks, but her lips were trembling and Charlotte knew she was thinking of the lost guinea.

She drove on and after a while she stopped.

'Poor woman,' she said. 'I suppose when one must beg for a living it is easy to lie.'

She waited until the woman came up.

'Here,' she said. 'Here is your guinea. But remember that you will prosper more by telling the truth than lies.'

She did not wait to hear the woman's thanks but whipped up the greys.

'I do not think it proper for Your Highness to bandy words with these people,' admonished Lady de Clifford.

'Bandy words! I was advising her always to tell the truth. Is that not a good thing? My lord Bish-Up tells me it is.'

'I do not think it wise to hold these conversations with beggars.'

'Jesus did. So why not the Princess Charlotte?'

'You blaspheme.'

'I don't see it. My lady, I don't indeed. According to you, it is at some times good to follow Jesus ... at others not. No, I think that was just how He would have behaved to that poor woman.'

Lady de Clifford put her hands over her ears. Sometimes she wondered with great trepidation what the Princess would do and say next.

What she did on this occasion was to whip up the greys and they galloped along at great speed while Lady de Clifford clutched the side of the carriage in terror and exclaimed in dismay as they turned into a field.

'Where are you going? This is Sir Thomas Troubridge's field.'

'I don't deny it.'

'I pray you turn back.'

'Too late, my lady, too late. Hold tight. That was a good one.'

The carriage went bouncing over the ruts.

'Heaven save us,' cried Lady de Clifford.

'Nothing like exercise, my lady,' Charlotte told her. 'Nothing like exercise!'

*   *   *

The shells on Bognor beach were numerous and of the most exquisite colours; the seaweed was of a kind Charlotte had never seen before; it had extraordinary hard black berries. She decided to add to the excitement of her rambles by collecting them and when she took them back to Mr. Wilson's mansion she made them into necklaces and painted some of them.

Mrs. Gagarin and Louisa declared they were lovely and that she was a true artist.

She made necklaces for both of them and one for herself, and promised that she would make one for Lady de Clifford. One day when searching for seaweed along the beach she found in one of the banks a layer of what looked like gold in its raw state. It had formed itself into strange patterns and while she was examining it three young ladies came along with their governess and excitedly she called to them to come and see what she had found. They all thought it was a great discovery and she told the girls and their governess that she was going to send two labourers along to get the metal out of the rock so that she might have it tested to see if it were gold.

'I will let you know the result,' she told them.

Meanwhile some of her attendants had come up and she excitedly explained to them.

She turned to the girls. 'You must come and see me tomorrow and I will tell you then the result of this discovery.' She nodded at the governesss. 'Pray bring them at three of the afternoon. We might play some games together. Do you like games?'

The girls said they did and listened attentively while she told them of the games she had played in Tilney Street with George Keppel, George Fitzclarence and Minney Seymour.

'So . . . tomorrow,' she cried as she went off.

Her attendants looked on with disapproval but she snapped her fingers at them and returning to the town she insisted on going to the house of a labourer whose wife she had talked with. The woman was heavily pregnant and Charlotte had been very interested in her condition, so she visited her often. The result of this visit was that the woman's husband should find a fellow worker and they would go down to the shore to see what it was the Princess had discovered.

Charlotte, pleased with the afternoon's work, returned to the house.

When Lady de Clifford heard what she had done she clicked and clucked and said it would not do.

'You forget your dignity.'

'Not entirely,' argued Charlotte. 'Now and then perhaps I throw it aside but I make sure it is never out of reach so that I can bring it back at a moment's notice if the need should arise.'

'I do not know what Her Majesty the Queen would say if she were to hear of this.'

'Nor shall you ever, my lady, for she will never know, because neither of us would dare tell her.' Charlotte laughed
aloud at her own cleverness and Lady de Clifford thought
anxiously: Is she growing more like her mother every day?

'I gather that you have asked these girls to visit you. Who
are they? You do not know. How can we be sure whom you
are inviting into the house?'

'Their governess is very stern. I am sure you would not
object to her.'

'I must point out that you condescended too much to
them by all accounts. You were too familiar. You must never
forget your station. I hope that when they come you will be
careful.'

'I promise you, dear Cliffy,' said Charlotte demurely.

*　　*　　*

The metal she had discovered turned out not to be precious
gold but the pieces the labourers had hewn out of the rock
were very pretty and she would keep them as ornaments. She
wished the labourers to be brought to her so that she could
give them two guineas for their work.

This was not the manner in which royal persons conducted
themselves, Lady de Clifford pointed out. A royal person gave
orders that money was to be paid to workmen. She did not
summon them and go through the sordid business of handing
them their pay.

'Very well,' conceded Charlotte. 'Let the money be paid to
them and tell them how pleased I am with my ornaments.'

She was at the pianoforte when the young ladies were
brought to her. Lady de Clifford had arranged to be present,
to make sure, thought Charlotte laughing inwardly, that I do
not become too familiar. Very well my lady! You shall see.

She continued to play.

'Your Highness,' said Lady de Clifford, 'the young ladies
are here.'

Charlotte went on playing and neither Lady de Clifford nor
the young ladies knew what to do. They could only stand
bewildered by the antics of royalty. Then turning, Charlotte
inclined her head haughtily at the girls and went on playing.

'Your Highness!' whispered Lady de Clifford.

Charlotte spun round on the stool and burst out laughing.

'My dear friends.' she said to the girls, 'I hope I have given
you enough royal dignity. It is necessary I am told for me to
use it now and then. But I'm heartily sick of it and so must
you be, so now that it's done, I will be myself and we'll play

one of the games I used to play with a very dear friend. It tests your wits.'

The young ladies looked alarmed at first at the prospect of having their wits tested by a princess, but very soon she had put them at their ease and Lady de Clifford looked on with some admiration and a great deal of dismay while the Princess took charge of the situation.

*　　*　　*

When the wife of the labourer who had worked for her was brought to bed Charlotte insisted that clothes for the baby should be taken to her cottage with bed linen and anything that she might like and need in the circumstances.

The woman was overcome with gratitude and when Charlotte called to see the new-born child she thanked her and said she had always known that Her Royal Highness was the most generous of ladies and had never believed for one moment she was not.

'Why should you have been expected to doubt it?' demanded Charlotte.

'Because my husband and his friend received no payment for the work they did for Your Highness. But this, Madam, is payment enough. Your goodness came to us at a time when we most needed it.'

'No payment,' cried Charlotte, a little colour coming into her pale cheeks. 'Why, I paid them two guineas for the work they did.'

'Two guineas, Your Highness? Why, they never set eyes on it.'

Charlotte was in a rage. She went straight back to the house and demanded an enquiry, and it was not long before she discovered the page who had pocketed the two guineas.

'You wicked dishonest boy!' she cried. 'You are no longer my servant. You ... you shall be beaten. Take him away. I n ... never want to see him again. And send two guineas to those men at once.'

Her fury was intense; but in a short while it had subsided and she began to wonder what had made the page do it. He was young but it was a wicked thing to do. She would not have him beaten however; he should simply be dismissed.

But the affair made her very unhappy.

'In future,' she declared to Mrs. Udney, 'I shall see that these debts are paid myself. Even if it does mean a little familiarity with those my lady does not think fit to mix with me.'

Mrs. Udney told Lady de Clifford what she had said and Lady de Clifford sighed and remarked that Charlotte was a wild creature and it was no use anyone's thinking they could instil discipline into such a girl.

'But her heart is good,' said Lady de Clifford, 'that is one thing which keeps me from despair.'

'My word,' said Mrs. Udney. 'Wait till the time comes to get her mated. Then the sparks will fly.'

'That time will come all too soon,' murmured Lady de Clifford. 'I pray God I am not in charge of her household when it does.'

Mrs. Udney licked her lips, contemplating Charlotte's fiery future while Lady de Clifford continued her silent prayer.

*   *   *

So passed those summer weeks by the sea. Charlotte enjoyed them and was sad to see the shortening of the days. But autumn was fast approaching and the chilly winds were springing up.

'It is time Charlotte left Bognor,' said the Queen to the Prince of Wales, who agreed, with some reluctance, that this was so.

So Charlotte left the sea and comparative freedom to return to the restricted life of an heiress to the throne.

The Arrival of Mercer

THE carriage rattled along through the streets. In it sat Charlotte simply dressed in a dark-green cloak and straw hat trimmed with rosebuds; she might have been any well-bred young lady taking a drive.

Beside her was Lady de Clifford, whose lips were a little pursed. She heartily disliked these excursions and believed they were bad for the Princess. But she agreed that something had to be done and perhaps it was better for Charlotte to go to Spring Gardens than to Blackheath. However, the King had given his permission, so there was no more to be said. Charlotte was going to pay her weekly visit to her grandmother, the Duchess of Brunswick; she would spend two hours there and during those two hours she would meet her mother.

The Princess herself looked forward to the visits; although she felt little affection for her grandmother, a silly old woman who chattered incessantly, she was excited by her mother. As for the Princess Caroline, she was in a state of hysterical joy to be reunited with her daughter.

It's all a little unhealthy, thought Lady de Clifford.

New Street, Spring Gardens! What a residence for a princess. And one must remember that the Duchess of Brunswick had once been the Princess Royal of England.

But her dignity turned the dingy old house into a palace. She received there and expected all the homage due to her rank. Poor thing, thought Lady de Clifford, I doubt she had much of that in Brunswick, by all accounts.

The carriage drew up and Charlotte and her governess alighted. Few people noticed them, but of course once the

papers began letting the people know that Charlotte visited
her grandmother once a week and there met her mother there
might be crowds to see her. Lady de Clifford shuddered. The
mob was so crude. They shouted such things . . . not fit for the
ears of a young girl.

Charlotte's heart beat fast as she entered the gloomy house.
Poor Grandmamma Brunswick had few servants but she made
the most of what she had. And her footman bowed as low and
with as much dignity as if he were ushering her into Carlton
House or St. James's.

But the Princess of Wales was noted for her contempt of
ceremony. She was waiting in the lower room for her
daughter and as soon as she saw her she flew at her.

Charlotte was aware of a highly coloured face, rouged and
daubed with white lead; the Princess's heavy brows owed
their existence to paint and her enormous black curly wig
always became a little awry in these emotional encounters.
Her low cut gown exposed a large white bosom which seemed
to overbalance her short body and give her a pear-shaped
look. She never appeared to be freshly clean, but the great
charm about her was the warmth of her love for her daughter.

'My darling, darling, darling!' she cried. 'My little Charlotte! Let me look at you.' Charlotte was strained to that
great bosom which was not exactly the best position for being
seen. 'It has seemed so long. And they give us two hours . . . It
is wicked and it is cruel. Torture designed by de old Begum,
I'll swear.'

She laughed wildly.

'Oh, Mamma,' said Charlotte, 'I am so happy to see you
again. I've missed you so much.'

'My Angel! My blessed love! My Lottie love!' The embrace was suffocating. 'And what do you think I have suffered,
eh? Kept from my own baby . . . my little Lottie girl. Ah, I
always longed for a child and when I had one they took her
away from me.'

'We're together now, Mamma, for two hours.'

Caroline grimaced and put up a hand. Charlotte noticed
the flashing rings, which looked incongruous because of the
grime under the nails. Her mother was the strangest and most
eccentric person she had ever known.

'They had to agree to this. Oh, the wicked old things!
They tried to prove Willie was my boy and they couldn't . . .
they couldn't!'

Nobody had ever been so frank with Charlotte as her
mother was. Caroline did not believe in hiding facts and

Charlotte was nearly twelve years old . . . old enough to know
what went on in the world.

'And how is Willie?' asked Charlotte.

'Willikins is adorable. What I should do without that angel
I can't tell you. Do you know this, my love, if I could have you
with me and Willikins too, I'd ask nothing more.'

'If only that were possible!' sighed Charlotte.

'But you are going to be a queen one day. Nothing is going
to alter that. My little Charlotte . . . Queen of England. Then
you won't keep your poor old Mamma in the background,
will you?'

'I would always have you with me.'

'My blessed angel! And soon we shall have done with this
two hours a week. It is ridiculous. Why only two hours a
week? I shall not accept it. One of these days I shall come and
carry you away by force and we will live at Montague House
happy ever after.'

But in spite of these protestations of affection Charlotte did
feel unsure about her mother. What had really happened
about that horrid little brat Willikins? She remembered him
from the days when she had been allowed to visit Montague
House, as a hideously spoiled child whom her mother doted
on and who kicked with rage when he couldn't have his own
way.

She would not have wanted to live at Montague House; one
was never quite sure what was going to happen there. There
were so many strange people coming and going and the wild
games they played at parties, while exciting for a time, left
one bewildered. Perhaps she had been too young in the old
days when she used to visit Blackheath to understand what it
was all about. Now it would be different. She was almost
grown up. And it seemed to her now that although she was
fascinated by Montague House she would not all the time
have wanted the kind of life which was lived there.

In her heart she longed for a quiet dignified household like
that in Tilney Street.

'I suppose,' said the Princess of Wales, with a grimace, 'that
we shall have to present ourselves to Madam the Duchess.'

She spoke ironically. Was that the way in which one should
speak of one's mother?

So they went to the dingy room where the Duchess of
Brunswick held her Drawing Room. It was pathetic. This was
no palace—just a room in a dingy old house. She had two
attendants but she behaved as though she had a retinue.

She sat in an old chair as though it were a throne and she

glanced haughtily about her as the attendant at the door
called: 'Her Highness the Princess of Wales and the Princess
Charlotte.'

The Duchess of Brunswick peered at her granddaughter.

'Come and sit near me, Charlotte,' she said. She added,
waving a hand: 'Chairs for the Princesses.'

These were brought. The Princess of Wales sat down, legs
apart, a hand on either knee, in exactly the manner Charlotte
had often been told princesses should not sit.

Charlotte looked round the room. She thought it was one of
the dirtiest she had ever seen and there was scarcely any furniture. She felt sorry for the old lady who was trying to cling to
her royalty in such surroundings and she was angry too when
she thought of all the apartments which could have been put
at her disposal. There was Kensington Palace, Windsor, Buckingham House, Kew, even St. James's. It was a shame.

'Grandmamma,' she said impulsively, 'You should not be
here. You should have a fine apartment.'

'My dear Charlotte, I am an exile. I must perforce take
what is given me.'

'But it's a . . . shame.'

'It's de old Begum's doing,' said Caroline with a short
laugh. 'She hates us all, and she's glad to think of an old
enemy living in such a place.'

What a wicked old woman the Queen was! thought Charlotte. How could she behave so to her own sister-in-law?

The Duchess suddenly became rather tearful. 'I had expected something different, Charlotte, my dear, I will confess.
Once I was a very important lady of this land. The Princess
Royal, and my brother doted on me. That's the King, you
know. This is not his fault. Poor man, I always said he had a
kind heart though an addled head. He would have done
better than this. But he's in a sad state, poor George. It was a
shock to me when I saw him. He goes on and on and on . . .
and one has no idea what he's talking about.'

' "Eh, what?" ' mimicked the Princess of Wales. 'But he's a
kind man and when I first came over I wished I'd come to
marry him instead of the Prince of Wales. Then it would have
been a different story, *I* can tell you. He had rather a fancy for
me. Charlotte, my pet, you would have had six or seven
brothers and sisters by now if I'd married dear addle-headed
George!'

'You were always so indiscreet,' said the Duchess, becoming
suddenly haughty. 'Restrain yourself, Caroline.' She turned to
her granddaughter. 'Your mother caused us great anxiety in

her childhood. She was so wild. I could tell you things. Perhaps I will one day. They used to say *I* was indiscreet. Madam de Hertzfeldt . . . she was my husband's mistress . . . was installed when I arrived. "I have no intention of giving up my mistress because I have acquired a wife," he told me. How would you have liked that?'

'Charlotte would have loved him,' said the Princess of Wales. 'He was a great man . . . a great soldier.'

'He fell at Jena. That wicked Napoleon! When shall we again sleep soundly in our beds? To think of his soldiers now . . . in our beautiful country . . . but I never thought much of it. England was my home . . . and it was consolation when I returned here. But I did not expect to return to this . . . squalor. How can I keep up the state due to my rank here? That is what I should like to know. But that wicked old woman . . . she always hated me. It was clear from the moment she arrived. Mecklenburg–Strelitz! She ought to have been humble. And so she appeared to be. Sly as a fox . . . though she looks more like a crocodile. *Queen* Charlotte! Oh, she would have liked to show her authority. "Oh no, no," I said . . . and my mother was alive then and George was in leading strings, you might say. It was our Mamma who said which way he should go, not little Charlotte.'

'De old Begum,' chuckled the Princess of Wales.

Charlotte was astonished by the freedom with which they both expressed their dislike of the Queen, and while she was a little repelled, she was fascinated. From the gossip of these two she could learn more than she could through the chatter of servants and even the cartoons and snippets from the papers which the sly Mrs. Udney brought to her notice.

'Someone called Jerome Bonaparte now rules in our palace . . . some relation of that man. He's splitting up Europe between them and we . . . the true rulers . . . are exiled wanderers on the face of the Earth. My dear child, I can't tell you what difficulty I had to escape. I came through Sweden . . . and so to England. I thought I should never arrive. What adventures . . . at my time of life! And when I came—what a welcome! George was kind, of course. A kind heart . . . though an adled head . . . but Charlotte . . . It's a pity they named you after her, but don't forget you have another name: Augusta. And that's mine . . . so although you were named for her you were named for me too. Is that not strange? You bear both our names.'

'Yes,' said Charlotte, 'it's true. I was named after my two grandmothers. Is my uncle here?'

She had met her mother's brother who was now the Duke of Brunswick, also in exile. He seemed different from the rest of his family—calmer, and yet a brave man. She had heard how he had fought with his men through the territory occupied by the French to the coast where a fleet of British ships were assembled to bring him to England with his motherless little boys.

That had seemed romantic and so had he in his dashing uniform and with his fine pair of moustaches giving him such a handsome look.

His little boys, Charles aged six and William four, were in this house occupying the upper rooms with their nurses and servants. Charlotte wondered whether she should go and see them before she left and suggested this.

'Poor mites,' said Caroline vaguely. 'Perhaps if there is time ... but we have only these two miserable hours and I suppose it will be reported if we try to make it longer. *I* want to spend every minute with my own sweet Charlotte.'

'Dear, dear,' said the Duchess. 'So you and the Prince are still at loggerheads. I must say it is a very odd way of going on. *I* found him charming. He invited me to Carlton House. "Dear Aunt," he said, "I shall be *desolate* if you don't attend." And so I went. How charming he is. What manners! I have never seen anyone bow with such grace and charm. I said to him: "My dear nephew, you are indeed the first Gentleman of Europe." '

'You should have seen him on his wedding night. Drunk. He had to be supported on his way to the altar. Yes he did. They had to stand very close to him to prevent his falling down.' Caroline burst into loud laughter.

'A charming man,' said the Duchess ignoring her. 'I do not think that in all my life I have ever met a more charming man than my nephew, the Prince of Wales.'

'He spent part of the wedding night under the grate. Very charming. I consider myself well off without him.'

Charlotte listened to this conversation with an eager horror. Her mother and her grandmother seemed to be carrying it on independently of each other and she wondered whether they were aware of her. But every now and then her mother would refer to her sweet Charlotte, her angel, her love, to remind her daughter that she was conscious of her presence.

Thus passed the two hours and Lady de Clifford was fidgeting to be off, for as she said to Charlotte, if they exceeded their stay the visits might be cut down to once a fortnight.

'How strange,' said Charlotte as the carriage carried them

back to Carlton House, 'that I am only allowed to visit my own mother once a week.'

Lady de Clifford did not think it strange at all when that mother was the Princess Caroline, when she had just emerged, scarcely unscathed from the Delicate Investigation, when it seemed almost certain that she was leading a very odd if not immoral life. It appeared to be very reasonable that her daughter—the future Queen of England—should be allowed only brief meetings with her.

Charlotte was silently thinking of her family.

'It's like a menagerie,' she said. 'A royal menagerie.'

*   *   *

Princess Charlotte was sickening for something. She was constantly shivering and to Lady de Clifford's alarm had developed a fever. She called the doctors and Charlotte was sent to bed; she was too listless to protest and a few days later the rash indicated that she was suffering from measles.

There was consternation throughout the family and the Prince of Wales sent his first physician to attend his daughter.

He said to Maria: 'If Charlotte should die they would tell me it was my duty to have another child. Maria, I could not do it. The thought of being near that woman makes me sick.'

Maria comforted him and said it was only the measles and most children recovered from this very quickly. Moreover, Charlotte was a strong child.

He scarcely left Maria's side. It was at times like this that he realized how much he needed her. Maria was happy too; it was going to be all right, she was sure. His ridiculous passion for Lady Hertford was not important. That woman was as cold as ice and would never become his mistress. Maria had nothing to fear. He was wayward by nature; it was a sort of compulsion for him to stray. It meant little. Maria was his lifelong companion and after that other separation when he had deserted her for Lady Jersey he had come to realize this.

Miss Pigot was called in and gave her views of the measles; she prepared a few possets which she was sure the doctors would say were beneficial. And the Prince talked of nothing but Charlotte's measles—not alas, Maria noted, because he cared so much for the child, but because he feared that her death would put him into a repulsive position.

The King and Queen discussed Charlotte's measles. The King was worried. 'She always seemed such a healthy child.

Romping here, jumping there ... eh, what? Measles. How
bad is it? Are they telling us the truth, eh, what?'

The Queen said it was a childish complaint and Charlotte
was in no danger. She was going to give very special instructions to Lady de Clifford and was sending some James's Powder for the child. It had wonderful healing properties; and
she was going to instruct Lady de Clifford not to allow the bed-
linen to be changed until she ordered that this should be
done.

'I could not sleep all night thinking of it,' said the King.
'The Princesses should not visit the child. That must be made
plain. It's a very contagious disease. Did you know that, eh,
what?'

'Indeed I know it, but once someone has had it they cannot
have it again, so you need not fear for the Princesses.'

'They'll be wanting to go and nurse her I daresay. I won't
have Amelia ...'

'Amelia shall not go and see her niece until it is perfectly
safe for her to do so. You must trust me.'

The King nodded. He was forced to trust to the Queen for
everything. A change from what it used to be, he thought, eh,
what?

*   *   *

The carriage of the Princess of Wales arrived at Carlton
House. Caroline alighted and brushed aside all who would
detain her.

'Where is my child?' she demanded. 'Take me at once to
the Princess Charlotte.'

The pages and footmen were in a quandary. They knew
that the Princess Caroline was not to be received at Carlton
House. What could they do? How refuse her? She was after
all the Princess of Wales.

'Come, don't try to obstruct me.' She spoke in an odd mix-
ture of French, German and English which they pretended
they could not understand, and they allowed her to push her
way into the house and to Charlotte's room.

She flung open the door.

'My angel. My little love!'

Charlotte said weakly: 'Mamma. It is you?'

'Of course it is me, my Lottie love. My baby ill and her
Mamma not with her. Why I should be with you every hour!
It should be my duty and my pleasure. How are you?'

'I'm getting better, Mamma. But I have lots of spots all
over me.'

'Why bless you, you'll soon be well again. I missed our two

hours together.' She grimaced and laughed aloud. 'Life is not the same for me without my little Lottie, you know.'

'Oh, Mamma, you are so . . . so . . .'

'So what, my love?'

Charlotte could not say 'So strange', which was what she had meant, and she was too weak to think of any other way of expressing what she meant. So she substituted: 'So . . . so dear to me.'

Caroline bent over her and kissed her.

'Oh, Mamma, I am con . . . contagious.'

'Dearest child, I wouldn't care if you were a leper. I'd still kiss you.'

Charlotte was so tired she could scarcely keep her eyes open but Caroline did not seem to notice this. She sat by the bed and talked of the good times they would have together when Charlotte was well and they had found some way of flouting the rule that they were to meet only once a week.

Lady de Clifford was pacing up and down in the next room asking herself how she could remove the Princess of Wales and what the Prince and the Queen were going to say when they knew that the woman had visited her daughter.

*   *   *

The Prince summoned Lady de Clifford. He bowed and bade her sit down. His manners, she thought, were impeccable. He had the gift of making one want to serve him with all one's power; and she was very unhappy because she knew that however charming he might be outwardly, inwardly he was displeased.

'My daughter is making a good recovery in your very capable hands,' he said, to put her at her ease. In spite of his bulk he was very handsome and Lady de Clifford was almost on the edge of tears because she had failed in her duty.

'Thank you, Lady de Clifford, for all your care of her.'

'Your Highness . . . if I could believe you were pleased with me I should be very happy but I fear . . .'

He was all concern. 'This unfortunate visit of the Princess of Wales?' he said, and coldness came into his voice when he said her name.

'Sir, I do not seek to excuse myself. I knew your wishes. I can only say that the Princess of Wales took us all by surprise. We had no notion . . .'

He nodded. 'I understand that. I understand full well. She stormed into the room before she could be prevented. That is the case, is it not?'

'Exactly so, sir.'

'I think,' he said, with that famous smile and the slight crinkling of the nose which made it lovable, 'that we had better forget it. We can say that the Princess of Wales had an excuse because her daughter was ill. But I think we should take precautions that it does not happen again, don't you?'

'I am sure it will not. I am sure all concerned must be upset because they fear they may have failed in their duty, which is to serve Your Highness.'

'Then that is well.'

With the utmost grace he had indicated that the interview was over; she rose and took her leave, feeling that whatever happened she would see that no one in her household ever displeased him again.

*   *   *

When Charlotte recovered she went to Bognor and there revelled in her freedom and was soon full of health again.

It was wonderful to be there, to sample Mr. Richardson's buns once more and to stroll along the shore looking for seaweed and anything the waves had washed up; she rode her carriage and four greys through the country lanes; she talked to the people.

Those were happy days; but back at Carlton House she soon discovered that there was a great deal of friction in her household.

The two chief combatants were Dr. Nott and Mrs. Udney; their dislike of each other had gradually grown and now they could scarcely hide it.

Quarrels constantly broke out between them; they criticized each other. Dr. Nott declared that Mrs. Udney was introducing the Princess to certain kinds of literature which should not be brought to her notice. Mrs. Udney retorted that Dr. Nott was trying to influence the Princess in the hope that later he might obtain certain benefits.

These petty quarrels were certain, sooner or later, to break out into a conflict which could not be ignored and it happened one day when Dr. Nott came in and found the Princess Charlotte and Mrs. Udney examining some cartoons which Mrs. Udney had acquired.

This love of what were known as 'prints' had made a bond between Charlotte and Mrs. Udney. It was not that Charlotte liked the woman—she never would do that—but she did find her conversation with its sly innuendoes irresistible; nor could she help being very interested in the cartoons and papers which Mrs. Udney was constantly showing her.

Mrs. Udney had just come from Gillray's in St. James's Street and was chatting with the Princess, telling her of her visit to this shop.

'He used to be in Old Bond Street and now he is moved to St. James's, which is even better. Your Highness would like to see Gillray's shop.'

Mrs. Udney's malicious smile played about her lips. Dare she take Charlotte there one day? It was a bit risky, for she could lose her position if discovered.

'Old Gillray is above, working away at his cartoons. I've seen him once. Such a quiet man, Your Highness—grey eyes and grey hair, but there is a sort of liveliness about him. You would never guess that he could do such clever ... wicked work.'

'He is undoubtedly clever,' said Charlotte.

'Yes, yes. Look at this one.'

It was a picture of the King—looking quite ridiculous and yet somehow so exactly like her grandfather that there was no mistaking him. He was seated at a bench making buttons. There were rows of them on the bench and beneath the picture was written 'The Royal Button Maker'. There was another of the King wearing leggings and with straws in his hair. It was called 'Farmer George'. There was one of the King and Queen—the Queen wearing an apron and frying sprats while the King toasted muffins. This was ridiculing the humble way they liked to live.

'They have some very wicked ones,' said Mrs. Udney with a laugh. 'Miss Humphrey serves below with Betty Marshall who can't stop giggling. They know me well. I'm a good customer.'

'I wonder my grandfather does not send him to prison.'

'Oh, we'd have all London up in arms and marching on St. James's if he did. No one would be allowed to lay a finger on Gillray. London would see to that. He makes the people laugh too much ... and they like to laugh. Miss Humphrey thinks he's a genius, which is not surprising, considering ...'

'Considering what?'

Mrs. Udney winked.

'She's his ... m ... mistress?' asked Charlotte.

Mrs. Udney nodded significantly. 'Well, you've got to know how your future subjects live, haven't you? Your Highness would be surprised. It's very respectable, mind. They're as good as married. Betty Marshall told me one day that he and

Miss Humphrey did start out for St. James's Church to get married and before they got there he got an idea for a cartoon and that made him change his mind. So they went back and things went on just as they had been.'

Charlotte was vitally interested and wanted to hear more about James Gillray and Miss Humphrey.

There was a great talent in his work, and he was very prolific. According to Mrs. Udney, he had made not only a name for himself but a fortune.

Mrs. Udney had brought an old cartoon with her of Mrs. Fitzherbert and the Prince with Mr. Fox and Mr. Pitt which had been done soon after the Prince's secret marriage to Mrs. Fitzherbert. Pitt and Fox were both dead now but Charlotte knew a great deal about them. A study of politics was essential to her education and no study of English politics could be complete without these two illustrious names.

The cartoon was called 'Dido Forsaken' and it showed Mrs. Fitzherbert—a good deal younger than she was today—standing on a pile of logs on the shore. A boat was sailing away from them and in it were Pitt, Fox and the Prince of Wales. From the Prince's mouth came a bubble in which were written the words: 'I never saw her in my life,' and from Fox's 'No, damme, never in his life.'

Charlotte was studying this intently when Dr. Nott came in so quietly that neither she nor Mrs. Udney heard him. This gave him the opportunity to see what it was they were so intent on and there spread on the table was not only 'Dido Forsaken' but 'The Royal Farmer' and 'Button Maker' and 'Frying Sprats and Toasting Muffins'.

As he stared at them his face grew scarlet. He tried to speak but he could only splutter.

Then he turned to Mrs. Udney and said in a voice cold with fury: 'You will hear more of this.'

*   *   *

The entire household was discussing the trouble between Dr. Nott and Mrs. Udney. The Bishop arrived and was closeted for a long time with Dr. Nott.

The general verdict was that Mrs. Udney would receive orders to leave the household. Dr. Nott had the Bishop on his side and everyone knew that Mrs. Udney was a scandalmonger and that the subjects she discussed with the Princess were unsuitable.

Charlotte was dismayed. She discovered that although she admired Dr. Nott she preferred the company of Mrs. Udney.

Dr. Nott was a good man and he had been selected by the King and approved by the Prince of Wales because of his piety; his lectures on Religious Enthusiasm had brought him fame; but he was a bore.

Hourly everyone was waiting for Mrs. Udney's dismissal, and Charlotte was sorry for her.

'I shall miss you if you go,' she said.

They were both thinking of that mention in her will. 'Nothing . . . for reasons.' Things had changed since then and Charlotte had realized that Mrs. Udney brought a great deal of amusement and enlightenment into her life.

'Your Highness should not be made unhappy by the loss of your servants,' said Mrs. Udney.

'Alas,' replied the Princess. 'I do not choose them.'

'That old man is very sensitive. I believe he would go if he thought Your Highness was displeased with him.'

'I *am* displeased with him.'

'Perhaps he does not know it.'

'Lady de Clifford is in a fret about this.'

'Lady de Clifford is always in a fret about something, Your Highness.'

Charlotte went thoughtfully away and when she met Dr. Nott she looked past him coldly to indicate that she blamed him for the trouble, and he was most upset.

All in the household thought the affair very strange for Dr. Nott suddenly made up his mind that he wished to retire, that he did not believe he was suitable for the task which had been given him, and that he could be of greater service elsewhere in his chosen profession.

So Dr. Nott went and the affair was suddenly over.

Mrs. Udney was very amused and gratified by the way everything had turned out.

It was pleasant to think she could still make her little trips to Mr. Gillray's shop in St. James's where she could buy his latest prints and see how his life was progressing with Miss Humphrey.

* * *

Dr. William Short was appointed to take Nott's place and the Prince of Wales decided that as Charlotte was now thirteen it was time she learned something about the laws and the government of the country; so in addition to Dr. Short, William Adam was sent to her to give her instruction. This was significant because Adam, lawyer and politician, had become Solicitor General and Attorney General to the Prince of Wales and Keeper of the Great Seal for the Duchy of Corn-

wall. He was a Whig and ardent admirer of the late Charles
James Fox—although at one time they had fought a duel.
Adam's task was to make a Whig of Charlotte and this he
found by no means difficult. Young and impressionable, she
was charmed with Adam who was a man of very easy manners
and personal attraction, though well advanced in his fifties.
He won Charlotte's affection immediately, for he was gay and
kind; and he had recently lost his wife which made him at
times attractively melancholy.

Charlotte was delighted by the change which had taken
away poor old Dr. Nott and put in his place this exciting personality, and it was through William Adam that Charlotte
made an important friendship.

One day after she and Adam had had their lesson on parliamentary affairs, Adam mentioned his niece Margaret Mercer
Elphinstone.

'Mercer,' he said, 'we've always called her Mercer—has
more personality than any woman I know. Mind you, she is a
girl yet. Well she would be some eight years older than Your
Highness. But she is intelligent and forthright . . . indeed a
young woman of great character. I think Your Highness
would be interested in meeting her, so if at some time you
will give me permission to present her . . .'

Charlotte thought everything that William Adam said was
full of wisdom and she could scarcely wait to meet his niece.

So very soon Margaret Mercer Elphinstone was presented.

Charlotte was enchanted. Mercer had the most wonderful
red hair; she was handsome and undeniably attractive; she
was certainly forthright, poised and extremely knowledgeable
of the world; she could talk politics with the utmost ease and
it was obvious that William Adam had a respect for her
opinions, *and* she was an ardent Whig.

The hour she spent with Charlotte passed all too quickly
and when it was over Charlotte declared: 'You *must* come
and see me again. Please . . . *when?*'

Mercer replied coolly that when the Princess chose to command her she would come.

'Command!' cried Charlotte impetuously. 'Let there be no
talk of command. I want you to be my friend.'

There was no doubt that Mercer was pleased. She said she
was glad of that because she had been hoping they would be
true friends and between friends rank meant nothing.

'I am so pleased you came,' said Charlotte; and Mercer said
she would call the next day.

*   *   *

Margaret Mercer Elphinstone was an exceedingly rich young woman; as the only child of Viscount Keith (whose sister William Adam had married) she was his heiress as well as her maternal grandfather's; and because of her wealth she was pursued by suitors who however admired her as well as coveting her fortune.

Mercer opened a new world for Charlotte. Mercer attended balls and all kinds of functions where she had met interesting people. She had stories to tell of that wild and extraordinary young man Lord Byron who, Mercer confessed, had it in his mind to become one of her suitors. He was handsome, witty and had some deformity in his foot of which he was most ashamed. 'I often wonder whether I should marry him,' said Mercer. 'I might be able to help him.'

'Does he need help?' Charlotte wanted to know eagerly. 'He seems to be so sought after.'

'Oh, everyone is amused and interested by him. But at the same time he is often melancholy. He will be a great poet one day and I am sure I could help him.'

Charlotte was equally sure Mercer would be able to; in fact there was nothing, according to Charlotte, that Mercer could not do.

She thought about Mercer constantly. She wanted to give her presents; when Mercer was absent she wrote long letters to her and could not be lured away from the writing table.

'It has made all the difference to me,' she declared, 'to have a friend of my own.' She quickly became passionately fond of Mercer; when Mercer was coming to see her she was filled with gaiety; when she went away she was melancholy.

She gave a ring to her friend in which she had had a message engraved stating her love for her friend and expressed the hope that Mercer would always keep it.

Mercer vowed she would and it would be a precious memento for the rest of her life; it would be a comfort if the day came when she was separated from Charlotte.

'That day shall never come,' declared Charlotte. 'I shall see to that. When I am queen you shall be chief minister.'

That made Mercer laugh. Would they allow a woman to be that? she asked.

'I am the one who shall make such decisions and I will have no one else.'

How pleasant it was to talk of the future. They also discussed the politics of the past; Mercer was widely informed on the Colonies question and she told how they would never have been lost if Fox had been in power. Fox was the greatest politician of the age and he had simply never had a chance to show his genius. Poor Lord North had vacillated—and the King with him—and so England had lost America. Mercer wanted to free the country from Tory influence, so Charlotte did too.

How exciting the world had become since she had known Mercer—and to think that she had once thought it the height of bliss to sit on a stool in Mr. Richardson's bakery and eat his buns!

Lady de Clifford reported the absorbing friendship to the Queen, who decided to speak to Charlotte.

'Future rulers,' said the Queen, 'should never make *particular* friendships. People are apt to presume on such . . . they may be the best of people but the fact that one is going one day to be in a position of importance should make one very careful.'

What is the old Begum talking about? thought Charlotte.

'Your great and only source of happiness comes from your father,' went on the Queen. 'You should not look for it in other directions until he advises you to do so.'

Now what did that mean? Until her father procured a man and said 'Marry him'? She would not allow herself to be forced into that, Mercer believed in independence. 'If you are weak people will impose on you,' said Mercer. How right she was. How right she always was. And how adorable! The best friend in the world.

Charlotte looked obliquely at her grandmother.

If she thought she was going to spoil her friendship with Mercer, she was very much mistaken.

*   *   *

Nothing was done to prevent the friendship which strengthened as the months passed. Then a series of tragedies struck the royal family and it seemed to Charlotte that she was jerked out of her childhood and nothing was ever quite the same again.

The trouble appeared to start because of a conflict between two of her uncles, Edward, Duke of Kent, whom she had never liked, and her favourite of them all, Uncle Fred, Duke of York.

It was such a scandal that try as they might they could not keep it from her; and that was the beginning.

The Rival Dukes and Mary Anne

EDWARD, DUKE OF KENT, was a frustrated man. His military career had been a bitter disappointment and the only one in the world who understood how he suffered was Julie—known as Madame de St. Laurent. She was the only person in the world for whom he cared; for years now he had regarded her as his wife; and he wanted no other. The family accepted her, for it was realized that as he was a royal Duke there could be no marriage ceremony, and Edward therefore must dispense with it. The affairs of the Prince of Wales and Mrs. Fitzherbert and the Duke of Sussex with his Goosey had shown how worthless such ceremonies were.

Julie was beautiful, discreet and in every way except one, worthy to marry into the royal family; and that one reason was that she was not royal. She would not allow this fact to give Edward the smallest cause for anxiety. Julie made it clear that she was content with her lot; and she wanted Edward to be the same. He was certainly content with Julie; it was the way in which he had been treated which angered him.

He was unlike the Prince of Wales in that he lacked that easy charm which was so much a part of his elder brother's character. Edward was a soldier who had been trained in the grimmest of schools. He was without humour; he behaved like a Prussian; and that had made him unpopular with Englishmen.

It was his Prussian attitudes which were responsible for his recall from Gibraltar.

Only to Julie could he talk of this matter; only to her could he explain the frustration. Julie understood it and it alarmed her because she sensed his growing jealousy of his brother, Frederick. 'Frederick, Duke of York, Commander-in-Chief of the Army!' He always gave him his full title when he spoke of him; and the bitterness he revealed made her shiver.

It would have been too wounding to point out that Frederick's easy-going nature ensured his popularity with the men—something which Edward, good soldier though he was, could never win.

He had begun to talk constantly of his brothers. 'George,' he would say with a sneer, 'thinks of nothing but his own pleasure. He's seen about with that ridiculous dandy Brummell and they discuss coats and neckcloths *ad nauseam*. And now he is creating a scandal with that Hertford woman, behaving like a love-sick schoolboy, following her round, gazing at her like a sick cow . . . tears in his eyes . . . and all the time living with Maria Fitzherbert. And this is the man who could one day be king . . . any day . . . by the state of my father's health. But Frederick . . . Commander-in-Chief of the Army . . .' He could not go on. His anger choked him.

'I think you should be careful not to quarrel with your brothers, Edward,' said Julie gently.

'My dear, I must say what I mean. I'm a blunt soldier. My feelings have not been considered. My father has treated me like a boy in the nursery.'

Julie tried to soothe him.

He had been sent from home when he was eighteen to Hanover, Luneburg and afterwards to Geneva because his father had believed that no young man could receive education or military instruction in England to compare with what he could get in Germany. Julie had heard all about the life he had led and the strictness of Baron Wangenheim's regime. But Edward always said with grudging admiration: 'He taught me how to be a soldier and I learned something that Frederick, Commander-in-Chief, never did.'

He had hated Geneva so much that he came home without permission and had been sent at once to Gibraltar where he had not been popular and his Prussian methods had almost caused a revolt. 'How like them,' he used to say, 'to send me to Prussia to learn German methods and then revile me for putting them into practice.' He had been recalled from Gibraltar and sent to Canada.

'The only piece of luck I ever had,' he used to say; for it was there that he met Mademoiselle de Montgenet—Julie herself—with whom he fell in love and who lived with him as his wife and changed her name then to Madame de St. Laurent after the St. Lawrence river, the scene of their blissful courtship.

Seventeen years they had been together and they still hated to be apart; when he was sick she nursed him; and when for health reasons he returned to England to take the waters of Bath she came with him.

He had to admit that his brothers, led by the Prince of Wales, rallied round him when he and Julie set up house in Knightsbridge, and Maria Fitzherbert became a particular friend of Julie's; and when Maria wanted to sell her house, Castle Hill in Ealing, Edward bought it and it became their home. Julie was the Duchess of Kent in all but name.

But of course he could not remain idle. He was a soldier and Frederick, Commander-in-Chief, had wanted to do something for him. Discipline on the rock of Gibraltar was bad and Edward was noted for his discipline. The Commander-in-Chief had talked to his brother—very jocular, very friendly, explaining to him the need to deal tactfully with the situation and reminding him of his unpopularity previously on the Rock.

He then began to scorn Frederick, who was in his opinion no true soldier; but he had believed he could reinstate himself in the eyes of the Army and the family and had accepted the challenge.

And the result was disaster.

He had quickly discovered that the reason for the trouble was drink. The soldiers spent half their time in the liquor shops and he found many drunk on duty. These he ordered to be severely flogged. He closed half the wine shops and forbade any but commissioned officers to go into those which remained open. His unpopularity soared. He did not realize how dangerously.

The soldiers hated him for depriving them of drink; the shopkeepers were furious because he took away their trade. Who was this man? they asked each other. The son of a king. They did not want to be commanded by kings' sons; they wanted to be commanded by soldiers. Where had he learned his army drill? In Germany. This was not Germany and they would not tolerate German ways.

The revolt was staged for Christmas Eve but it was ill-planned and the Duke, if stern, was competent. He had soon captured the ringleaders and without hesitation stood them up before a firing squad. The sound of those shots sobered the mutineers as he had guessed they would.

But within a month he was recalled to England.

'By God, Edward,' said Fred—jolly, good-humoured Fred —'things are damned awkward at Gib. Worse than they were before you went. Better if you'd stayed at home, perhaps.'

This from Frederick—a careless pleasure-loving Fred—who cared more for his numerous mistresses than he did for the Army. It was an insult; it was a deep wound; it was an open sore. For whichever way he looked at it he had once again been recalled from Gibraltar in disgrace.

The King received him with much shaking of the head. 'Discipline ... very good, but it has to be *reasonable* discipline, eh, what? You've got to have tact, eh, judgment, eh what?' He glared at his son as he spoke, and those protuberant eyes were wild beneath the bushy white brows. He was half mad, thought Edward, but that did not heal the wound. He had done his best. He could have kept order in Gibraltar; he could have restored discipline; but they had recalled him after he had stifled the revolt because they said he was too severe; when he remembered the disgrace of it, he was furious. And there was Fred—unfit for command if ever anyone was—Commander-in-Chief of the Army!

*　　*　　*

The incompetence of Fred therefore became an obsession; he had to occupy his mind with something, cut off as he was from the career he loved.

Then one day a certain Colonel Wardle came to him with a startling story.

'Your Highness,' said the Colonel, 'there is a matter which causes me great uneasiness and puts me in a very delicate position, but I have come to the conclusion that it is my duty to bring it to your notice. It concerns certain practices which are being carried out to the detriment of the army which we both serve.'

'Certainly tell me,' said Edward.

The Colonel coughed. 'It is a little embarrassing, Your Highness. This concerns the conduct of the Duke of York.'

Edward tried to suppress his excitement. 'I trust it is nothing ... discreditable.' His very expression denied the sentiment showing clearly that he hoped it did.

'So discreditable, Your Highness, that I think perhaps I should not talk of it.'

'You have made an accusation against my brother. I must insist.'

'Not against the Duke, Your Highness. It is a certain woman who was once his mistress.'

Edward licked his lips. 'I command you to proceed, Colonel.'

'I know for a fact that a certain Mary Anne Clarke has been selling commissions in the Army. Her position as mistress of the Commander-in-Chief has put her into a position to do this.'

'Selling commissions. It is monstrous!'

'So I thought, Your Highness.'

'And how long has this been going on?'

'Doubtless it is no longer happening because His Highness pensioned off the woman some time ago. But it did happen. I have irrefutable evidence of this.'

'It is something which must not be allowed to pass. It is trickery of the worst kind. Where is this woman now?'

Colonel Wardle twirled his moustaches. 'Passing from one man to another in the process of her profession, Your Highness.'

'And my brother?'

'They parted good friends. He gave her a pension of four hundred a year but she is in debt. I fear he instilled in her a taste for extravagance.'

'Coupled with a taste for trickery,' said Edward, his eyes protruding and his face growing so red that he looked remarkably like his father.

'You know where to find this woman?' he asked.

'Yes, sir.'

'She should be asked ... bribed if need be ... to tell the truth.'

'I will try her out, Your Highness. I think I know how to make her talk.'

'It is deplorable, highly regrettable, but even though my own brother and a royal Duke is involved I do not see how I can allow this to pass.'

We are in for an exciting scandal, thought Colonel Wardle, and went off to set it in motion.

*   *   *

Mary Anne Clarke, vivacious, extremely pretty and, according to the men of her acquaintance, infinitely desirable though now nearer forty than thirty, was finding it difficult to satisfy her creditors. It was true that though she came from the establishment of a stonemason—her husband—in Snow Hill, that was long ago and she had grown accustomed to living with a Duke—and a royal one at that. She had four children—the stonemason's—to whom she was devoted and she was determined to have the best for them. She would like nice respectable marriages for the three girls and a good career for the boy. If Frederick had stayed with her this could have been achieved but Frederick had left. They had been together for three years—which was a long time for Frederick —and she had always been well aware of his penchant for variety. He had been an easy-going, pleasant lover, not very intelligent, but one must not expect too much; he had royalty to offer and that meant prestige even if there had not been all the money she would have liked. Poor Fred, like his brother the Prince of Wales he was constantly in debt, and although he had promised his dear Mary Anne a good income, it was rarely paid.

'Simply haven't the money, my angel,' he would tell her blithely; and she knew it was true.

But she had insisted on her pension of four hundred pounds a year on which she delicately called her retirement from his service. It had all been arranged legally; she had been determined on that.

Sometimes she read through his letters. They made her laugh, for writing was not one of his accomplishments. They were crude and ill-spelt, but one thing they did show was his devotion, for Fred had been a very devoted lover, while it lasted.

The letters she kept carefully tied up with ribbon and in a locked box. The ribbon was for sentiment and the locked box for prudence. Remembering Perdita Robinson who had dealt very profitably with the letters of the Prince of Wales, she did not see why Mary Anne Clarke might not fare equally so with the letters of Frederick Duke of York. Well, perhaps not equally but should she say adequately—for she must not lose sight of the fact that a Duke of York was not quite a Prince of Wales.

And a woman in her position had to consider her assets. Her looking-glass told her that they were still considerable. Her cheeky nose, her full sensuous lips, her big blue eyes and her fair unblemished skin were more than charming; they were inviting; and her thick fair curly hair was youthful still. No one would guess that she was nearly forty. But she was ... and that was why it was comforting to think of those letters with their pretty pink ribbon and their strong box.

She had very little money and extravagant tastes. Having lived in an establishment with twenty servants to wait on her, it was hard to wait on herself. But even at the height of her extravagance and when Frederick was at his most adoring she had been short of money because she had entertained him so lavishly and so many people had flocked to her house. The wild Barry Brothers were constant visitors although she never penetrated the sedate Maria Fitzherbert set. And who wanted to? was Mary Anne's comment. What Mary Anne wanted was fun . . . and money to enjoy it.

The royal brothers had an unpractical attitude to money. For them it was almost an abstract quality. They ordered what they wanted as a privilege of royalty and forgot that it had to be paid for.

'My darling shall have an allowance,' Frederick had declared; but it never seemed to occur to him that an allowance was an amount of money which had to be paid regularly.

When she asked him for it, he was bewildered. He hadn't got it.

Mary Anne sighed, but she was experienced enough to know that constantly to demand money was the quickest way to kill sentiment. Therefore she found her own means of supplying her purse.

Through Frederick she learned a little of Army matters. He told her that his staff sold commissions and that there were regular rates for these. The money was collected and used to help orphans and widows of soldiers who had lost their lives in the Service.

What did soldiers pay for those commissions? Mary Anne wanted to know.

'Well, for a Major it would be somewhere in the neighbourhood of £2,500, for a Captain half that ... well, say £1,500.'

'And less for lesser ranks naturally,' said Mary Anne. 'What a lot of money must be coming in to your fund.'

'It trickles in, I believe,' said the Duke. 'I know nothing about it.'

Mary Anne went on thinking about that money. She was in the service of the Army in a way since she delightfully charmed the leisure hours of the Commander-in-Chief, so she did not see why she should not benefit from some of this money which was coming in.

The more she thought of it, the more it appealed to her. Suppose she cut the price as an inducement? That should be tempting. As adored mistress of the Commander-in-Chief she could make sure that the commissions were supplied. She could make it clear to those whose duties it was to look after these matters that if they did not work with her she would find some reason to complain against them to the Commander-in-Chief. It was so easy to whisper a word into the royal ear during tender interludes, when he would be ready to promise her anything she asked for.

It was a brilliant idea and Mary Anne lost no time in putting it into practice.

In a short time she had found a friend to help her, and so great was the flow of business that she took an office and employed a clerk or two. Business flourished and she would have been enabled to pay her debts, but the more money that came in the more extravagant she became.

Still, it was a prosperous concern. In addition to commissions, she sold transfers from one regiment to another; and she began to look for fresh loopholes in the system which would enable her to add to her activities.

All was going well when Frederick's great passion for his Mary Anne came to an end, and once that happened Mary Anne's creditors were at her door. What could she do? Her lucrative business had come to an end; she was heavily in debt; and what security had she to offer now? She could see no answer but in flight.

The Duke with unexpected shrewdness had called in his financial adviser to arrange for her pension; and this was to be paid to her, subject to her good conduct. Rather unfair, she thought; and not in the original bargain; but she did not underestimate her awkward position. She went to Devonshire, but Mary Anne was not meant for the country life and very soon, stifled with boredom, she was back in London. She had her children's future to think of—always a great concern—so she went to live with her mother in Bloomsbury. Mrs. Thompson took lodgers and one of her lodgers was a friend of Colonel Wardle.

Calling at Mrs. Thompson's house Colonel Wardle met Mary Anne whom he had known in the days of her glory and he expressed his concern to see her so reduced in circumstances. She was comforted to talk of her sorrows.

'But for my creditors,' she declared, 'you would not find me skulking here. I should be out in the world.'

'So you would and so you should be.' Colonel Wardle implied that he was not unaffected by her charm. It was a sin, he said, that such beauty had to remain hidden. She had not been exactly generously treated by the Duke of York.

'Poor Fred,' she said with a smile. 'He was always short of money himself.'

'A man has his obligations. The royal Duke whom I serve would honour his commitments.'

'Your royal Duke?'

'Edward, Duke of Kent.'

'So he is your friend.'

Colonel Wardle retorted airily: 'Oh, yes, we are on terms of friendship. He is not very pleased with his brother. I have it from Major Dodd—you must meet the Major who is in close attendance on the Duke—I have it from him that His Highness of Kent would very much like the position held by His Highness of York and feels himself much more capable of fulfilling it.'

'Fred is very popular with the men.'

'His brother thinks discipline is very lax in the Army. What they need is a strong man at the head.'

Mary Anne shrugged her shoulders. 'Where do I come into this?'

'It may be that you have certain information. Major Dodd, through a higher authority, would be very willing to pay you for it.'

'You mean enough money to settle these creditors of mine?'

'But certainly.'

'And to set me up afresh.' Mary Anne's eyes sparkled at the prospect. This might be treachery towards poor Fred, but what had he done to her—left her with a pension of four hundred a year after teaching her to live at the rate of thousands! A woman had to look after herself in this world.

Mary Anne would do what she could.

From then on it was easy.

* * *

Frederick's first action when he realized what accusations were going to be brought against him was to call on the Prince of Wales.

The Prince was in a mood of despair. Lady Hertford had not become his mistress and Maria was being what he called extremely unreasonable.

Ever since the end of the Seymour case he had been constantly in the company of the Hertfords. It was maddening. No matter how much he pleaded with that frigid lady she would not relent. It was no use offering her jewels or riches; she had plenty from the long-suffering Lord Hertford. She cared for three things only: her appearance, her reputation and the Tory Party. The Whigs were watching anxiously, for they knew that Lady Hertford intended to interfere with the Prince's politics; in fact it was only through politics that he

stood the slightest chance of gaining his ends. Maria Fitzherbert was a Tory, but Maria had never sought to force her
views on anyone. The Whigs were hoping that Maria would
continue to hold sway.

The Prince would not have been so unhappy if she had. He
was not averse to this platonic relationship with Lady Hertford. It gratified the sentimental romantic side of his nature
which was strong. He wanted Maria, though, to remain in the
background of his life. The last thing he wanted was for
Maria to leave him.

And this was exactly what Maria was suggesting she would
do.

He had just received a note from her.

He had read it through several times, refusing to accept
what it conveyed. It was true he had seen less of her lately. She
should understand that. Lady Hertford kept him dancing
continual attendance; and she always insisted that for 'propriety's sake' Maria should be present when they met. Why
could not women be reasonable?

It was ironical that women who to him were the most delightful of all God's creations should plague him so. He had
always loved women more than anything else on Earth. Better
than horses, better than drinking, and the conversation and
companionship of men like Fox—ah, why had that genius had
to die! Why was he not here to give him the benefit of his
advice now? He forgot that his relationship with the brilliant
statesman had deteriorated in later years—but then he always
forgot what it was convenient to. Now it soothed him a little
to think of Fox who had been his mentor and his friend. Why
could not the women in his life be more kind and understanding? There was his wife . . . Ah, no, he could not bear to think
of that creature! There was his daughter, always difficult, not
what he would have wished for a daughter to be, and he could
see trouble increasing from that quarter as she grew older;
there was Maria behaving now in an aloof manner and with
her quick temper which had been responsible for that other
regrettable break in their relationship, and even Isabella
Hertford frustrated him because she was so pure that her
reputation meant more to her than the devotion of the Prince
of Wales. Who could have believed that women whom he had
always idolized as a sex could bring so much anguish to a man
who only wanted to please them and make them all happy?

He read Maria's letter once more:

'The constant state of anxiety I am perpetually kept in

with respect to your proceedings, and the little satisfaction I experience when occasionally you make partial communications with me, have determined me to address you by letter.

'You must be well aware of the misery we have both suffered for the past three or four years on a subject most painful to me, and to all those who are attached and interested about you. It has quite destroyed the entire comfort and happiness of both our lives; it has so completely destroyed mine that neither my health nor my spirits can bear it any longer. What am I to think of the inconsistency of your conduct when scarcely three weeks ago you voluntarily declared to me that this sad affair was quite at an end and in less than a week the whole business was begun all over again? The purport of my writing to you is to implore you to come to a resolution upon this business. You must decide, and that decision must be done immediately, that I may know what line to pursue. I beg your answer may be a written one to avoid all the unpleasant conversations upon a subject so heartrending to one whose whole life has been dedicated to you, and whose affection for you none can surpass.'

He threw the letter down and stamped on it. He wanted to burst into tears and would have done so if there had been anyone there to witness the depth of his emotion. How could Maria behave like this? Why could she not be patient with him? All he asked her to do was act as chaperon because Lady Hertford insisted.

His page was at the door. His brother the Duke of York was asking to be admitted.

The Prince picked up the letter, put it into a drawer and turned to greet Frederick.

Frederick's woebegone face told the Prince immediately that his brother had troubles and he was probably going to be denied the luxury of bemoaning his own.

Frederick burst out as soon as they were alone: 'George, I'm in the most fearful mess. It's that fellow Wardle. He's one of Edward's men. They're going to ask a question in the House.'

'What about, for God's sake?'

'Well there was a woman I was on terms with ... pretty creature. It's a long time since we parted but it seems they've got hold of her. She'd been selling commissions in the Army.'

The Prince stared at his brother. 'Good God, Fred. What have you got yourself into?'

'That,' said Frederick, 'remains to be seen.'

'Can nothing be done to stop this?'

Frederick shook his head. 'Wardle's determined. Behaving like a self-righteous martyr. Nothing is going to stop him. This is Edward's doing.'

'Our own brother—surely not! I can't believe it.'

'Oh, Edward's changed. He's become embittered. It was that Gibraltar business. He doesn't forgive me for recalling him. He wants to show he's a better soldier than I am. He'd like to be Commander-in-Chief, I don't doubt. George, what am I going to do?'

The Prince was silent. He would do anything for his brother, but what help could he offer? Once they started asking questions in the House one had to take the consequences. He remembered when a question had been asked in that holy of holies by some bumbling old country member which had led to Fox's denial of his marriage with Maria. And look what trouble that had caused.

He looked at Frederick helplessly. 'Fred, if there's anything I can do . . .'

Frederick grasped his hands. They could always rely on each other; of all the brothers they had been the closest, and they were almost as horrified by Edward's treachery as by the situation itself.

They both knew that the least that could happen to Frederick would be to lose his position in the Army.

Trouble, thought the Prince. Just trouble all round.

*　　*　　*

So the storm broke. There had rarely been such a scandal in the royal family. Colonel Wardle, as he had threatened, delivered his bombshell in the House, doing as he declared 'his duty' to the Army and the country.

The people were both outraged and amused. Yet another indiscreet love affair of the royal family. One had to admit they were entertaining. Even the stolid Duke of Kent had a mistress, although he lived most respectably with her, as did Clarence with Dorothy Jordan. Now they were going to hear something of the adventures of the Duke of York.

Within the royal family as throughout the country the main topic of conversation was the Army scandal.

The King had grown visibly older and more incoherent.

'I can't believe this of Frederick,' he told the Queen. 'If it had been George . . .'

'George would never have been such a fool as that,' insisted the Queen. But would he? she wondered. These sons of hers seemed capable of the utmost follies over women.

'Frederick,' babbled the King. 'Hope of the House . . . Best of the bunch, eh, what?'

'It's to be hoped not,' retorted the Queen. 'If he is the best, heaven help the rest.'

'Why do they do these things, eh? What happens to them? They have no sense of duty. It makes me think we failed somewhere . . . in the way we brought them up, eh, what?'

'Your Majesty was always the strictest of fathers,' replied the Queen, determined not to take the blame. He was the one who had laid down the laws; he had never allowed her to disagree with him. Often she had wanted to protest against the canings that had been administered. It had turned them against him, she was sure; it had made them wild. It was never good to restrict high-spirited young people too much. Yes, it was his fault, silly old man. She could scarcely be sorry for him; she had never loved him; but she was concerned now for his health for if he broke down it could mean a Regency and when that had almost happened before (and would have been established but for the King's recovery) she and her eldest son had become the bitterest of enemies.

So she tried to soothe him.

'This woman seems to be an adventuress. Perhaps she is not telling the truth.'

'Adventuresses! Why do they get themselves mixed up with adventuresses, eh, what?'

'I don't think William's actress is exactly that. From all accounts she seems to be keeping *him*. And Edward's Madame de St. Laurent is a very worthy creature. As for Maria Fitzherbert, Your Majesty has always had a certain admiration for her. And Lady Hertford, whom George seems to be pursuing now, is very jealous of her reputation. So they are not all mixed up with adventuresses—although I do agree with Your Majesty that these liaisons are not exactly desirable.'

'And there's the Princess of Wales . . .'

'Oh, she is a monster! And to think that she is Charlotte's mother. I hope and pray the child doesn't take after her. Although I must say Charlotte often causes me misgivings.'

'She's a sweet child. I am fond of my granddaughter.'

'She needs a great deal of correction, I do assure Your Majesty. The Princesses and I are deeply concerned. Now if you please she has shown a tendency to make *particular* friendships. We shall have to watch over her very carefully.'

Anything, thought the Queen, any topic to turn his mind from this terrible affair of Frederick's.

And she had managed it. The King's mind wandered so much nowadays. She had set him thinking of Charlotte who for all her faults was a pleasanter subject than Frederick's horrible affair with this low woman.

*   *   *

The Princesses whispered together.

'Have you heard the latest news? She is to appear before the Select Committee. She will have to give evidence at the Bar of the House. What a scandal.' Augusta had left her embroidery to fall to the floor in her excitement.

'Even George has never given us such a scandal as this,' added Elizabeth.

'They say she had produced his love letters,' said Mary.

'Just fancy having your love letters read in public.' Sophia was aghast.

'And I daresay Frederick's are rather silly,' put in Elizabeth. 'He could never spell.'

The sisters started to laugh; but Amelia said: 'I tremble to think what effect this is going to have on Papa.'

*   *   *

Mary Anne was rather pleased with all the limelight.

'It's somewhat different from the dreary life in the country,' she said.

Mrs. Thompson, her mother, who had ceased to marvel at the adventures of her daughter, asked timidly: 'Isn't it something of a disgrace?'

'For poor Fred. Not for me. Do you know gentlemen are writing me notes making me the most attractive offers.'

'Oh, Mary Anne! Will you take them?'

'I have so much to consider,' she replied. 'In the meantime I must make a good impression at the Bar.'

She did. She chose her costume with care. Blue silk—to bring out the blue in her eyes—edged with white fur. Her muff was of white fur, too. She looked exciting, very pretty and quite ten years younger than she actually was. Excitement always improved her; and she had never been at a loss for words. In fact it was her quick wit—often quite clever—which had helped her to her place in society as surely as her beauty had. On her fair curls she wore a white fur hat with the most tantalizing veil. And thus she was ready to face the assembly.

She enchanted most of them. She was so completely feminine, both demure and saucy; and she successfully dealt with those who tried to bully her, scoring over them to the amusement and delight of so many onlookers. If this was disaster for the Duke of York, it was triumph for Mary Anne.

Corruption there had been. That much was evident. The point was how much had the Duke of York been involved in it? Had he been completely innocent of it? This was hardly likely but it was of great importance to the royal family and to Frederick that he should be proved a fool rather than a knave.

Mary Anne, urged by her supporters to bring her former lover to ridicule, produced some of his letters, which were read aloud in the court. This was the highlight of the case; for Frederick was no scholar; his letters were ungrammatical ill-spelt but intensely illuminating; and gave a picture of his intimate relationship with his fascinating Mary Anne. They were quoted in all the coffee houses and the taverns.

The King ranted for hours at a time. He sent for Frederick; he demanded to know what he thought he was doing. 'No sense of duty, no sense of propriety. Can't settle down like a good husband. Got a wife ... what was wrong with that? All those animals it was true. Barren ... No children. Very unsatisfactory, eh, what? But not as unsatisfactory ... as *criminally* unsatisfactory as trafficking with this woman and undermining the discipline of the Army, eh, what?'

Frederick was wretched. He couldn't understand how he had got himself so entangled. He went to Carlton House and talked endlessly to the Prince of Wales who while he sympathized had to admit that it was the worst scandal that had hit the House. He reckoned it was this sort of thing which could start a revolution. They hadn't to look very far back across the Channel. Mary Anne was a beauty—the Prince conceded that; and he was no stranger to the sudden and irresistible passions for a woman which could beset a man, but Frederick had gone a little far in letting her become involved with the Army. So there was no great comfort even there.

As for William, he shrugged his shoulders. Really Fred was a fool. The other brothers were sorry for him but they did think he had been too absentminded or indulgent or plain stupid. Edward did not come near his brother; he couldn't help chuckling when he remembered Frederick's recalling

him from Gibraltar. Was Frederick remembering that now?
To think he had complained of Edward's behaviour.

'Ha, ha,' said Edward to himself; but not to Julie who
might have been a little shocked. Dear Julie, he wouldn't
have liked her to be otherwise. But she couldn't understand a
man's pride in the profession for which he lived and worked;
and what it meant to see an inferior placed above him—just
because he was older, just because their father doted on him,
just because he was easy-going and good-natured. This would
teach them.

So poor Frederick was wretchedly unhappy while the case
was being tried. There was no comfort anywhere ... except
with George, though even he couldn't entirely hide the fact
that he thought Frederick had acted like a fool; he couldn't go
out to any of his clubs because he knew that people were talking about him, remembering phrases from his letters to Mary
Anne, tittering over the banal manner in which he expressed
his sentiments.

Frederick stood before his mirror and said to himself:
'Damn it, I'm not a writer. I'm a soldier.' His reflection
mocked him. A soldier. He was an even worse soldier than a
writer it seemed; at least that was what his enemies were
trying to prove.

There was no one who really stood with him. He had never
felt so friendless in his life. George—yes, George— but he
knew that things had never been the same between them
since their quarrel over Maria Fitzherbert and the Duchess of
York.

The door of his bedroom was quietly opened and someone
was standing there looking at him. He stared at his wife. 'You
here?' he stammered.

'Yes.' She came into the room and sat down on the bed.

'You have been hearing of this ... affair,' he said; and he
thought: She has come to mock me, which is understandable.
She is my wife but I never loved her and I showed it quite
clearly. As for her, she always preferred her animals.

She nodded. 'I have heard,' she said. 'And I think at such
time it is well that we are under the same roof.'

'What?' he cried.

'Oh, yes,' she said. 'It is why I have come to London.'

'But you hate London.'

'I prefer the country.'

'And your dogs and cats and birds and monkeys ... you
prefer them.'

'They are well looked after. They do not need me now.'

'And . . . I do.'

'It is well at such times that a wife should be with her husband . . . to show that she believes him innocent of what is being proved against him. They should be seen *together*. At other times, let them go their own ways . . . but in times of trouble they should be together.'

He looked at her rather mistily. He was sentimental like the Prince of Wales, and now he was deeply touched that she of all those near to him, should have been the one to stand by his side.

* * *

The case ended with Frederick's being acquitted of complicity in corrupt practices by 278 votes to 196.

Pacing up and down the drawing room at Castle Hill Edward received the verdict with jubilation.

'He'll have to resign his command,' he told Julie. 'It's not possible for a Commander-in-Chief to have suffered the indignity of such a case.'

'Even though he is not proved guilty?'

'My dearest Julie, 196 people believed he was guilty. He'll have to resign.'

'Will they give you the command?' she asked.

His mouth was grim. 'Who can say? It may be that they'll have had enough of royal dukes. Frederick has disgraced the family as well as himself.'

'Never mind,' soothed Julie. 'They must appreciate you one day.'

'At least,' he said with satisfaction, 'Frederick has got his deserts. I doubt my father is calling him the Hope of the House now. As for George, he's making a regular fool of himself over that Hertford woman.'

'What a pity, Edward, that you were not born the eldest. But if you had been they would have married you to the Princess Caroline.'

'God forbid!' cried Edward. 'There could never have been anyone for me but you, Julie.'

She knew and she was contented.

'I am thankful that they at least had a child. Otherwise they might not have left us in peace,' she said.

'Yes, they have that girl. A hoyden by all accounts. She wants a little discipline.'

'Poor Charlotte,' said the tender-hearted Julie. 'Don't forget how difficult it must be for her with such a father . . . and such a mother; and this antagonism between them.'

'It doesn't seem to affect Madame Charlotte. I heard she is giving herself more airs every day and behaving as though she is already Queen of England.'

'Poor dear! It's a great burden for her.'

Soon came the news that Frederick Duke of York had resigned his post as Commander-in-Chief of the Army.

'Operation completed,' murmured the Duke of Kent.

*   *   *

But this was not quite the case; there was scandal to come. Mary Anne had been promised rewards, but where were these rewards? Colonel Wardle could not provide them; nor could Major Dodd for he knew how hard pressed his master was. Martinet that Edward was he had the family habit of living beyond his means.

Mary Anne was furious. She had emerged from her hiding place so that she was an obvious target for her creditors; she had gone to some expense to provide the adequate wardrobe for her act in the House of Commons—and no one could deny that she had given a first class performance—and now, here she was, tricked. The £5,000 promised was not forthcoming.

Her first plan was to write to the Prince of Wales to tell him that there was information in her possession that she was sure would be of interest to him. The Prince of Wales's fondness for pretty women was well known and if he could chase that old piece of ice Lady Hertford and still be living with Maria Fitzherbert who was decidedly old and who had lost her teeth—and replaced them by a set which were obviously false—surely he would be a little interested in enchanting Mary Anne?

But the Prince of Wales had no desire to be involved in the unsavoury affair; he was in any case too deeply committed to Lady Hertford, and too anxious about his relations with Maria to think of a possible romance with Mary Anne. He sent his equerry to see what Mary Anne had to say and when he returned with a tale of rivalry between his brothers he was doubly determined to have nothing to do with her.

Mary Anne in desperation wrote and published a book which she called *The Rival Princes* and in which she dealt with the relationship between the Dukes of York and Kent. That there should have been friction between the brothers and that this was behind the investigation was a source of great interest to the public and many copies of the book were sold. Mary Anne was thus able to placate her creditors for a while. She had now developed a taste for writing sensational and profitable literature so she produced another book *The Rival Dukes* or *Who is the Dupe?* In this she attacked Colonel Wardle for his part in the affair and as a result Wardle brought a libel action against her.

She had no objection to appearing in Court again; she had been such a success as a witness in the case against the Duke of York that she was certain that she was going to win against Wardle, and she was right, for she was found Not Guilty.

But her pressing need was for money. She had always known that her greatest asset was those letters which she had so carefully preserved. She now announced her intention of publishing them.

Frederick, disillusioned and disgusted that 'his dearest angel', 'his sweetest darling love' could have written what she did and so shown her true grasping nature, had discontinued her pension. He was seen everywhere with the Duchess who had left her animals to be with him. They were the best of friends and seemed to enjoy each other's company. They had not become lovers. That would have been asking too much on either side; but he would never forget her loyalty and coming to his aid when he needed her. They would be good friends as long as they lived and he was grateful to her. And the more grateful he became to Frederica the more he despised Mary Anne.

When he heard that she was about to publish his letters he went at once to Frederica and told her.

'This will be worse than ever,' he told her. 'I have said the most foolish things to that woman in the most foolish manner. The whole country will be laughing at me. I'll never hold my head up again.'

But Frederica consoled him. 'Nonsense. It's not the first time a man of rank has written foolish letters. There is only one way of dealing with it—and it will be dealt with in this way because it is not only what is best for you but what is best for that odious woman. And it is what she is striving for. The letters will be bought.'

Frederica was right. They were bought for £7,000 down and a pension of £400 a year.

Mary Anne paid her debts and decided that it was time she set about preparing her daughters to make good marriages. Frederica returned to her animals; the Duke of Kent discussed his hopes of the future with Julie de St. Laurent and hoped to catch the prize which he had helped to take from his brother. Great was his disappointment when it was awarded to Sir David Dundas. His consolation must be, said Julie, that he

had done his duty. It was a pleasant way of looking at it and
Julie as usual brought him some comfort. As for the Duke of
York, he took a new mistress and tried to reconcile himself to
having lost his post.

Maria Triumphant

CHARLOTTE was very much aware of the scandals through the cartoons and pamphlets Mrs. Udney brought into the household, and her mother was constantly showing them to her. Caroline laughed gleefully at the Mary Anne Clarke affair.

'I thought I was the one who brought trouble into the family. I'd like to know what de old Begum says about her Frederick.'

'Frederick doesn't want to know,' said Charlotte. 'I hear he keeps out of her way. We don't see him in the royal apartments since all this happened.'

That made Caroline laugh louder and Charlotte felt that she and her mother were conspirators against the rest of the family.

It was pleasant to belong and be so fiercely and passionately loved, but she sometimes wondered how much deep feeling there was behind those outward demonstrations. Caroline was so wild, so fervent in all her declarations, that she called her servants 'my love' and 'my angel' indiscriminately.

And the manner in which she discussed the Prince of Wales was rather embarrassing for Charlotte disliked hearing her father disparaged.

There were always men at Caroline's apartments in Kensington Palace. Caroline would push Charlotte at them and say: 'Is she not a little charmer, this Charlotte of mine? Ah, she is going to be a fascinator. Like her Mamma, did you say, naughty boy? Then you should.'

Odd, thought Charlotte, yet fascinating. And when she reported it to Mercer, her dear friend was disapproving. And because of her attitude Charlotte began to feel the same because all her views were being coloured by Mercer.

Visits to Spring Gardens were of dubious pleasure, although they enlivened the days a little. Grandmamma Brunswick had settled into that dreadful house as though it were a palace and Charlotte often thought that she saw it as such. She was sure poor Grandmamma was unaware of the shabbiness and the lack of furniture and where there was nothing she saw gilded stools; the old chair in which she sat was a throne; her shabby clothes were velvet and ermine; and there in Spring Gardens she was a queen. Poor Grandmamma, she had always longed to be a queen and if she had had no brothers she would have been.

The only member of the family who was really kind to her was the King. He called on her occasionally and was received with ceremony—royalty visiting royalty. He wanted the Queen to be kinder to her, but the wicked old Begum refused and the Old Girls followed their mother in everything.

It was a pity that the King was so vague. He wanted to help and he was determined to and then he would go away and forget; which was not surprising for he called people by the oddest names. He had called Charlotte Sarah once and said she had pretty hair. So of course when he went away from Spring Gardens it was only natural that he should forget all about poor Grandmamma Brunswick.

'Poor George!' repeated the Duchess. 'A kind heart but an addled head.'

She made Charlotte come and stand near her so that she might talk to her; and Charlotte would sit on a stool at her feet and look round that room which had scarcely any furniture in it but had cobwebs in the corner. Couldn't they have done something better for poor Grandmamma? Charlotte was so sorry that it was not in her power to provide a better lodging that she tried to please the old lady as much as she could by appearing to be interested in her repetitious chatter.

'An invitation from the Prince of Wales, if you please. "Dearest Aunt," he says, "pray come to Carlton House. Stay as long as you please. I will have a suite reserved for you." So charming ... so utterly charming. I do believe he is the most charming man in the world. Of course some people do not think so. Some people cannot get along with him at all. I cannot think why. It's a mystery to me.'

'If you knew him as well as I do,' cried Caroline, 'you wouldn't be in any doubt.'

'His elegance ... and his manners. I never saw the like. And so charming to his old aunt.'

'Why did you not go to Carlton House, Grandmamma?' asked Charlotte. 'There you could have lived in state.'

The Duchess sighed. She brought her lips down to Charlotte's ear. 'It was prevented.' She threw a sly look at her daughter. 'My son was against it, too. The relationship being what it is ... and so on and so on ... and so I must decline the most gracious invitation so graciously given. And I remain here.' She threw out her arms in a dramatic gesture and Charlotte thought that in comparing this dingy old place with Carlton House, she saw it as it really was.

What a strange family I have! thought Charlotte. She must discuss them with Mercer. It might well be that all families were as strange as this. No, she couldn't believe that. There was only one menagerie—and that was the royal one.

* * *

'The position is becoming intolerable,' said Maria Fitzherbert to the faithful Pigot. 'I will not continue in this way.'

Miss Pigot looked worried. She could not bear conflict between her beloved Maria and the Prince who was almost equally beloved. Why could they not go on as they had in the past? Why could he not be content? He was a foolish boy to think that he could ever find the happiness with that cold ambitious Hertford woman that he had known with dear Maria. And there was Minney. He loved Minney. He always looked for her when he arrived; and sometimes she would spring out on him from some unexpected corner, or wait until he was seated and then put her hands over his eyes and cry 'Guess who?' in a voice unmistakably Minney's; and he would go through all the ladies of society pretending that he was trying to guess. It did you good to see them, thought Miss Pigot. And now it was all spoilt by that lump of dressed-up ice, the Hertford woman.

Maria was getting touchy and that meant that she really was beginning to think seriously of breaking with him.

That's just something I couldn't bear, thought Miss Pigot.

'It'll pass,' she kept telling Maria. 'It's just another of those little wickednesses of his. My goodness, we know enough about them, or we ought to by now.'

But this was not just a little wickedness. It had been going on too long; and Maria had already written to him very seriously telling him that she would not continue to tolerate it.

And he had ignored the letter, as he ignored so much that he did not want to accept. He wanted to go on paying his pleasant morning calls to the house on the Steyne chatting with Maria, playing with Minney; and then at the evening entertainment at the Pavilion he would be at Lady Hertford's side all the evening so that Maria would be there merely as the chaperon that very virtuous icicle desired.

It was really asking too much and no man but the Prince of Wales would think of subjecting a woman whom he had once loved so wholeheartedly—and still did in his way, insisted Miss Pigot—to such an indignity.

And now the climax was close.

Maria had returned from a drive with Minney and before the child, of course, she pretended that all was well. Miss Pigot thanked God every day for Minney. Because, reasoned that faithful friend and companion, if ever the break did come there would be Minney to comfort her; and Miss Pigot was beginning to think that Maria's love for that child was greater than the love she had for the Prince. Well, the foolish man was showing himself unappreciative of Maria's devotion, whereas little Minney was never really happy unless she was with Maria. She could not have felt closer to her own mother; and perhaps the fact that they had once been in danger of losing each other had made them all the more aware of the value of their devotion.

Minney had gone to her room to change her gown and Maria came into the drawing room to speak to Miss Pigot whom she had seen from the window as they were getting out of the carriage.

'My word,' said Miss Pigot, 'Minney looks the picture of health. Brighton agrees with her.' She was anxiously regarding Maria's face. 'Brighton agrees with so many. His Highness called while you were out.'

Maria's lip curled coldly. Oh dear, thought Miss Pigot. Trouble!

'I daresay he was surprised to find us not here.'

'Surprised and hurt.'

'He should not be surprised. But what a child he is. He thinks he can behave to me intolerably in public and then he comes through his tunnel like an adventurous schoolboy and expects Minney and me to be waiting to pounce on him and play childish games.'

'Couldn't you be patient a little longer?'

'I've been patient too long.'

'If you could have seen his face when he heard you weren't here.'

'I wish I had seen it. Oh, Pig, don't make excuses for him.

You know he has behaved abominably. I'm sorry I ever went back to him. That was a great mistake.'

'Have you forgotten how happy you were?'

'For a little while we were happy.'

'It was for six years or more ... before this ... this ... woman came along.'

'But before her there was the Jersey affair. Oh, it's hopeless. Don't let us pretend. This sort of thing would happen constantly, and I have had enough. I should never have given in in the first place. I told him it was impossible.'

'And he wouldn't accept that,' said Miss Pigot firmly. 'He was determined, and when he's determined...'

'As he is now with Lady Hertford.'

'Oh, that woman. If she had not been such a prude the affair would have been over and forgotten by now.'

'That doesn't make it more pleasant. No, I have come to a decision. I am not going to endure the present position. I am not going to be chaperon to Lady Hertford. If he wishes to make her his mistress, let him do so, but I am not going to be a party to his amours. Dear Pig, we have been together so long and you have seen what I have had to endure.'

'There are faults on both sides,' said Miss Pigot quickly.

Maria laughed. 'Oh, trust you to stand up for him. But you must admit that this is asking too much. Now do you admit this?'

'Well ... I do think he shouldn't ask your help in courting the woman.'

'You see, he is quite ridiculous. I know you're going to say he is the Prince of Wales and people have always made allowances for him. Well, I have finished making allowances. I have been thinking of this for a long time, and I've come to the conclusion that I shall appear less and less in society. Minney and I are very happy together. The three of us should make a good life, eh, Piggy?'

Miss Pigot nodded.

'And,' went on Maria, 'I believe that once we have recovered from the break we should be happier without him. This constant friction, this perpetual straying ... I am too old, Pig, to cope with it. I really believe that I prefer a quiet life. There is Minney's education to think of ... I want to supervise that myself. What an intelligent child she is. Then I shall launch her and hope that she makes a good marriage ... by that I mean a happy marriage. You see, this is different from when he left me for Lady Jersey. Then I was desolate and alone. Now I have Minney and I do believe that I can come to a more peaceful happiness with the dear child than I ever could with him.'

Miss Pigot nodded. She was beginning to believe this was true.

*　　　*　　　*

A carriage had drawn up at Mrs. Fitzherbert's house. Peeping through a window Miss Pigot was startled to see Lady Hertford stepping out.

She ran at once to Maria's dressing room, thinking to find her there, but Maria was already in the drawing room with Minney, which meant that Lady Hertford would be brought to her there.

What could this mean? Had the Prince sent her? How she wished she was there to see what was happening.

Maria was no less astonished than Miss Pigot. She did not expect to receive visits from her rival. Lady Hertford exquisitely dressed with an aura of delicate perfume about her asked Mrs. Fitzherbert's indulgence for calling unexpectedly.

Maria hid her dismay with perfect poise and her manner was as cool as Lady Hertford's.

'And this is, of course, Mary.'

Minney came forward and made a charming curtsey. 'My dear child,' said Lady Hertford, 'How pleasant to see you. We should meet more frequently. Don't forget that I am your aunt.'

Maria was pleased to see that Minney did not show the concern she must be feeling, for Minney was well aware of the danger there had been of defeat which would have meant that she would be separated from Maria.

But this was her Aunt Isabella who, with her husband, had stepped in and allowed her to come to Maria. Still, there was something about her which warned Minney as it did Maria.

Would Lady Hertford drink a dish of tea? asked Maria.

Lady Hertford graciously declared that she would be delighted to do so, and Minney pulled the bellrope.

They talked of the weather, the amenities of Brighton, the newest additions to the Pavilion until tea was brought; then Lady Hertford, her eyes on Minney said: 'Relations I think should be together. There is nothing like family ties.'

Maria conceded that it was ideal for families to be together if circumstances made this possible.

'Families should adjust themselves to circumstances,' Lady Hertford replied with authority.

'And accept the best arrangements that can be made,' put in Maria growing more and more uneasy every minute.

She had seen a certain fear in Minney's face. Minney was exceptionally intelligent; she would be seeing beneath the innuendoes. What did it mean? wondered Maria. Was the battle going to start all over again? Was this woman not content with the Prince? Did she want Minney as well?

'My dear Mary,' said Lady Hertford, 'pray come here. Why, how like your mother you are! Your Uncle Hertford and I were speaking of you only the other day. What about your religious instruction?'

'Minney studies with her teachers and she is being brought up in her parents' religion.'

'How important that is! And since it is well known that you, my dear Mrs. Fitzherbert, are a Catholic, I believe all the family will be happy to know that Mary is not having . . .' she smiled deprecatingly, '. . . secret instruction in the Catholic faith. Of course, I know, my dear Mrs. Fitzherbert, that you have given your word that this should be so, but we have been—and you will be the first to admit justifiably—a little anxious that Mary might be influenced.'

'I do not attempt to influence her in any way as far as her religious instruction is concerned.'

Lady Hertford waved a hand about the room. 'I am sure that is so but, as Lord Hertford was saying to me, influence is . . . insidious.'

'Lady Hertford, pray tell me, are you complaining of the manner in which I am bringing up Minney?'

Minney had swiftly crossed the room to stand beside Maria. Maria thought then: If they try to take her away from me I will fight them all. I'll never give her up.

Lady Hertford smiled icily. 'Well, it has been *so* pleasant talking to you. Thank you. The tea was delicious. And Mary, my dear niece, we must see each other more frequently. I fancy we *shall* in the future.'

She had gone, leaving disquiet behind her.

She was threatening of course.

As the sound of carriage wheels died away Minney threw herself into Maria's arms.

'Don't be frightened, Minney,' said Maria. 'I'll never let you go.'

*   *   *

Maria could not wait; she presented herself at the Pavilion and asked to see the Prince of Wales, who received her in his

own apartments—in the ante room leading to the library and
his bedroom. He was examining a picture on the walls and
when she was announced he came to her and embraced her
warmly.

'My dearest love, you are just in time to advise me about
this picture. And what do you think of that looking-glass? It's
silvered beech. Rather fine don't you think?'

Maria said: 'I did not come to look at pictures and looking-
glasses, but to talk to you very seriously.'

A haughty expression touched his features and his face
grew a little pinker than usual. He tried to whip up an indignation. Here he was trying to be friendly with Maria,
trying to behave as though she had not sent him an unkind
letter, as though she had not refused an invitation to dine at
the Pavilion. Why, if anyone else had behaved in such a way
he would never have spoken to them again. And she was
being censorious!

'Let us stop prevaricating for Heaven's sake,' said Maria.
'Let us have done with pretence. I have had a visit from Lady
Hertford.'

'Is that so?'

He knew, she thought in panic. They had arranged it
together!

'During which she made some alarming implications. Poor
Minney was present and aware of these. The poor child is most
unhappy.'

'Minney unhappy! That will never do. What is the stupid
little goose frightened of?'

'That Lady Hertford is going to demand that she leaves me
and goes to her.'

The Prince was silent. 'That is something,' he said, 'that
she could do.'

'But she shall not do.'

'My dearest love ...'

'Please do not call me that. It is so *false*. Let us be truthful.
That woman who may or may not be your mistress but whom
you are endeavouring to raise ... or lower ... to that ques-
tionably enviable position ... is going to take Minney from
me to spite me. She has made that clear. And you—are you
trying to help her? I cannot believe that you would be so
cruel. You have always pretended to care for Minney. Play
your childish games if you wish, continue to submit me to
these humiliations ... at least you may attempt to, but I have
made up my mind that I will endure no more ... but for
God's sake don't tamper with a child's happiness.'

He was angry. How dared she say such things to him! And on the other hand no one could be quite as magnificent as Maria in her rages. He did not want to lose Maria and he knew her pride and determination. If she said she was going to leave him she meant it. Why could she not be reasonable? The relationship between them was too strong to be broken over a silly quarrel. Why couldn't she wait patiently for him? Why couldn't she allow him this little flutter with Lady Hertford and remain stolidly in the background so that he would always know she was there?

But how dared she speak to him in this manner. 'You seem to think that you are the only one in the world who can make Minney happy.'

'I do think that and I know it's true.'

'I happen to think that Minney has some affection for me.'

'She has—but if she were aware that you were in this diabolical plot to separate her from me, you would lose that affection, let me warn you.'

'*You* warn *me!*' ·

'Certainly. If you wish to keep Minney's affection do not make plans with your paramour to take her from me.'

This was too much. Tears filled his eyes. He—the Prince of Wales—had tried to talk to her reasonably and she had come here to abuse him.

'You forget,' he said, 'that you were allowed to take Minney because of *my* intervention. *I* persuaded Lord and Lady Hertford that it was *my* pleasure that the child should come to you. And this I did solely to please you because your comfort and happiness had always meant so much to me.'

'And for Minney's too, I hope. You know how frightened the child was at the prospect of leaving me.'

'Children forget. She will be happy with the Hertfords.'

'You talk as though the matter is already settled.'

He went on as though she had not spoken. 'Minney will see me . . . frequently. I daresay that if you do not displease the Hertfords they would allow you to call.'

Maria's eyes were blazing with rage and determination.

'Let me tell you this: Minney is not leaving me. Understand this and make the Hertfords understand it. She is happy with me; she feels secure . . . or she did until that woman came with her sly and cruel suggestions. Minney was disturbed when the case was in progress. I shall not allow her to be upset again. I will do anything . . . simply anything to prevent this. You may go to Lady Hertford. Do so if you so wish it. But let

me tell you this: If you attempt to take Minney from me I
shall fight for her with all my power and I do not think you
will succeed in taking her from me.'

'There is the justice of this case. Hertford is the head of
Minney's family. It was he who allowed you to take her.'

'And you will make him see that it would be wise for him to
allow matters to stay as they are.

'I fear I do not understand you.'

'I think you do. I do not forget that you and I were married
in my house in Park Street on the 15th December 1785. I have
a certificate to prove this. I have never produced this evidence
because I did not think it proper to do so. I allowed you to
permit a denial of our marriage. I have never published the
true facts. I considered it beneath my dignity to do so. You are
not very popular with the people. They used to cheer you
wherever you went. You have no one but yourself to blame.
Pray do not look at me like that. I tell you truths which others
dare not. You may be the Prince of Wales but you are also my
husband and I will speak my mind. You are my husband . . .
whatever you say to the contrary. I should have been stronger
and refused to go through that ceremony with you. I should
have gone away as I intended to. You will remember that it
was you who persuaded me that you could not live without
me. So . . . there was that ceremony. You married a Catholic.
And what if I publish evidence of this? What if your marriage
to the Princess Caroline is in question? What if Charlotte is a
bastard? What then? Oh, you will say that our marriage was
no marriage in the eyes of the State though it was in those of
the Church. Perhaps some will agree with you but there will
be many who do not. What a storm about the ears of a prince
who will one day be king. Is he married or is he not? Yes, say
some. No, say others. And what of your father? What of Charlotte? Is she the true heiress to the throne. You see what a
storm you will be raising if you allow me to publish that important certificate of marriage.'

'You would not do it, Maria. You have always said you
would not do it.'

'I have said so and I have kept my word all these years, have
I not? But Minney is my child. I love her as my own
daughter. I know she needs me . . . as I need her. If she were
torn from me she would suffer . . . terribly. Minney is not
going to suffer. I have decided on that. I will do *anything* to
prevent it. You will admit that I have evidence which could
possibly make your throne rock. Now is your chance to choose
again. Your *dear* Lady Hertford would love to wound me and

clever woman that she is she sees that the best way of achieving this is through Minney. But my child is not going to be used for the sport of that woman. Perhaps you wish to please her . . . If you do remember that you could lose your crown through doing it in this instance.'

'I never heard such dramatics over a matter that has not been *thought* of in any seriousness.'

Maria smiled relieved.

'I am delighted that this absurd and cruel plot was not seriously thought of. I hope you will explain this to Lady Hertford.'

'Maria . . .' His eyes had filled with tears. Maria was magnificent; she was a good woman; he had always known that. It was her goodness which often irritated him.

'Well?' She was imperious as though she were royalty and he the subject.

'You have been behaving very badly lately. How dared you refuse my invitations to the Pavilion?'

'Because I did not wish to accept them. I will not be chaperon to your mistress. Do make that plain to her.'

'I have suffered a great deal for you,' he began.

'Then you will be relieved that you need suffer no more. Pray do not invite me to the Pavilion for I have no intention of coming while Lady Hertford is your guest of honour. And I beg of Your Highness to understand that Minney is my child and I would die rather than give her up.'

With that she swept out of the ante room leaving the Prince staring after her.

He wanted to burst into tears. How dare she talk to him in such a manner! His dear magnificent Maria? She knew that she would always have a special place in his heart and she did not seem to care.

She will be placated, he thought. He would tell the Hertfords that Minney stayed with Maria. Then she would see that he was in truth her friend.

Back in Tilney Street Minney was anxiously awaiting the return of Maria. As soon as she came in Minney flung herself into her arms.

'It's all right, darling,' said Maria. 'Everything is all right now.'

Minney looked up into Maria's face and knew that this was true.

'You have seen Prinney?'

'Yes, dearest. I have seen Prinney and he is going to stop the Hertfords taking you from me.'

'Oh, dearest Prinney!'

Maria stroked Minney's hair. No point in telling her that Prinney had had to be blackmailed into allowing her to stay and that when he was enamoured of a woman he would brush aside a child's happiness to please her.

What did it matter? thought Maria. Minney was her child. She had won.

Minney was the most important thing on Earth to her. That was a discovery. Through this case she had gained a child and lost a husband. But if she could keep Minney she would not complain.

She had reached a new stage of her life. She would no longer be dominated by the Prince. Once she had loved him exclusively; but now Minney came first.

Mystery in St. James's

IN the year 1809 Charlotte celebrated her thirteenth birthday. 'Another year,' she told Mercer, 'and I shall cease to be a child.'

'That,' replied Mercer with her sound good sense, 'will rather depend on how you develop in the meantime.'

Charlotte was sure that continued association with her beloved Mercer would enable her to grow up more quickly than anything else. Between Mercer, who was so high-minded, and Mrs. Udney, who was perhaps a little low-minded, one could grasp life in its various layers which, reasoned Charlotte, was rather necessary if one was to understand it in all its aspects.

One February day Mercer arrived to tell her that Drury Lane theatre had been burned down. This was a terrible calamity, for the place had been gutted and the reservoir on the roof was quite useless.

'Poor Mr. Sheridan!' sighed Mercer. 'I am so sorry for him. So brilliant, so clever! But the theatre was insured against fire for which I am indeed thankful. I hear the House of Commons expressed its sympathy; so I am sure all help will be given in building a new theatre.' From this Mercer went on to talk of Mr. Sheridan's exciting career and how he and Mr. Fox had worked together. Fox, being one of Mercer's heroes, was one of Charlotte's too—and Charlotte was delighted because her father had been so fond of him.

'A good Whig,' said Mercer, which was high praise from her. 'And the finest playwright of his age. There are many politicians, but I have heard it said that there is no man living who can write plays to equal Sheridan's. But perhaps he does well to continue in politics, for it is better to lead the people than to amuse them.'

Charlotte agreed wholeheartedly as she did with everything Mercer said.

Mercer knew exactly what was happening throughout the world; she could talk excitingly of Napoleon's exploits; she gave her opinions freely and she taught Charlotte to be a good Whig.

She made Charlotte long for the days when she would be able to appear in public, to attend the opera or the theatre. In Mercer's opinion she should always have been allowed to attend these places if only for special performances. Not that Mercer believed she should have gone to the first night of the new theatre at Covent Garden, where Mercer told her, they had opened with *Macbeth*. Mr. Kemble had spoken the address though the uproar had been so great that no one had heard him. That was not suitable for a princess, but the opera certainly was, thought Mercer. She feared that the Princess's education was neglected in some respects. She, Mercer, would try to remedy that.

She it was who told the Princess of the duel between Mr. Canning and Lord Castlereagh, which had taken place because it had reached the noble lord's ears that Mr. Canning had thought him unfit for office.

'Do you mean they fought . . . with pistols?' cried Charlotte. Her eyes round with wonder.

'I mean exactly that,' replied Mercer. 'And Mr. Canning's bullet took the button off Lord Castlereagh's coat and Mr. Canning was wounded in the thigh.'

'Poor Mr. Canning! I trust he did not bleed to death.'

'No, he walked off the field. But can you imagine such folly? Two grown-up men . . . using such a means to settle a quarrel!'

'Men have always settled their quarrels in this way,' Charlotte reminded her friend.

'There is no need for them to continue in such folly.'

'When I am Queen I shall forbid men to fight duels,' declared Charlotte, and Mercer looked at her pupil with approval.

Yes, it was very pleasant, talking to Mercer, and Charlotte felt that she was becoming really knowledgeable under her tuition.

She told Mercer how Mr. Canning used to bow to her when she was held up to the window to wave to him.

'I used to tear my caps imitating him,' she said, and

laughed boisterously to remember it; but Mercer liked her to
be serious.

So from Mercer she learned much of politics and the affairs
of the world and from Mrs. Udney those secrets which others
sought to keep from her.

'Do you know,' whispered Mrs. Udney, 'Mary Anne Clarke
had a service of plate which once belonged to a prince of the
Bourbon family. My word, she did well for herself!'

'Do you think she's doing well for herself now?'

'Ha, ha. Those very saleable letters. You can bet your life
she will be very highly paid for them.'

'Poor Uncle Fred! He must be feeling dreadful. I'm glad
Aunt Frederica came up to London to be with him.'

'I doubt he ever wrote such letters to *her*.'

'All the more reason why she is to be praised for standing
by him,' retorted Charlotte.

But although she snubbed the woman she was often
friendly towards her because she wanted to hear all that Mrs.
Udney had to tell as well as learn from Mercer. So it was Mrs.
Udney who showed her the cartoons about Uncle Fred and
Mary Anne Clarke and told her how cheeky the woman had
been at the Bar.

It is all very regrettable, said Charlotte, but one has to know
about one's own family.

She liked to hear stories about the people. How a sailor had
died in Guy's Hospital and when his body had been opened
up eighteen clasp knives had been found in him.

'He'd swallowed them all when he was drunk. It was for a
wager,' said Mrs. Udney. 'The things people do!'

There were stories of thieves, one of whom had broken into
the house of a pelisse maker and murdered him and his
family; there was another of a man who had shot a young girl
when she refused to marry him.

It was all exciting and highly entertaining if, thought Charlotte, one did not know the people personally, for she would
not have cared for any of her acquaintances to be shot dead by
disappointed lovers.

But this, she assured herself, was as much a part of life as
what Napoleon was doing in Europe.

In October began the great jubilee year. The King had
been on the throne for fifty years. Fifty years! thought Charlotte. It was a lifetime. But poor Grandpapa was hardly in a fit
state to enjoy a jubilee.

'And,' said Mercer, 'who wants this jubilee? The Tories of
course. And for what reason? Because there is so much

trouble at home and abroad that they want to turn people's attention from that to these celebrations at home.'

Charlotte settled down to hear an account of the troubles at home. The loss of trade because of the Napoleonic wars; the difficulty of calling a halt to Napoleon's domination of Europe. The general ineffectiveness of Tory rule. Mercer would have liked to mention the state of the King's health, but that was hardly a subject fit for his granddaughter's ears. There were rumours that his strangeness was increasing; everyone would be prepared now for a return of his malady. He had aged so much in the last few years and was now almost blind and quite often wandering in his mind.

Hardly the man to wish to celebrate his jubilee. But there were banquets and fireworks and festivities everywhere. The Queen and the Princesses had given an open air fête at Windsor, in spite of the fact that it was autumn; there were coloured lamps in the city of London and fireworks constantly lighted up the sky accompanied by the red glow from bonfires. The various houses of business illuminated their premises with signs of their trade; and in addition to all this there were many thanksgiving services in the church all over the country. The theme was 'God Save the King'.

Exciting times, thought Charlotte, in which anything might happen.

But she was unprepared for the great scandal which hit the family and put even the Mary Anne Clarke scandal into the shade.

It was Mrs. Udney who told her of this.

As soon as Charlotte saw the woman she knew that something especially exciting had happened.

'I don't know if I should tell Your Highness. It'll be common knowledge soon enough ... but there's been a terrible tragedy in your Uncle Ernest's apartments at St. James's.'

'Do you mean Uncle Ernest is dead?' asked Charlotte, her eyes round with horror.

'He's come pretty near it.'

Then she told the terrible story of how Uncle Ernest had been found in his bed with a great wound in his head which, so it was said, was meant to have killed him. But it did not kill him.

'Providence was looking after him,' said Mrs. Udney with a knowing smile. 'And lying in the next room was his valet Sellis ... with his throat cut.'

Charlotte cried: 'Did he try to kill Uncle Ernest? And who killed *him*?'

Mrs. Udney shrugged her shoulders. Who could say? There would be a trial of course. This was murder ... royalty or not.

There was a hushed atmosphere through Carlton House and at Windsor, in fact wherever the family were. If Charlotte attempted to mention the matter she was hastily silenced by one of the Old Girls. But that did not prevent rumours reaching her. Her mother showed her some of the cartoons, and some of the sly allusions in the papers.

It was being said that the Duke's valet had a very pretty wife and that the valet had found her in bed with the Duke. The valet had almost killed the Duke and then committed suicide.

It was the biggest scandal that had ever touched the royal family. The romantic affairs of the Prince of Wales had never gone as far as murder. It was true he had once let it be believed that he had attempted suicide when Mrs. Fitzherbert threatened to leave the country to elude him. But was that true? And in any case it was very different from murder.

Was Uncle Ernest, Duke of Cumberland, a murderer?

Aunt Amelia was very melancholy. She said once: 'This has upset your poor Grandpapa more than anything that has ever happened.'

And poor Grandpapa *was* upset. He mumbled quite incoherently to Charlotte and did not seem at all clear who she was.

Amelia herself was looking more wan than ever. She was very melancholy, and Charlotte wondered what it was that made her so.

I don't really know very much about them, she thought. They had been the old aunts to her for as long as she could remember; but when she thought of the sadness of Amelia she wondered if there was any cause besides her illness and that of her father.

Poor Amelia, thought Charlotte. It must be dreadful to be twenty-six and never to have been anywhere, never to have married, just ceasing to be a young girl and becoming an old girl.

But that, of course, was the fate of all the aunts.

Death of an Old Girl

AMELIA sat in her window looking out at the sea. She was
feeling no better in spite of the sea breezes; but she was happy
because her eldest brother had promised to ride over from
Brighton.

Her embroidery lay in her lap. She was, in fact, too tired
even for such work. Her tiredness increased with every week
and she had a premonition that this time next year she would
not be here.

Her sister Mary was with her. What would she do without
Mary—the favourite among her sisters as George was among
her brothers. Yet she supposed she had grown accustomed to
Mary. George was a being from another world, a world of gay
romance, whereas poor Mary who had been so pretty when
she was young and who was now like a faded flower, was one
of the frustrated sisterhood.

Mary came in to the room and saw her sister's hands lying
idly in her lap.

'You should sleep a little,' she said.

'I have slept all morning. I don't want to sleep my life away
. . . what's left of it.'

'Don't speak like that, I beg you.'

'Oh, Mary, let us be frank. You know it can't be long now.'

'I know nothing of the sort.'

'But you do, dearest sister, and you won't accept it.'

Mary shook her head almost angrily and Amelia said
gently: 'Come and sit down and talk awhile.' Mary picked up
a footstool and leaning it against Amelia's chair sat down.

'What a lovely day,' she said. 'I hope it will be as pleasant
for George's journey tomorrow.'

'It will be wonderful to see him. I wish he were happier though.'

'Why shouldn't George be happy. He has everything he could wish for. He is *free*.'

'Freedom only seems good when you don't possess it . . . like good health and riches . . . like youth.'

Mary sighed. 'We are all getting old now. Even you, Amelia, are twenty-six. Twenty-six and the youngest of us all. As for George, if he is not content it is his own fault. They say he is breaking with Mrs. Fitzherbert. I am sure that will not make him very happy.'

'He thinks he will be happier with Lady Hertford.'

'Our charming brother can be a little foolish sometimes.'

Amelia was not going to have him criticized. 'His life is so full. It is natural that he should often act in a way we do not understand.'

Mary softened towards her brother. All the sisters were fond of him. She said: 'He always said that the first thing he would do on coming to power would be to find husbands for us. I think he is sorry for us. He has a kind heart although he does not let his pity for us disturb his pleasures.'

'It would be foolish if he did, for what help would that be?'

'Oh, Amelia, sometimes I feel so frustrated, so full of resentment that I will do something really wild. Run away, perhaps, something like that.'

'I understand,' said Amelia. 'But it would kill Papa.'

'Amelia, has it ever occurred to you that Papa has killed something in us? He has kept us here. He has never allowed us to marry. It is like shutting birds in cages and letting them see other birds flying about around them in the sunshine . . . soaring, swooping, mating . . .'

'Yes, it always comes back to that,' said Amelia. 'We should have married . . . all of us.'

'But Papa does not wish it. We are royal Princesses. There is no one royal enough. Our sister Charlotte was the only one who found a husband. And do you remember how we feared that her marriage would not come off because her husband had had a wife who died mysteriously and they weren't quite sure that she was dead?'

'Poor Charlotte, she was so ill when she thought it was going to come to nothing. I could weep to think of her terror. It all seems so clear to me.'

Mary regarded her sister anxiously. 'Does such talk upset you?'

'Pray don't change the subject. I want to talk about us . . .

us and our lives. But it does not make me love dear Papa any the less.'

'You were always his favourite.'

'The youngest. Papa's girl.' Amelia smiled. 'They used to send me in to amuse him when he was melancholy.'

'And you always made him happy.'

'He used to hold me so tightly that I was afraid. Do you remember the time when he clung to me so fiercely that they thought he would do me some harm?'

'I remember it well. They put him into a straitjacket because he cried so much when they took you from him. That was when he was very ill.'

'Mary, do you think . . . he will be ill again?'

'I often wonder. I think of it often.'

'So do I. We ought to remember it. We ought never to do anything that would upset him.'

'Yet we are young . . . or we were once. Didn't we have lives of our own to lead?'

'Sophia thought so.'

'Sophia!' murmured Mary. 'She was more daring than the rest of us.'

'Poor Sophia. Is she happy, do you think? Oh Mary, what must it feel like to be the mother of a child you must never acknowledge?'

'At least one would have been a mother. Better that . . . than to grow old and never have lived . . . just to have been a princess in a cage . . . sitting with Mamma, reading with Mamma, looking after the dogs, stitching, filling the snuff-boxes. Sophia is perhaps not to be pitied.'

'But she looks so tragic sometimes. Do you think that one day she will marry the General? Suppose they did . . . and the boy was with them. Do you think they would be happy?'

Mary looked over her shoulder. 'Someone might hear.'

'They know,' said Amelia. 'You cannot have a secret like that and keep it from your household.'

They were thinking of that day some ten years ago when Sophia had confessed to them that she was to have a child. Poor Sophia—almost out of her mind with worry. What would Papa say? What would the Queen say? She had feared the Queen more than their father, for since his illness he had become very meek and sometimes unaware of what was going on around him. 'It is Papa's own fault,' Elizabeth had said. 'He shuts us away and expects us to live like nuns in a convent. But we are not nuns and this is not a convent.'

Sophia was in love; and to think that the partner in her

adventure was one of their father's equerries and that he was
still with them . . . a member of the suite which had accompanied Amelia to Weymouth. It made him seem like one of
the family, Sophia had been just twenty-three then and she
had been reckless, for at that age they might have found a
husband for her. But as if they would! There were Augusta,
Elizabeth and Mary all to come before her. She had been in
love with Sir Thomas Garth and despairing of marriage had
decided to do without it.

A royal Princess pregnant! It would have to be kept secret.
Papa must never know. It would kill him, said Augusta, and
Elizabeth believed her. Tom Garth was resourceful. He
would make all the arrangements, Sophia must hide her condition, which was not difficult with the fashion for voluminous
skirts; she must feign sickness, which was not difficult either
for the poor girl was very worried and this in addition to the
trials of pregnancy meant that she had little acting to do. The
doctor—a friend of Tom's—had suggested a change of air.
Weymouth—a favourite spot, was suggested; and here Sophia
had come with Mary, who was always delegated to care for the
sick members of the family, and there she had given birth to
her boy. It had all been very cleverly arranged. A gentleman's
tailor named Sharland who lived in the town had a pregnant
wife and when this wife gave birth to a boy, there was no
reason why it should not be believed that she had had twins.

Thus were these matters arranged in royal families.

And Sophia had carried this great secret for ten years. Her
boy was growing up. She saw him now and then. Mary was
always afraid that she would betray her secret by the very
manner in which she looked at him.

As for Tom Garth he was devoted to the boy. He had
already taken him from the Sharlands' and 'adopted' him. He
was constantly talking of him and planning his education;
and indeed young Tom had the stamp of Hanover on his
round rather vapid face, and in his wide blue eyes; his lashes
were dark though and this was not a Hanoverian feature.
(Poor Charlotte's eyelashes were so pale that one could
scarcely see them.) His lips had that sullen expression, except
when he smiled and his jaw was heavy, but on the whole he
was a handsome youth.

He seemed to wheedle what he wanted out of Tom Garth
and the General appeared to want to spoil him in every way
because he had royal blood in his veins.

What secrets there were in the family! thought Amelia. The
boys were not the only ones who had adventures.

She thought sadly of dear Charles Fitzroy, whom she loved and who loved her—but they were not for each other and they had known it. Charles had married twice, for his first wife had died young after giving him a son and now he had married Frances Anne Stewart, the eldest daughter of the Marquis of Londonderry. He had his boys, George and Robert, and a daughter as well. What was the use of regretting, of saying to oneself: 'Those should have been mine.' She was a Princess and although he was a son of the Duke of Grafton and descended from Charles II and his mistress Barbara Villiers, he was not considered worthy to marry the King's daughter. But was that so? Was it that George III could not bear to think of any of his daughters in the marriage bed? He was a man with strange dark thoughts which sometimes harassed and tormented him to such an extent that they drove him into madness.

For her there might have been marriage with Charles Fitzroy; and dear Mary, her sister who insisted on being with her, nursing her herself, was in love with her cousin the Duke of Gloucester. Why could they not be permitted to marry? Why must they remain in what her brother George called the Band of Spinsterhood.

Was it her father's strange obsession which sent him on the verge of madness to contemplate his daughters married? Or was it their mother who wanted to keep them about her—her handmaidens, whom she governed and treated as though they were still children in the nursery?

What did it matter? Amelia asked herself wearily. The result is that we remain here in our prisons and even Sophia who briefly stepped outside hers could only step back into it when the inevitable result overtook her.

'My poor Amelia,' said Mary suddenly. 'I *have* tired you with all this talk.'

No, thought Amelia. It is *poor* Mary. For I shall die young; and as they become older the resentment will grow. And when George is ready to find husbands for them they will be too old.

There was a discreet scratching on the door.

Mary gave permission for whoever was there to enter.

It was Sir Thomas Garth himself, a loyal member of her suite. Mary said he never forgot anything that was necessary to Amelia's comfort and if Dr. Pope ordered something he would see that it was procured however difficult. He looked upon Amelia as a young sister.

Both sisters looked a little guilty as he entered, since they had so recently talked of him. He was far from handsome and well advanced into his fifties—a good deal older than Sophia. Couldn't she have chosen someone more handsome? wondered Amelia. Someone more like her dearest Charles Fitzroy. One could not imagine gentle Sophia with that bluff old soldier; he was scarcely handsome either and had an ugly birthmark on his face.

Poor Sophia! thought Amelia. Poor all of us!

Thomas bowed as well as the package he was carrying would allow.

'A present, Your Highness, from Brighton. His Royal Highness has sent it on in advance of himself.'

Amelia gave a little cry of joy and held out her hands for the package. Mary came close and Thomas stood watching while she opened it—very unceremoniously, thought Mary, but what could one say to the father of one's nephew?

There were five pelisses all in delicate and charming colours. Amelia flushed and wrapped a delicate blue one about her shoulders.

'It's most becoming,' said Mary.

'Trust His Highness to choose the right colours,' said Thomas.

A letter had fluttered to the floor and Thomas picked it up and handed it to the Princess.

Amelia glanced at the flourishing handwriting, and read the fulsome phrases with pleasure. He could scarcely wait to see his dearest sister. He was coming with all speed the next day. He would be delighted if his dearest Amelia were wearing one of these pelisses which he, with Brummell's help, had spent two hours in choosing. And so on . . . flowery phrases from the most charming brother in the world.

Mary smiled to see her sister happy. One could almost believe she were well again.

* * *

'My dearest sister!'

Amelia rose from her chair and was enfolded in his scented arms.

'George, dearest, let me look at you. Oh . . . you are magnificent!'

He laughed. 'What do you think of this cloth? Brummell brought my notice to it.'

'You are constantly in the company of that fellow, I hear.'

'He's a wizard, I tell you. Have you heard of the new cravat he has invented?'

'I am glad you find such pleasure in these things.'

'Which sounds a little censorious, sister.'

'Not in the least. If there are things in life which give pleasure without harming others it is foolish to turn one's back on them. Besides, think of what pleasure *I* get from wondering what you will appear in next and having little games with myself to guess. There is one thing I can always be sure of. You will look elegant, and more than that—magnificent ... all that a Prince of Wales should. Pray turn that I may have a better view.'

He did so. The epitome of elegance. The cloth of his coat fine and of pleasant moss green, his neckcloth snowy white to match his buckskin breeches, moulded to a fine though plump thigh; the diamond star flashing on his breast and few diamonds adorning his white and shapely hands.

'Oh, George,' cried Amelia. 'I'm so *proud* of you.'

He embraced her, the tears in his eyes. This was a scene such as he loved. From his parents he had nothing but criticism and when he rode into the streets the crowds were either silent or hostile; Maria in the last year had thrown plenty of home-truths at his head. But here he was with his favourite sister who adored him.

'The pelisses are lovely. I shall think of you every time I wear them. Not that I need a pelisse to remind me of you. Oh, George, sit down, and let us be alone to talk. There is so much I want to say to you.'

He sat down and looked at her. She was growing very frail. He wanted to weep for Amelia, his little sister who had never had a chance to live and was now not far from death. What could he do for her?

'Dearest Amelia, if there is anything on this earth that I can do for you ...'

'There is something, George. Let us face the truth. I am not going to live much longer.'

'I won't allow you to talk in such a way.'

'Then I shall do so without your permission. The time is passing and I have certain affairs to settle. George, help me.'

He brought a handkerchief from his pocket and wiped his eyes. 'Anything,' he declared brokenly. 'Anything.'

'I want everything I have to go to Charles ...'

George nodded. He knew of her hopeless love for Charles Fitzroy. He was genuinely sorry for his sisters and definitely intended to do something for them when it was in his power. He often thought—when he was not concerned with his own affairs—how sad their position was. They had no allowances

they could call their own, no freedom; they were the complete
slaves of their parents. His brothers were fortunate; they had
escaped that thraldom; but George would never cease to be
sorry for his sisters and he swore that when he was in control
the first thing he would do was to see what could be done for
them.

'I borrowed five thousand pounds from Charles and have
only paid back one. He must be paid back.'

The Prince nodded. He was not very fond of Charles Fitzroy, but since Amelia was enamoured of him he would do his
duty.

'You should have another executor,' he told his sister.
'What about Adolphus? I'll tell him that he will act with me.
Now let us have done with this painful subject.'

'Oh, George,' she said, 'how I love you! How grateful I am
to have such a brother.'

There were the tears again, the flurry of the beautiful
handkerchief, the emotion which did not mar his fresh complexion or dull the brilliance of his eyes.

It was pleasant to bask in his sister's adoration. If only some
people were as appreciative of him he would be less troubled.
Maria for instance who was being so difficult and determined
to quarrel and had refused his invitations. Even Lady Hertford was as cold as ever, determined not to be the mistress of
the Prince of Wales until he became a Tory—he, who had
been a Whig from the earliest days when he had had his tuition from the famous Fox—and who insisted on Maria's acting as a chaperon whenever she visited him, a task which
Maria refused point blank to accept. However, for the time he
would enjoy the undemanding homage of his favourite sister.

'Then,' he said, 'let us talk no more of this doleful subject. I
will tell you of the new alterations I am planning at my
Pavilion, and I am going to insist on your coming to Brighton.'

'I should enjoy that . . . if I were well enough. But I should
hate to be ill at Brighton. Brighton is such a gay place. And
how is darling Charlotte?'

'As full of whims and fancies as ever. She is a troublesome
girl. I fear she takes after her mother.'

'When I last saw her I thought you must have looked
exactly like her when you were her age.'

'I'm not complaining of her looks. It's her spirits. She has
too many and they are too high.'

'Well, she is her father's daughter. Would you expect a
meek little creature without an original thought in her head?'

'Certainly not, but I wish she would not be troublesome.
There's trouble enough in the family.'

'Oh, George, what news of Ernest?'

'He's getting on. You know he is recuperating at the Pavilion.' The Prince frowned slightly. Brighton was his town.
There at least the people were loyal to him; he feared that
Ernest was impairing his popularity in Brighton. There were
so many rumours about that unfortunate affair of the valet
and when scandal touched one member of the family it
touched the rest. It was particularly disastrous following so
quickly on Fred's scandal with Mary Anne Clarke.

Still, what could he do? Ernest had had to get away from
Town; he had to recover from his very serious accident ... if
that was the right word for it ... and none of the brothers
refused to help each other when the need arose.

This unpleasantness would pass.

'It's good of you to look after him,' said Amelia. 'But you
are always good to your poor brothers and sisters.'

'I wish to God I'd been able to do something for you girls.
It's not much of a life for any of you.'

'There were too many of us.' She laughed. 'How strange are
the lives of kings and queens. So many have suffered because
they could not get one child; and our parents had fifteen.
Thirteen of us growing into adults to cause them trouble.'

'You have never given any cause for trouble.'

'Have I not? Papa continually worries about my health and
what he would say if he knew that I loved Charles I cannot
imagine.'

'He wants you to love only him.'

'How was he when you last saw him?'

'Poor Papa!'

She shook her head and did not speak for a moment; she
was aware of that somewhat eager look in her brother's eyes.

'Very bad,' she said. 'Worse. He can scarcely see now. He is
almost blind and the other ...'

'The rambling,' supplied the Prince.

'*That*,' she said, 'is worse, far worse. He keeps asking me
how I am and embracing me and weeping over me and I keep
telling him that I am getting stronger every day, which is a lie,
George.'

'Yet it comforts him. Poor old man, he is in need of comfort. Can it be much longer?'

'People are noticing. Not only the family ... but his ministers. There will be a Regency soon. I am sure of it, though it
may be that I shall not be here to see it.'

'How you harp on that,' he said almost pettishly, 'when you know how it grieves me.'

She held out a hand and pleaded forgiveness. 'When the Regency comes you will be too busy to miss me.'

'That could never be.'

'Wherever I may be, my love and hopes for your success will follow you.'

'My blessed Amelia!'

She looked at him tenderly. Dared she attempt to advise him? Could she say: Be careful with Maria. Maria is the one for you. No other woman will be as she is to you, none will love you as well.

How could she? She knew the fervour that possessed him when he was in pursuit of a woman and Lady Hertford was cold and cruel—Maria Fitzherbert warm and loving. And in his heart he knew that whatever fancies he had, it would always be Maria whom he loved. Maria whom he looked upon as his true wife.

Frederick and William had mentioned this to her. They both admired Maria Fitzherbert greatly and they were fond enough of their brother to wish for his happiness. She knew that they had tried to bring George and Maria together—to make Maria more tolerant of his weakness, to make him see the folly of his ways. But it was useless. They could do nothing against Maria's pride and his infatuation for a woman who would bring no good to him.

How she would like to see him happy with Maria, bringing her tales of little Minney Seymour whom he had looked upon as a daughter. She would have liked to see Maria's good sense made of use to Princess Charlotte. But how could she, a poor invalid, who had not been able to suppress her hopeless love for Charles Fitzroy, hope to guide the lives of others?

She thought of the trials of the family, the scandals that beset the brothers. Was there to be no end to them and were they not of their own making? But the young Princess Charlotte needed guidance. She was torn between her parents—her father who could not take to her because she reminded him of her mother, and her mother who smothered her with affection and saw nothing wrong in luring the girl into that scandalous household which she had built up at Montague House.

It was better to talk of lighter matters: of the *objets d'art* he had acquired; of the Chinese decorations he was having done in the Pavilion.

But her thoughts ran on the sorrows of her family; and

there was one whom she could not banish from her mind : the poor ailing King, who loved her more dearly than he loved any other.

When I die, she wondered, what will become of him?

*   *   *

That October Amelia was afflicted with erysipelas—the doctors called it St. Anthony's Fire—and it became clear that she was approaching her end. The Princess Mary was broken-hearted; she had nursed Amelia since she had become so ill and although she had known what the end must be—and that it could not be long delayed—nevertheless the shock was great.

There was mourning throughout the royal family. Amelia had been the best loved of them all, but none mourned her as deeply as the King. She alone, in the last year, had been able to soothe his troubled mind; only is beloved youngest daughter had been able to bring a smile to his lips. That she had been thinking of him at the end, that she had had made for him a ring containing a lock of her own hair under crystal and set with diamonds, could only accentuate his loss.

He took her ring; he slipped it on his finger and shut himself in his apartments. The Queen could hear him talking and talking all through the night.

He was moving fast into twilight. The anxieties of the world were too much for him; and the loss of his dearly beloved Amelia was beyond bearing.

One day his equerries came to him to find him smiling happily. 'My darling Amelia is not dead,' he told them. 'She has gone to Hanover with her little brother Octavius.'

As Octavius was the son who had died when he was four years old some twenty-six years before, it was known that the King's mind was wandering.

That was the beginning. His situation worsened. His troubles had been too much for him and he could no longer keep up the pretence of sanity.

The time had come for him to retire from the scene. The need for the Regency had once more arisen and this time it was brought into effect.

The Prince of Wales became the Prince Regent.

The Gallant Captain Hesse

It was inevitable that life should change for Charlotte with the Regency. Instead of being the frivolous Prince of Wales, her father was now, in all but name, the ruler of the Kingdom, which implied that she herself had, in a way, taken a step nearer to the throne.

She was now seen in public more often than before and the people took a lively interest in everything she did. She was very popular and although she was constantly reproved by poor old Lady de Clifford for her inelegance, her impetuousness, her boisterous manners, at least the people did not mind these failings.

They liked her a great deal more than they liked her father, for all his perfect manners. They were in fact annoyed with him; they did not like Lady Hertford, his new inamorata, and would have preferred him to have stayed with Maria Fitzherbert, which in Charlotte's opinion showed their good sense, for she herself would have much preferred it. She never saw Maria now and she often thought enviously of Minney Seymour to whom that lady devoted herself. So instead of visiting Maria as he used to, the Regent was constantly in the company of Lady Hertford who, although she might be exquisitely dressed, and look like a china figure, had little charm for the people, and did not help the Regent to regain their esteem one little bit.

The lampoons which were circulating about them were very malicious and Charlotte couldn't help chuckling over them when Mrs. Udney brought them to her notice. She liked particularly the references to Lord Yarmouth, Lady Hertford's son, as 'The Yarmouth Bloater'.

She would have liked to ask her father why he did not go to

see Maria Fitzherbert now; she wanted to say to him: 'But can't you see she is so much more pleasant to be with.' Imagine her daring to do that! It was only when she was not in his company that she imagined all sorts of daring conversations with him; when he was present she seemed to become petrified, unable even to walk with grace, and these were the occasions when the stutter was apt to return.

Oh, what is the use? she asked herself. He'll never like me. It's all pretence that he does. He can't forgive me for being my mother's daughter.

She was regretful, but there was so much in life to make it enjoyable, especially now she was growing up. Mercer kept her informed on politics and many a joyful discussion they had together. She was a staunch Whig and her father was beginning—under the influence of Lady Hertford—to forget his loyalty to that party.

It was fun to ride out in the park at Windsor and to flirt with George Fitzclarence who was really quite taken with her. Not that she was with him. It was his background which fascinated her. He was her cousin—though he was only half royal —his mother being the beautiful Dorothy Jordan. How interesting to have an actress for a mother! She made him tell her all about her. How she studied her parts and acted them at odd moments when her family were around her and how Uncle William used to love to hear her and would tell her whether she was good or bad. How exciting some people's lives were—and how dull others! Compare Maria Fitzherbert and Dorothy Jordan with the Old Girls. And yet they were supposed to be virtuous and Maria and Dorothy not really so—although no one could call Maria anything but a good woman. It was very interesting and she liked to tease George and flutter her eyes at him and gallop off in a way which made him spur his horse and come after her. They gave the grooms the slip sometimes and went off by themselves, which would of course be forbidden if it were known. But they both enjoyed it—chiefly because it was forbidden.

'You're a flirt, Charlotte,' George told her.

Was she? She certainly liked attention . . . masculine attention. And it amused her to tease George a little and perhaps made him think that he might marry her one day not because *They* would say he might for *They* never would, but because the Princess Charlottte herself insisted.

Poor Lady de Clifford would have a fit if she knew the conversations which went on in the Park between the Princess Charlotte and George Fitzclarence.

She was thinking of this as Louisa and Mrs. Gagarin were dressing her for the visit to the New Drury Lane theatre where she was going with her father, the Queen and the Princesses. This was one of those public occasions which she so much enjoyed. Lots of people would be there and her father would ceremoniously view the theatre before it was opened to the public. The day before there had been a ceremony in Whitehall Chapel at which she had played a prominent part.

'There now,' the fond Louisa was saying, 'they'll have eyes for no one but you.'

'Well, they'll spare a glance for Papa, I shouldn't wonder, for he will look most splendid.'

'They'll like you better.'

'I should hope so, for they don't like him one little bit.'

'Hush!'

'Really, Louisa, I am not a child now, remember. I am really growing up, and you will have to treat me with just a little more respect. I shall have to insist on it, you know.'

They looked so alarmed that she laughed at them and threw herself into a chair, her legs stretched out before her.

To reassure them she began to tell them about yesterday's ceremony in the chapel and was in the midst of this when Lady de Clifford entered and seeing her stretched out in such an inelegant pose cried out in horror: 'Princess Charlotte, you are showing your drawers.'

'I never do but when I can put myself at ease,' retorted Charlotte.

'You are showing them now.'

'But I am at ease.'

'And when you get in and out of a carriage you show them.'

'I don't care.'

'Your drawers are too long.'

Charlotte lifted her skirts and surveyed the lace edging of the offending garments. 'I don't agree,' she said, 'and I've seen longer drawers. The Duchess of Bedford's for one. She wears them long because she wants to show off the Brussels lace with which they are bordered. I like to show mine too.' She stood up and drawing herself to her full height and lifting her skirts to her knees declared: 'If I wish to show my drawers I shall ... and there is an end of the matter.'

Lady de Clifford looked as though she were about to burst into tears; she shook her head in desperation.

She really could not continue to cope with the waywardness of the Princess Charlotte.

*　　*　　*

It was pleasant travelling down to Oatlands, inevitably accompanied by Lady de Clifford. Charlotte was amused watching her guardian who appeared to have an unpleasant smell under her nose. Anticipation perhaps, Charlotte laughed to herself. The house *did* smell like a zoo, but she for one would forget the smells because in spite of Aunt Frederica's odd ways there was a warmth of affection in her which was rare.

'I should not fondle the dogs so much, Princess Charlotte, if I were you,' said Lady de Clifford.

'No, I don't suppose *you* would,' countered Charlotte.

'I have heard that sometimes ... er ... unpleasantness ... can be passed on through such a habit. I do recommend your not forgetting this, at the same time not allowing Her Highness to be aware of it.'

'Oh,' laughed Charlotte, 'you are teaching me to be deceitful.'

Poor Cliffy! She raised her eyebrows in the well-remembered way and that helpless look came into her face. One shouldn't tease her really, but if one did take her seriously nothing exciting would ever be allowed to happen. All the same Charlotte was sorry for poor Lady de Clifford's impossible task and for the rest of the journey sat with her hands quietly resting on her lap.

When they arrived it was delightful to be made immediately aware of the lack of ceremony. Aunt Frederica did not appear to greet her. One of the dogs, in the charge of the pensioner whose duty it was to care for him, was sick and so Aunt Frederica could not be expected to spare much thought for visitors, even if one of these was the heiress to the throne.

Never mind. Charlotte was delighted. She immediately walked out to the cottage with Lady de Clifford panting behind her and helped Aunt Frederica with the sick animal, while Lady de Clifford tutt-tutted and wondered what the world was coming to and Aunt Frederica was completely unaware of her.

It was certainly good fun to be at Oatlands. Charlotte made a pilgrimage to the pets' cemetery near the grotto where there were about sixty little tombstones each bearing the name of a beloved pet. She laid a small posy on the newest grave which she knew would please Aunt Frederica who could not fail to see it when she paid her daily visit to the little graveyard.

She sat with Aunt Frederica while that lady busied herself with her needlework. In this she was different from the Old Girls because she did not expect Charlotte to sew with her.

Charlotte could sit on a footstool and select the skeins of silk
for her and idly lure the conversation away from animals to
the family.

Such a strange family, thought Charlotte; and Aunt
Frederica one of the strangest. Looking at her Charlotte wondered how she had felt when she had known she was to be
married, for being married was a matter which constantly
occupied Charlotte's thoughts nowadays; she discussed it endlessly with Mercer. How she wished Mercer were with her
now; there was no one on earth to compare with Mercer and
she was forever grateful that they had become friends. She
would write and tell Mercer all about this visit to Oatlands
because she could not bear that they should be apart, and
when they were the next best thing was to write to Mercer as
though she were talking to her.

She would be luckier than Aunt Frederica, who, poor soul,
had had to leave her home and come to a strange land. Not for
me, Charlotte told herself. They'll never be able to make me
leave England. I'm here forever, and no one would dare say
otherwise. Poor Aunt Frederica was so small that she looked
quite incongruous when with Uncle Fred; and no one could
call her pretty with her skin spoilt by the pox, and her brown
teeth. How had she felt about Mary Anne Clark? Oh, yes,
Charlotte knew all about that—thanks to Mrs. Udney and her
own Mamma! How they had gloated! And neither of them
had spared a thought for poor Aunt Frederica. Not that she
cared, perhaps. It was not like an animal being sick and
everyone knew that Uncle Fred didn't live with her, so why
shouldn't he have a mistress? But those love letters! Of course
he would never have written letters like that to poor Aunt
Frederica.

And, thought Charlotte, she grows stranger and stranger—
wandering out at night with all the dogs, never wanting to go
to bed because she can't sleep; making the servants read to her
in the night, and having the animals living in the house. But
she was good because she did care for the poor and all those in
the neighbourhood who benefited from her goodness were
devoted to her.

Now as she stitched away, three of the dogs were lying close
to her; one had leaped on to her lap and was nuzzling against
her. Occasionally she stopped work to pat the animal and
murmur some endearment.

Charlotte said dreamily: 'I do wonder whom they will
choose for me.'

'Choose for you?'

'To marry. Do you realize how old I am?'

Frederica wrinkled her brows. She remembered the age of all the dogs but not of her niece.

'Sixteen,' said Charlotte dramatically. 'You have to admit it is quite an age.'

'They will find suitors for you soon, never fear!'

'I don't exactly fear it,' said Charlotte, 'but I confess I look forward to it with some apprehension, although no one shall make me marry where I do not wish.'

'Let us hope not.'

'Indeed it is a certainty.'

Frederica lifted her eyes, her needle poised.

'Oh,' demanded Charlotte, 'you do not think so? You think Papa might *find* a suitor for me and I should be *obliged* to accept him.'

'It is often the way with royal princesses.'

'I am heir to the throne.'

'You should not forget that you are not the heir apparent.'

'W ... what?'

'But the heir presumptive.'

'You mean that if my parents had a son ...'

Frederica nodded.

'But they do not live together. How is it possible for them to have a son if they never see each other?'

Frederica hesitated and shrugged her shoulders. 'If the Regent married again,' she said ... 'Well, it is a possibility.'

'How ... when he is married to my mother? You mean if she should *die*.'

'I did not. But we must not discuss such things.'

'Aunt Frederica, please don't you be like the Old Girls.'

After another slight hesitation Aunt Frederica decided that she would not be like the Old Girls and she said: 'What the Regent hopes for is a divorce that he might marry again. In which case if he had a son, you my dear Charlotte, would no longer be heiress to the throne.'

'A d ... divorce. The Prince of Wales!'

'Royal people are sometimes divorced. But it is foolish to speculate.'

A divorce! thought Charlotte. The Delicate Investigation. Willie Austin; and the wild strange life her mother led. It was a possibility.

She could not endure it. Always she had believed she would be the Queen. She wanted to be another Elizabeth—a great queen who inspired brave men to go out and conquer the world for her. It was a dream she had always had, a dream which had comforted her more than anything else in those days when she had been so jealous of Minney Seymour and had wished her father to love her. And it could happen. A divorce. A young princess for a stepmother; a child born to them . . . a brother . . . who would come before her!

'But . . . she is his wife,' she stammered.

'Of course. Of course. I talk nonsense. Look at this artful fellow. He is jealous. He wants to have the place on my lap. Oh, you are a crafty old man!'

A divorce, thought Charlotte. It is possible.

'Soon,' Aunt Frederica was saying, 'we shall have to be a little social. We are going to celebrate your stay here, my dear. We are going to have a ball for you here at Oatlands.'

'A ball! For me. Oh, what fun!' But she was thinking: He hates her. He wants to be rid of her. He will marry and have a son and he will love *him* dearly. And that will make him hate me all the more.

'Yes, a ball my dear. And who, do you think, will be our guest of honour?'

'Not . . . my father.'

'But of course. Who would think of giving a ball without him?'

*　　*　　*

The Prince Regent drove down to Oatlands in the company of William Adam, whom he had some years before made his Solicitor General and whose company he found interesting. Another member of his party was Richard Brinsley Sheridan.

The Prince was in a sombre mood. A party at Oatlands for his daughter Charlotte was not a very enlivening prospect. He was always ill at ease with the girl, although he was determined to feel an affection for her. That such a child should have been his daughter seemed incongruous; the only characteristic she had inherited from him was her daring on a horse. If it were not for the fact that she looked so much like him he would say she was not his daughter. The great desire of his life was to be rid of her mother; to remarry, to get a son. They would relegate Charlotte to a position he would very much like to see her occupy.

He was now in all but name the King; and it was becoming more and more obvious that his father would never be fit to rule again. The old man was afflicted with incipient blindness to add to his other disabilities. No, he would never rule again. The Prince Regent was the ruler. But what had the supreme power brought him? A break with Maria. Yes, it had been inevitable. It was not only that Isabella Hertford insisted, but there could not be rumours that the King (though he was not being given that title yet) was married to a Catholic; and people would insist that he was married while he continued to live with Maria So he had broken with Maria—and this could often depress him. He was flirting with the Tories and had allowed them to continue in office 'My God,' his mother had said, 'if the King recovered and found the Whigs in power it would send him mad again.' Still, he kept the bust of Fox in his apartments. Isabella was being charming to the ruler yet still keeping the lover at arm's length. He was uncertain of the future, but one thing he had done was make sure that his sisters had separate allowances so that they were no longer dependent on the Queen. It was something he had always promised himself, for he had long been very sorry for them and they would bless him for it; for the first time in their lives they had a measure of independence, and, he promised himself, there should be more, because at this late stage if it was possible for any of them to find a suitor, he would not stand in their way of marriage.

At least he could do this for his family.

And now to Oatlands, to a sort of children's ball. Charlotte was growing up, no doubt to be a plague to him. Maria had warned him that if he did not show some affection towards her she would turn to her mother and as soon us she was free to do so might ally herself openly with that woman. Who knew what consequences that would entail!

Maria, his good angel...with a devilish temper. He had provoked her, of course. But she had never really understood that however he strayed—and how could he help his own nature?—it was Maria to whom he always wanted to return. He wanted to return to her now—to Minney and old Pig. But how could he? If he tried to get back now what a stream of complications would ensue. But he still kept her picture and he looked at it often.

Here they were at Oatlands. A monstrosity of a place. A pity they had not asked *his* advice after the old place had been burned down. He'd scold Fred about that. What was it now though, but a home for animals? Frederica was an odd creature; but he did not dislike her as much now as he had at one time.

A flutter of excitement ran through the house because the Regent had arrived. He was aware of it and expected it but it always pleased him. Even Frederica would have to stand on a

little ceremony today. There she was waiting to greet him and
Charlotte was beside her, a demure Charlotte, he was glad to
see.

Frederica swept a deep curtsey.

'Oh, come,' he said, 'this is a family affair.' He kissed her
hastily. She did not attract him with her pockmarks and smell
of dog. And Charlotte. He embraced her. The poor girl clung
awkwardly for a moment.

'Your looks assure me that you are well, Charlotte,' he
said.

And then into the house with Adam and Sherry—a
changed house, thought Charlotte, with its atmosphere of awe
because it was offering hospitality to the Prince Regent.

*   *   *

'Oh,' sighed Charlotte to Louisa Louis, 'How I love gaiety!'

'And the gentlemen,' added Louisa quietly.

'And the. gentlemen,' conceded Charlotte. 'I confess to a
fondness for Mr. Adam.'

'As he would to Your Highness.'

'Come, Louisa, you must not let your mind run on. Mr.
Adam is a very proper gentleman *and* some forty years older
than I ... more perhaps. So a little flirtation with such a
gentleman cannot come amiss surely? It will put me in practice for the younger ones.'

'Such as Master Fitzclarence and Captain Hesse, I daresay.'

Charlotte lowered her eyes at the mention of Captain
Charles Hesse. There was indeed a charming young man and
she confessed inwardly that she was a little taken with him.
He looked splendid in his uniform of the Light Dragoons and
he was very sure of himself because he claimed to be a son of
the Duke of York. It was almost certain that he was and therefore half royal like George Fitzclarence and like George,
her cousin. Oh, these wicked uncles, what lives they led! She
was not sure that her father behaved more scandalously than
his brothers; it was merely that he was a more prominent
target for gossip.

And that brought her to Charles Hesse again. How amusing to ride in Windsor Great Park with Charles one day and
George the next—and another day with both, each vying for
her favour. Growing up *was* amusing.

She was sorry they were not at Oatlands now; still, she
would have to turn her wiles on ancient Mr. Adam who was,
perhaps because of his age, more skilful in the arts of flirtation than either George or Charles.

'Well,' sighed Louisa to Mrs. Gagarin, 'we have to face the fact that our young lady is growing up.'

'It is always desirable to face facts,' Charlotte reminded them.

She was excited. Now that her father was here it would be different. There would be no more singing duets with those two young girls Aunt Frederica had had brought to the house as companions for her. Silly little things Charlotte thought them in their simple muslin dresses and with their innocent chatter. She would have much preferred Charles Hesse or George Fitzclarence. The girls reminded her of the young Minney Seymour; sometimes she wondered about Minney but not often. It was all rather long ago.

She liked the sight of her bare shoulders. If she were not so pale she would be very pretty; her brows and lashes were so light that it was almost as though she had none; but her hair was good and so was her skin. On the whole she was a fairly handsome girl on whom a pretty dress could work wonders.

'I must look my best tonight, Louisa,' she said, 'because the Regent will open the ball with me.'

'He'll be so proud of you.'

Charlotte grimaced to hide her emotion. If only that could be true, how pleasant it would be! She pictured his telling her how pretty she looked and how proud he was to have such a daughter. If Mrs. Fitzherbert were here perhaps she would have called attention to Charlotte's dress, her hair, her skin and how pretty she was growing. But there was no one else who could, because there was no one else to whom he would listen.

Perhaps if he saw how Mr. Adam liked her, he would begin to think she was not so stupid and unattractive after all.

*   *   *

The Prince took her hand and led her on to the floor. How magnificent he was with the diamond star on his breast and the diamond buckles on his shoes; and everyone was looking at him, Charlotte was sure. She herself was a glittering figure because she was allowed to wear her diamonds for this occasion and her dress seemed almost as becoming here in the ballroom as it had under the adoring eyes of Louisa Lewis and Mrs. Gagarin.

He danced exquisitely in spite of his bulk; he was so light on his feet and of course she must seem clumsy beside him. But when she caught the eyes of kind Mr. Adam he conveyed the fact that he thought her very charming and she was grateful to him. After all, she thought, the Regent is a fat old man and I am young and as royal as he is and if he is King in all but name one day I shall be the Queen.

Poor Sheridan was looking on with bleary eyes. He had been in a state of semi-intoxication since his arrival. It was difficult to believe that he was the brilliant author of *The School for Scandal* and *The Rivals*, which she had read so many times and longed to see played; but of course he had suffered terribly after the burning down of Drury Lane and was always in debt and couldn't sleep and was often in cruel pain, so she'd heard, from his varicose veins. It was hard to see in him the romantic young figure who had eloped with Elizabeth Linley, herself long since dead. But men such as Sheridan were talked of and their past glories remembered. She was glad Papa was still friendly with him because although he was witty and clever, he was no longer handsome and, thought Charlotte severely, his poor second wife cannot find him a very good husband.

Charlotte much preferred the gallant Mr. Adam.

She glanced at her father's profile as they danced, plump and pleasant, with that attractive nose which gave such a jolly look to his face, and made one feel there was no need to fear a man with a nose like that. At least that was how Minney had felt—and George Keppel too. She had made them admit it. But of course they were not *his* children.

The others were falling in behind them now and the ball was open, and after a while the Prince led her back to the Duchess and said that she danced well; and after that she danced with Uncle Fred, which was good fun, and they tried the waltz.

'Said to be most improper,' Uncle Fred told her, 'except when the partners are a lady and her uncle. Then it is quite proper.'

'Then it gives you a chance to be proper for once, Uncle Fred,' she retorted, and that made him laugh, for Uncle Fred laughed easily.

After that she waltzed with Mr. Adam, which was a little daring, but delightful because he danced well for such an elderly man; and he told her she was looking exceedingly charming and that he was sure the Regent on this occasion must find his daughter the most beautiful young lady in the ballroom.

Very pleasant to hear; and they could talk of Mercer, too, because Mercer was related to Mr. Adam's wife, who was now dead; so that there was a family connection. Charlotte could

extol Mercer's many virtues; she could tell Mr. Adam that
Mercer was her greatest friend and she could not imagine how
she could ever have existed without that friendship; to which
Mr. Adam replied that he was delighted that a connection of
his—although only by marriage—could be of such good
service to the Princess, but he advised her to modify her
language when discussing Mercer's good qualities with people
other than himself, for with such an important young lady as
Charlotte there were spies all about her and there would be
many who might try to spoil the friendship if they knew how
deep it was.

Charlotte listened intently; she was remembering her
grandmother's references to 'particular friendships'.

The music stopped and the Prince Regent was heard trying
to explain the movement of the Highland Fling to the
Duchess.

He glanced towards them. Charlotte's heart beat faster because she thought he was going to ask her to join him in the
Highland Fling, and because she had no idea how this dance
was performed and would have hated to confess ignorance to
her father she tried to hide herself behind Mr. Adam. Apparently she was successful, for the Prince cried: 'Come, Adam,
you know the dance. We will give an exhibition.'

So Mr. Adam went on the floor with the Prince and one
hand lightly on his hip and the other held above his head Mr.
Adam executed a few steps of the Highland Fling. The Prince
said that was the idea and greatly to the amusement of the
entire company the two of them danced, when suddenly the
Prince gave a cry of pain and would have fallen had not Mr.
Adam caught him.

The Duke and Duchess came hurrying over.

'I've done my foot some damage,' cried the Prince. 'Stab
me, Fred, the pain is intense.'

The Duchess called to her servants and in a moment the
atmosphere of the ballroom had changed. Charlotte stood by
helplessly watching, longing to be the one who looked after
him and amazed them all by her calm competence. But
clearly her services were not needed; and the Prince was
carried to the best of the bedrooms where he lay groaning
until the doctors came and gave the verdict that he had injured his ankle and must rest for a few days.

Uncle Fred said that he must stay at Oatlands where it
would be his privilege—and that of the Duchess—to look
after him.

*　　　*　　　*

Since it was necessary to care for the Regent, the Duchess had no time to devote to Charlotte, so she and her retinue returned to Warwick House.

Warwick House, as the Princess said, was not her favourite residence. She had always hated it and was constantly planning to get away from it. For some years now she had spent a certain amount of time there and it was recognized as her particular residence. It was an old house and in fact part of the out-buildings of Carlton House; and it had been alloted to her because it was so close to her father's mansion. Charlotte had said that her father had put her there so that he could, when he thought of her, keep an eye on her; and at the same time not be bothered with her. She never went back to Warwick House without a sense of grievance.

The house was in a cul-de-sac at the end of a narrow lane, and the buildings which surrounded it made it gloomy. The two sentries stationed at the entrance of the lane, Charlotte said, made her feel like a prisoner. It was not pleasant to come back to Warwick House after the jollities of Oatlands.

'I think I prefer the smell of animals to that of damp,' she complained to Lady de Clifford.

Lady de Clifford was also disappointed. Warwick House did her rheumatics no good; in fact, as she said often to her daughter, the Countess of Albermarle, she could not go on much longer and was only waiting for the right opportunity to relinquish her post. If it were not for the fact that dear Princess Charlotte needed her she would have done so long ago.

'I'd almost rather be at Windsor,' Charlotte told Mrs. Udney.

'I'm not surprised at that,' replied that lady with a wink. 'Your Highness does so enjoy her rides in the Park and finds the company so congenial.'

'Company?' said Charlotte, flushing.

'Delightful company, I believe,' went on the incorrigible Mrs. Udney. 'And in particular the gallant Captain Hesse.'

'You have seen us riding together?'

Mrs. Udney laughed. 'Your Highness should not be alarmed. I should not dream of mentioning the matter to Lady de Clifford, and if I did . . . she would not know what to do about it. It strikes me that her ladyship becomes more and more flustered every day.'

It was true, thought Charlotte. And a good thing too. One must have the opportunity to exercise a little freedom.

'How I wish I could go to Windsor,' she sighed, at which Mrs. Udney laughed conspiratorially.

Later that day she produced a note which she said the gallant Captain had asked her to give to the Princess.

Charlotte read it through with pleasure. It was very daring of him. He missed their rides. He longed to talk to her. She was not only the most beautiful of Princesses but the most witty.

Oh, how daring of him! And what Lady de Clifford would say if she knew. Or her father for that matter.

But I'm growing up and I must live, she told herself. I do not want to become like one of the Old Girls.

*   *   *

She rode to Oatlands to see her father. He lay on a couch looking large and unusually pale. Mr. Adam was with him. She kissed his hand and enquired anxiously after his health.

'Not good,' he said languidly. 'Not good.'

'Oh, Papa ... if there is anything I can do ...'

He looked at her in amazement. Anything she could do? What was she talking about? She blushed and stammered: 'I ... j ... just thought ...' She did not know how to continue and he, who was so articulate, despised incoherence.

The Duchess who was present came to her rescue. 'Charlotte is naturally disturbed by your Highness's indisposition. But don't fret, Charlotte my dear. His Highness is improving every day.'

'I'm not sure that I am,' said the Regent crossly. He frowned at the Duchess. He had never really liked her since she had refused to receive Maria. All those animals she kept about the place were disgusting; she was not pretty and her dignity reminded him of Maria and made him wish that he were in Tilney Street or at the house on the Steyne, going to it through the secret passage from the Pavilion. How well Maria would have nursed him!

He closed his eyes, indicating that he wished to speak to no one; he felt languid and bored and sorry for himself.

Charlotte, dismissed, wandered out of the room and sat alone in a window seat. When one of the dogs came and thrust his damp nose into her hand, she caressed him absently, feeling depressed. How different it would have been if they were all together—herself, her mother and her father. She imagined herself making a posset for him and taking it to him and when he drank it he declared he felt so much better because she had made it.

'The Princess unattended!' It was Mr. Adam smiling, bowing, very much the courtier.

'I don't think my presence is really required in the sick room.'

'Good. We can be much more at ease here.'

'*You* are at ease in any place.'

'It's a state that comes with age.'

'Then I shall not regret growing old.'

'I am sure you will be far too wise to do that, for with age comes experience—which is perhaps a more valuable asset even than youth.'

'Yes,' said Charlotte quickly. 'I believe it is. I'd much rather be sixteen than ten.'

'Then you have begun to make the discovery too.'

It was very pleasant talking to Mr. Adam, whose eyes so admired her. She told him about the dreariness of life at Warwick House and the odd quirks of the members of her household. Her laughter rose immediately and she found she was really enjoying herself.

But when she went back to Warwick House she was sad again thinking of the conflict between her mother and father, which now she was growing older she was beginning to realize was too great ever to change.

*   *   *

The rumours were rife. The Regent was ill. What was the matter with him? He had been dancing the Highland Fling and had hurt his ankle!

Hurt his ankle! said the lampoonists. That was just a tale. More likely the Yarmouth Bloater had lost his temper and attacked his benefactor. And the reason? Because His Highness was far too interested in the Bloater's wife.

That was a great joke. The son of the Prince's latest flame to attack him for casting eyes on his wife! What lives Royalty led! It was too good a story not to exploit. After all, was the comment, it was a mild echo of the Sellis affair when it was widely believed Cumberland had come close to being murdered because he had been found in bed with his valet's wife.

Charlotte heard of these rumours and was deeply disturbed by them. At the same time stories were still circulating about her mother and her supposed lovers. There were many who believed that Willie Austin was the son of the Princess of Wales.

Hurt and bewildered she longed to know the truth and yet dreaded it.

'My word,' said the informative Mrs. Udney one day, 'there are rumours about the Regent. Not that I believe them. They'll say the maddest things.'

'What things?' asked Charlotte.

'Not that I'd repeat . . .' began Mrs. Udney, but Charlotte was not deluded; she knew that those words were the preliminary to a confidence. 'You must not mention that I told. You must never repeat . . .' Charlotte gave the promise which she knew she would wish afterwards that she had not allowed to be extracted because when she heard these vile slanders she would want to trace them to their sources; she would want to demand that the lies be retracted. Lies! How she wished she could believe they were lies!

It came out after a certain amount of wheedling.

'They are saying that the Regent has inherited his father's illness and that he is *mad*.'

Charlotte stared at Mrs. Udney for a few seconds in silence, then she cried: 'Don't dare say that again.'

Mrs. Udney was alarmed 'Of course not. I only told you because you got it out of me.'

'Who . . . who dared say it?'

'Well, don't tell a soul, but they are saying the rumour started with Cumberland.'

His own brother, her uncle Cumberland whom she had never liked! In fact she had found him a little sinister with his one glittering eye (he had lost the other before she was born, at the battle of Tournay) and she had always felt that he resented her.

But what a wicked thing to say about her father!

She turned on Mrs. Udney and would have struck her if the woman had not hastily retreated.

'I'm only telling you what you asked,' began Mrs. Udney.

'Don't ever say that again,' cried Charlotte. 'Don't ever say it. I . . . I'll kill anyone who says it.'

She ran to her bedroom and threw herself on to her bed.

She kept thinking of her mother and her father and how they hated each other and how so many people seemed to hate them.

*   *   *

In her apartments at Kensington Palace the Princess of Wales embraced her daughter.

'If you only knew how I long for these hours, my little Charlotte. Oh, if you only knew,' she cooed. 'But I am allowed so little. It's a scandal. Of all the scandals in this family this is the greatest. To be allowed to see my own daughter for an hour now and then. I tell you I will not endure it. I will make such a big noise one day that they'll be sorry. Oh, yes, they will.'

Charlotte gave herself up to the warm, almost suffocating hug. Mamma's wig as usual was a little awry and strands of her own grey hair were visible beneath it. It was so black that her heavily painted cheeks made her look like a grotesque doll. The dress she was wearing—mauve satin trimmed with ribbons and lace—was very low cut and none too clean, being stained with food, and Charlotte could quite understand how the immaculate and fastidious Regent was disgusted.

But she loves me, thought Charlotte; she is warmhearted to me and he is so cold. Yet it was his love she wanted. Why could she not be satisfied with her mother's love which, whenever they met, seemed to be so intense?

'Well, tell me all your news, my angel. How is de old Begum. Pestering you, I know. Interfering old crocodile, saying "This shall be done" and "That shall be done" and making my little Charlotte's life a burden. I know de old Begum.'

'When I'm at Warwick House I don't have to see her often. It's at Windsor.'

'Ah, Windsor . . . gloomy old place! Cold and draughty . . . ugh! I was saying to darling Willie only the other day, "Willie," I said, "they can keep their castle. We're much better at Blackheath." '

'And how is Willie?' A purely rhetorical question, for she had no wish to know how the obnoxious child fared.

'Willie!' called the Princess. 'Come here, Willie. Charlotte wants to see you. Oh, the naughty boy. He does not come.'

'Never mind, Mamma. I want you to myself for the little time I have with you.'

'My sweet, sweet Charlotte.' More damp kisses and displays of affection which set the wig more awry and the gown slipping farther off the shoulders.

'So what are they doing to you, eh? What is Madame de Clifford saying now? Trying to stop you having a little fun, eh? It is time you are done with governesses. Governesses! Dey are for children. And my Lottie is a young woman now, eh? And she has her little flirtations. Oh, I know. George Fitzclarence . . . Captain Hesse. Now there is a young man I have one big fancy for. Captain Hesse—he is not very tall but he is a very attractive man.' Caroline burst out laughing. 'You find him so . . . and so does your Mamma.'

'Captain . . . Hesse has visited you?'

'Often he comes. He is a very great favourite here "You are very welcome, Captain Hesse," I say to him. "Come whenever you care to. We are always happy to see you." And he comes often. Sometimes I think he comes hoping to have a word with you. He thinks how much more *comfortable* here than in the forest where you may be seen and spied on ... Oh, yes, my Charlotte, you are surrounded by spies.'

Charlotte was taken aback that so much should be known of her friendship with Captain Hesse—those secret meetings in the forest, the letters which Mrs. Udney helped to smuggle in to her. The occasional kiss when they thought no one was watching them.

Had they been seen and reported to her mother? She was horrified at the thought of such conduct coming to her father's ears. He would despise her and dislike her more than ever.

'Mamma,' she began, but the Princess of Wales was not listening.

'You are treated like a child,' she went on. 'It is time you are free. My poor little Charlotte who is watched over and spied on by these stern old women. They are all under the rule of de old Begum. Charlotte, my love, you must not let them crush you. Get rid of that silly snuffling de Clifford. Tell her she's an old idiot and tell your father too. Does he visit you? Ha! What a spectacle he is making of himself, running after that lump of ice. He'll never get into her bed. He would have done better to stay with the Fitzherbert. I've always said it and I say it now. She was the one for him and the people would have thought a lot more of him if he'd stuck to her.'

A lady at the door was announcing an arrival. Charlotte looked up eagerly. One never knew what kind of people one was going to meet in her mother's apartments. The most colourful characters mingled with the most disreputable and there was a sprinkling of politicians, all of whom Charlotte suspected were endeavouring to stir up strife between her mother and father.

But here was a surprise which sent the blood to her cheeks. Captain Hesse came into the room. He bowed from the waist, German fashion.

Charlotte cried inelegantly: 'Oh, so it's you.'

'Always at Your Highness's service,' he responded gallantly.

He looked very handsome in his uniform of an officer of the Light Dragoons, and although he was short there was a look of the Duke of York about him.

'A surprise for you both, you naughty children!' cried Caroline archly.

*   *   *

After that whenever Charlotte visited her mother Captain Hesse would be there also.

It was a shame, declared Caroline, that Charlotte was treated like a child by her father and his mother. She had no fun at all. Her Mamma was going to make sure that when she came to her she should enjoy herself.

She was soon conveying letters from the Captain to her daughter and Charlotte, always ready to take up her pen, responded.

This was romantic adventure and it gave a spice to life. The monotony of Warwick House was considerably relieved; she would laugh to herself when she listened to the Queen's lectures. They might treat her like a child and she was amused thinking of what they would say if they could read those letters which were passing between her and Captain Hesse.

It was all so simple, with her mother acting as the go-between and making it possible for them to meet.

Charlotte often wondered what her father would say if he knew of this. Serve him right, she thought. *He takes* no interest in me.

There came a day when even Charlotte began to feel some alarm. Her mother behaved in such an odd way but perhaps never so dangerously odd as she did on this occasion.

Charlotte had paid the prescribed visit to find Captain Hesse in her mother's drawing room where Caroline made them sit together on a sofa very close while she talked of the manner in which Charlotte was treated by her father and grandmother.

'Like a child, you understand, *mon capitan*. And she is not a child. But they would lock her up and say No to this and No to that ... No to everything that is nice and pleasant, and Yes, Yes, Yes to everything that is a tiresome bore. She has de old fool de Clifford always at her elbow. Is it not a shame, *mon capitan*? But when she comes to see her mother ... which is not often enough because her wicked father keeps her from me ... she is going to enjoy herself. Someone must be kind to my darling Charlotte.'

The Captain said he believed everyone would want to be kind to the Princess Charlotte.

That made the Princess Caroline laugh; she fell back in her

chair and her short legs, which did not reach the floor unless
she sat forward, shot up rather indecorously showing grubby
lace petticoats.

The Captain pretended not to see and asked Charlotte
whether she had ridden lately. The Princess of Wales sat
listening to them for a while, sly amusement on her face.
Then she went to the window where she stood fingering the
heavy curtains.

'New ones I have in some parts of this place. Charlotte, I
want your opinion.' Charlotte rose and her mother said: 'You
too, Captain. Your opinion is sought also.'

Charlotte was surprised when her mother led them to her
bedroom.

'Come in, come in,' she said. 'Oh, that wicked Willie. He
has been playing with my paint and lead. Naughty boy!' She
left them standing in the middle of the room and suddenly
she was at the door crying: 'Amuse yourselves!'

They were alone for the door had shut on them and with
something like panic Charlotte heard the key turn in the lock.

The Captain's panic was as great as Charlotte's. Here he
was locked in a bedroom with the heiress to the throne of
England. He could be accused of treason. Suppose Charlotte
had been in similar circumstances before. Suppose . . .

He grew faint with apprehension at the thought.

Charlotte herself spoke: 'We . . . we must get out of here . . .
at . . . at once . . .'

The Captain nodded.

He went to the door and rapped on it.

'Open this door. Your Highness, I beg of you open this door
at once.'

They heard Caroline chuckling.

Had they said her father was mad? thought Charlotte.
They could say that of her mother and perhaps it would be
true.

'Mamma,' she cried. 'I am frightened. I beg of you open
this door at once.'

There was a pause before the key was turned in the lock.
There was the Princess of Wales laughing immoderately.

'Well, my children,' she cried, 'all I say is that you did not
make the most of your chances.'

'It is time for me to leave,' said Charlotte.

'Not yet. We have a little longer.'

They went back to the Princess's drawing room and sat un-
easily and very soon the Captain was making his excuses and
begging leave to retire.

When he had left Caroline embraced her daughter.

'My love, you shouldn't have been frightened. I should not have left you there . . . unless you had wanted to stay. I wanted to think what Madame de Clifford or de old Begum would have said if they had known you were locked in a bedroom with the dear little Captain. Oh, I am a wicked one you think. But no, you do not. You know your poor Mamma too well. You know she loves her darling Charlotte as she loves no one else and she cannot bear this separation and she wants most of all for us to be together. She is wild and foolish and does mad, mad things . . . but she loves too. Here is a warm heart, dearest Charlotte, a heart that wants to give love all the time and is kept from her treasure. Oh Charlotte, my little girl, tell me you understand.'

'Y . . . yes, Mamma, I understand but please do not try to shut me up with Captain Hesse . . . or with any man, again.'

'Never, unless my angel wishes it. It was Mamma's silly way of saying she loves her little girl and wants to give her all that the others take away from her. Say you understand. Say you love your Mamma. It is the only thing she has . . . her little Charlotte.'

'You have Willie, Mamma. He is as a son to you.'

'I have Willie . . . but he is the substitute for my own little girl. Try to understand me, Charlotte, and love me.'

'I do, Mamma, I do.'

They wept together. I do love her, Charlotte told herself, I do.

'Promise me, dearest, that when you are your own mistress you will not forget your mother.'

'I promise,' said Charlotte.

'So perhaps it is not so long to wait, eh?' Mischievous lights shot up in the eyes of the Princess of Wales. 'And in the meantime we plague them in all ways we know, eh?'

Charlotte did not answer.

Poor Mamma, she thought, she is starved of love. I must try to understand and help her.

But when she went back to Warwick House, sitting in the carriage with Lady de Clifford, she wondered what that lady would say if she knew what had happened in her mother's bedroom and she shivered with apprehension.

It was a great trial to be a princess and heiress—though only presumptive—to the throne of England and at the same time to be a buffer between two such strange parents.

Charlotte in Revolt

MRS. GAGARIN and Louisa Lewis were dressing the Princess for her birthday ball. It was to be a grand occasion at Carlton House given by the Prince of Wales because she was sixteen years old.

'Soon,' she was saying, 'they will have to stop treating me as a child. I'm longing to wear *feathers*. When I do, you will know then that I really am no longer regarded as a child.'

'Don't you be in such a hurry to grow up,' advised Louisa. 'It'll come soon enough.'

'Not soon enough for me. Do you think the Prince R. will be proud of me tonight? Now don't say "Yes yes yes" Stop and think. Think of him and all his elegance. I have to be rather good to come up to his standards. Why, what's the matter with Gagy?'

'It's all right, Your Highness, just a stitch in my side.'

'Better sit down,' advised Louisa. 'You know . . .'

Mrs. Gagarin flashed her a warning look which Charlotte intercepted.

'Now what is this?' she demanded imperiously. 'Gagy, you are not ill are you?'

'No, no. It's nothing. My dinner did not agree with me.'

Charlotte looked suspicious and felt a sudden touch of panic. Birthdays made one realize that time was passing. It did not seem so long since her last; and some of these people who had been with her for so long that she thought they would be with her forever, were getting old.

Mrs. Gagarin had a grey tinge to her face today. Charlotte threw her arms about her and said: 'Gagy, you mustn't die. Don't forget I made you want to live after you lost Mr. Gagarin, didn't I? I still want you. You mustn't be ill.'

'What a fuss,' said Mrs. Gagarin, 'About a touch of indigestion. Anyone would think I was on my death bed.'

'Don't talk about death,' commanded Charlotte. 'I don't like it.'

'All right,' said Mrs. Gagarin. 'Let's see that you look your best for this party.'

'Do I?'

'Lovely,' cried Mrs. Gagarin. 'Doesn't she, Louisa?'

Louisa adoringly agreed.

It was silly, Charlotte assured herself, to think poor Gagy was going to die just because she had indigestion. There were years and years left yet to them all.

She was in a slightly sombre mood, however, on the journey to Carlton House, but she was soon elated, for her father had determined this should be a special occasion. The people who had gathered to watch her alight from her carriage cheered her and she waved as Lady de Clifford had told her many times she should not—instead of bowing regally. But the people liked her for her free and easy ways and she was not going to obey Lady de Clifford's orders much longer.

Her father looked splendid and she was thrilled as always to see him and proud that he was her father; and the odd feelings of resentment and pride fought together in the familiar way; but resentment was defeated on this night, because he smiled as he embraced her affectionately, even with a glint of tears in his eyes, and told her that she looked charming.

She was happy as, holding her lightly by the hand, he led her into that house which the old gossip, Horace Walpole, had described as the most perfect in Europe. She was proud of the tasteful decorations; they had all been done under *his* supervision; and from the moment she passed through the front porch with its Corinthian portico, because he was leading her there and seemed pleased to have her, she knew this was going to be a happy evening, a birthday to remember.

Carlton House was her birthplace and *his* home where she wished they could all live together—her father, her mother and herself, like an affectionate family. It was what she had always wanted more than anything and she had confided this to Mercer.

'Papa,' she said, 'whenever I come to Carlton House I am struck afresh by its beauty.'

He was pleased. 'I confess to a fondness for the place myself.'

'Everything is p ... perfect,' she cried, and for once he did not frown at her stammer. She went on: 'The lovely apart-

ments, and best of all I think I love the dear little music room
that opens on to the gardens. I never saw a room as pretty as
that music room.'

He began to tell her how the idea had come to him to create
such a room; and this was one of the rare occasions when they
were able to chat easily together.

During dinner when she sat on his right hand he talked
almost exclusively to her and told her how for the banquet to
celebrate his accession to the Regency he had entertained two
thousand guests here in Carlton House.

'I had the idea that a canal should be made to run right
down the central table and in it was a stream in which fish
swam—they were silver and gold and I can tell you were
extremely beautiful.'

'How wonderful it must have looked. That was a great
occasion.'

He was sad momentarily, thinking about Maria who had
refused to come because she had been denied a place at the
stream-decorated table. Why could she not understand that as
Regent he dared not bring into prominence one who was a
Catholic and suspected of being his wife? It was not really
because Isabella had not wished her to be at the top table.
Maria could not understand that. How shackled one was
when one was royal! Why the legitimacy of this girl seated
beside him might be in question if that ceremony in Maria's
drawing room was accepted as a true marriage.

He wished he had not reminded himself of the Regency
banquet.

'Papa,' Charlotte was saying. 'You have grown more
slender. I trust you are well.'

He was pleased with the remark, although he disliked
people to hint that he had ever been 'fat' which he considered
an unpleasant word. He had lost a little weight, yet lying up
at Oatlands had not improved his health.

Later when he led her into the dance she noticed that he
limped a little and did not call attention to this; by that time
she was thinking that this was one of the happiest days of her
life. Her father was fonder of her than he had been for a long
time and as this was, she hoped, the beginning of the gratification of one of her dearest wishes, she could forget her misgivings caused by Mrs. Gagarin's grey looks and the odd
eccentric behaviour of her mother.

For once her father approved of her—and that was perhaps
what she most wanted in life.

*   *   *

Mercer was a constant visitor to Warwick House. Charlotte often wondered what she would do without her. She confided in Mercer—not everything, of course, but a great deal. She could never talk of her feelings for her parents but perhaps this was because she did not fully understand them herself. She had not mentioned that occasion when her mother had shut her in the bedroom with Captain Hesse. That was something she could scarcely bring herself to think of—let alone talk about.

But in almost everything else Mercer was her confidante, her *alter ego*; and she often thought that while she could have Mercer for her friend she could bear everything else—the criticisms of her paternal grandmother and the dreary boredom of her maternal one; the alternate scoldings and gushing affection of the Old Girls; the sadness that came to her when she thought of poor mad Grandpapa and most of all her mingled feelings for her parents.

Sometimes Mercer would describe the dresses she had seen at a ball. Then they would talk of clothes—a subject of which Mercer was a past mistress, as of everything else, and they would perhaps call in Mrs. Gagarin and Louisa Lewis to discuss what could be made for Charlotte out of what Mercer sternly called her 'somewhat inadequate allowance'.

'Never mind,' cried Charlotte, 'I shall soon have an establishment of my own and that will mean a good allowance. They can't keep me in the nursery forever.'

'It will be on your eighteenth birthday,' prophesied Mercer, 'which is not really very far away.'

Charlotte's eyes sparkled at the thought of growing up.

'One thing you must promise me, Mercer. When I am queen you will always be with me.'

Mercer said it was not really very becoming to talk of being queen when one considered what must happen before she was.

There were times when Mercer was a little self-righteous, and Charlotte was glad of it. It would not have been good for them both to be as impulsive as she was.

She confided in Mercer that her Uncle Cumberland had said her father was suffering from *his* father's malady.

'That is a treasonable and most wicked statement,' announced Mercer. 'I have always been suspicious of the Duke of Cumberland.'

Charlotte had declared that she too had always been suspicious of him. There was something definitely *sinister* about the man. The fact that he had only one eye made him look a real villain.

Mercer agreed. 'He's a Tory too.' Heinous sin in Mercer's opinion. She could always be angry with anyone who might seek to turn Charlotte from the Whig cause.

They spent a hilarious half hour talking of Uncle Cumberland's many failings and building up a quite horrifying picture of him which eventually sent them into fits of laughter, for Mercer had her lighter moments.

Louisa, hearing them laughing together, commented that it seemed to her that that Miss Elphinstone was the Queen of Warwick House and that if they didn't look out they would soon be taking their orders from her.

Mrs. Gagarin, who was looking more frail than ever, replied that it was pleasant to hear dearest Charlotte laugh. Her life was not all Mrs. Gagarin would wish for a young high spirited girl. Let her enjoy herself while she could.

But when Charlotte told Mercer of the cartoons Mrs. Udney had brought in for her, Mercer's lips were set into lines of disapproval. 'I don't like Mrs. Udney,' she said.

'Nor do I,' admitted Charlotte, and told Mercer about the will she had once made. Soon they were laughing again, but Mercer added that she thought it was not suited to Charlotte's *dignity* to look at these scurrilous cartoons about her own family. She should reprimand Mrs. Udney for bringing them into her household; and Mercer for one would like to see Mrs. Udney *replaced*.

Charlotte nodded gravely. 'As for the cartoons,' she said, 'I only had a little peep. I shan't look at them any more, dearest Mercer, if you think I should not.'

As Mercer would prefer the Princess Charlotte not to so demean herself, Charlotte declared she would do nothing of which dearest Mercer would not approve.

Mercer allowed the conversation to become lighthearted again and talked of Lord Byron, who had the good sense to admire Mercer very much. He also admired the Princess Charlotte whom he had once had the honour of meeting.

'I remember him well,' cried Charlotte. 'The most handsome man I ever met . . . or one of them. He is like a Greek God and that limp makes him exciting in some way. They say he is very wicked.'

'What he needs is a woman to look after him.' Mercer smiled complacently and Charlotte was ready to believe that he needed Mercer as she herself did. Everyone must be in need of Mercer.

'Oh, Mercer,' she cried in an excess of affection, 'how glad I am that you are my friend.'

'It's useful,' admitted Mercer. 'Being so much older, I can help you.'

*   *   *

The Prince Regent was reading a poem to his friend Sheridan who, having a great belief in the power of the pen—particularly when wielded by the celebrated Lord Byron—was disturbed.

It was called *Lines to a Young Lady Weeping.*

> *'Weep, daughter of a royal line,*
> *A Sire's disgrace, a realm's decay:*
> *Ah, happy if each tear of thine*
> *Could wash a father's fault away.*
>
> *Weep, for thy tears are virtue's tears,*
> *Auspicious to these suffering isles:*
> *And be each drop in future years*
> *Repaid thee by a people's smiles.'*

The Prince's face had flushed scarlet and his eyes filled with tears of anger.

'This is referring to that disgraceful scene the other night. Sometimes I think my daughter is determined to anger me.'

'There are too many seeking to take sides, sir,' said Sheridan.

'They are giving her ideas of her own importance. By God, she has no importance and she *shall* have none if I say so.'

Sheridan knew when to be silent. It would have been folly to remind the Prince that Charlotte was his daughter and unless by a miracle in the form of divorce from the Princess of Wales he was able to get a son, Charlotte must in due course inherit the throne.

'You know what happened. I was speaking of those rogues Grey and Grenville, who had refused my offer to join the government. Lauderdale defended them and declared he would have refused in their place. He was a true Whig and so on and hoped he would always remain faithful to the cause. And what does Charlotte do but burst into tears. Tears, Sherry, at a dinner party! How is the girl being brought up?'

Sherry refrained from pointing out that the shedding of tears was a family habit and said that the Princess must be taught to behave in accordance with her position.

'Taught indeed . . . and so she shall be. But you see . . . she burst into tears and this fellow Byron has to write a verse about it, showing her as a heroine and me as a scoundrel . . . and the whole country is reading it, I don't doubt.'

Sheridan could only admit to the popularity of Byron's work.

'And in the past I've recommended his poetry. I liked the fellow. Why should he behave so . . . against me?'

Sheridan shrugged his shoulders. 'She is a young girl, sir, not without charm. The people are determined to take sides and some of them will take hers.'

'But why should they take sides?'

One might reply: Because we are concerned with the House of Hanover and in this House it is the custom for parents to quarrel with children. Hadn't the Regent himself set an example to his daughter?

'They will always take sides, sir. The people like a battle, and if there is not one they will set about contriving it.'

'Charlotte should have behaved with more decorum. But when does she? She is now a staunch Whig. Soon we shall have her interfering in politics.'

It was her father who had wished her to become a Whig in the first place; if now that he had become Regent he was looking for some compromise between Whig and Tory and was inclining very much towards the latter, could he expect Charlotte to follow without a protest? Lady Hertford had decided to make a Tory of him and Lady Hertford must be placated at all costs. But one could hardly expect Charlotte to care for Lady Hertford's views.

'Stab me,' said the Prince, 'I have been too lenient with that young woman. I must let her see who is master.'

'I think she is aware of that already, Sir.'

'Then it's more than she appears to be. I want to know who it is who is feeding her her politics. Her governess seems a fool to me.'

'Lady de Clifford is perhaps not adequate to the task of controlling a princess like Her Royal Highness.'

'And she sees her mother too frequently.'

'Once a week, Sir.'

'Too frequently,' retorted the Prince with a frown. 'I'll warrant it is there she is taught how to plague me. But I'll tell you this, Sherry: It is not going on. No, it is not going on. Keep your ears open and see if you can discover who is encouraging her to behave in this way. Once I know I shall put that person somewhere where he—or she—will have no power to instruct the Princess and to plague me.'

Sheridan would, he declared, as always do his best to serve his Prince.

'And I shall see that someone in her household keeps an eye open,' said the Prince.

*   *   *

The Duchess of York arrived at Warwick House to accompany Charlotte to the Opera. The Princess was excited.

'At this rate,' she told Louisa, 'I shall soon be wearing *feathers.*'

'Time enough,' soothed Louisa, which made the Princess laugh.

'I expect the people will cheer me when I go into my box. I shall let them see how pleased I am that they like me. I think one of Papa's faults is the haughty way he behaves in public. Of course he *looks* magnificent. But that is why everyone would recognize him as the Prince Regent so he has no need to keep reminding them by his manner that he is. He will be a little hurt I think if they cheer me more than they cheer him, but he won't be there. I wish he would be. Do you know, Louisa,' she added wistfully, 'no event seems quite the same without him.'

She thought how pleasant it would be if they were all in their box together: He magnificent in one of his more colourful uniforms, Mamma looking elegant like Lady Hertford for instance or Maria Fitzherbert; and herself between them— the beloved daughter. It was an old dream and a foolish one because all dreams were foolish if there wasn't a hope of their coming true.

The Duchess was scarcely elegant. She was happier at Oatlands with all the animals than chaperoning her niece to the Opera.

'Dearest Aunt, and how are the darling dogs and are they not going to miss you?' she demanded.

The Duchess settled down happily to give her an account of the illnesses and cleverness of her pets and Charlotte listened with interest so that the Duchess was pleased and suggested that as soon as it could be arranged she must come to Oatlands for a rest. That was satisfactory because anything was preferable to the boredom of Windsor or the monotony of Warwick House.

Lady de Clifford was flustered and nervous as usual. She really was becoming more and more stupid, thought Charlotte. She was ready to accompany them to the opera with Colonel Bloomfield who as a clever 'cellist was particularly interested in music.

It was exciting to be going out into the world and Charlotte chattered lightheartedly to the Duchess as they rode through the streets and was delighted when she was recognized.

'It's Charlotte!' cried the people, and there was a special cheer for her after Lord Byron's poem. She was good Princess Charlotte as opposed to the wicked Regent. Sometimes she was pleased about that, sometimes sorry; it was all part of her mixed feelings for her father. She could not really decide how she felt about him when sometimes she was saddened by his unpopularity, at others elated by it.

At the opera house she was received with ceremony and conducted to her box.

How they cheered as she stepped into it. She came to the front, bowing and smiling and waving in an exuberant if not exactly a regal manner. The people did not mind. She was young and fresh and so obviously pleased to be among them.

'God bless the Princess Charlotte!' they called. And there were cries of 'Down with the Prince Regent.'

Lady de Clifford was in a fever of anxiety, but the Duchess was as calm as ever; and Colonel Bloomfield decided that it was his duty to report to the Regent how she had been applauded, for fear he should hear through some other source.

During the intervals people looked up at her box and she could not resist waving to them. There was excitement throughout the opera house, and it was clear that the audience was delighted to have the Princess among them and to see her in a new light—no longer a girl but a young woman destined to be their queen.

When she left they crowded round her carriage cheering her; she waved and smiled and even threw kisses.

'Princess Charlotte!' murmured Lady de Clifford in embarrassment, and was certain that Colonel Bloomfield would report to the Prince that she had no control over her charge.

She was right. He did.

Thus the Prince learned that Lady de Clifford was nervous with the Princess and had no control over her; that she was constantly in the company of that forthright and most forceful young woman Miss Margaret Mercer Elphinstone who was a fervent Whig and determined that Princess Charlotte should be the same.

As a result the Regent paid an unexpected call at Warwick House.

There was a flutter of excitement throughout the Princess's establishment. Lady de Clifford was visibly trembling; she ran into the room where Louisa and Mrs. Gagarin were mending

one of the Princess's gowns and asked if they had any idea why
His Royal Highness should have called.

They were astonished. Surely Lady de Clifford should have
more idea than they. But had the Princess any notion that her
father was coming? None that she had imparted to them, said
Louisa.

She ran out distractedly.

'Dear me,' said Louisa, 'I do fear the task really is becoming
too much for her ladyship.'

'Charlotte has no respect for her,' said Mrs. Gagarin sadly.
'It is time she went.'

'But for whom would Charlotte have respect? I am not sure
that Miss Elphinstone is good for her.'

'You're jealous, Louisa,' said Mrs. Gagarin. 'Perhaps we
both are. She's like our very own child, I suppose . . . and we
don't like to see others taking too much of her attention. I
hope and pray I live to see her happily married.'

'Don't talk like that,' said Louisa sharply. She could not
imagine the apartments without Mrs. Gagarin and she was
angry with her when she talked as though her end was not
far off. Louisa could not bear the thought of change. She
wanted to go on with Charlotte their own dear tomboy forever.

Meanwhile the Prince had summoned his daughter to his
presence.

He looked at her coldly.

'I have come to tell you,' he said, 'that you are to leave for
Windsor without delay.'

'W . . . Windsor,' she stammered, and he frowned. After all
the teachers she had had she had never completely mastered
that unbecoming hesitation in her speech. It was most trying.

'I said Windsor,' he repeated, enunciating very clearly.

'I hate W . . . Windsor.' There! She had been so determined not to stutter. That was why she had repeated the
name of the hateful place; and she had done it again.

'Nonsense,' said the Prince. 'How can you hate Windsor?'
And as he spoke he knew perfectly well why she hated Windsor. He had always hated it himself.

'It's cold and draughty and . . . dull, and the old . . .' She
stopped in time. 'I want to stay here,' she added boldly.

'That is unfortunate,' he retorted coldly, 'since you are
going to Windsor. Pray, let us have no more childish scenes.
You will leave tomorrow. And there is one friendship you
have made which shall be discontinued, I refer to this unseemly familiarity with Miss Elphinstone.'

'M . . . Mercer,' she cried.

'I said Miss Elphinstone. I wish all contact with her to cease.'

'That's not p . . . possible.'

'Charlotte, pray don't be absurd. I shall expect you to see no more of this young person until I give you permission to do so.'

'B . . . but she is my greatest friend.'

'You are too old for foolishness now. You have been making yourself familiar with the people. That means that your actions are under supervision. There is no place in them for sentimental friendships.

'Friendship is a very good thing. So I have been taught.'

'I believe this woman would seek to direct you. That is something I cannot have—nor should you. You will see no more of her. Do you understand what I say?'

She hesitated; her lower lip jutting out defiantly. Then she said 'Yes, Papa.'

'Very well. I am most displeased with your conduct. That tearful scene of which so much has been made quite disgusted me. Pray try to be a little more responsible. Remember that you happen to be *my* daughter. Now you may go. Tomorrow you shall leave for Windsor and you understand me when I say that you shall make no further contact with Miss Elphinstone until I give my permission for you to do so.'

'Yes, Papa,' she said meekly.

*   *   *

Of course, she said to herself, I *understood* what he said. Does he think I am a fool who can't understand English? I understood but I didn't promise. And in any case if I *implied* I promised, promises given in such circumstances are not binding.

To prove to herself that she was not going to be dictated to by him she took out a piece of paper and picked up a pen to write to her dearest Mercer to tell her that she was to leave for Windsor the next day and that the 'P.R.' had instructed her to cut off all communication with her dearest Mercer.

'He thought I promised but I did not. And I should never promise such a thing, my best of friends. I would die rather than give you up, as you well know.'

Mercer's response was to send her a bracelet which was engraved with their names.

Charlotte wept over it when she received it and declared that it would always be a great joy to her. She needed some solace because by that time she was at Windsor, and what was there to do at Windsor but attend dreary Drawing Rooms presided over by the Queen who was becoming more and more stern with her granddaughter and was even more critical than the Prince Regent; and when she rode out it was usually with one of the Old Girls.

What a life! Her visits to her mother were less frequent and the Princess of Wales was growing restive. She was hinting that she would not much longer endure the situation and was giving out dark hints as to what she would do.

Then Mrs. Udney brought her a note which had come through the Princess Caroline. It was from Captain Hesse who was coming to Windsor when he hoped he would have the pleasure of seeing the Princess Charlotte. Charlotte was delighted and after that she often contrived to give the grooms the slip and meet Captain Hesse in the forest.

*   *   *

One must make the most of dull old Windsor. What was there to do but ride and practise dancing and write to Mercer telling her how she longed for her company? George Fitz-clarence had arrived and what fun it was to divide her smiles between the two young men.

The aunts were shocked.

'I do declare, Charlotte,' said Aunt Mary, who had once been the prettiest of the Old Girls and still was, though faded, 'that you are a regular *flirt*.'

Poor Aunt Mary who hoped to marry her cousin the Duke of Gloucester. Charlotte wondered why they didn't because surely the Prince Regent would put no obstacles in their way. It was only poor mad Grandpapa who had done that—and of course the Begum. That wicked old woman did not wish her daughters to marry because she did not want them to have any independence and wanted to keep them dancing attendance on her. But if Mary and Gloucester were ever going to marry they should do so now before it was too late. Perhaps the Regent would give his consent if they asked it, but it might be that having waited so long they had lost the urge to marry.

Poor old things! thought Charlotte. When one was approaching the charming age of seventeen one could be sorry for these old people—particularly such as Aunt Mary who had never lived any life but one in subservience to the old Begum. So what did she know of flirts? Though, considered Charlotte, I believe I am inclined to be one. She would write and tell Mercer. Dear Mercer, who meant more to her than anyone.

During that stay at Windsor when she was not reading Mercer's letters smuggled in to her very often by the services of Mrs. Udney, or writing her own to be smuggled out by the same ready hand, when she was not writing to Captain Hesse —and how much more familiar she could be on paper than in conversation when they were so spied upon (and in any case she had inherited her father's gift for letter-writing and his indiscretion in the art, because after all it was indiscretion which made a correspondence exciting)—she became aware of a certain tension in the atmosphere. Poor old Lady de Clifford seemed to have become more scatter-brained than ever; Mrs. Gagarin was remote and Charlotte feared she was sometimes in pain, a fact which disturbed her greatly; Louisa was worried about Mrs. Gagarin; and there was something secretive about the aunts. As for the Queen, she was more tight-lipped than ever, more disapproving, and attendances on her were becoming intolerable.

Something was about to happen, thought Charlotte.

One day when she came in from riding in the forest Mrs. Udney said: 'Talk about scenes. We've had some excitement while you've been out. Who do you think called? None other than the Princess of Wales. And what do you think? Her Majesty refused to receive her. Of course it's not the first time. The Princess was furious, shook her fist at our stone walls as she got back into her carriage and talked a lot of German, but I did understand her to say that she was not going to allow things to remain as they were. She was going to see her daughter when she wished. She was not going to be kept away and she had *friends* to help her.'

'I should like to have seen her.'

'Trouble's brewing,' said Mrs. Udney and the sparkle in her eye proved that she was one who felt that to be rather a desirable state of affairs.

*   *   *

One could not keep the girl at Windsor indefinitely, ruminated the Regent. However troublesome, she had to be brought back. She would be seventeen at the beginning of the new year and that was but a year from her coming of age.

It had been more comfortable when she was a child.

His advisers had said that she must be seen now and then; she must begin to take a part in public affairs. 'So, we shall have to bring her back to be a plague and torment, I suppose,' he had remarked to his Lord Chancellor, Lord Eldon. 'We must bring her back and put her on show.'

Lord Eldon, who was well aware that the Princess would soon have powerful advisers in parliamentary circles and that they would be opponents of his, reluctantly agreed.

'My sisters can be her chaperons,' said the Prince. 'I think they will be pleased to come out a little themselves, poor souls. They lead very dull lives.'

So it was agreed that Augusta, Elizabeth and Mary should, with the Princess Charlotte, attend the opening of Parliament.

The Regent was not looking forward to the occasion as his valet prepared him for it. It was tiresome because this was an occasion which he should have enjoyed. Position and power still excited him. He could have been content to be the centre of some splendid scene, magnificently apparelled—the benign and charming Regent—King in all but name. This is how he had pictured it in the days of his youth when he had assuredly not thought of a Regency but of reigning in his own right. After all he had been reared for that purpose. He had always known from those early days when he strutted about the nursery that he was to be a king one day. He had not foreseen the tragic illness of his father. Poor old man, living out his clouded existence in the hands of keepers . . . for that was what it amounted to, almost totally blind now and struggling to grope a way out of his madness. What a fate to overtake a man—and a king at that!

The Regent was sorry the relationship had not been more amicable between them; but he had made occasional attempts and the old man had always been a sore trial. Moreover, parents and their children were rarely good friends in this family—in fact often open enemies. And this brought him back to his own tiresome Charlotte. Why could not the girl behave with decorum? Why did she have to be such a bouncing indiscreet hoyden? The answer was simple. Because she was That Woman's daughter and although she might have inherited some admirable qualities from the paternal side of the family no one could deny the fact that she was her mother's child.

Charlotte must be kept in her place which she must understand that for another year or so was not an important one. Until she was of age she must be treated as a minor; and she must not forget—for God knows he never did—that the much-longed-for divorce was not an impossibility and that if by some heaven-sent opportunity he was able to achieve it, he would marry with all speed, get a son and then young Charlotte would be of no more importance than one of his sisters whom she seemed to despise.

But Charlotte had more spirit than his sisters. She was, after all, his daughter. And they had been brought up without hopes whereas it seemed very likely to everyone that Charlotte would one day be a queen.

Trying creature! Oh, what an unhappy day when he had married her mother! It all came back to that odious, revolting, vulgar, ill-smelling creature who was known as the Princess of Wales.

Well, now to the opening of Parliament and very splendid he looked in the uniform of a Field Marshal. He himself had designed the cocked hat and had he still been on terms of friendship with Brummell he would have challenged him to produce a better.

Surely they must applaud such a figure. He was aware of the interest and admiration in everyone's eyes. Whatever they said of him they must admit that he graced an occasion. He might be a little portly but a lean man would not have been so impressive.

The horses were restive but how beautiful—all matching in colour. A few people had gathered to see him get into his coach but they stood in silence, which was of course preferable to vulgar insults—but he would have preferred a little enthusiasm.

The coachman whipped up those beautiful light-coloured horses and as they started off he was remembering the old days when he was young and how the people had stopped his carriage to cheer him.

He wondered whether Maria would see him today and if so what she would think. Happy days when he had called on her and it had been like coming home. Home was something he had missed in life. Carlton House and the Pavilion might be the most splendid residences in the country but they were scarcely homes. If only Maria . . . but that was an old story. Maria had failed him. He had almost lost the crown for her sake and she had left him all because of his friendship with Isabella—that pure friendship which was one of the mind. And she had taken Minney with her—Minney, his gift to her. And Minney had loved her Prinney.

There were tears in his eyes and he hated the woman who, he assured himself, had ruined his life because he blamed Caroline for everything, even Maria's desertion. He was ashamed of the German Princess to whom they had married him. That he, the most fastidious and elegant of princes, should have been given that drab was cruelly incongruous. And the fact was that whenever he saw Charlotte he was reminded of her. She might have his looks but she never failed to recall her mother to his mind.

Suddenly he was thrown forward. The coachman, still clutching the reins, had been thrown to the ground and the coach swayed dangerously for some seconds before righting itself.

The crowds were beginning to gather. The Prince, realizing that he was unhurt, looked through the window and called to those who were helping the coachman to his feet: 'Is he hurt?'

'No, Your Highness,' the coachman answered for himself. 'It was the post, Sir. We struck it and it all but overturned us.' He was still clutching the reins which had no doubt prevented the horses from bolting.

The unsavoury crowd, the curious eyes, he hated it all. So different from the old days. He wanted to give immediate orders to drive on but that consideration for his servants for which he was noted and which endeared them to him no matter how unpopular he might be outside his own household, was second nature to him.

'Are you fit to go on or would you like another driver to take over?'

The coachman's eyes were a little reproachful. 'I'm all right, Your Highness. It wasn't what you'd call a spill. Just that old post, Sir.'

'Then let us go.'

So the coachman got on to the box and they were off; the entire incident had only taken up five minutes.

Still, it had shaken him a little, not the accident of course but the sullen looks of the people. They no longer liked him. They would be glad when it was Charlotte's turn. How had the change come about and what was the precise reason? Why were monarchs so popular in their youth and why did that popularity almost inevitably wane as they grew older?

Walking between the peers, the crown carried before him on its cushion, he felt better; he would deliver his speech effortlessly and in his beautifully modulated voice. His manner would remind them that they could always rely on him to grace an occasion.

Charlotte watched him with those feelings to which she was now accustomed. She hoped that when the time came for her to perform a similar duty she would do so with the same elegant panache. She was proud to be his daughter and at the same time she had to fight those waves of resentment. She was fiercely proud of him and yet ashamed; she loved him and she hated him.

If he would only show that he cared a little for her, it might be so different; but often it seemed that he enjoyed humiliating her. Even on this occasion he had commanded that on their way from the Speaker's House she must walk *behind* the Old Girls. She, the heir-presumptive to the throne, to walk behind old women who were not and never could be of any significance. It was done surely to humiliate her, to remind her that as yet he considered her of no importance.

Very well, she would show him that *she* was the one the people liked. She would do everything she possibly could to win their cheers when they rode back to Carlton House.

She could have wept when she heard him reading the speech. It was so beautiful. Surely they must admire him. But then of course he had behaved so badly to poor Mamma and the cartoons were becoming more and more scurrilous although, having promised Mercer, she did not look at them . . . well, only a quick glance when Mrs. Udney brought them in or her mother sent them, not what one could call a real look.

It was fun riding through the streets. What a lot of people there were about!

'God bless the good Princess Charlotte.'

Good? Well, perhaps that was a bit too much. But it was pleasant, particularly as, when the Regent's magnificent carriage drove by, they were silent. She had heard that when he left his coach outside the Hertfords' house it had been pelted with mud and rotten eggs. Who was he to tell her how to live when he lived so scandalously himself? All the same he was the most *exciting* man in the world and if only he would let her into his confidence just a little, if only he would let her see that he was a loving father . . .

But how her thoughts ran on!

'God bless Charlotte. Our queen to be. And may it not be long.'

How shocking, and yet in a way pleasant because it would show him that if he did not appreciate his daughter they did.

Here they were at Carlton House, through the vestibule, to marvel at what Horace Walpole had called 'its august simplicity' and into the music room with the lovely view of the garden's winding paths.

The Prince Regent was in a rage. First the accident had

upset him and then his reception by the crowds. He had been fully aware of the disloyal looks directed at him and the cheers which had come his daughter's way.

He took off that wonderful cocked hat and threw it on to a chair. The poor Old Girls looked terrified. Charlotte was expectant.

'That farce is over, thank God. I should be glad to retire to the country and have done with these boring ceremonies. I am plagued on all sides.' He looked at Charlotte and the tears came into his eyes. She had a mad impulse to throw herself into his arms and cry: 'Papa, don't let us be a plague to each other. Let us love each other. It is what I've always wanted.' But how could she do such a thing? He would think she had inherited poor Grandpapa's madness and despise her more than ever. He strode past her. 'And you . . .' he turned back to glare at Charlotte, 'aggravate me. I know of course who encourages you in this. Do not think I do not understand. Of course I know. It is that woman . . . your mother. Ever since I married her there has been trouble. It was the greatest mistake of my life. That woman . . . that loathsome woman . . .'

Poor Aunt Mary shivered and Aunt Augusta uttered a little cry of protest but he dismissed them with a look. He was weary of pretence. He was going to let this wayward daughter of his know what a mother she had, that the source of all his troubles came from her.

He seemed to lose all control. 'She is vulgar; she is immoral. Let us not pretend. We know the kind of life she leads. We know she keeps that gross creature with her . . . and why. She says he is the son of some low woman . . . but that is not so. He is her son and the father is Smith, Manby, Lawrence . . . what does it matter which?'

Charlotte said in a high excited voice: 'It was proved this was not so.'

He turned on her in anger. 'Indeed it was not. It was simply not proved that it was so . . . which is a very different matter. By God, one day I'll have the proof I need and when I have it I'll be rid of her.'

Charlotte felt that irresistible urge to protect her mother. It was always so. When in the presence of one she always felt she owed her allegiance to the other. 'She is my mother . . .' she began.

But he would not let her speak. He cried: 'You shall see all the papers. You will have no doubt then. Have you ever heard of the Delicate Investigation?'

'Y . . . yes, I've heard of it.'

'And very *in*delicate were the facts revealed. If you feel you
must speak for *her* there is only one thing to be done. You
must read the papers. And you shall. You shall know what sort
of woman you have for a mother. No doubt we know only half
the truth but what we do know is reason for divorce and if it
were not for my accursed enemies . . .'

Tears of self-pity filled his eyes; the Old Girls stood by
shocked, unable to speak. In front of Charlotte! Mary was
thinking; but Charlotte herself put an end to the scene. All
ceremony forgotten, she ran from the room. She imperiously
summoned Lady de Clifford and demanded that she be taken
to Warwick House without delay.

She heard the Prince's ejaculation as she ran: 'By God, she
grows more like her mother every day.'

Back at Warwick House she started to shiver. Lady de
Clifford was flustered. She must be put to bed. The doctors
must be sent for. What was this mysterious 'attack'?

Charlotte lay thinking of them both—hating each other,
producing her. They had hated each other even then. She had
been born simply because there was a need—in his opinion a
revolting need—to produce an heir.

And I am that, she thought.

And then: I hate him. He is cruel. I must help her because
he is going to try and rid himself of her.

She believed in that moment that it was to her mother that
she owed her allegiance; and today it had become clear to her
that she could not be the friend of both of them.

In Carlton House the Prince had grown a little calmer.

He said: 'Charlotte's manners are disgraceful. What is
Lady de Clifford thinking of? She is no use at all. As for Charlotte, she is no longer so young. It is time I found a husband
for her.'

*   *   *

The Prince paced up and down his bedroom in Carlton
House. There was no doubt that he would be happier in his
mind if Charlotte were married. That would be one burden
less. Let a husband be responsible for the girl. And if it were a
husband who could take her out of England, so much the
better. He'd have his brothers' support for such a plan. They
often hinted that it was a sorry state of affairs when England's
heir was a girl and the daughter of such a mother. If he could
rid himself of her and marry and produce a son what a happy
solution that would be! But his brothers would doubtless like
to see him tied to that woman and Charlotte out of the way

and one of them take the crown. Fred had no children and never would have. And the others—there was not one of them who was respectably married. They had never attempted to make suitable marriages; that burden had fallen on him. Suitable! My God! he thought.

But he had been over that many times.

The outlook was a little brighter than usual. Napoleon was bitterly engaged in his campaign against Russia and from the accounts that were coming in all was not going well for him. Wellington was scoring successes in Spain. If things were as bad as rumour declared this could well be the beginning of the end for Napoleon. The Regent regretted as he had so many times that he was not able to prove himself a military hero. Reflected glory was the next best thing and he was proud of Wellington, as he had been of Nelson.

Now what he must do was to find a husband for Charlotte and he believed he knew the ideal suitor. He had hinted to the Dutch Stadholder William VI that a match between the Stadholder's son William, Hereditary Prince of Orange, and his own daughter Charlotte might be desirable.

The Dutch were all in favour and a Protestant match would be bound to have the approval of the English. Young William had distinguished himself on the field, had been educated at Oxford—for the possibility of such a match was not a new one—and he was in all ways ideally suited.

Not least of his attractions in the mind of the Regent was the fact that if she married him Charlotte would be expected to reside in Holland.

And that, thought the Regent, would be one of them out of the way. Caroline might even wish to live in Holland to be near her daughter; and if she were away from England, Heaven alone knew what indiscretions she might be capable of.

It was an excellent scheme; and the brothers would be in favour for they would feel that once the Princess was settled out of the country it might follow that the crown would pass to the King's other sons should by some unfortunate accident the Regent be no more.

The Regent did not see why some proposals should not be put to the Stadholder.

*   *   *

The Queen was not insensible to the fact of Charlotte's growing maturity.

'There are faults in her household,' she said to her daughter

Mary. 'That woman de Clifford seems to me a poor helpless creature.'

'There is no doubt of it, Mamma,' replied Mary. 'She hates Windsor and is always complaining of the cold. She says that her rheumatism grows worse every time she is there.'

'I am sure,' said the Queen, 'that she is responsible for Charlotte's dislike of the place. She has *taught* her to dislike it. Most reprehensible.'

'Indeed, yes, Mamma. I have even heard rumours that she is so lax as to allow Charlotte all kinds of undesirable liberties.'

'And with such a mother one must be very careful of the girl. What undesirable liberties, pray?'

'Well, Mamma, I hesitate to mention it, but Charlotte is inclined to flirt.'

The Queen looked intensely shocked.

'Yes, Mamma. I have even seen her myself. With people like George Fitzclarence and young Captain Hesse.'

'Both the results of indiscretions themselves! Oh dear, I cannot understand why your brothers behave as they do.'

'And with William . . .' Mary flushed a little. 'With the Duke of Gloucester.'

'Oh!' The Queen spoke sharply. She knew of Mary's penchant for her cousin. There was some suggestion that they wanted to marry. Ridiculous! thought the Queen. As for Mary she was decidedly piqued. Charlotte *was* a flirt and she behaved towards many in a manner which Mary could only call arch. Her uncles for instance—so perhaps that was why she behaved in that manner to William. But it had wounded her because of that very special understanding and the fact that they hoped to be allowed to marry one day. And to see that young girl—scarcely out of the nursery—attempting to flirt with William, was well . . . it had shaken her; and for that reason, perhaps, she was now speaking of her in this way to the Queen.

'Charlotte has inherited so much from That Woman,' said the Queen, and her mouth shut like a trap. After a second she opened it and continued: 'It cannot be allowed to go on. Something will have to be done. I shall speak to George. As her father he will have to order some changes in her household I think. And what about that particular friendship of Charlotte's? I did not care for that in the least.'

'I understand it still goes on, Mamma, although Charlotte has had her warning and promised, so I believe, not to communicate with the woman. But she receives letters and presents from her and they write regularly.'

'It is a most disturbing state of affairs and it must be stopped. I consider Lady de Clifford largely to blame. The woman is useless. It would be much better for everyone concerned—and not least my granddaughter—if I chose a new household for her.'

'I am sure that is so, Mamma.'

The Queen looked surprised that there should be any question of it.

'My snuffbox, Mary,' she said. 'Oh dear, how trying family affairs can be.'

* * *

'Oh dear,' sighed Lady de Clifford to her daughter Lady Albemarle, 'something is wrong . . . very, very wrong, I fear. The Queen was very cool to me and the Prince Regent looked at me as if I simply did not exist. There is trouble brewing.'

'You should resign, Mamma. If you don't you will go mad.'

'My dear, I cannot tell you what I suffer. Charlotte is becoming more and more difficult. It is not that she means to. Her nature has always been a sweet one—but she terrifies me. I can never be sure what she is going to do next. And do you know she has been sending *notes* to that Captain Hesse . . . and receiving them from him. And although the Prince has strictly forbidden her to have any communication with Mercer Elphinstone she writes to her regularly.'

'Mamma, you should not allow it.'

Lady de Clifford raised her hands to the ceiling. 'But how can I stop Charlotte doing what she intends to? Surely you know that's impossible. Of course if she has really been sending notes to that man . . . and if the Prince should hear of it . . .' Lady de Clifford put a trembling hand to her lips. 'Do you suppose he *has* heard of it?'

'It is possible, Mamma. After all you are sure to be surrounded by spies.'

'If I thought he knew . . . It will be the end. He will never trust me again. How could she? And to promise him that she would not communicate with Mercer and then to do so . . . but worst of all is sending notes to that man. Oh dear, I cannot tell you . . . My dear, you have no idea. And her petticoats are far too short. She is constantly showing her drawers.'

Lady Albemarle said soothingly: 'Mamma, I know what I should do if I were you.'

'What is that?'

'Resign before you get your marching orders.'

Lady de Clifford clasped her hands together and raised her

eyes to the ceiling; her turban had slipped slightly to one side of her head; she said in a trembling voice: 'Oh, the peace of being free! And yet . . . and yet. I have been with her so long. She is like my own child . . . and in spite of everything she is so lovable.'

'Mamma,' went on Lady Albemarle sternly, 'offer your resignation . . . now. Don't wait.'

*   *   *

Lady de Clifford watched Charlotte tenderly. How would she feel when the Princess was no longer in her charge? What an emptiness there would be! Dear, dear Charlotte, so wayward and yet so lovable!

'My dear Princess Charlotte,' she began timidly, 'I hope and trust that you have not been seeing too much of Captain Hesse.'

'It is always good to hope, they say,' retorted Charlotte, 'and greatly comforting to trust.'

Oh dear, she was in one of her perverse moods, thought Lady de Clifford, but went on: 'Because it is not seemly that a princess in your position should be talked about.'

'Who is talking about me?'

'There are always those to talk about a princess.'

'But who, who, who? You implied that someone was talking about me. I want to know who it is.'

'I meant that people will talk.'

'You hinted that they *were* talking. So it is merely guess work on your part. Pray remember that I do not wish to be told what I must and must not do.'

'As your governess . . .'

'Governess,' cried the Princess, 'I am too old for governesses. Whoever heard of a g . . . girl . . . a woman of seventeen . . . or nearly . . . with a governess!'

'It is not unusual. People in your position . . .'

'I am thinking of myself, my lady, and I say that I am too old to be told do this and do that by some g . . . governess.'

'You mean that you no longer desire me to remain in your service?'

'I mean that I am too old to have a governess.'

'So you want me to go?'

'I did not say that. I said I am too old for governesses, and moreover, I will not have one.'

'But Your Highness can only be referring to me. I am afraid you no longer have any confidence in me. I am afraid that you . . .'

There was a high colour in the Princess's cheeks.

'Lady de Clifford,' she said haughtily, 'you are too much afraid.'

And with that she walked out of the room.

It is the end, thought Lady de Clifford. I have no alterna·tive now but to resign.

*   *   *

When Charlotte paid her weekly visit to her mother at the latter's newly acquired residence Connaught House, which was not far from Kensington Palace, Caroline was eager to know what was going on at Warwick House. She had heard rumours, she said, and they concerned Madam de Clifford.

'Oh, yes,' declared Charlotte, 'she is acting very strangely. She is more absentminded than ever and almost put snuff into the tea pot.'

This made Caroline shriek with laughter and as usual Charlotte joined in. Her mother made her feel witty and clever which was exactly the opposite effect her father had on her. It was certainly rather pleasant.

'She goes about muttering to herself and shaking her head. Do you know, Mamma, I think she is going to resign. She has hinted it. Perhaps she has already spoken to my father . . . or to the Queen or the Old Girls.'

'And de old Begum I don't doubt is looking round for someone to take her place.'

'I think I am old enough to have done with governesses,' said Charlotte. 'In fact I told Lady de Clifford so. She seemed to take it as a slight on her but it wasn't. It isn't just one governess I don't want—it's any governess.'

'And quite right too, my angel. You're no longer a baby. Though they would like to keep you one forever I don't doubt. They'll keep you in the nursery for as long as they can. And why? Because the people like you too much, that's why. It was the same with me. When I first came here the people used to cheer me. They were silent when he rode by, but you should have heard the cheers for me, and they hate him more every day. You should see the latest crop of papers. I've saved them for you . . .'

'I don't think I'll look at them . . . now, Mamma.' Mercer's stern face rose before her. Just a quick look perhaps, she pleaded with that reproachful image. After all as the future Queen of England I should know what's going on. But most important was to stand firm and refuse to have another gover·ness. There was no point in de Clifford's going if she was to be replaced. She might have someone worse. At least she could keep her ladyship in order. She said quickly: 'I'm afraid they are already choosing Lady de Clifford's successor.'

'My darling, you must stand firm. You must say No, no, no! No more governesses. You must say: I'm seventeen years old. Why, most girls are married at that age. Governesses! Poof! You should be enjoying life not listening to governesses.'

'I know, Mamma, but when they get on to me . . . it's not always easy.'

Caroline's eyes narrowed and she burst into sudden wild laughter.

'Well, my pet, so I thought, so I have asked two very clever gentlemen to call on me today. They will come . . . by accident of course . . . at the precise time that you are visiting me. And no one is responsible for that if it is an accident. And poor old de Clifford dozing away in her arm chair is not going to know that you have seen them until the interview is over.'

'What gentlemen are these, Mamma?' asked Charlotte thinking of that occasion when her mother had shut her into the bedroom with Captain Hesse and all the occasions when he had called 'by accident' during her visits.

Caroline lifted her finger archly. 'Oh, very serious gentlemen. You will see.' She ran to the window and looked out. 'We shall hear their carriages at any moment. They are *my* friends, my love; and I tell them that no one is my friend unless they are my daughter's friends as well.'

'Mamma, please tell me who these gentlemen are so that I shall know something of them before they arrive.'

Caroline drew her daughter's arm through hers and they sat down on a couch together.

'First there is old Brougham,' she said. 'A politician and a lawyer. He is going to fight for me. He is going to see that I get my rights and he is a very clever man. He's reckoned to be the best barrister of the day. He's defending Leigh Hunt and I hope he gets him off. I hope it indeed. Have you seen what he said about your dear Papa?'

'N . . . no,' said Charlotte.

'Ah, you must read it. I have it here. I'd like to frame it. The *Morning Post* printed a poem about your respected Papa calling him an Adonis and glory of his people and goodness knows what. Then Leigh Hunt writes this . . . Here. I'll read it for you. "This Adonis in loveliness is a corpulent man of fifty." I'll swear he liked that. If ever you want to annoy your father call him fat. He hates the word. He thinks if no one uses it it just is not. So he'll love this. Corpulent man of fifty.

And him behaving like a young man of twenty-one! "This delightful, blissful, wise, honourable, virtuous, true and immortal Prince is a violator of his word, a libertine over head and ears in disgrace, despiser of domestic ties, the companion of gamblers and demireps, a man who has just closed half a century without one single claim on the gratitude of his country or the respect of posterity." There's your Papa for you.'

'They actually wrote that about the P . . . Prince Regent!'

'They did, my pet, and are being prosecuted for Libel and my Brougham is going to get them off.'

'Papa will never permit it.'

'There is one thing that is of more importance than he is, my pet, and that is the law. Mr. Brougham knows a great deal about the law—far more than Adonis does. And then there is my dear Sam Whitbread. He's a Member of Parliament and a very clever gentleman and he is my friend. He has sworn to stand by me and to help me to my rights. So you see, my sweet child, we are not alone, you and I. Nobody is going to trample on us. We have protectors. Listen! Do I hear carriage wheels?'

Charlotte said that she did. And in a very short time Mr. Brougham was ushered into the room to be followed a little later by Samuel Whitbread; and after treating her with the utmost respect as though she were not only a Princess but an adult, they began to talk of her rights and the need for her to have an establishment of her own.

There was nothing she wanted so much. She wanted freedom from restraint; but she felt very uneasy when she wondered what her father would say if he could see her here with these people who had openly declared themselves to be his enemies.

The Battle for Miss Knight

MRS. GAGARIN lay in bed gazing sadly at Charlotte who was seated beside her, an expression of great sadness in her eyes. Dear Gagy, thought Charlotte, it was clear that she was growing more and more wan every day. Louisa had told her sadly that she did not think she would be with them this time next year.

'You must take more care,' said Charlotte severely.

Mrs. Gagarin smiled and held out her hand. 'It's my dearest Highness I'm concerned about.'

'You were always foolish about me. I'm old enough now to take care of myself. You know there is talk of Cliffy's resigning.'

'Yes. Louisa told me. And then. . . ?'

'And then I shall be free. I'll never have another governess. I'm quite determined.' Charlotte hesitated. Better not to mention those important men she had met at her mother's house. Poor Gagy would start to worry if she did; and that would be no good for her in her present state.

Louisa Lewis who was hovering near the bed said: 'Don't tire yourself. You should be sleeping.'

'So you should,' added Charlotte, 'and I am keeping you awake. Oh, darling Gagy, do get well.' She knelt by the bed and taking Mrs. Gagarin's hand kissed it fervently. Louisa laid a hand on her shoulder and Charlotte rose and leaning over gently kissed Mrs. Gagarin's forehead. Then she tiptoed away with Louisa into the adjoining room.

'Is she dying, Louisa?' she asked.

'Fading away,' replied Louisa. 'But she'll be with us a little longer.'

'I used to think she would always be there. When I became

queen I was going to give her a house of her own—and you were to share it, Louisa.'

'I know, my dearest, but things don't always work out as we plan. There are changes.'

'Changes,' agreed Charlotte. 'Changes everywhere. Where is Mrs. Udney? I have not seen her for days.'

Louisa pressed her lips tightly together. 'So,' said Charlotte, 'she has gone. I suppose this is my grandmother's doing. Louisa, I am afraid that she will try to force another governess on me. I won't have it. I shall stand firm.'

Louisa was silent, wondering how Charlotte would successfully oppose such forces as the Queen and the Prince Regent. There was certainly a new determination about the Princess. She was growing up and she had always known that it was very likely that one day she would be Queen.

'I suppose changes come about all the time,' she mused. 'It makes one a little sad. Mrs. Udney . . . gone. I'm sure she has. But they didn't tell me. They should have told me. She was of *my* household. Actually I'm not sure whether I'm glad or sorry. I didn't really like her but she made life exciting in a way with all the gossip and the cartoons and things like that. And now she has gone without saying goodbye. And my mother says I'm too old to have a governess, and there are people like Brougham and Whitbread who will help me to get my independence and what is due to me. Louisa, I'll tell you something: Mercer is coming to see me.'

'But your father forbade her to.'

'I know, but I am growing up and I really don't see why my friends should be chosen for me.'

'Oh, my dearest, take care.'

'That is exactly what I intend to do . . . take care that I am no longer treated as a child.'

* * *

'Mercer!' The friends embraced. 'How wonderful to see you! Your letters have been *such* a comfort—and how brave of you to come here.'

Mercer shrugged aside the compliment. 'I don't think the Regent would be very harsh on us if he knew. He is kind at heart and I expect he is sometimes sorry that he stopped our meetings.'

Charlotte glowed with pleasure as she always did when his virtues were referred to. 'He is,' she agreed warmly. 'He really is kind at heart.'

'Now,' said Mercer practically, 'it is certain that Lady de

Clifford is going. She has had her congé and although I daresay she is hoping you'll make a scene and beg her to stay,
in certain quarters it has been decided that the matter is
settled.'

'How clever of you to find out!'

'I have heard it from several sources and that they are
thinking of appointing the Duchess of Leeds to take her place
as your governess.'

'The Duchess of Leeds!'

'She is a meek creature and would give you little trouble.'

'But as governess! I have sworn I'll never have another.'

'They are going to insist on it.'

'They? You mean the Queen. I suppose *she* is behind this.'

'Your only chance would be to appeal to your father.'

'Of course. I'll write to him. You'll help me to compose a
letter, Mercer?'

Mercer inclined her head like a wise mandarin. That was
in fact what she had intended to suggest.

Mercer said: 'A letter such as this is of the utmost importance. Your affairs are, after all, the concern of the State. A
copy of this should be sent to Lord Liverpool.'

'Lord Liverpool!'

'Certainly. He's the Prime Minister, is he not?'

*　　*　　*

For comfort Lady de Clifford took a larger pinch of snuff
than usual. After all these years, she was thinking, to be dismissed more or less, for that was what in her heart she felt it to
be. All the years I have looked after the Princess . . . and then
to be thrust aside.

Seeing her governess so dejected, Charlotte tried to cheer
her and smiled at her brightly.

'My dear Princess Charlotte, it does me so much good to see
you,' sighed Lady de Clifford. 'A privilege I fear I shall soon
have to do without.'

Charlotte nodded with an almost ready resignation.

'Of course,' went on Lady de Clifford, 'it is a great wrench
for me.'

'These separations are inevitable.'

'And very sad.'

Charlotte could not honestly concede that. 'You'll be happier without me,' she consoled. 'Think of the trial I was to
you. All the wicked things I did.'

'One expects waywardness from children.'

'All my unsuitable friendships,' continued Charlotte. 'My

lack of dignity. It may well be what is known as a happy release.'

Lady de Clifford was shocked. She had expected a pleasantly tearful scene with Charlotte imploring her not to go. This was very different. So ungrateful! thought Lady de Clifford. And how typical of royalty!

Guessing her thoughts Charlotte tried to placate her without pretending. 'You see, Cliffy, I am too old for governesses. It is not just you. It's that I want to be free. I'm too old to have a governess and that's a fact.'

It was the right angle. Poor Cliffy brightened considerably. If the Princess were too old to have a governess there would be no slight implied by her dismissal. It was only if another was appointed that people would say she had failed.

'Your Highness is right, of course. You are no longer of an age to have a governess. If I might offer a word of advice I would say that should they try to inflict one on you you should refuse.'

'That's the sort of advice I can accept because it accords entirely with my intentions,' replied Charlotte; and wondered what poor ineffectual Cliffy would say if she knew that letters were on the way to the Regent and the Prime Minister.

* * *

That day Charlotte was visited by her Aunt Mary and she could not resist the opportunity to speak of that matter which was uppermost in her mind. Mary was shocked. Charlotte had not been officially told. How, she wanted to know, had Charlotte learned of this.

'Cliffy herself told me she'd resigned and that her resignation was accepted. I think she was hoping I would implore her to stay and was hurt when I did not.'

'You don't regret her leaving you then?'

'Dear Aunt, I am not a child any more and I have done with governesses. Nothing will induce me to accept another.'

The Princess Mary felt it her duty to inform the Queen of this conversation. Mary was enjoying a certain amount of independence, largely because of the Regent's action in settling an income on her and her sisters, but the habit of a lifetime was strong and the Queen had trained her daughters to report immediately anything that might be of the slightest interest to her. Matters which concerned the Princess Charlotte were of vital importance to her and her immediate action was to send for Charlotte and Lady de Clifford.

When they arrived at Windsor where the Queen impatiently awaited them, they were received coldly, and scarcely glancing at Lady de Clifford the Queen expressed her surprise that a governess should have felt the necessity of telling Charlotte she had resigned.

'A matter,' she added, 'which the Princess should have heard from myself or the Prince Regent.'

'But what does it matter from what source I heard it?' demanded Charlotte. 'Besides, I knew about it. Everyone is talking about it.'

'*Everyone*, Charlotte. I beg of you do not exaggerate. This is a most distressing affair and made unnecessarily so, I fear.'

'It is inevitable,' retorted Charlotte. 'I am too old for governesses.'

The Queen said: 'I am surprised that you feel so little regret at the prospect of Lady de Clifford's departure. She has been with you so many years. I'm afraid this shows a most *unfeeling* nature.'

'It doesn't,' contradicted Charlotte. 'It's merely that the time has come for me to do without a governess.'

'That,' replied the Queen shortly, 'is not a matter for you to decide. Your father will doubtless convey his decision to you in due course.'

'His decision! I hope Your Majesty does not mean that he has another governess in mind for me!'

'A father is in no way bound to explain his decision to a daughter and a daughter has only to concern herself with obedience.'

Charlotte was angry but, as always in the presence of the Queen, was unable to explain her feelings.

But those letters which she and Mercer had composed would, by now—or very nearly—be in the hands of her father and his Prime Minister. Then the trouble would begin.

* * *

The Regent read his daughter's letter with an astonishment which quickly turned to fury. So she would lay down instructions to him! She would plague him! Was it not enough that he should have to tolerate the wife an unkind fate had given him! Must he be cursed as well with a disobedient troublemaking daughter!

She would soon discover that it was not her prerogative to order him, and as soon as a new governess was appointed and her present household completely reorganized the better.

He sent for his Lord Chancellor, Lord Eldon, and gave him Charlotte's letter to read.

'Well?' demanded the Prince.

Eldon grunted. 'Her Highness will need very firm treatment,' he said.

The regent nodded. He could trust the wily lawyer to stand by him in this matter which was an important one when there were such rival factions at work. Charlotte might be a minor just now but she was an heiress to the throne—and this was doubtless the reason for her defiance for she was fully aware of her position. But 'Bags'—his nickname for Eldon—could be relied on. He was the best sort of henchman, perhaps because his roots were in trade rather than the aristocracy, and he had had to rely on his own abilities to reach his present position. His father had been 'in coal' as Newcastle-upon-Tyne whatever that meant. The Regent thought of it vaguely as 'Trade'. However he was not one to look closely into a man's origins. Old Bags was his Chancellor and his man.

'We shall go at once to Windsor to see my daughter,' announced the Prince.

'And explain to her doubtless that it is not for her to dictate to Your Highness.'

'Precisely.'

'And that Your Highness sees clearly how much she is in need of a governess?'

'It is obvious, is it not?'

'Your Highness has chosen?'

'I am considering the Duchess of Leeds.'

Eldon inclined his head. 'And the rest of her household?'

'I think a clean sweep, don't you, Bags? We have already dismissed some of them.'

'Your Highness shows your usual insight. My daughter . . .'

'Would like a place in Charlotte's household? I don't see why not.'

Bags was well satisfied.

*   *   *

Charlotte stood before her father, cowering a little in the face of his fury which he was showing with great dramatic effect—not entirely assumed for he really was annoyed with her. The Queen, snuffling from a cold (and no wonder, thought Charlotte, when one considered those horrible draughty corridors at Windsor. 'Enough to drive a man o' war,' someone had said) sat watching her granddaughter with baleful satisfaction.

Lord Eldon stood close by the Regent as though to support him. (Silly old man. As if the powerful Regent needed protecting from his daughter!)

'This letter,' the Prince was saying, 'which you have had the effrontery to send to me and worse still to my Lord Liverpool is the most foolish, ineffectual, disloyal and ridiculous document it has ever been my misfortune to read.'

'It . . . it is what I mean,' stammered Charlotte.

'What you mean! What exactly do you mean? You will have no more governesses, you say. Let me tell you, that is not a matter for you to decide. Lady de Clifford is resigning and may I say it is time, too, since she seems unable to induce you to behave with the dignity due to your rank. Your conduct shocks us all. Her Majesty . . .' The Queen nodded sharply and looked malevolently at Charlotte . . . 'My lord Chancellor . . .' Lord Eldon raised his eyes to the ceiling and Charlotte would have liked to throw something at him. 'Myself . . .' The Prince held a lace kerchief to his eyes to wipe away an imaginary tear . . . 'We are all deeply *wounded* by your thoughtless and indeed callous behaviour.'

'Papa, Your Highness, I am nearly seventeen . . .'

'We are fully aware of your age and that makes your conduct all the more to be deplored. I should have thought you were old enough to realize the pain you are causing us all . . .'

'It causes *me* pain that I should be treated as a child.'

There were shocked looks from the Queen and Eldon because she had interrupted the Prince Regent.

'It is clear,' commented the Queen grimly, 'that you have not yet finished with governesses. You are in *sore* need of correction.'

'Exactly so,' agreed the Regent. 'You are headstrong and perverse. So pray let us hear no more of your folly.'

Charlotte stamped her foot. She had to stand firm now or they would keep her shackled for years. Mercer had said she must put her case clearly. Her mother had told her to defy the Regent and the old Begum. They would have to realize that there were powerful men ready to help her.

'But,' she began. 'I . . . I will never submit to another governess. A . . . lady companion I might consider, but never a governess.'

'There you are wrong,' corrected the Regent, 'for a governess you shall have. Pray do not attempt to go against my wishes. I may tell you that I know of certain very unfortunate scenes which have passed between you and certain young

men, and for this alone I could have you shut up for life if I
felt so inclined.'

'S . . . shut up for life!'

'I am referring to Hesse and Fitzclarence and certain meetings in Windsor Forest. Utterly disgraceful. Utterly unworthy
of a princess of your rank. There has been correspondence
with people whom I have forbidden you to know. Can you
deny this?'

Charlotte was silent and the Regent went on triumphantly: 'There! You see! You show your guilt.'

'If you . . . shut me up like a prisoner, what can you expect?'

'My lord Eldon,' cried the Regent, 'what would you do if
you had such a daughter?'

'Your Highness,' replied Eldon, 'I should lock her up.'

Charlotte looked at Eldon in silence for some seconds then
turning to her father asked if she might retire.

'You may if you have come to your senses.'

She made a somewhat clumsy curtsey in his direction and
another to the Queen's and left them.

In her apartment she threw herself on to her bed and burst
into tears.

Lady de Clifford, eager to know what had taken place, came
hurrying in.

'What is it, my dearest Princess? What has happened to
upset you?'

Charlotte sat up and stared fiercely before her. 'That coal
heaver said I should be locked up. Let him wait until I'm
Queen. I'll make him wish he had *died* before he had said
that.'

'Lock you up!' tittered Lady de Clifford. 'Rather unseemly
words for a coal heaver to use when referring to the future
Queen of England.'

Charlotte pummelled her pillow as though it were the
offending Eldon's head. But she was really thinking that she
had lost her battle. She was no match for them and they had
decided to saddle her with another governess no matter what
she said.

It was now not a question of Shall I have another governess?
but Who will it be?

*   *   *

The Regent had made his decision. It was to be the Duchess
of Leeds.

'Her daughter,' said the Queen, 'will be a companion for
Charlotte. She is exactly fifteen—a little younger than my

granddaughter, but I do not care for her to make friendships with older women. They can be most unsuitable.'

The Princess Charlotte sullenly received the news.

'The Duchess of Leeds!' she cried to Louisa. 'She's a foolish woman.'

Mercer, who was calling now and then at Warwick House as secretly as could be contrived, reminded the Princess that the Duchess, while a stupid woman, was also a meek one and that could be to her advantage.

'You may well find that you can flout her as easily as you did Lady de Clifford. I am sure she will have no spirit whatsoever. She is certainly stupid—and a Tory. I do not think though that we need fear a great deal of trouble from her.'

'They have suggested that her daughter, that silly little Catherine Osborne, might be a suitable companion for me. That's an insult.'

'You will ignore the child, of course.'

'Of course. But what I will not have in my household, although they are trying to force her on me, is Lord Eldon's daughter. My mother says I am being treated shamefully and should not endure it. And at least if I have to accept the Leeds woman I shall refuse that Scott girl.'

Mercer thought she should certainly insist on that and to Charlotte's surprise the Regent conceded this request.

Old Bags would have to be disappointed, for this matter of Charlotte's household was arousing public interest and the people egged on by the press were taking sides—and naturally they were on Charlotte's.

She should have the Duchess of Leeds and her daughter, but he was well aware that what she needed was a sensible woman whom he could trust. He had spoken to his sisters about this and they, who had always adored him, now that he had given them some measure of independence, if it came to a tussle between him and their mother, could be relied upon to give him their support. And he might need it for his choice had fallen on Miss Cornelia Knight.

Miss Knight was in her mid-fifties, a strong-minded and intelligent woman—even a much-travelled one. She and her mother, for reasons of economy, had lived abroad for some years after the death of her father Admiral Sir Joseph Knight; she was of a literary turn of mind and had even published her writings, some of which were of an erudite nature. During her prime she had been a friend of some of the leading literary and artistic figures among them Dr. Johnson and Joshua Reynolds; and there had even been a friendship with Lord Nelson and the Hamiltons while Cornelia was in Naples. Altogether a woman with whom Charlotte could improve her mind. Moreover, Charlotte was not prejudiced against her and even had an affection for her. Mercer Elphinstone admired Miss Knight, not only because there was a similarity in their characters but because Cornelia had been a friend of Admiral Keith, Mercer's father.

There was, however, an obstacle to the appointment. For more than six years Cornelia had been a member of the Queen's household—somewhat in the role played some years earlier by Fanny Burney, and the Queen decided that if she lost Miss Knight she would miss her very much. It was not that she had any specified duties. Like other ladies she received her £300 a year, lodging and the services of a maid; but to have such a discreet, sensible, much travelled woman about her greatly pleased the Queen who was certainly not going to relinquish her lightly.

The Regent told his sister Mary of his decision to appoint Miss Knight to Charlotte's household.

'It's an excellent idea!' declared Mary. 'How like you to select the person she most needs.'

'And the Queen?'

'Mamma has heard of this.'

'It's astonishing how nothing can be kept secret in this place.'

'It's true,' sighed Mary. 'I was saying so to William only yesterday.'

William, her cousin, thought the Regent, whom she hoped to marry. Poor thing! He would see what could be arranged one day, but that would be an even greater battle with the Queen than this for Cornelia Knight—and after all, Mary and her cousin should fight their own battles. If they were really bent on marriage, they should agitate and he would most certainly come down on their side; but at the moment he was too concerned with more pressing affairs and if Meek Mary and Silly Billy would make no move for themselves they must wait. Meanwhile there was this matter of his own wayward daughter.'

'And what does the Queen say?'

'She declares that she has no intention of relinquishing Miss Knight.'

'And Miss Knight herself?'

'Well, secretly she would be delighted to go to Charlotte. You know how exacting Mamma can be and really she has only begun to show her appreciation of Cornelia now there is a prospect of losing her.'

'I think we need Miss Knight. Charlotte must have a steadying influence and the Duchess will require her help. I will speak to her.'.

*   *   *

Miss Knight received the Regent's command with an inner satisfaction and an outward equanimity. She was a wise woman and she had found waiting on the Queen stultifying. The Princess Charlotte—a lively young girl and heiress to the throne in her own right—was so obviously a more exciting project and the task before her appealed to Cornelia's adventurous spirit. Immediately it was offered she knew she was going to take it. The Queen might be annoyed but Miss Knight felt strengthened in her decision. It was a matter of displeasing either the Queen or the Regent.

There was, however, an unpleasant scene with Her Majesty to be endured.

'I am surprised, Miss Knight,' said the Queen, taking a pinch of snuff as though to fortify herself against the sorrows inspired by ingratitude, 'that you have decided to give up a post which you have filled to *my* satisfaction for so many years. It is an astonishing thing to me that you should have come to this decision, knowing my wishes.'

There was a pause—an indication that Miss Knight might speak.

'Your Majesty, when I received a command from His Royal Highness, the Prince Regent, I believed I had no alternative but to obey it. It did not occur to me that Your Majesty was not in complete agreement with His Highness, and although I have always striven to perform my duties to the best of my ability, I was not aware that my poor performance had been worthy of Your Majesty's special notice.'

Clever creature! thought the Queen. She reminds me of Miss Burney and although *she* was not well versed in Court ways when she first came to us and often behaved quite oddly, I have missed her and regret her departure. She was sensitive and *feeling*, and Miss Knight has a similar quality; and now my son has taken her from me I have no power to keep her. Unless she wishes to remain, I have lost her.

There was a last hope. Suppose Miss Knight *wished* to remain with her.

'His Highness is eager for you to join the Princess Charlotte's household, I know,' she said, 'but I am sure, Miss

Knight, that if you wished to stay in mine and made this clear to His Highness, and I added my wishes to yours, this decision could be reversed.'

'Your Majesty is most gracious,' replied Miss Knight, 'but His Highness made his wishes so clear to me, and having given my word, I am sure Your Majesty will understand that I could not break that now.'

The Queen nodded. One did not plead with one's subjects. It was not the first time that she and her eldest son had been at variance. She must be grateful now that they were in closer harmony and a small matter like this must not be allowed to ruffle the smoothness of their relationship.

She contented herself with a warning. 'You will not find your new post a comfortable one. The Princess Charlotte can be a great *concern* to her household. I am sure poor Lady de Clifford had a most trying time attempting to control her. The poor creature was almost driven out of her wits. The Duchess of Leeds does not seem to me to be a very *determined* woman and a great deal of responsibility might fall on *your* shoulders.'

The intrepid Miss Knight perceptibly squared that part of her frame and a confident smile touched her lips. She who had travelled widely, had been the friend of Lord Nelson and his Emma, who had enjoyed many an animated discussion with Dr. Johnson, was not going to be beaten by young Princess Charlotte. She could look to the future with confidence.

The Queen knew that she had lost Miss Knight to the Regent.

In any case, she consoled herself, the tiresome matter of Charlotte's household could now be settled with the Duchess of Leeds and the able Miss Knight in control and many of the old household replaced—so the Queen hoped—by wiser women. Poor Mrs. Gagarin was very ill and would soon no longer be with them. As for Louisa Lewis she was too insignificant to cause anxiety.

The matter was over. Charlotte who had declared she would not have another governess had been made to realize she must submit to her father's wishes. The Queen trusted her granddaughter had learned a lesson. If that were so, she told herself virtuously, she would be fully compensated for the loss of Miss Knight.

A *Letter to the* Morning Chronicle

THE Princess Charlotte stood before her mirror to admire her feathers.

'This,' she told the admiring Louisa, 'is an outward sign of age. The first time I have ever worn them—and how do they become me?'

'Admirably,' declared Louisa wholeheartedly.

'My dear Louisa, I do believe you mean that. You do think I look beautiful, don't you? But it's only because you love me. You look at me through the eyes of love, dear Louisa, and that is a very pleasant way to be looked at. How I wish my father could be made to look at me in the same doting way. He looks with the eyes of criticism. Sometimes I think he wants to find something wrong. Yet perhaps he is changing. Is he not giving this ball for me? In my honour! Think of that! And at Carlton House. All that splendour and me... in feathers!'

She laughed loudly and Louisa joined with her. Charlotte was sober suddenly. 'I must go to show myself to dear Gagy. She'll be hurt if I don't.'

Louisa turned away sharply. She did not want the Princess to be depressed on such an occasion as she would certainly be when she saw the change in Mrs. Gagarin even in the last few days.

Miss Knight went with Charlotte to the carriage. She was more often accompanied by Miss Knight than the Duchess whom she showed she resented. Anyone who bore the hated title of governess would be resented but the Duchess lacked the personality to win Charlotte's respect. She thought her *nouveau riche*, for her marriage to the Duke of Leeds had, Charlotte had commented to Louisa, been a high step up for a lawyer's daughter. 'And what airs the woman gives herself—

in her meek way of course. She's anxious that everyone should know she's a duchess.'

Moreover Mercer disliked her—mainly because she was a Tory and Mercer feared she might try to influence Charlotte's political views.

'No danger of that,' Charlotte had declared hotly. 'I'd be more Whiggish than ever just because she is a Tory.' Which, Mercer could not refrain from pointing out, was scarcely a logical reason for forming a political opinion.

So the Duchess was a trial to be endured—though not one to give Charlotte any real qualms. In addition there was her daughter Catherine Osborne—a sly child whom Charlotte despised not only for her somewhat devious nature but because it had been suggested that the girl might be a companion for her. And she was fifteen years old! How could they insult a seventeen-year-old heiress to the throne by offering her a fifteen-year-old nonentity as a playmate! A playmate indeed—when her fancy was for a brilliant woman older than herself like the adored Mercer, and yes—she would admit it— Cornelia Knight, for she was growing more and more fond of Cornelia and she felt that one compensation which had come out of the recent shuffling of her household was the acquisition of Cornelia.

'Dear Notte' as she called her—an affectionate form of Knight—was a treasure. She had been to interesting places and was *persona grata* with fascinating people and she never hesitated, when prompted, to talk of her exciting past. The Prince liked her. He called her playfully 'The Chevalier'. Because she was *sans reproche*? wondered Charlotte. Or because she went into battle for what she thought was right?

In any case, Charlotte was glad to have her, and when she was unable to be with Mercer, Notte made a good substitute.

Now riding in the carriage to Carlton House she was delighted to have Miss Knight beside her. It put the Regent in a good mood to see his daughter in such capable hands and Charlotte herself was pleased because dear old Notte was becoming so fond of her. She was always anxious that Charlotte should enjoy life as much as possible.

'Oh dear,' sighed Charlotte. 'I do hope Papa will like my feathers.'

'It is more important that he should like *you*,' Cornelia reminded her, and it might have been Mercer speaking, Charlotte noted delightedly.

'But the Prince Regent cares so much for the right costume

that his affections could be swayed by such considerations, don't you think?'

Miss Knight was not going to be drawn into that.

'I'm glad you came and not Leeds,' went on Charlotte. 'How I wish I could be rid of her. As for her odious daughter —I hate the child. I'm sure she listens at doors. She is always prowling around at night. Little beast! One of these days I shall let my lady Catherine know what I think of her.'

'Do remember when you sit down not to expose your undergarments.'

Charlotte laughed. 'My drawers—or rather the showing of them—always caused poor Cliffy such concern. Don't you start worrying about them, dear Notte.'

'People watch. They talk of these things.'

'I'm continually spied on. If it is not the odious Catherine creeping round corners, it's people.'

'The penalty of royalty.'

'I've been discovering the penalties all my life. Soon I hope to enjoy the privileges. Oh dear, I wonder if Devonshire will be there tonight.'

'Your fondness for the Duke of Devonshire has been noticed.'

'Well, he is rather charming. Not handsome, I grant you, but very pleasant to be with.'

'Your Highness should be careful.'

'People notice,' mimicked Charlotte. 'Let them. I am after all the heiress to the throne. Why shouldn't I be with people I like!'

'Your father would not wish you to be too friendly with the Duke.'

'Why not? He was once friendly with his mother. Not now, of course. My father is almost a Tory now. What a turncoat!'

The manner in which Miss Knight set her lips conveyed that this was a subject she did not wish to discuss, and when she looked like that nothing could shift her. Charlotte smiled. Cornelia became more and more her dear Notte every day and grew less and less like her father's Chevalier. Cornelia was going to be *her* devoted friend, not his. It was strange how everything seemed to turn itself into a battle between them.

Here they were at Carlton House. The Prince was waiting to greet her and the people who had gathered to see the arrival of the *ton* had loud cheers for the Princess Charlotte in her feathers.

* * *

Back at Warwick House Charlotte decided it had been a disappointing evening in spite of the feathers. The Duke of Devonshire had not been present. He had been unwell, she had heard. Was this the truth or had be been informed that his presence would not be welcome? One could never be sure and if people were beginning to notice that she liked him and it reached her father's ears it was very possible that the Duke had received a hint to keep away. What a bore to be royal! All the fun one had must be enjoyed surreptitiously.

So the ball had been dull in spite of the presence of a number of French exiles and her father's being particularly gracious to her. 'Now that you are seventeen,' he had said, 'there must be more such balls.' She hoped her demeanour and deportment had pleased him. It had appeared to—but one never knew. He had probably been warned by his ministers that it would be wise to show that his relationship with his daughter was amicable.

She yawned as Louisa removed the feathers.

'Tired,' soothed Louisa, 'after all that dancing?'

Charlotte nodded. 'It's tiring if you don't dance with those with whom you want to dance.'

'Any special one?'

Charlotte laughed. 'I confess to an interest in Devonshire. He's not good-looking but I like him all the same. And he likes me, too. But perhaps he doesn't. Perhaps it's just because he feels he must.'

'Of course he likes you. He couldn't help it.'

'Louisa, I believe that if I were a foundling who had been left at your door—the child of a fish porter and a flower girl—you would still love me.'

'Of course I would.'

'You *are* a comforting creature,' declared Charlotte and on that note of satisfaction retired to bed.

* * *

She was dozing when she heard the sound of light creeping footsteps. Someone was coming along the corridor. Charlotte snatched up a wrap and leaped out of bed. Now that she was fully awake she guessed who the intruder was because she had found Catherine Osborne wandering about at night before. 'I thought I heard Your Highness call,' she would say if caught. 'I thought Your Highness wanted something.' Sly creature! What did she expect to find? What did she *hope* to find.

There was a certain amount of gossip about Hesse and Fitzclarence and now Devonshire . . . Could she really think . . . ?

Charlotte flushed scarlet at the thought.

The door was slowly pushed open and Catherine Osborne looked in.

'Your Highness!' she was startled and Charlotte smiled grimly.

'What's wrong, Lady Catherine? You look as if you expected to find someone different from myself in my bedroom.'

'I . . . thought Your Highness called.'

'Indeed I did not.'

'It must have been someone . . . or perhaps I dreamed it.'

'Perhaps,' said Charlotte tersely. Lady Catherine's eyes wandered about the room. Did she expect to see De____ire lurking in a cupboard, Fitzclarence crouching behind the curtains or Captain Hesse under the bed? How the sly creature would have enjoyed reporting something like that to her Mamma.

'Well, Lady Catherine, having satisfied yourself that I did not summon you and your hearing is at fault or you are the victim of a nightmare, you may escort me to the water closet.'

'Yes, Your Highness.'

The creature was looking complacent. She thought she had cleverly extricated herself from a delicate situation.

Charlotte took her arm and led her along the corridor which was cold and draughty, but not as cold as the water closet. Having reached this, Charlotte gave Lady Catherine a little push and sending her in shut the door on her. Lady Catherine gasped as she heard Charlotte turn the lock from outside.

Charlotte went back to her room. And that, she thought, will teach my lady Catherine not to prowl at night.

After half an hour she would go and release her. She did not want the silly girl to die of cold—only to teach her that the Princess Charlotte would not tolerate spies in her own household.

*　　　*　　　*

The Princess of Wales had decided, with the backing of Brougham and Whitbread, that this was the time for action. Charlotte was at variance with her father over this matter of her household; the spate of comment in the newspapers was growing; and the Prince was more unpopular than ever. As for herself she was treated shamefully both by her husband and the Queen who never invited her to her Drawing Rooms or any state occasion and who had taken the care of her daughter out of her hands.

Brougham had drafted a letter of complaint which she was to send to the Prince of Wales at the appropriate moment: and that moment had come.

She read the letter through. 'This will make him take notice,' she murmured, and smiled to herself. She was ready to go to any lengths to get her darling Charlotte back. It was wicked to keep a mother from her daughter. Occasional visits were not good enough; she wanted to have Charlotte constantly under her roof; she wanted them to be seen together. And why not? It was what the people expected. She had heard that when Charlotte drove out in her carriage the cry of 'Don't forget your mother! Cherish and love your mother!' had been shouted more than once.

That fat coxcomb she had married must be grinding his teeth in rage. They didn't say 'Cherish your father' did they? Oh, it was easy to see whose side the people were on, and Princes—be they Prince Regents and all but Kings—had to consider the people.

What a letter! Laboriously she copied Brougham's close writing.

'I should continue, in silence and retirement, to lead the life which has been prescribed for me and console myself for that loss of society and those domestic comforts to which I have so long been a stranger . . .'

She chuckled, thinking of life at Blackheath, Connaught House and the apartments in Kensington where she received her friends. Far more interesting than Carlton House and the Pavilion! Amusing people came to her parties . . . unshockable, witty, unconventional. But that was not the point. In this letter she was a woman complaining of her miserable and unnatural state and stressing her willingness to accept it but for one consideration: her daughter.

'But, sir, there are considerations of a higher nature than any in regard to my own happiness which render this address a duty to myself and my daughter. May I venture to say—a duty also to my husband and the people committed to his care. There is a point beyond which a guiltless woman cannot with safety carry her forbearance . . .'

She laughed. Brougham could certainly write. She imagined the Prince reading this missive. The anger, the irritation, the fury . . . but he would applaud the style and of course know it was not hers which was all to the good. He would know clever people were supporting her.

She went on writing. He would have to notice this. If not, she would publish it. That would be a good idea. Then there would be trouble. Wait until the people read this letter which they would think she had composed herself and which showed her so clearly as the wronged wife and the heart-broken mother..

'...the separation which every succeeding month is made wider, of the mother and daughter, is equally injurious to my character and her education. I say nothing of the deep wounds which so cruel an arrangement inflicts upon my feelings, though I would fain hope that few persons will be found of a disposition to think lightly of these. To see myself cut off from one of the few domestic enjoyments left me—certainly the only one upon which I set any value, the society of my child—involves me in such misery as I well know Your Highness could never inflict on me if you were aware of its bitterness. Our intercourse has been gradually diminishing. A single interview weekly seemed sufficiently hard allowance for a Mother's affection ... that, however, was reduced to our meeting once a fortnight; and I now learn that even this most rigorous interdiction is to be still more rigidly enforced ...'

She was enjoying this. Brougham was making her aware of emotions she had never understood. Of course, she told herself, I wanted my daughter with me. What a dear little baby she was and all my own then ... for a time ... a little time. Then they took her from me. I wasn't good enough to bring up a future Queen of England even though she might be my own child.

She went on writing in the same strain, stressing her wrongs and the theme of that letter was: Consider a mother's feelings and do not separate her from her child.

When she had finished it she sealed it and despatched it to Lords Eldon and Liverpool with the request that they should lay it before the Prince of Wales.

She laughed at the thought of his receiving it. He would pick it up as though it were infected with the smallpox, that expression of disgust on his face because he would be thinking of her.

In her bedroom she took a small figure from a drawer. She set it up against a looking glass and laughed at it. The likeness was good—the portly figure, the well-shaped calves, the pert

nose and the pouting lips. It was the Regent to the life—and
exquisitely dressed of course with a necktie worn high up to
his chin; the coat was of the finest velvet; even the breeches
were of buckskin.

Caroline picked up a pin and thrust it into the figure where
his heart would have been. The heads of several pins were
visible in this spot.

'At least,' she said aloud, 'it relieves the feelings. Take that,
my fat prince. And that . . . and that . . .'

She laughed so much that Willie came in to see what was
the matter.

'Oh,' he said, 'You're playing the pin game again, Mamma.'

She picked him up and gave him loud kisses all over his face
to which he submitted resignedly. He was accustomed to these
outbursts of affection.

She put him down at length and threw the figure face down
into a drawer.

'Now,' she said, 'we shall see what His Highness has to reply
to that!'

*   *   *

When the Prince saw the sealed letter he looked at it in
much the same manner as Caroline had imagined.

'I have sworn that I will never receive any document from
the Princess of Wales,' he reminded Eldon and Liverpool.

'We do not forget this, Sir,' said Liverpool, 'but we were in
duty bound to inform Your Highness of its arrival. We believe it to be Your Highness's wish that this . . . missive . . .
should be returned whence it came . . . unopened.'

'This is my wish,' replied the Prince.

'Then,' said Liverpool, 'so be it, and I will inform the
Princess that any communication she wishes to make must be
made through the Chancellor and myself.'

The Regent nodded. 'Let that be done, but *I* wish to have
nothing to do with the woman.'

The ministers nodded.

It was deplorable, Lord Eldon remarked to Lord Liverpool later, that statesmen like themselves should have to
occupy themselves with such matters.

*   *   *

The Princess Caroline laughed aloud when she heard.

'So he won't read my letters, eh? He can't bear to talk to
me. I'm not dainty enough. Come here, Willie . . . do you find
me dainty . . . or dirty?'

Willie dutifully came and was seized in a suffocating hug. 'You love your old Mamma, eh, Willie?'

Willie declared that he did.

'I've had nothing but insults from that man since I came here. Prince Regent! Prancing Tailor's Dummy more like! And my own blessed Charlotte snatched from her mother's arms. How would you like that?'

Willie said that what he would like was some of the special sweetmeats which were kept in her apartments.

She hugged him afresh and said he should have his sweetmeats, and she would have her darling daughter.

Brougham called.

'My dear, faithful Brougham!' she cried distractedly. 'What should I do without you? What do you think that dreadful man has done now? He refuses to read my letter . . . our letter . . . and he has sent it back by way of Liverpool and Eldon. He'll communicate only through them if you please. His Highness is afraid *I* might contaminate him.'

Brougham listened cautiously.

'We will send the letter back to the noble lords,' he said, 'with instructions that if the Prince will not open the letter, they must do so and read its contents to him.'

*   *   *

'Well, my lord?' demanded Caroline.

Lord Eldon, the arrogant creature who always seemed to look scornfully down his nose as though to say 'My goodness, what outsider have we brought into the royal family!' said coldly: 'Your Highness's communication has been read to His Highness the Prince Regent.'

'At last! And what did his noble Highness say?'

Eldon smiled complacently. 'Nothing whatever, Your Highness.'

When the insolent man had gone Caroline gave vent to her fury, stamping up and down the room, abusing the royal family, her cheeks under their rouge red with emotion, her wig awry so that her own straggling grey hairs showed under the wayward black curls.

Her fury did not last long and soon she was laughing. 'They will be sorry,' she told Willie.

She was soon able to gloat over her revenge when on the advice of her friends, led by Brougham, the letter was sent to the *Morning Chronicle* and on February 10th was published prominently on the front page.

*   *   *

The whole country was talking about the scandalous state of affairs which existed between the Regent and his wife. What effect was it having on their daughter? the readers of the *Morning Chronicle* asked each other. The poor Princess was like a shuttlecock, batted back and forth between a pair of irresponsible players. But the letter appealed to public sentiment. It was not right, was the verdict, to keep a child from its mother.

The Regent was more unpopular than ever and was greeted with boos and catcalls in the streets. His carriage, standing outside the Hertfords' was once again pelted with refuse and spattered with mud. His standing had never been so low.

Then Brougham brought up the matter in Parliament and the letter was freely discussed.

It was, declared the Regent to the Queen, one of the most humiliating occasions of his life. 'I wish to God I had never seen that woman. I would give anything to undo this marriage.'

The Queen, her hands folded in her lap, could not resist a self-satisfied smile which reminded him that if they had listened to her that woman would not be here now. She had wanted her son to take her niece instead of his father's. How different if he had married Louise of Mecklenburg-Strelitz instead of Caroline of Brunswick.

If she did not say it now she had said it a hundred times in the past, but who knew, wondered the Regent, what marriage with Louise would have been like? It could not have been worse, he supposed, for Caroline surely must be the most unsuitable wife in the world. He despised and detested her and his greatest desire was to be rid of her. The only benefit she had brought him was to give him his heir—Charlotte—and Charlotte with her waywardness was a mixed blessing. His poor mad father had had a quiverful—too full—so that his progeny were a great expense to the nation; and he, the First Gentleman of Europe, had succeeded in producing only one —and that a girl.

This brought him back to the great problem of his life—if only he could rid himself of Caroline, If only he could re-marry while he was still young enough to get a male heir! A new wife...a male heir...and neither Caroline nor Charlotte would be of importance in his life.

The Queen was saying: 'It is disgraceful to publish such a letter. It means of course that she has supporters, otherwise she would not dare and if they are going to discuss the matter fully in Parliament . . . oh dear.' She reached for her snuffbox, her greatest solace in trouble.

The Regent suddenly made up his mind. 'I shall insist on another examination of those documents concerned in the Delicate Investigation. I am sure there is something there which will give me the information I need. If I can only find proof that William Austin is her son I'd have my evidence.'

'And meanwhile,' put in the Queen, 'she will be poisoning Charlotte's mind against us all. Charlotte has to be considered now. Next year she will be eighteen and that will be her coming of age. I do believe that prompt action should be taken.'

'Charlotte shall not see her mother while the investigation is in progress. I will go to her myself and tell her that they are not to meet for a while.'

'Charlotte,' said the Queen decisively, 'needs a very firm hand.'

Encounter of Two Carriages

THEY faced each other in Charlotte's drawing room in Warwick House—he seated in a chair, elegant as ever, she standing before him, awkward as always in his presence. He
appeared to avoid looking at her as he spoke.

'You will have heard of the distressing turn of affairs,' he
was saying. 'Your mother has seen fit to publish a letter setting out her imagined wrongs. It cannot be ignored and in
self-defence there must be an investigation of her conduct.'

'But . . . there . . . was . . .'

'A further investigation,' went on the Prince. 'We cannot
go on in this unsatisfactory state and while the investigation is
progressing it is not suitable for you and your mother to
meet.'

Rebellion rose in Charlotte. Why was it that when one
parent attacked another she always wanted to defend the
attacked? Why was it she had to show her affection for her
mother and her antagonism for her father when it was his
approval that she craved? She could not understand herself.
She only knew that when she was in his company she longed
for some show of affection from him and when she could not
get it she wanted to oppose him and stir up a hatred.

'But I love my mother. Why should I be kept from her?'

She could not have said anything to anger him more.

'You wish to see her? How can you wish to see such a vulgar
person?'

'She is my mother.'

'Alas!'

'And she is your wife. You must have had some regard for
her since I was born to you.'

He shuddered. Charlotte could be really vulgar.

'I shall speak to the Duchess and Miss Knight,' he said. 'I
cannot imagine why you are not taught restraint. Such manners I would not have believed possible in a daughter of
mine.'

'Not with such a mother?'

She was on the point of tears. Why was it that she was
always in this state of emotion when they were together? Why
could she not be elegantly calm—the sort of daughter he
wanted? She had come near to being that under Mrs. Fitzherbert's guidance. But Mrs. Fitzherbert had left him now
and was living, so she had heard, peacefully, her only concern
for her darling Minney's future. Mrs. Fitzherbert had escaped
from the storm which beset those in royal circles. Charlotte
felt a twinge of envy for Minney.

'It is clear to me that you have inherited too many of her
characteristics and that makes me feel how justified I am in
imposing this ban.'

'Ban? What ban?'

'Pray restrain yourself. In the interests of all concerned it
has been decided that you and your mother shall not meet for
a while.'

'Why, it's that old Investigation all over again.' The urge to
shock was irresistible. He thought her crude. Well, she would
be crude; and because he hated her to show affection for her
mother she would show it.

'It is a further investigation and we do not know what
shocking details will be brought to light. I do hope that you
understand what is expected of you. Obedience. This shall be
impressed on your governess.' . . . (She winced at the word) '. . .
and those who serve you. You will not suffer,' he added with
an attempt at kindness. 'You shall have the balls and entertainments which have been planned for you. And I shall see
you frequently, and all that is expected of you is that you
should not see your mother during the investigation and if
any shocking details should be revealed . . .'

'For which you ardently hope,' she could not resist putting
in, but he pretended not to have heard her.

'. . . you will cease to see her altogether.'

'I shall soon be eighteen,' she reminded him, 'and then I
cannot be forbidden to see my own mother.'

'I must remind you that your eighteenth birthday is still a
year away and even when you reach it it will still be necessary
for you to obey your father.'

He could see no reason for prolonging the interview. He
embraced her, repeated that she should be seen in public

more frequently—and in his company. He would visit her
and she should visit him.

He left her disturbed but secretly pleased at the prospect of
more meetings.

But of course, she told herself scornfully, it is only what his
ministers advise him is wise. If he wants to regain a little of
the popularity he has lost he must be seen with his daughter.
It must appear that in the Great Quarrel, she is on his side.

And I won't do it, she told herself fiercely. I won't let him
use me. He doesn't want to see *me* at all. It's only to placate
his ministers and the people that he does so.

If only he had cared for her . . .

But what was the use of dreaming. She must face facts.

*   *   *

She remained in bed. She was not going out. If she could
not see her mother she would see no one.

A whole week went by and Cornelia at length spoke to her.
'There is a lot of gossip,' she said, 'and comments in the
papers.'

Oh, those papers! thought Charlotte. Now that Mrs.
Udney had gone and she was not visiting her mother she
never saw them.

'There are really shocking hints,' went on Cornelia.

'About my mother and the Prince, I suppose.'

'About *you*!' retorted Cornelia.

'What about me?'

'You have been rather indiscreet with certain gentlemen.'
Charlotte looked startled.

'Captain Hesse, Captain Fitzclarence and the Duke of
Devonshire.'

Charlotte started to laugh.

'It's no laughing matter,' said Cornelia severely. 'Such
rumours can be dangerous.'

'Are they saying I am like my mother? Are they preparing
a Delicate Investigation?'

'What they are saying is too indelicate for me to repeat. I
suggest we go out this very day for a drive in the Park that you
may show yourself. That will be the best way to prove these
rumours false.'

That morning the Princess Charlotte was seen with Miss
Knight, riding in the Park.

*   *   *

Charlotte sat back in her carriage. It was pleasant when she
was recognized and the people cheered her. They were satisfied

that the rumours about her were false. What had they imagined? wondered Charlotte. That she was about to bear an illegitimate child? She giggled at the thought. Well, she had been a little indiscreet. She thought of the letters she had written to Hesse and which her mother had passed on to him. It had been exciting at the time but now that she was growing up she was beginning to wonder.

She was now passing along Piccadilly on the way to Hyde Park when she was aware of a carriage coming along Constitution Hill at a rattling speed, heading, Charlotte realized, straight in her direction. Before the carriage reached her she recognized it as her mother's; so had many others, and as the carriage of the Princess of Wales drew level with that of the Princess Charlotte, a crowd had gathered.

The Princess Caroline put her head out of the window of her carriage with some difficulty, adorned as it was by a large hat trailing highly-coloured feathers.

Charlotte put her head out of her window and her mother's arms were round her. Charlotte's usually pale face was faintly pink and the colour gave beauty to her fresh young face.

Caroline was shrieking with pleasure. 'My darling. My own little girl!'

They embraced, kissing again and again with passionate fervour, while the crowd roared its approval. God bless them both. Why should they be kept apart? It was wicked to separate a mother from her child.

Caroline was laughing exultantly and mischievously. 'My darling, how can I bear this separation!'

'Shame!' echoed the crowd like a chorus in a play. 'To keep a mother from her child.'

'Shame indeed, good folks,' cried Caroline, tears of emotion threatening havoc to rouge and white lead.

'I shall come and see you as soon as I'm able,' said Charlotte.

'Of course my angel will. I shall live for that day.'

The crowd had grown larger. 'God bless you both,' the people cried. 'And love your mother, Charlotte.' Charlotte, always conscious of the applause of the people, played her part with a verve worthy of her father.

'I will, I will,' she cried. 'Nothing will prevent me.'

Then she embraced her mother again to the accompaniment of cheers. Caroline clung to her daughter's hand and gradually released it.

'*Au revoir*, Mamma,' said Charlotte. 'This separation shall not last.'

'We shall soon be together again,' declared Caroline.

Caroline's carriage moved forwards and Charlotte fell in behind. They rode along to the cheering of the crowds.

*   *   *

Mercer called at Warwick House and was received by Charlotte with her usual enthusiasm. Cornelia was not so pleased. What would the Regent say if he knew that Miss Elphinstone, of whose friendship with his daughter he was somewhat suspicious, had been allowed by his daughter's guardians to enter her household, he had said nothing to Cornelia nor to the Duchess of Leeds about that scene in Hyde Park, although he was doubtless asking himself what her guardians were doing to allow it to happen. He was therefore neither pleased with Cornelia nor the Duchess, and Madame Elphinstone had to threaten more trouble by coming to the house against his wishes. If she were discovered, his displeasure would mean little to Mercer; it would be the unfortunate governesses on whose heads his wrath would expend itself.

Charlotte was aware of the antagonism between Cornelia and Mercer and deplored it. She adored Mercer, of course, but she was also growing very accustomed to and fond of Cornelia. How she wished that they would be friends; and she could not understand why they were not for there was a similarity in their characters which she had thought would make them appreciative of each other.

But she was too pleased to see Mercer now to worry about Cornelia's reactions.

'I am so happy to see you, dear Mercer,' she declared with deep feeling.

'One day I hope that I shall be able to stay with you,' said Mercer, 'so that I don't have to pay these rather embarrassing secret visits.'

'What a wonderful arrangement that would be! But now you are here don't let's waste a minute. Oh, my dear, you look so *handsome*!'

Mercer accepted the compliments graciously and assured the Princess that she looked charming herself and in good health.

'Quite belying the rumours,' she added.

'So you have heard rumours.'

'There will always be these stories of royalty but, my dearest Charlotte, you must do nothing to provoke them.'

'That seems impossible. One only has to *look* at a man and one is accused of having a fondness for him.'

'You were a little indiscreet at Windsor, I believe.'

'What pleasures do I get in life ... when I don't see my dearest Mercer? These were just little flirtations. And now they are talking about Devonshire.'

'Oh ... Devonshire!' Mercer laughed just a little self-consciously. Had Devonshire been paying attention to Mercer? She was very attractive. Lord Byron had been in love with her; but Lord Byron was in love with so many women; and Charlotte could understand *anyone's* being in love with Mercer who was so beautiful and talented. All the same she would have liked to think that Devonshire was faithful to her.

'Do you find him attractive?' she asked.

'In a way. He is unusual. Do you know, I have heard—but don't whisper a word of this—that he is not the Duchess's son after all.'

'How could that be?'

'I heard that the Duchess wanted to cover up her husband's infidelity and for him to have his heir. Devonshire is the son of the Duke's mistress, they say.'

'In that case he's a bastard and not the true duke.'

'Hush. These things should not be spoken of.'

Mercer had spoken of it, of course, but then Mercer was outside criticism. What an exciting person she was! She discovered the most intriguing news and not being Royal she had such freedom. She went to balls, met interesting people and was not fettered by governesses.

But poor Devonshire! What a position! To be called the Duke and to know he was not. And how strange that true scandal often remained a secret and it was the imaginary ones which were openly discussed!

'Cornelia insisted on my driving in the Park when she heard of the rumours,' she said.

Mercer's lips tightened at the mention of Cornelia. 'I hope you don't allow that woman to *order* you.'

'Oh, no, Cornelia would never do that. Dear Mercer, she reminds me of you.'

But Mercer was not pleased by the comparison.

'Why, she is an old woman. Because I am a few years older than you, do you see me as of an age with this Miss Knight?'

'Of course not. You're young and beautiful and dear Notte is old. Look, Mercer, I am wearing your bracelet. I do every day.'

Mercer was placated and passed on to the subject which she had come to discuss.

'I have heard rumours about Orange.'

'The Prince, you mean?'

Mercer nodded. 'They have chosen him as a possible husband for you.'

'I have heard he is very young and graceless,' said Charlotte.

'He is both.'

'Oh, Mercer, what a bother it is to be royal. I shall not accept him.'

'They might insist.'

'They?'

'Your father, of course.'

'I would not have Orange. I hate the whole family.'

'Still if the Prince Regent insisted . . .'

'I should have to worm my way out of that.'

'Could you?'

'Trust me,' retorted Charlotte.

But she was uneasy. She would find out all she could about William of Orange, son of the Stadholder—but she knew she was not going to like what she heard. They have forced me to have a governess, she thought, but they'll not force me to take a husband I don't want.

* * *

On a bleak March day Mercer again called at Warwick House, this time with the news that she had come openly. She had heard, through the Regent's equerry, that she had his master's permission to visit the Princess Charlotte.

Charlotte laughed gleefully. 'My father is trying to please me. Perhaps,' she added wistfully, 'it isn't for the sake of pleasing the people but because he wants to please me.' Mercer brought sad news. The old Duchess of Brunswick was very ill and in fact not expected to live.

'It's a long time since I saw her,' said Charlotte. 'Poor Grandmamma. Not seeing my mother has meant that I didn't see her either.'

A few days later the Queen sent for the Princess to tell her that her grandmother was dead. 'A death in the family is always an occasion for mourning,' she said, 'but I think we may say that this is not a very *important* death.'

Poor Grandmamma, who had once been Princess Royal and had had such a humiliating life! Charlotte's mother had talked of her now and then—how she had left England for Brunswick and found her husband's mistress installed there, and how Grandpapa Brunswick would not give up his mistress, and the poor Duchess had to accept a *ménage à trois*. And she had had her strange wild children—none of whom had been quite normal (for Mamma was a little odd, Charlotte had to admit), and then when Napoleon had captured Brunswick the old Duchess had come to the country of her birth to find no welcome there for her, for her kind brother was on the verge of madness and his queen was indifferent to the plight of a sister-in-law whom she had always disliked. So the Duchess had lived in that dingy dark house which was not at all like a royal residence, but there she had held court as though it were a palace—and perhaps lived in illusions.

Now she was lying in her coffin—neglected in death as in life. Not a very *important* death, so the old Begum had said.

Charlotte was sorry and wished she had seen more of her.

She went to Cornelia and talked of her grandmother.

'She used to sit on a chair in that cold and ill-furnished room and receive us. Oh Notte, dear, it was pathetic. And now she is dead and I might have been kinder to her.'

'It is no use regretting now,' soothed Cornelia. 'What could you have done? The situation was so awkward.'

'I should like to see her in her coffin. Would that be frowned on?'

'I don't see why it should.'

'I will pay my last respects, as they say. It's not much use, is it, but if she is watching she will be pleased.'

'Then we will go,' said Cornelia, 'for you will feel happier for it.'

*　　*　　*

'You were on the point of going out?' cried Mercer who had just arrived.

'To pay my last respects to Grandmamma Brunswick.'

Mercer gave Cornelia a cold glance. 'You think that wise?'

'I see no harm in it,' said Cornelia. 'It's a natural thing.'

'Natural to gaze on the dead!'

'It is the Princess's wish,' Cornelia reminded her coldly. Really, one would think the woman was the Queen at least.

'*I* consider it quite ghoulish!'

Charlotte looked from one to the other in dismay. She had wanted to see her grandmother in her coffin but clearly Mercer did not approve and perhaps it was ghoulish. Now she was wondering whether she really did want to see the dead Duchess—certainly not so much that she would offend Mercer by doing it.

She took off her cloak. 'I think Mercer is right, dear Notte. Perhaps I should not go.'

It was triumph for Mercer and defeat for Cornelia.

Really, thought Cornelia indignantly, that woman rules the household!

*   *   *

Charlotte drove to Blackheath with Cornelia and the Duchess of Leeds beside her for she had received her father's permission, in these special circumstances, to visit her mother.

The Prince and the Queen had come to the conclusion that because of the death of Caroline's mother that permission could not be withheld. The meeting in Hyde Park had been the main item of news in the papers for a few days; the lampoons had intensified. The Prince's enemies gloated over his callous treatment of his wife. To separate a mother and daughter! they reiterated. And to see the affection of those two leaning out of their carriages to embrace was so touching.

'Devil take them both,' cried the Prince. 'Not only have I the most vulgar woman in the world for a wife but I have also the most capricious of daughters.'

But in view of the fact that his mother-in-law was dead he had lifted the ban on meetings because there was nothing like a death to arouse public sentimentality.

The Princess of Wales wore purple for mourning and it did not become her. Charlotte always forgot how grotesquely colourful her mother was until she came face to face with her. The brilliantly rouged cheeks, the painted black brows, the black wig with its profusion of curls always gave her a fresh shock.

'So my angel has come,' cried the Princess, fiercely embracing her.

'Papa gave me permission.'

'The wicked old devil!' She laughed. 'What I have to endure from him! But nothing he can do to me hurts me like separating me from my dearest Charlotte.'

'And how is Willie?' Charlotte always had to remind her mother of Willie when she became too effusively affectionate. Was she jealous of Willie? She did not think so but she was not sure. There was so much which bewildered her in this strange relationship with her parents.

'Willie is adorable,' declared Caroline. 'He is my solace. But it is of you, my precious, that I wish to talk today. You are no longer a child, you know.'

'I know it well,' cried Charlotte. 'My complaint is that others forget it.'

'You heard the people cheering as you alighted from your carriage. We have them on our side . . . against *him*.'

'But it is not good that they should be against him. He is after all the King in a way... until Grandpapa recovers at least and we all know he never will.'

'Poor old King,' said Caroline. 'He was always my friend. The only one of the whole miserable family who showed me any kindness.' She broke into one of her bursts of loud laughter. 'He had a fancy for me. His mind was wandering half the time, I do believe, but he had a fancy for me. If I'd come as his bride that would have been a different story.'

Charlotte drew slightly away from her mother—repelled yet fascinated as she was so often.

Caroline had noticed. 'They have made a Mistress Prim of you. That's de old Begum. You've forgotten Captain Hesse ... and those pleasant meetings you had and the letters I helped you exchange. What would de old Begum say to that, I wonder? Or His High and Mighty Highness. Imagine the scene.' She laughed even louder at the thought. 'He can have his games, oh yes! There's not a bigger libertine in the kingdom. But it all has to be done like a piece of fancy play-acting.'

Charlotte was not listening. She was thinking of the meeting with Hesse which had given her such pleasure. Innocent meetings when she had felt herself to be living dangerously. They had been alone together so often in her mother's house; and there had been that occasion when her mother had locked them in the bedroom.

What had brought this home to her with such a shock was the thought of her father's hearing of this. He would be disgusted. He would find her as vulgar as he found her mother.

She shivered.

'It is better to forget that,' she said.

'Forget your romances. Why they're the best things in life, my angel. Ask your father. The scandals about him. Have you ever heard of Perdita Robinson? Ha! What a scandal. And then there is the biggest and best of all: Maria Fitzherbert. Did he or did he not marry her? He should not be the one to deny us a little fun, eh? But he would. He would be the first.'

Charlotte wanted to shut her ears.

Her mother, her arm about her, led her to the table. They must eat, she said, before that Leeds woman poked her sly nose in and said it was time for Charlotte to leave.

'Silly old fool,' cried the Princess of Wales. 'She likes shower baths, I hear.' Her contempt for anyone taking baths frequently was great. 'I hope she does not try to persuade you to bathe too often, Charlotte. That could be injurious to the health.'

Charlotte did not answer that regular baths were a rule of the household and she knew that one of the reasons why her father had been so disgusted with her mother was due to her dislike of washing herself. 'And I hear she's no horsewoman,' went on the Princess of Wales. 'Chooses the quietest horse to amble along on. What a woman! And she is given to you in place of your mother!'

Willie joined them and sat under the doting eye of the Princess Caroline. She does in fact prefer him to me, thought Charlotte jealously. She looks on him as her very own. Is he? She shivered. These investigations had not proved that he was Caroline's son, but they had left some very unpleasant doubts in everyone's mind.

While they ate Charlotte was thinking of past visits, of her mother smiling secretively when Captain Hesse was announced as though she were a conjuror who had brought forth a very pleasant gift for her daughter.

What an inflammable situation existed in this house—and she, Charlotte, when she had paid those lighthearted visits and had been so charmed with the company of Captain Hesse, had been playing with fire among the gunpowder.

Yet her mother had allowed it. Why? Because she was sorry for her daughter. Because she wanted to make her happy and give her some pleasure in life.

And she had. Charlotte was not going to deny that—dangerous pleasure though it might have been.

Willie was guzzling as usual. He was not the least bit impressed that the Princess Charlotte was seated at the table and that she was the future Queen of England . . . unless her father succeeded in divorcing her mother, marrying again and having a son.

And suppose he were in truth married to Maria Fitzherbert and his marriage to Caroline had been no true marriage, then she herself had no more claim to the throne than guzzling Willie.

What a strange household this was.

Caroline was drinking freely and her laughter was becoming louder.

'Oh, Mamma,' said Charlotte, 'how I wish that there need not be this conflict in the family! How I wish that you and my father could be friends.'

Caroline looked at her daughter as though she suspected her sanity.

'What! Me be friends with that man.' She picked up her glass of wine and threw it across the table. Charlotte stared at the pools of red liquid staining the white cloth. 'You may as well attempt to put that wine back in its bottle as stop my fury against people who have so maliciously used me.'

And there it was . . . the stained cloth, her mother laughing immoderately, Willie putting his finger into a nearby pool of wine and conveying it to his mouth, and the servants not in the least disturbed because they were so accustomed to the wild behaviour of the Princess of Wales.

Going back in the carriage Charlotte was thinking: If he knew about my friendship with Captain Hesse, what would he say? What would the people say? She thought of the things they had said because she had not appeared in public for a while.

Growing up was sometimes alarming.

Slender Billy

WILLIAM, Hereditary Prince of Holland was on his way to London. He travelled with little enthusiasm for he was fully aware of the reason for his journey. His father, the Stadholder, was in England at this time 'on a mission'; and young William could guess what that mission was.

They had chosen him to be the husband of the Princess Charlotte and although his father was delighted at the prospect, young William himself was not so sure. He was a good soldier; he had distinguished himself under Wellington but he wanted to carry on with his career, not settle down as the consort of an imperious young woman. He had heard reports of her—and she was certainly not the wife he would have chosen.

His father had written of his future as the husband of the heiress presumptive to England as though he were giving him a glimpse of Paradise. Napoleon was on the point of defeat; and when that happy event took place, Holland would be returned to the Stadholder. As future ruler he would have to spend the greater part of his time there; but he would also be the consort of the Queen of England. He would realize the benefits of such an alliance: the Dutch and the English joined in marriage—a William of Orange once more in control of England, for he would know how to handle Charlotte and although she would in name be Queen, he would be her husband. He would be a fool if he did not understand how very advantageous such a match would be.

Advantageous, yes. William was ready to concede that. But he would be Charlotte's husband and by all accounts she was a handful.

He was too young, he reasoned with himself as he knew he

would not dare reason with his father. He was by no means prepossessing and hardly the sort of young man to appeal to a high-spirited girl. He was too thin and his teeth were not good and he was nervous and shy.

No, the Hereditary Prince of Orange would have preferred to stay with the army than to visit the English Court.

*   *   *

By God, thought the Regent, the young fellow can scarcely be called handsome. What's Charlotte going to say to him?

He received young William graciously enough, hoping that his own natural elegance would set a good example.

He was delighted, he said, to welcome the Prince to England and he hoped that his stay would be a happy one.

William mumbled that His Highness was gracious and the Stadholder looked on anxiously guessing the impression his son was making.

Gauche or not, the Regent was thinking, he would do for Charlotte who was scarcely a model of deportment herself. Married to this young man she would be obliged to spend months in Holland. What a pleasure to pass on the responsibility to a husband! At least one of the tiresome females who haunted his life would be removed from it. And yet . . . she was his daughter; and sometimes when he was with her his paternal feelings would arise and he would remember that he was fond of her. If she had had a different mother . . .

But this was repetition of a wearying and depressing theme. Charlotte unfortunately *was* Caroline's daughter as well as his and it was something he could never entirely forgive her.

So . . . this thin boy with his gaucheries and not very good teeth (but perhaps these could be rectified?) would do very well for Charlotte. The boy was a Protestant and that would please the people—indeed anything but a Protestant marriage was unthinkable. It was time she was married, and when she had children they would occupy her time and thoughts; and this marriage, while not a bad thing for England, would be a relief for the Prince Regent.

They chatted for a while of Wellington's successes, and the boy became more attractive talking of soldiering. There was no doubt where his heart was.

The Regent remarked on this and added: 'I have also been with Wellington . . . in spirit. I cannot tell you how bitterly I railed against the fate which denied me the right to serve my country. When I was your age I implored my father to allow me to join the Army. But I was forbidden. My position

as Prince of Wales made it impossible. How fortunate you are
to suffer no such bans. I trust you realize this.'

The Prince did realize it. The Regent questioned him and
they talked of past battles in which the enemy had been
routed. It surprised young William to find how knowledgeable
the Regent was and how he could discuss an action as though
he had actually taken part in it.

The Regent on his part exerted all the famous charm and
before the interview was over William was thinking that if
only the Princess Charlotte appealed to him half as much as
her father did he would be happy enough to go on with this
betrothal.

When he had gone the Regent discussed him with Eldon
and Liverpool.

'Hardly Adonis. I wonder what she will say when they
meet. Frankly, I'm not looking forward to that meeting.'

'If Your Highness makes known his wishes,' said Eldon,
'that will be enough.'

'I know, I know,' said the Regent testily. 'It is my wish that
this betrothal shall take place and if I say so, it shall. But she is
my daughter, Eldon, and I should like her to be pleased with
her future husband. Perhaps I'm too indulgent ... but I
shouldn't want to see her forced into a marriage which displeased her.'

'Your Highness, when the Stadholder is restored to Holland
it will be a good match.'

'I know. I'm not thinking of the match so much as the
bridegroom. Not a romantic prince, you must admit. And
Charlotte can be perverse, as you well know. I have qualms, I
must tell you. I am not at all sure how my daughter will like
her Slender Billy.'

From that moment William, Hereditary Prince of Holland,
had his nickname and was more often referred to as Slender
Billy than by his own name.

* * *

'I won't have him,' declared Charlotte. 'Orange! I always
hated what I heard of his family. And they tell me he is very
unattractive ... little and thin ... with nothing to say for himself.'

'You can always supply the conversation,' Cornelia reminded her.

She laughed aloud. 'I'm not having it, Notte. I will make it
perfectly clear that I will not be forced to marry where I don't
wish to.'

'Has your father talked to you of the Prince?'

'No, and that is strange. I know why he's here. It's to win my approval. Yet I have not seen him . . . and I'm not going to if I can help it. And my father says nothing.'

'I think he is trying to be kind to you.'

'Do you really?' asked Charlotte ecstatically.

'I do indeed,' replied Cornelia. 'When he speaks to me of you he seems most earnest.'

Charlotte said suddenly: 'Dear Notte, there is something very serious I have to say to you.'

Cornelia looked slightly alarmed at the seriousness of Charlotte's voice and the Princess hurried on: 'I was once friendly with Captain Hesse—*very* friendly.'

'My dear Princess Charlotte, what do you mean?'

'I mean that I had a . . . romantic attachment.'

'My God!' cried Cornelia.

'Oh, you should not be alarmed. There was nothing wrong. And I see now that he behaved with great respect towards me. I was very young and foolish and inexperienced and because of this there might so easily have been . . . trouble. As a matter of fact there were letters.'

'Letters!'

'Don't repeat me like that, dear Notte. It irritates me. As I said we exchanged letters. I have destroyed his.'

'But he still has yours?'

'Unless he has destroyed them. I don't feel very easy in my mind when I remember what I wrote.'

Cornelia was aghast. The fact that this correspondence had taken place before her appointment was the one bright spot in the affair as far as she was concerned. But it was alarming to think that that adventurer . . . for he might well be one . . . had letters . . . and knowing the Princess they were likely to be indiscreet letters . . . in his possession.

Cornelia thought quickly. 'Have you mentioned this to Miss Elphinstone?'

'No, but I shall when I see her. I did not want to write it. I don't think it wise to write of such things.'

'Then you have learned a lesson,' said Cornelia rather sharply.

Dear Notte, thought Charlotte, she spoke so because she was anxious!

Cornelia was thoughtful. 'When you tell Miss Elphinstone perhaps you will let her know that you have also spoken to me. It may well be that she will wish to consult with me. If so, tell her that I should welcome that.'

Charlotte put her arms round Cornelia and kissed her. In a crisis Cornelia wished to do what was best for Charlotte and could thrust aside petty differences with Mercer for the sake of her charge.

* * *

Cornelia was delighted when Mercer came to her room. She had expected it, for arrogant and self-sufficient as Mercer was, she was a true friend to the Princess.

'She has told you,' said Cornelia.

Mercer nodded. 'It is alarming.'

'There is obviously one thing that must be done.'

'Obviously. We must get those letters back.'

'In your position . . .' began Cornelia.

'Yes, in my position I could do a great deal. I suggest that we mention this to no one. I will get to work immediately. I know that Captain Hesse is on the Continent serving with the Army. My father will help me.'

'I am so thankful that she has seen fit to confide in us.'

The two women looked at each other. They were far too sensible to wish to continue their feud—and too fond of Charlotte. The Princess needed their care and they could serve her much better if they worked together than if they indulged in petty jealousies.

They were both relieved to have come to such an understanding. The immediate task was to get the letters back from Captain Hesse.

* * *

Charlotte was also relieved that those two in whom she had great trust were now aware of her folly. She could shelve the unfortunate matter of Captain Hesse and give all her thoughts to avoiding Orange.

She was more seriously worried than she had admitted, for she knew that her father was set on the match; and she was well aware of his power. He was not only her father but her sovereign. If poor dear Grandpapa could be approached it might have been possible to explain her feelings, but how could she do this to her father or the old Begum?

Her health was beginning to suffer. There was a pain in her knee which worried Louisa a great deal because her aunt Amelia, who had died when she was twenty-six, had had a similar pain in the same place. She had a pain in her side too, and although it always became worse when there was a prospect of meeting Orange, it was, even without this fear, extremely painful.

Cornelia and Mercer, now allies, discovered that Orange was to be at a ball given by Lord Liverpool and his wife which Charlotte was to attend, and there she was to be given an opportunity of seeing him. This threw her into such a panic that the pain in her side became worse and Cornelia sent for the doctor, Sir Henry Halford, who was a great favourite with the Regent and the leading physician of the Court. Sir Henry, who had long been popular with all the family and whom George III had made a baronet, was more than a physician; he was a courtier, and he was well aware of the Regent's desire for a betrothal between Orange and his daughter.

Charlotte certainly looked very pale and far from well. She needed a stay at the sea, Sir Henry decided, but the Regent would scarcely agree to that at this time. He listened to her description of the pain and said that a blister should be applied.

'Very well,' said Charlotte. 'I shall be unable to attend the Liverpools' ball. But as I don't feel well enough to go I should miss it in any case.'

'Rest!' prescribed Sir Henry. 'That's what Your Highness needs.'

He began to tell her about a matter which excited him greatly. Charles I's coffin was about to be opened and as a leading doctor he was going to be present at the ceremony.

'How . . . gruesome!' cried Charlotte.

'Sometimes gruesome things have to be witnessed in the name of my profession.'

Charlotte smiled benignly. She let him run on about the ceremony which excited him so for she was grateful to him for having given her the excuse of the blister not to have to see Orange.

Halford reported to the Regent that the Princess Charlotte was by no means well and he thought a change would do her good—and rest. She needed rest.

The Regent was a little concerned. He was by no means abandoning the thought of the Orange match, but he could see that she would have to be prepared for it gradually, so Orange returned to his regiment without having seen Charlotte and Charlotte's spirits rose considerably. Dear Mercer was in communication with Captain Hesse who she was sure would never be so ungallant as to refuse to return her letters. Her two dear watchdogs were friends and that made her very happy.

Orange had gone and the Regent was behaving towards her with more affection than he had ever shown before.

*   *   *

One hot July day when Louisa went in to wake Mrs. Gagarin she found her dead. That was a great sadness. The Princess and Louisa wept together and kept reminding each other of the past when they had all been together.

Charlotte missed her old dresser more than she had realized possible and it was only the fact that Mercer and Cornelia were getting on so well together and that her father was showing her some affection that could comfort her.

The Prince, hearing of the death of Mrs. Gagarin from Charlotte expressed suitable grief and even shed a tear for her.

'She was a good creature,' he said. 'I know she served you well.'

And when Charlotte broke down and wept he put an arm about her and said that if it was any comfort to her he shared her sorrow. And although he did not feel one hundredth part of it she was charmed that he should say so.

The next day he sent her a sapphire which he said she could have made into any ornament she pleased. She was delighted —not with the stone which was very valuable but because he had sent it.

'And because I know how fond you are of your pets,' he said, 'I am sending you a white greyhound. I think you will find it a graceful and beautiful creature.'

She was delighted with the greyhound and loved it from the moment she saw it; She would allow no one to feed it but herself. The dog must know he was entirely hers and occupied a very special place in her affections—because he was so beautiful. But it was more than that, she told herself; it was because her father had given the dog to her.

She felt well again. The summer was gloriously warm and now that Mrs. Gagarin was dead she found it a relief not to have to notice every day how wan she was becoming.

In June the whole country had rejoiced over the victory at Vittoria. Napoleon's end was in sight and everyone but himself seemed to see it. The combined forces under the command of Wellington had put the French—under Joseph Bonaparte—to flight and they had been driven across the river Bidassoa into France.

The Regent was delighted and behaved as though it was he instead of Wellington who was the victor. He wanted to know every detail of the battle and would talk of it, sketching maps as he did so. 'We were here.' 'We advanced there . . .' His eyes alight with excitement, much to the amusement of some of his cynical courtiers.

There was to be a public festival in Vauxhall Gardens to celebrate the victory but the Regent decided that he himself would give an open air fête at which Princess Charlotte should preside. This would be held at Carlton House and was to celebrate the victory.

Charlotte arrived in great spirits in a gown sparkling with jewels. The people who had gathered to see her step from her carriage cheered her wildly and as she lifted her skirts to get down from her carriage displaying an expanse of frilly drawers there was a laugh and a cheer and she smiled and waved and thought of poor Lady de Clifford who would have deplored such conduct which nevertheless pleased the dear people.

The Prince was waiting to embrace her—looking magnificent as ever. One always felt awkward in face of his elegance she thought, but she was pleased; and the people did not seem to hate him so much when he showed affection for her.

And glory! There was the Duke of Devonshire looking more fascinating than ever and clearly deeply moved at the sight of her.

She was going to dance with him. After all, she was the principal guest so why should she not dance with whom she pleased?

What a happy occasion—herself looking beautiful, for she knew she did in that glorious gown (and now she was grown-up she would have many such gowns) and she was flushed—and that always helped because it was her pallor which spoilt her looks—and she danced with Devonshire, charming Devonshire who looked at her so tenderly and hopelessly. But how exciting a hopeless love could be! If only Orange could love her *hopelessly* she would view him so much more favourably. But why think of Orange on such an occasion?

Her father was glowering at Devonshire. Oh dear, she hoped he was not going to make the dear Duke *aware* of his displeasure. That might mean the sweet creature would be banned from appearing where the Regent was—and that could be disastrous, for Charlotte knew that she would in the future be very often in her father's company.

'Come, Papa,' she said, 'let us have a Highland Fling on the lawn and as it is my fête I command you to dance with me.'

The Prince hesitated, remembering that other occasion when he had hurt his ankle and been laid up for a time at Oatlands, which had given rise to the usual distressing rumours.

Then he decided to dance with Charlotte and she found

herself laughing with him, and everyone who looked on declared that the relationship between the Prince and his daughter was taking a more satisfactory turn.

Driving back to Warwick House with Cornelia and the Duchess, Charlotte chattered about all that happened. It had been a ball of balls. Had not her father looked elegant when he was dancing with her? And did they notice how attentive the Duke of Devonshire was? Did they not think he was a most attractive man?

The Duchess listened fearfully; she was constantly apprehensive of trouble. Cornelia was uneasy, too, remembering the Hesse affair.

* * *

The letters had not arrived from Hesse and Mercer was beginning to be uneasy. She had heard from the Captain that he had letters and presents from the Princess and that he kept them in a strong box. He had given instructions that if he should die these were to be returned to the Princess Charlotte or if that were not possible dropped into the sea. He did not believe he could entrust such a precious box in the hands of a messenger.

'What do you think?' asked Mercer.

Cornelia replied that she thought the young man might be something of an adventurer.

'I don't like it at all,' went on Mercer. 'I remember so well when she was attracted by him. Her letters to me contained accounts of his charm. In fact, she scarcely mentioned anything else at the time. I persuaded her eventually that it was a dangerous flirtation and gradually persuaded her to drop it. How I wish I had managed that earlier.'

'It may be that he *is* afraid to entrust the box to anyone,' put in Cornelia. 'Imagine what could happen if it did fall into the hands of some wicked person.'

'Letters!' groaned Mercer. 'They have been the curse of the family—her father's to Perdita Robinson were costly . . . and think of the Duke of York's to Mary Anne Clarke.'

'This is different,' said Cornelia. 'This is nothing but innocent flirtation.'

'We know it, but who else would accept it? We must get those letters. They're important.'

When Charlotte heard that Captain Hesse had not returned the letters she was uneasy. She had visions of terrible scenes with her father just as he was beginning to like her a little. The pain in her knee was so bad that it was necessary to call in Dr. Halford again and he recommended rest.

Mercer visited her and told her about the breakfast party Devonshire was giving at his Chiswick Mansion and Charlotte sighed and wished that she might go, knowing of course that the reason why she had not been invited was because for Devonshire to have asked her to be his guest would have brought a reprimand from the Regent—and she would most certainly have been forbidden to go.

She was depressed. How boring to be royal!

She was looking so listless that Cornelia suggested a drive and she agreed with alacrity. And when they were in the carriage Charlotte directed the driver to make his way towards Chiswick.

'Chiswick!' cried Cornelia aghast.

'I want to see the *ton* all in their carriages and what the ladies are wearing for Devonshire's breakfast.'

So they went rattling along the Chiswick road and were soon in that stream which was making its way to Devonshire House. No one could be unaware of the royal carriage and even though when it came to the Devonshire mansion it did not stop but went straight on to turn and come back shortly afterwards, everyone knew that the Princess Charlotte had been on the road.

*   *   *

The Regent called at Warwick House. He would see Miss Knight, he said.

Cornelia found him, large, imposing, glittering and coldly displeased.

'I want an explanation, Miss Knight,' he said, 'of this driving to and from Chiswick.'

'The Princess and I did drive that way. Let me see, it was on the...'

'It was on the day of Devonshire's breakfast.'

'Oh, yes, sir. I remember the carriages on the road.'

'I am sure you do. And I want to know why this drive was taken.'

'The Princess was feeling low, sir, and I thought a drive would do her good.'

'And she suggested that you go to Chiswick.'

'It was my idea that we should go for a drive, sir. I had suggested that she might like to see the carriages...' Cornelia floundered. He looked at her witheringly. Clearly he did not believe her.

Turning angrily he went from the room.

*   *   *

The Queen was pleased that he came to her.

'Devonshire,' he said. 'It's Devonshire! Do you think the fellow can have ideas? Who would have believed it of him. I shall have to speak to him. It seems she has a fancy for him. A fancy for Devonshire!'

'It would seem to me,' said the Queen, 'that she is ready to have a fancy for anyone whom you do not favour. Why could she not have had such a fancy for Orange? Is Devonshire so much more handsome?'

'One has to admit that he has something Orange lacks. But it is no use for Charlotte. She is going to have Orange, I shall see to that. In the meantime, though, this Devonshire nonsense must be stopped.'

'It should not be difficult. A word to Devonshire should warn him. He is not a fool, I take it, and would not go against your wishes.'

'I am surprised that her women don't keep her in better order. Miss Knight drove with her, if you please, to Chiswick.'

'Miss Knight!' The queen gave a short sharp laugh. 'I think that woman was more suitable serving *me*.'

She looked at him fondly. They were good friends now after the terrible enmities of the past. Her feelings for him had passed through three stages, intense love, violent hatred and now a placid affection; but he would always be her first-born, the only person who had ever really found a place in her cold heart. All the same she relished stressing the mistakes he made. Marrying Caroline was the greatest and to take Miss Knight from her had been of course of much less magnitude, but a false move all the same. She was glad he realized it; and if she could do anything to bring home to him the fact that Miss Knight was not the most suitable companion for Charlotte she would do so.

*   *   *

Charlotte was beginning to feel desperate. Hesse would not return the letters and she never met the Duke of Devonshire anywhere. It was understood that if she were present, he was not. He made no effort to see her. Clearly he had had orders.

When she saw her father he talked to her of Orange all the time, the desirability of the match and the bravery of young William on the battlefield.

Something would have to be done. They wanted her married and unless she could find a husband of her own choice they would make her take Orange. So she must look around and an idea came to her that if she allowed them to think her fancy had alighted on someone really unsuitable they would be obliged to consider her choice and thus she could play for time.

With this idea in mind she looked about her and when at her grandmother's Drawing Room she caught sight of her Aunt Mary in conversation with her father's cousin William Duke of Gloucester. A mischievous idea came to Charlotte. Silly Billy, as the Regent with his love of nicknames had called him, was attached to Mary in a luke-warm way; as for Mary she hoped to marry her cousin; and would have done so had not the Queen stood out firmly against it. The old King of course in his day had been against any of his daughters marrying. Poor things, thought Charlotte, for they had wanted to . . . desperately.

The more she thought of Silly Billy the better she liked the idea. Mary had been rather actively spying for her mother recently and it would teach her a lesson; and when the little joke was over—for over it would be in due course—it might well be that the Queen would not attempt to stand in her daughter's way any longer.

The more she thought of the idea the better she liked it. It would create a diversion and some amusement and heaven knew she was in need of that.

She selected Lord Yarmouth for her confidence. As Lady Hertford's son he was on good terms with the Regent; and he really was a rather stupid dandy so it would be easy to try it out on him. Moreover he had, in a rather clumsy way, been trying to gain her confidence lately and knowing her fondness for dogs had given her a delightful French poodle. She loved the poodle but it did not change her opinion of the 'Yarmouth Bloater' as the writers called him in their lampoons.

She did not have to wait long for Yarmouth to call upon her. He said he came to enquire about the little French dog.

Charlotte assured him that her poodle was adorable and showed him to Yarmouth who pretended to be most affectionate towards the animal. Superciliously Charlotte watched him patting her dog. Then she said: 'I have something to confide in you, Lord Yarmouth.'

His bloater face was suffused with gratification. All his efforts were to be rewarded. Charlotte was going to make him her confidant and the Regent would realize his importance.

'You know, my lord, I am not eager for the Orange match.'

Yarmouth looked grave. It was his duty as the Regent's friend to make her realize the advantages of union with Holland.

'Because,' she went on, 'I have a fancy for another.'

Lord Yarmouth's whiskers bristled. 'Your Highness, if you would tell me the name . . .'

'It is the Duke of Gloucester.'

'The d . . . d . . . d . . .' spluttered Yarmouth.

'Yes,' giggled Charlotte. 'The . . . d . . . d . . . d . . . of Gloucester of course.'

'Your father's cousin!'

'Why not?'

'But Your Highness cannot really mean this!'

'I have always liked the Duke of Gloucester.'

'Your Highness he is twenty years older than you are.'

'If I do not mind why should other people?'

'I do not think His Highness, the Regent . . .'

Charlotte shrugged her shoulders. 'I know very well,' she said, 'that he can prevent my marrying the Duke of Glouces-ter by withholding his consent, but if he does I shall state publicly that I refuse to marry anyone else.'

Lord Yarmouth could scarcely wait to report to the Regent.

*   *   *

The Prince strode up and down his apartment.

'Why should I be cursed with such a daughter. Gloucester! Is she mad? He's thirty seven years old. I never liked him. He's a fool. Silly Billy to be the husband of my daughter! I think she has gone raving mad. Why should I be surrounded by such women? What have I done?' Floods of self-pity overwhelmed him. He, who had been ready to be friendly with her, to indulge her. Hadn't he given her that magnifi-cent sapphire? And what about the greyhound and all the fêtes and balls he planned for her? And she repaid him by refusing suitable Orange and declaring her preference for Gloucester. 'Gloucester Cheese,' he cried, rounding on Yar-mouth. 'Indeed, he's nothing but a cheese. He has no sense . . . or little of it. The fellow's a pompous fool; and why, because of his origins! They say his mother was a milliner. My uncle had no right to marry so low. He did it against my father's wish, as you know. And it was due to him that we had this accursed Marriage Act. His mother might have been a beauty but she was illegitimate . . . and my uncle had no right to bring her into the family. And this daughter of mine chooses her son in preference to the Prince of Orange. The Cheese instead of the Orange. Did you ever hear of such folly, eh?'

Lord Yarmouth replied that he had been thunderstruck when the Princess told him of her preference. He had not believed her and insisted that she was joking. But no, she had said; she preferred Gloucester to Orange and if she couldn't have him, she would have no one.

'I don't believe it,' cried the Regent. 'How could a young girl like Charlotte fancy that fool Silly Billy? Besides he's been dancing attendance on the Princess Mary for years. It's time he married her.'

'Her Majesty . . .'

'Oh, I know, Her Majesty is against the match. Her Majesty is against all matches for her daughters, but while Silly Billy might do well enough for Mary he is no match for Charlotte.'

'What does Your Highness wish me to do?'

'To tell her I say No! And the sooner she comes to her senses and takes Orange the better.'

*   *   *

The Duke of Gloucester could not help but be flattered. The young Princess wanted to marry him—and she the future Queen of England!

It was true that he had been attached to Mary for years, but that had never come to anything; and such a dazzling prospect as marriage with the heiress presumptive was enough to turn anyone's head, certainly such an unbalanced one as Gloucester's.

He had always been conscious of the humble origins of his mother because there had been plenty to remind him of them; and although she had been a good woman of remarkable beauty and had conducted her life with more decorum and dignity than most members of the family, her birth had been a handicap—particularly as she was not even legitimate.

Here was a chance to wipe out that stain. He would be the husband of the Queen . . . for Charlotte would be that one day. The King was growing more feeble every day and the Regent was scarcely robust. He could look fine enough in all his elegant glitter but he was constantly being bled and was subject to mysterious illnesses. Gloucester could not help walking around with his head held high and a new arrogance had crept into his manner.

The Princess Mary drooped visibly as she saw her chance of marriage disappearing. William had been her comfort; and they had resigned themselves to the fact they could not yet be married, but she had always believed they would in time. And now that hope was threatened by Charlotte's extraordinary statement.

The Regent went to his mother to talk of Charlotte.

'I believe,' he said, 'that it is just a cover. It's Devonshire she's after. No girl could seriously contemplate marrying Silly Billy.'

'I believe Charlotte would go to any lengths to disturb us.'

'But she is thinking of marriage! Billy should have been married years ago . . . to Mary.' It was a reproof to his mother. She was constantly referring to his mistake in marrying Caroline instead of her niece and now of course that he was not so pleased with Miss Knight she was giving little digs about his taking her away. So this was just a gentle retaliation. They worked together nowadays, which was more agreeable to them both. Sentimental as he was, it suited his moods and ideals to be devoted to his mother and to know that she was to him. With such a relationship which existed between himself and his wife and daughter, he could not afford trouble with his mother in addition.

'William is a fool,' said the Queen tersely. 'He sways this way and that. First he wants to marry Mary . . . but Charlotte only has to mention his name in this ridiculous way and he turns to her.'

'He's ambitious as well as silly,' said the Prince. 'Think what it would mean to him. But the whole thing is a plot of Charlotte's. She's turned against Orange and she's after Devonshire. I wish to God I could get the Orange match settled.'

'We must try to bring this about,' said the Queen. 'And Charlotte must be made to see that no one takes this Gloucester affair seriously.'

* * *

Meanwhile Charlotte was writing gleefully to Mercer telling her all about the consternation, but being careful not to put her true feelings on to paper. Those letters she had written to Hesse and which were still in his possession haunted her a little. They reminded her too that she must exercise a little caution—even to Mercer.

But she talked to Cornelia about the affair. 'Poor Mary!' she said. 'I know she has not always been my friend and I don't trust her. I don't really trust any of the aunts. The old Begum trained them all to spy for her and they can't stop themselves doing it. But I am sorry for her, because she is old and would like to be married . . . and free from bondage, for while they remain spinsters, poor old aunts, they will have to do what the Queen tells them. My uncle Brunswick has lost his wife. Now why should he not marry Mary? Don't you think that's a good idea?'

'It has always been believed that one day she would marry Gloucester.'

'But how can she if I marry him?'

'You are not serious.'

That made Charlotte laugh. 'Well, I think until she does marry Gloucester Mary ought to have another hope. Put it about, Notte dear, that there is a chance of her marrying Brunswick. That would cheer her a great deal.'

'My dear Princess, what plots are you considering!'

'My dear Notte, you must admit that it has made life just a little less dull. I am sure all the writers are pleased with me. I have given them plenty to write about.'

It was true. The press was full of the Princess Charlotte's matrimonial prospects.

'Is it to be the Cheese or the Orange?' was the question on everyone's lips.

The Hasty Betrothal

THE Regent temporarily forgot his daughter's affairs, for glorious news was reaching him every day. Napoleon was being routed everywhere. The battle of Leipzig had taken place and this was to prove decisive. In Napoleon's disastrous retreat from Moscow he had left behind him over a thousand pieces of cannon and these the Russian Emperor was setting up as a memorial to their great victory. At Dresden the French had surrendered and the entire German Empire was liberated from the conqueror. In Amsterdam the Dutch had turned out the invader and were shouting for the return of the House of Orange.

The Regent who looked upon these victories as his, who had followed in detail the manoeuvring of the British Armies, was exultant. He rode to open Parliament with his usual pomp and this time no voice was raised against him, although there was none for him. He could not greatly care. He was seeing himself as the victorious general, for he had always longed to lead an army to victory and if he could not do so in fact had done so a thousand times in his imagination.

His speech was fired with eloquence. He dwelt lovingly on the recent victories, of the hardships that had been endured, of the years of strain and trial which that man Napoleon had imposed on the world. But we had stood firm against him; we had come through magnificently.

He was acting a part as he could do so well. He was the great soldier who had never fought a battle; he was the man who had led his country to victory and brought freedom to the world.

He was magnanimous in victory, declaring: 'We shall not require sacrifices from the French of any description inconsistent with her honour or just pretensions as a nation.'

His eyes filled with tears as he thought of his dear friend and cousin Louis XVIII of France who had been holding his court in Aylesbury and would soon now be returning to his country.

Afterwards he went to his mother, for she was willing to share his illusion that he was the main architect of peace.

He walked up and down her apartment, his arm through hers. 'The Corsican's star has set,' he declared. 'This is new freedom for the world. All our struggles have not been in vain. We have fought and won.'

He took from his pocket a snuffbox on which was a miniature of himself.

'I hope when you use this you will not feel ashamed of the face that adorns it,' he said emotionally.

The Queen replied that she would be proud ... proud indeed.

'I believe,' he replied, 'that now you may think me worthy of my family and this country.'

'I am proud of you,' replied the Queen, 'proud of you and the country which has stood for so long alone ... facing this tyrant. And now I hear his glory is over. Is it true that they are sending him into exile?'

'Exile in Elba,' confirmed the Prince. 'Thus ends all his pride.'

'The sun is shining,' replied the Queen with more sentiment than she usually expressed. 'May God bless you.'

The Regent took her hand and kissed it.

How pleasant, she thought, to be on these terms with him. How in the old days she had longed for his affection. She wished that she was not aware of his superficiality. But no matter—he was her first-born; he was the same George whose charms as a baby she had had modelled in wax and kept under a glass case on her dressing table. She did not love him the less because she knew him perhaps as well as anyone did.

How delighted she was to see him flushed with victory. His unpopularity hurt him a good deal; and perhaps now he would be less so. If only he could be rid of Caroline, marry again, produce an heir; or even come to some happier relationship with Charlotte.

'This will mean that many sovereigns will be claiming their own,' he was saying. 'They will bless us forever because we have restored their kingdoms to them. Not only the King of France, but there's Spain, Sardinia, the elector of Hanover and Orange ...'

A cloud touched his brow. This was a reminder. Orange! Something must be done soon about Charlotte's marriage to Orange.

*   *   *

The Prince of Orange was coming back to England. He was a better match than ever, the Regent declared to his mother. Now that his House was restored to its own, he did not know of a better opportunity for Charlotte.

He was not going to have any more nonsense about her preference for Gloucester—which he knew was a cover to hide her foolish infatuation for Devonshire—he was going to insist on a meeting with Orange, and Charlotte was going to discover that she approved of the match.

He called on his daughter frequently. He put himself out to charm and of course he did. He explained the tactics of victorious battles to her and she listened, not caring for the details but enjoying his endeavours to please. Once at Carlton House he showed her a picture of the Prince of Orange.

'You have to admit,' he said with a smile, 'that he is quite a pleasant looking young man.'

Charlotte was silent.

'Come,' said her father. 'You must agree with me.'

That was the trouble; he wanted everyone to agree with him, and when they did he was so charming.

'He is not ugly,' she admitted; and the Regent was not dissatisfied with that answer.

'Soon,' he said, 'your own eyes will tell you that he is far from ugly.'

She set her lips in a stubborn line, but he was intent on charming her and pretended not to notice.

Mercer who was travelling at the time saw the Prince of Orange when he passed through Plymouth and wrote to Charlotte to tell her so.

She was agreeably surprised. He was a shy young man, but Mercer thought that was not a disadvantage, and he could look very pleasant when he smiled. He was by no means dour and seemed to enjoy a joke. Mercer had had an opportunity of observing him closely and found that he could converse very agreeably. She hoped that Charlotte would think so.

This letter from Mercer had more effect on Charlotte than all the Regent's attempts to make a fine picture of Orange. She believed Mercer; and if Mercer thought the young man possible, perhaps he was.

*   *   *

The Regent called at Warwick House. He scarcely gave
Cornelia a glance; he had not been very friendly since the
Devonshire breakfast. He had come, he said, to speak to his
daughter.

Charlotte received him with apprehension. She guessed
that he had come to talk about the evening's reception when
he had arranged for the Prince of Orange to be presented to
her.

When he saw her he embraced her with more affection than
usual; she was immediately softened as always, although in
her heart she knew that he wanted something from her and
experience had taught him that he was more likely to get it by
being tender than stern.

'My dearest child,' he said, 'how well you are looking, and I
am glad. Your health has been giving me much concern.
Moreover, you will wish to look your best for tonight.'

'Shall I?' she asked fearfully.

'You know you always like to look your best when many
people see you and tonight is rather a special occasion.'

'All visits to Carlton House are special occasions,' she reminded him, and the comment pleased him.

'Tonight you will see William.' He held up an admonitory
finger. 'Now, don't be alarmed. There is nothing alarming in
this. I merely wish you to give me an opinion of the young
man. You understand, my dear Charlotte, that we cannot
shilly-shally forever. We have to make up our minds, don't
we?'

'I suppose we do.'

'Certainly we do. And tonight I shall want you to tell me
whether or not it will do. Just that. And then if it does you
will get to know this young man and decide whether you can
marry him.'

'Papa . . .'

'Oh, I know, you are grateful, for all I have done. I have
been very patient, now haven't I, Charlotte? What an indulgent parent I am! But then of course you are my dearest
daughter and I happen to love you.'

She was pink with pleasure.

'Now let us try that Highland Fling together, eh? You can
hum the music.'

It was hilarious. Large as he was, he was so graceful that he
made her, for all her boisterous youth, feel awkward.

'No, you are wrong,' he cried. 'Charlotte you are out of
step.'

'It is you! It is you!' she shrieked. And they danced to-

gether, hallo-ing at the appropriate moments until he was
breathless and sat down.

She sat beside him.

'There,' he said, 'we did that rather well together.'

'I shall never dance as gracefully as you, Papa,' she said.

He smiled, acknowledging the truth of this.

He patted her hand. 'You do very well,' he said. 'And tonight you will tell me that . . . it will do.'

*　　　　*　　　　*

When he had gone her spirits sank.

She went to her dressing room and called to Louisa.

'What shall I wear, Louisa?' she asked.

'Your most becoming gown, I should think.'

'Leave me and I will look through my gowns and choose
myself.'

When she was alone, she thought of him dancing with her.
She had been really happy then; it was how she had always
wanted him to be in her childhood when she had striven so
much to please him. It had seemed while they were dancing
like that that they were friends. But of course it was really
because he wanted her to say it would do.

Would she have been happier living with her mother? At
least there would have been a show of affection.

If she went to Carlton House tonight and said 'It will do,'
he would be very affectionate. He would always be affectionate if she did what he asked.

She turned over her dresses. This lovely lama one—how
becoming that was! It made her look like a fairy princess.
Then there was one sewn with pearls. That and feathers in
her hair . . . she could look quite beautiful.

There was the purple satin with the black lace. It was like a
dress one would wear in mourning, but Mercer had said that
only a very fair person could wear it.

A mourning dress!

She took it up and held it against her.

'Not that!' Louisa had come and was staring at her.

'Why not?'

'It is hardly suitable for . . .'

'For what, Louisa?'

'When you are going to meet . . .'

Charlotte laid the dress on the bed. 'I have chosen to wear
it,' she said.

*　　　　*　　　　*

The Regent embraced her, but she saw by his eyes that he
did not like the dress.

'It s a dinner party, though a small one,' he said. 'Not a
funeral.'

She did not answer as he led her to his guests. There were
not more than a dozen so; it was indeed a small party according to Carlton House standards; and there—a little awkward,
perhaps a little overpowered by the splendour of Carlton
House, was the Prince of Orange.

'It is time you two young people met,' said the Regent
jovially.

They faced each other. He was small and pale; he had
scarcely any chin and his teeth were uneven and not good; but
there was about him a desire to please and his smile, even
though it exposed the teeth, illuminated his face and made it
quite pleasant. The fact that Mercer had found something to
praise influenced Charlotte in his favour.

'I have heard so much of you . . . for some time,' she said;
and he smiled, understanding in what manner she must have
heard and for what purpose.

They had been placed side by side at the dinner table and
the rest of the guests made sure—on the Regent's instructions
—that they had an opportunity to talk together. At the same
time the Regent himself engaged the young Prince in conversation about his army experiences and drew him out so that
he was able to show himself as a good soldier and a modest
man, for the Regent chided him for being too reticent about
his successes in the field.

'I have heard,' he declared, 'from Wellington what a brave
soldier you were, so do not attempt to tell us the reverse.'

Charlotte liked him better than she had thought possible
and was wishing that she had worn a more becoming gown.

The Regent was obviously impatient for the guests to leave
the table and this meant that they did so in record time.
According to the custom the guests strolled about Carlton
House admiring the latest acquisitions, and the Regent took
this opportunity to draw Charlotte aside and hustle her into
his drawing room.

'Well,' he demanded as soon as they were alone, 'what is the
verdict? What do you say?'

She stared at the yellow silk walls. 'Papa, I . . . I . . .'

He cried: 'You are telling me it will not do. You were
determined that it would not! It is for this reason that you
came dressed in . . . mourning!'

His face had grown scarlet with anger; she could not bear

it. She cried out: 'No, no. You are mistaken. I like his manner. I like it very well . . . what I have seen of it.'

His face relaxed. She was seized and held against him. He
turned and called: 'Liverpool.'

Lord and Lady Liverpool who could not have been far off,
came into the drawing room immediately.

'My daughter has just made me the happiest man alive.
You may congratulate her.'

Liverpool declared that he did so with all his heart. He was
sure that the match would be blessed. He shared His Highness's emotion, for he believed that the Princess had acted
with good sense which would bring joy not only to herself but
to the nation.

Charlotte opened her mouth to protest, but the Regent
forestalled her. 'Liverpool!' he cried. 'Bring Orange. I am so
overcome by emotion. I declare I have never, never been so
happy.'

Liverpool had already disappeared and Lady Liverpool was
murmuring her congratulations. It was indeed wonderful she
said that the Princess had chosen in such a way which so
gratified His Highness her father. She was sure that her
father's pleasure must give her almost as great a happiness as
that which would be hers with this most wise and virtuous
Prince of Orange.

Orange arrived with Liverpool, bewildered but aware of
what had happened. The rather aloof young woman in the
purple satin had accepted him—and he was to be the consort
of the future Queen of England.

The Regent immediately took the centre of the stage. He
seized the hands of Charlotte and Orange.

'There,' he said, 'my two dear children!' He made Orange
clasp Charlotte's hand; the two young people looked at each
other—Orange fearfully, Charlotte sullenly. 'Happy, happy
moment,' cried the Regent. 'I declare I feel young again. I am
touched by the happiness of you two young people. Ah, Liverpool . . . and you, Clarence . . . you cannot guess my emotions
at this moment! What a wonderful thing it is to be a parent
and to be certain of a child's future happiness.'

He went on in this strain, walking up and down, pausing
every now and then to look at Orange and Charlotte, to smile
at them, to weep, which he did all the time, in that expert
manner so that the tears never fell from his eyes but were
neatly despatched into the most exquisitely worked and delicately scented handkerchief.

It was his scene and he played it as only he could. No one else said very much.

We are like the furniture on the stage, thought Charlotte. We are only there to enhance his performance.

But she admired him. How she would have liked to be as he was. Only one who did not feel deeply could give such a display of deep affection.

Orange looked on with some astonishment. She hoped that he was admiring her father.

With perfect timing the Regent stopped his act and became statesmanlike.

'The engagement shall not yet be made public,' he said. 'Her Majesty would be put out if she heard through any other means than by my special messenger. I think perhaps the Duke of York should take the news to her.' He smiled charmingly at Clarence. 'She would expect it from my eldest brother.'

Clarence said he would inform the Duke of York without delay.

'And now,' said the Regent expansively,' I think our betrothed young people might have an opportunity of sauntering through the rooms . . . alone.'

So they sauntered, shyly, wondering what to say to each other. The Regent's display of eloquence had left them tongue-tied.

'I . . . I had expected you to be a little different,' said Charlotte awkwardly, implying that he was not so bad as she had expected.

'And I had thought you would be different from what you are.'

They smiled and suddenly it struck Charlotte that just as she had heard about the lack of charm of Slender Billy he had doubtless heard stories of her.

It struck her as funny and she burst out laughing, rather hysterical laughter, for it was very disconcerting to have made up one's mind to refuse a suitor and then find oneself affianced to him.

But Orange was laughing.

Yes, thought Charlotte, he is not so bad.

And she began to feel better.

*   *   *

When she returned to Warwick House she would talk to no one. Louisa helped her out of the purple satin; Cornelia wanted to speak to her; but she was silent.

They were disturbed, knowing something had happened, but she refused to allow them to question her.

The next morning the Prince of Orange called at Warwick House.

When he was announced Charlotte said to Cornelia: 'He is my betrothed.'

'You cannot mean . . .' began Cornelia.

'I do. It happened last night at Carlton House.'

'So you agreed.'

'Well, not exactly. It happened. I did not quite know how but one moment my father asked me how I felt and the next I was engaged.'

Cornelia stared in horror at Charlotte, who swept past her, and Cornelia following went down to greet the Prince.

Oh dear, thought Cornelia, hardly prepossessing. Really plain . . . and he does not look healthy. She cannot really be in love with him. In love with him! But of course she is not.

But perhaps she is, for she loves strange people. Gloucester for instance. But that was not serious. Devonshire, Hesse, Fitzclarence. They all except Gloucester, who did not count, had a romantic air about them which this young boy from Holland lacked.

She could hear the betrothed pair talking together. They sounded like two ordinary young people getting to know each other. Charlotte did not seem desperately unhappy so perhaps she was reconciled to her father's wishes.

When he had left the Princess was uncommunicative—but quiet and serious. Cornelia wished that Mercer were here so that they could discuss the matter together.

* * *

The next day the Prince of Orange came again and with him was the Prince Regent.

The latter was more cordial to Cornelia than he had been for some time; he was clearly good humoured and delighted with himself and the young people.

'The Prince of Orange was so eager to call on the Princess,' he told Cornelia, 'that I thought I would accompany him here. Charlotte, you and the Prince will have a great deal to say to each other and I will sit awhile and talk to the Chevalier. I have something to say to *her*.'

Cornelia felt a twinge of apprehension, wondering what the Regent had to say to her.

She soon discovered. He had not forgotten her rather careless conduct in riding out to Chiswick with the Princess. He

wanted her to be especially careful, particularly now that
Charlotte was affianced. He had noticed that his daughter's
behaviour was sometimes what he would call 'light'. He did
not think those who had been put in charge of her should
allow her to behave in this way. She was an innocent young
girl, he was fully aware of that. But he did not want people to
suppose for one moment that it could be otherwise. And
people were inclined to put unfortunate constructions on the
most innocent actions. He did not want to have to lay the
blame at any door, but there were so many who would say
that there was some fault in her household.

Cornelia thought of the Hesse letters and shivered.

This rather disturbing conversation was brought to an end
by the sound of violent sobbing in the next room. The Regent
sprang to his feet and hurried in the direction of the sobs.
Charlotte had thrown herself on to a sofa and was crying
bitterly while the Prince of Orange was standing helplessly
by.

'Is he taking his leave of you?' asked the Regent. 'Well,
well, you must not be distressed. You will have plenty of
chances to be alone with him.' He turned to Orange. 'In spite
of her protests I fear we must depart now. Don't forget you
have an important engagement.'

How like him! He did not want to know the cause of her
tears and had implied it was because Orange was saying
goodbye to her. He decided how people should act to give him
most comfort, and that was the way he pretended they did.

When they had gone Charlotte said: 'I don't want to be
engaged to him, Cornelia. I never wanted it. And he told me
that I shall have to live part of the year in Holland. I won't. I
swear I won't.'

Cornelia did her best to comfort her, but they were both
conscious of how implacable could be the will of the plump
and benign-looking Regent.

*   *   *

Charlotte lay listlessly in her bed. For some days she had
felt very unwell. The pain in her knee had intensified; she
had no desire to go out. Louisa tried to mother her, but she
did not respond. Cornelia, who knew the cause of her apprehension, wrote to Mercer and told her how uneasy she was.

When Mercer arrived Charlotte brightened considerably
and the two of them discussed her affairs with Cornelia. Charlotte admitted that she did not want to marry Orange although she did not dislike him as much as she had thought she

would, and she knew she had to marry someone; but the thought of having to leave England horrified her.

'Imagine,' she cried, 'to be in a strange land, parted from all one's friends. Besides, my place is here. One day I shall be the Queen. Should the Queen of England live abroad?'

Mercer was thoughtful. 'You could not, as Queen of England, live abroad.'

'And could he, as ruler of Holland which he will one day be, live in England?'

There was silence and then Mercer said: 'Don't worry, let things go for the moment and do not let the Regent know that you are determined on this point. You could not possibly go abroad for a long time. The state of Europe would not permit it. And your betrothal has not yet been publicly announced. I would say wait and see what happens.'

Cornelia was nodding her approval of this idea; and Charlotte felt relieved. Her two friends had comforted her as they always did.

Enter and Exit Leopold

THE following January was the coldest Charlotte ever remembered. By the middle of the month the Thames was frozen and booths were set up on the ice that a fair might be held. It was impossible to travel outside London for the roads were blocked with snow; trade was coming to a standstill; but the mood of the people continued exultant because the end of the Napoleonic wars was in sight.

The Regent was stricken with influenza and gout. He was peevish and his doctors were constantly at his bedside; Charlotte herself was far from well; she said she only had to put her nose outside the door to shrivel up like a lemon.

But by the end of the month the thaw had set in and everyone's spirits rose.

On her birthday Charlotte went to visit her mother. She was feeling hurt because she had not seen her father. It was true he had remembered her birthday and had explained to her that he would be unable to see her on that day as he had promised to attend a christening. But, Charlotte asked herself, if he had really wished to be with her he would not have allowed this other engagement to be made. He had given her a splendid diamond bracelet for a birthday present when he had told her that he would be unable to see her; it was very grand and valuable and she had worn it constantly since— even on unsuitable occasions—but she could not tell him that his presence would have meant more to her than the glittering gift.

At least she could see her mother and Caroline received her with many explanations of delight and affection. If her little girl had not come to her on her birthday she would have

called in Brougham and Whitbread to do something about
it, she declared. She was not going to be kept away from her
darling in this way. And now Caroline must come and see her
library which had just been completed. Connaught House delighted her. It was far far better than stuffy old Kensington
Palace.

Charlotte admired the library which was ornate in the extreme with its six large bookcases designed by the Princess of
Wales herself. Caroline called Charlotte's attention to the
pedestals at the end of the bookcases on each of which was a
statue holding a lamp. There were many statues in the room
and such a quantity of pictures that there was hardly a space
on the wall which was not occupied.

'There!' cried Caroline. 'What do you think of it, my
cherub?'

'It is very splendid, Mamma.'

'I was determined it should be. Why should I not surround
myself with splendour . . . and people . . . and amusing, clever
people, eh? Because he despises me that does not mean the
rest of the world does. Oh, no!'

'Of course not, Mamma.'

'Not my little Charlotte, eh? She loves her old mother, and
I do believe that if it were possible she would come and live
with me tomorrow. Is that not so?'

'If it were possible,' said Charlotte hesitantly.

'One of these days it may be. They can't treat you like a
child forever, can they?'

'When I am married . . .'

'Married. These rumours!'

Charlotte realized that her mother had not been informed
of her betrothal; and indeed it had not been publicly announced, but she thought her mother should have been told.

'So,' cried Caroline, 'they are true!'

'Well, Mamma, there is an understanding between myself
and the Prince of Orange.'

'Orange! That thin little boy . . . without a chin and a
kingdom too, until a little while ago.'

'My father is eager for the match.'

'The old rogue! Why? Why should my precious daughter
be thrown away on that stripling! It's monstrous! And the
Regent wants it. You can't want it, Charlotte. You can't want
him. He'll be no good to you.'

'I . . . don't find him unpleasant.'

'You don't find him unpleasant! Why, bless you, that's no
way to talk about your future husband. Do you find him

pleasant? Of course you don't. I know what he wants, the old devil. He wants you out of the way. He's jealous of you, Charlotte. He knows the people are fond of you and he knows they hate him. So he wants you out of the way . . . so that they'll forget you.'

'I don't want to go to Holland.'

'You must not go to Holland. You must stand out against it, my pet. And to think they did not tell me of the betrothal of my own daughter!'

'I shall refuse to leave England.'

'That's right. You refuse. And refuse him too. You're throwing yourself away, Charlotte . . . and why should you? You should choose your own husband . . . someone like little Hesse, eh?' Caroline nudged her daughter slyly. 'Oh, there was one you felt very fondly for, eh? And I'm not surprised, a little charmer, he was.'

Charlotte thought of the letters which he had not returned and drew away from her mother, remembering that it was she who had fostered that friendship.

'And Fitzclarence too; and I hear that Sussex's bastard has been casting eyes at you.'

Charlotte laughed. 'Oh, d'Este,' she said. 'He has written me a most passionate letter.'

'The young rip. What hope has he, eh?'

'None at all, but he writes very charmingly.'

'I'll warrant he does and fancies himself as your cousin . . . although from the wrong side of the blanket . . . for although that woman insists she's married to Sussex she's not, you know, and they'd never let you have young d'Este though he may insist he's your cousin.'

'I am affianced to Orange in any case.'

'And you're not happy about it. I can see that. Tell your Mamma.'

Charlotte explained her feelings and Caroline sat nodding sympathetically. It was easy to talk to her mother, she found.

'Why, my love,' said the Princess of Wales, 'if I had any say in this, which as a mother I should have, I'd never let them marry you to a man you didn't fancy. I know the miseries of an unhappy marriage; and I should have thought he would know, too. I cannot understand his forcing you into this . . . for forcing you it is.'

'I don't think he believes he actually forced me. I did see Orange and said that I found I liked him . . . just a little.' Again that need to protect one parent in the presence of the other. But her mother was certainly soothing.

'My dearest,' she said, 'you shall never be forced to do what is distasteful to you. You must always come to me and we will find a way out.'

'I have some good friends. Miss Knight and Miss Elphinstone are very calm and practical and they think always of my good. They say that I should wait and see what happens. My betrothal has not even been made public yet.'

'Dear good people!' cried Caroline. 'I'm glad they are with you. But never forget—you always have your mother.'

'I don't forget, Mamma. I know you are always there and would always help me . . . if you could.'

'With all my heart, my precious. And to think they are trying to force you into a marriage you do not fancy. It must not be. Look at your Mamma. I was married . . . not exactly against my will. I was told I was to have the best match in Europe. Oh, my dear, what tales I heard! And the picture they sent me of him! Framed in diamonds and must have been painted twenty years before. What a rude awakening! They didn't tell me how *fat* he was; and his manners. He took one look at me and asked for brandy to sustain him. That was your First Gentleman of Europe. I've had the fortune-teller. She should read your hand, Charlotte. Do you know that she told me that I'd be rid of him, that I'd travel. I always wanted to, Charlotte. It was one of my dreams. To travel and have lots of babies . . . babies of my own to look after and love. "Yes, Madam," she said, "you'll travel the world and you'll have a husband . . . a new husband who dotes on you." So there.'

Charlotte looked uneasy. 'Papa would have to die first.'

Caroline put her head on one side. 'Not necessarily, my pet. You know he's been longing to divorce me for years. Perhaps he'll succeed. He won't if I can help it . . . but he might. He's got the powers-that-be with him . . . but then so have I. Ha, that would be amusing, would it not? A new husband who adored me! Perhaps we'd have a child. Why not? There's time. But I'd never have anyone I cared for as I do for my dearest Charlotte.'

Charlotte was uneasy and Caroline, for once, seemed to sense this and started to talk of that day eighteen years ago when they had come to her bedside and said to her: 'You have a baby girl.' 'And they put you in my arms, my dearest, and I knew what it meant to be really happy. Nothing else in the world mattered. He was preparing to throw me aside . . . but I didn't care. I had my baby . . . my own Charlotte . . . and there wasn't a happier woman in London.'

Then she talked of Charlotte's endearing ways; she had

many stories most of which Charlotte had heard before, but she enjoyed hearing them again; and when it was time for her to leave she clung to her mother tenderly. Caroline supplied, oddly enough, a certain security. She was the most unstable of women, but her attitude towards her daughter had always been predictable. Charlotte believed that her mother would always willingly do her utmost to help her. It was a very pleasant feeling. Caroline seemed to sense her thoughts, for she said: 'Never forget, dearest Charlotte, that when you need help, there is always your mother.'

'I shall remember,' replied Charlotte soberly.

And she felt contented as her carriage took her along the icy roads to Warwick House.

* * *

This was victory year and from all over the Continent visitors came to England to pay their respects to the Prince Regent because of the significant role England had played in the downfall of Napoleon. Wellington was the military hero and the Regent associated himself with the great general to such an extent that it seemed sometimes as though he actually believed he had been on the battlefield directing Wellington himself.

There should, he decided, be lavish entertainment for the foreigners. Carlton House and the Pavilion should be the setting for many a fête and banquet. The bells would ring out; the cannons should be fired; and this reminder of the country's glory might even win back a little of that popularity which had been so lavishly bestowed on him in earlier days.

Charlotte must play a part in these entertainments, he decided. Orange had returned to Holland and no date had been fixed for the wedding which, said Cornelia, and Mercer agreed with her in this, was all to the good and showed that the Princess was wise not to worry at this stage about leaving England.

With the coming of April Napoleon signed his abdication of the French throne and he was given sovereignty of the island of Elba with a pension of 2,000,000 francs. Louis XVIII left his country retreat and came to London accompanied by the lifeguards en route for France—where he was received by the Regent. There was a touching meeting between them during which the King bestowed the order of St. Esprit on the Regent. It was an occasion such as the Regent loved; magnificent and beneficent, tears in his eyes, flowery phrases on his lips, constant expression of friendship—all these he lavished

on Louis who, plump and unctuous, swore undying friendship to his cousin of England who had made his exile so pleasant and who now rejoiced even as he did at the return of the
monarchy to France.

The Regent declared that nothing would please him better
than to accompany his dear cousin to Dover; and with great
pomp, the King and the Regent riding together, the caval-
cade set out while Napoleon left Fontainebleau for Elba.

The foreign visitors began to arrive and one of the first of
these was Catherine, Duchess of Oldenburg, the sister of the
Tsar of Russia (the Tsar was to follow later). She was twenty-
four at this time, widowed and reputed to be very beautiful,
although the British ambassador at the Hague described her
as being 'platter-faced'. This was an allusion to her Mongo-
lian cast of features which others said was one of the reasons
why, to western eyes, she was considered so fascinating.

The Duchess arrived after a somewhat uncomfortable journey, during which she had wished that she had never set out.
The sea was rough; she had been dreadfully ill; and she did
not consider she had been given the warm welcome in England which was the right of a sister of the Tsar—and a favourite sister at that.

She had decided to make her home in London the Pulteney
Hotel and to this she came on an April day which was cold
and blustery, and this did not improve her temper. She was
not sure that she liked the English, but she was looking
forward to seeing the Regent of whom she had heard so
much.

'An interesting ménage,' she commented to one of her
attendants. 'He is by all accounts a most exquisite gentleman
and there is this hoyden of a daughter and the most vulgar of
wives of whom he seeks to rid himself.'

The Duchess's long narrow eyes glittered. The Prince
Regent would be king in due course; and she was a widow. He
had only to rid himself of that woman who created such
scandal. Surely not an impossibility.

She was looking for excitement in London.

She had not been a day in London when the Regent's
equerry called at the Pulteney Hotel to tell her that his
master begged permission to call on his most distinguished
visitor.

Catherine was excited. He was, it was said, the perfect
lover—impeccably mannered, romantic, the First Gentleman
of Europe. It would be amusing when her brother Alexander
arrived to tell him that the Prince Regent was devoted to her

and between them they would put their heads together and find a way of ridding him of the obstacle which stood between them and marriage.

She replied that she would be delighted to receive His Royal Highness and planned a magnificent toilette to astonish him. Unfortunately one of her servants had made a foolish error about the time and the Prince arrived half an hour early with the result that she was not ready and had to keep him waiting, which did not please him; and then instead of receiving him graciously as she had planned, she was obliged to go into the drawing room, where he had been taken, and there greet him as though she were some ordinary hostess.

In the drawing room she found a somewhat peevish fat gentleman who, had she been the vision of beauty he had been expecting, would have readily forgiven the delay. But she was not. She was dark, slit-eyed and flat-faced; not in the least like his own Maria Fitzherbert, with whom he still unconsciously compared all women. She was not to his taste. Where was the luscious white arms and bosoms that he so admired; the golden hair, the blue eyes, the brilliant complexion? She was dressed in some dark and exotic garment. No doubt striking, but not to his taste at all.

His dismay was obvious to her immediately and she was a woman who could hate fiercely; in that moment she hated the Regent. A fat dandy, she thought. Where is all this much vaunted charm?

I've seen flower girls in cotton smocks prettier than she is, thought the Regent; and his disappointment was acute.

He gave her his famous bow, however, which even she had to admit to herself was a masterpiece of elegance; and they talked desultorily, he of the war and the battles—as though he had been present and won the lot, she thought derisively—and very shortly he took his leave.

Nothing will come of this, thought the Duchess. She would have to find other means of amusing herself in London than with the Prince Regent.

*   *   *

She found them in his daughter, Charlotte, for naturally the girl must call on her and pay her respects. Sitting at her window brooding on her situation, waiting impatiently for the arrival of her brother Alexander, looking out across Green Park, she had decided to cultivate the Princess. She had learned of the situation between the Prince and his daughter; it was full of tensions; Charlotte was betrothed to Orange and the girl was obviously not ecstatically happy about that. It had been a match of the Regent's arranging.

Interesting, thought the Duchess. Orange was a sickly youth but now that his father had been reinstated and the young man would be the ruler of Holland, he was not to be despised and she had thought he would make an excellent match for her sister, the Grand Duchess Anna. Quite clearly this could not be if he married young Charlotte; and the obvious answer to that was that he must not marry young Charlotte.

As she had shown her indifference to the Regent so she showed friendship to his daughter. She set out to charm the child and Charlotte—innocent, frank, ready to laugh and believe the best of everyone—was an easy victim.

Returning home in her carriage, Cornelia beside her, Charlotte said: 'I do believe that the Duchess of Oldenburg must be one of the most amusing and charming women in the world.'

'Your Highness can scarcely make such a hasty assessment of character.'

'Stuff and nonsense, Notte,' cried Charlotte. 'I tell you she is charming. I like her very much.'

'Time will either confirm or deny that.'

Charlotte was filled with irritation. 'Really, I don't know what has become of you. Ever since Devonshire's breakfast you have been so touchy and irritable that I find it difficult to tolerate your moods.'

Cornelia was shocked. Charlotte had never spoken to her in that way before. She was immediately contrite. 'Oh, I'm sorry, Notte. I didn't quite mean that. But the Duchess *is* charming and she was so pleasant to me and I find her so interesting. It's silly for you to carp.'

Cornelia was silent for the rest of the journey.

*　　*　　*

In spite of his dislike for her, the Regent must entertain the important sister of the Tsar, so he gave a dinner for her at Carlton House to which he invited the most important of his ministers and members of the nobility.

Her entrance was a shock to them all for she appeared in the long flowing black draperies associated with widowhood. Even the Regent could not hide his surprise, and she determined to assail his reputation for perfect manners in all circumstances and asked in a loud voice why he disapproved of her gown.

It was most becoming, he declared, and far from disapproving, he admired. But he did wonder whether it resembled the costumes worn by widows.

'I am a widow,' she said.

'One so young and beautiful will not remain a widow for long,' he announced coldly, to which she replied pointedly that at the moment she felt no temptation to change that state.

The dinner party was not a success.

At every function she tried to draw him into verbal battles and he often had difficulty in extricating himself gracefully. He declared to Liverpool that he would be glad when the Tsar arrived, for then he would devote his attention to him and the devil could take his waspish sister.

Meanwhile Charlotte was invited frequently to the Pulteney Hotel and there the Duchess exerted all her charm.

Cornelia was wrong, said Charlotte. The Duchess was fast becoming one of her best friends. Cornelia did not like her. Poor Notte, thought Charlotte, she was actually jealous! Was she to be denied interesting company just because a lady's companion was jealous?

Certainly not, said Charlotte.

*   *   *

In June Alexander, Tsar of Russia, arrived in London with a magnificent suite among which were many princes of European States. Now the real hospitality began. The Regent was delighted to find Alexander handsome and affable—very different from his sister; he was easy to entertain and the Regent forgot the unpleasant Catherine and devoted himself to Alexander. The most extravagant entertainments were given at Carlton House. The bankers and merchants gave banquets for the visitors, and Alexander declared his desire to see all that his dear cousin of England would allow him to see. There were visits to the Bank of England, Westminster Abbey, the dockyards and the Arsenal at Woolwich; there were grand reviews in Hyde Park. The visit was not to be a long one so that there were a great deal to be crowded into a short time. Everywhere he went the Tsar was cheered; his good looks and pleasant manners endeared him to the people; and the Regent was able to bask in his reflected popularity. No longer were there sullen silences and it pleased him to imagine that he was included in the cheers.

The Duchess had not forgotten Charlotte and continued to be charming to her.

One day when the Princess came to the Pulteney Hotel as she had been encouraged to do informally, she found one of the most handsome young men she had ever seen seated beside the Duchess in animated conversation with her.

Charlotte, who had entered unannounced—for one of the most delightful things about the Duchess was the informality that could be enjoyed with her—started, somewhat awkwardly and wondered how to proceed. The young man immediately rose to his feet, bowed, kissed the Duchess's hand and walked to the door. Coming face to face with Charlotte he clicked his heels, bowed from the waist and departed.

Charlotte's cheeks were pink, and the Duchess laughed. 'Why, my dearest Charlotte, you are blushing. Well, it is most becoming. I am sure Leopold thought so.'

'Who is that young man?'

'A young prince and a delightful one, I do assure you. One of my favourite princes. And in fact a family connection. His sister Juliana is married to my brother Constantine. I am so glad Alexander brought him in his suite. He is so charming— interesting and intelligent too.'

There was no subterfuge about Charlotte, and being in-terested in the young man she made no attempt to hide the fact.

'Tell me more of him.'

'Sit down my dear and make yourself comfortable and we will talk of Leopold of Saxe-Coburg.'

'A German?'

'Well, is there anything wrong with that? You yourself have much German blood in you.'

'I think of myself as English. But pray, dear Duchess, tell me about this Leopold.'

'He is the youngest of a large family . . . well six or seven of them.'

'The youngest.'

'You are thinking he will be a poor young Prince. That may be, but what he lacks in worldly possessions he makes up for by his handsome face. Do you agree?'

'I thought him handsome.'

'Why, he's the best looking Prince in Europe.' She leaned over and touched Charlotte's hand. 'I believe you are already comparing him with poor Orange. *Poor* Orange! *He* won't come very well out of the comparison. Not many would with Leopold. Now if you were not betrothed I would say: "There is the man for you." He's a Protestant too so there would be no trouble on that score.'

Charlotte giggled. 'I don't know what my father would say if he could hear us.'

'Well, is that not why we enjoy each other's company ... because we don't have to stand on ceremony, because we can say what we mean ... and if we wish to discuss the most handsome prince in Europe I don't see why we shouldn't ... and compare him with others less fortunate ... if we wish to. Don't you agree?'

'I do agree,' said Charlotte fiercely.

*　　*　　*

The Duchess was smiling secretly when Charlotte took her leave, for she had a shrewd suspicion as to who would be waiting at the door of the chamber. Leopold would surely not miss such an opportunity, for he was a very ambitious young man.

Thus when Charlotte passed out of the room she immediately saw the young Prince of Saxe-Coburg standing at attention. Again that military bow which was very attractive—less elegant but more masculine than that famous one of the Regent's.

He looked at her, her eyes brilliant with excitement and he said: 'I waited in the hope that Your Royal Highness would allow me to conduct you to your carriage.'

'That is good of you,' Charlotte said graciously.

She laid her hand on his arm and he declared that he was extremely sensible of the honour done to him. How serious he was! There was no sign of gaiety in his eyes; it was a very solemn occasion.

Cornelia stared in amazement to see Charlotte's escort, but Charlotte did not look in her direction as Leopold handed her into her carriage.

'I shall be glad to see you at Warwick House,' she told him.

At which he made another of his solemn bows and stood back to watch the carriage as it drove away.

Cornelia said: 'Who was that?'

'His Serene Highness, Leopold of Saxe-Coburg,' said Charlotte grandly.

'I see, and he was presented to you by the Duchess I presume?'

'He was with the Duchess when I called. Cornelia, don't you think he is the most handsome man you ever saw?'

'I think I could be accused of hyperbole if I agreed to that.'

'I wouldn't accuse you. Don't be so stuffy, Cornelia. You must admit he is very charming.'

Cornelia sighed. Was this going to be another Hesse affair? Charlotte looked at her companion coldly. What had happened to old Notte? She just wanted to spoil everything. She might have agreed that Leopold was handsome. It was so obvious.

How charmingly he had bowed and what an exciting day!

*   *   *

She must find out all about Saxe-Coburg and the ruling family. The Duchess was informative. The House of Saxe-Coburg occupied a small territory of some eight towns and two hundred and seventy villages, and it ruled over less than sixty thousand subjects.

'Very small,' commented Charlotte, 'compared with England . . . or Holland for that matter.' Oh yes, Leopold was a minor Prince as far as worldly possessions were concerned.

'But he is a Protestant,' pointed out the Duchess, 'and that is in his favour. He is a very serious young man and has proved his courage on the battlefield. His brother Ernest, the reigning Duke, is devoted to him—as are all his family. They constantly sing the praises of their dear young Leopold. He has been such a good son to his widowed mother for he has a strong sense of duty.'

'It is a quality I greatly admire in a man,' said Charlotte.

'My brother, the Tsar, has given him rank in our army. You should see him in his uniform. My dear, it would quite take your breath away.'

Charlotte was almost breathless contemplating the sight of godlike Leopold in the uniform of a Russian general.

'My brother has a very high opinion of him and presented him in the battlefield with the cross of a Commander of the Military Order of St. George.'

'He is indeed a hero,' said Charlotte wistfully.

*   *   *

But she was piqued when he did not call at Warwick House.

She had supposed he would accept her invitation without delay and had waited for him expectantly. Every time one of her household came to her, she had hoped that they would announce the arrival of Leopold.

How strange that he should have waited to conduct her to her carriage and then not accept her invitation!

Sometimes driving in the park she would see him and he always endeavoured to ride near her carriage as though hoping she would notice him.

She did, of course, but she was not going to let him know this. She was hurt with him. She had offered an invitation and it had not been taken up. But if she was angry with him that did not mean she liked him any less.

He was constantly in her thoughts.

* * *

One day in the Park he rode near her carriage and lifting her eyes she looked straight into his. On impulse she ordered the coachman to stop.

'Good day,' she said coolly. 'I wonder why, having received an invitation from me, you neglect it.'

Leopold looked startled. He was unused to such direct manners.

He said: 'Your Highness, I did not understand that it was a formal invitation. I was under the impression that Your Highness was speaking lightly . . . and merely intended your comment as a kindly gesture.'

'I always say what I mean.' She was smiling for he was every bit as handsome as she had been thinking him—and he had scarcely been out of her thoughts since their first meeting.

Cornelia was apprehensive. Charlotte would never behave with necessary decorum. Did she not realize that they were being watched even now and it would very likely be reported to her father that she had been seen chatting in a very friendly manner with one of the insignificant princes of the Tsar's suite.

Charlotte went on: 'Well, you know now that I mean what I say so I will say it again. I shall expect to see you at Warwick House.'

Leopold inclined his head and Charlotte instructed the coachman to drive on.

Cornelia said: 'Was that wise?'

Charlotte turned on her in anger. 'What do you mean— *wise*?'

'To ask him to come to Warwick House. It was not in accordance with the usual . . .'

'Oh Notte, you make me cross. Do stop carping. He will come this time. He won't be able to avoid it.'

'Have you realized that you have put him into a very awkward position?'

'How absurd!'

'Not absurd at all,' said Cornelia. 'The Prince of Saxe-Coburg cannot call at Warwick House unless he has permission from the Regent to do so.'

'You forget that I am no longer a child. Warwick House is my residence and I shall ask whom I please.'

'If he called without your father's permission he could be sent out of the country.'

'Stuff!' said Charlotte, and she added: 'And nonsense too.'

But she was not really angry because she was so looking forward to seeing him.

* * *

Leopold's feelings were very mixed as he rode off and went back to his rooms over a greengrocer's shop in Marylebone which was all that had been available for him. She was an enchanting creature this Princess Charlotte and obviously interested in him; and her interest made him think of a most exciting possibility. But was it possible? The Duchess Catherine had told him that Charlotte was betrothed to the Prince of Orange and if that were so she was not free. Moreover would they consider a humble prince of Saxe-Coburg as suitable?

Why not? His family was a noble one; Orange was a sickly creature by all accounts and Charlotte did not like him. Whereas she was naïve enough not to hide her interest in Leopold. Clearly she liked him very much indeed.

Ever since their first meeting he had been turning over in his mind the possibility of calling at Warwick House as she had suggested. How could he who had been brought up in the strict German manner commit such a breach of court etiquette—even though the Princess asked it? If he called without her father's consent he would never be forgiven.

He was ambitious—and there was something more which influenced him. She *was* charming; and he would have to marry one day. The future Queen of England! He felt almost giddy at the prospect. But it was hopeless. Nothing was hopeless. What about Orange? Something which had glinted in the Grand Duchess Catherine's eyes when she talked of Charlotte's future had made him feel that Orange might not be an obstacle after all. Catherine was one of the cleverest women he knew and fortunately she did not dislike him; and for some reason she would like to substitute another bridegroom for Orange.

How could she—a visitor to this land—alter the plans which the rulers had laid down for their princess? And yet . . .

Leopold was aware of his good looks. There were not many princes who were tall, slim and handsome, brave, serious and Protestant.

What a chance! What a dizzy prospect! He could not spoil

it right at the start by behaving in a manner which would make that important gentleman, that arbiter of manners, the Prince Regent, dismiss him as a boor.

There was the Duke of York, affable, approachable, always ready to help a good soldier. Suppose he told the Duke of York of his predicament and asked his advice. The idea was an excellent one and he begged for an audience without delay.

The Duke received him with pleasure; he had heard of his exploits in the army and congratulated him on his decoration by the Tsar.

Leopold then told the reason for his call and begged the Duke of York to tell him what he should do.

The Duke stuck out his heavy jaw thoughtfully. 'There is only one thing you can do, my dear fellow,' he said, 'and that is to write to the Regent, tell him what has happened and request his permission to call on the Princess.'

'It is what I thought should be done,' replied Leopold, 'and I will lose no time in doing it.'

* * *

The Regent stormed up and down his study. The impertinence! This penniless fellow from Saxe-Coburg—a younger son of an insignificant House—craved his indulgence and asked to be allowed to call on the Princess Charlotte. He felt it his duty to inform the Regent that he had received an invitation to visit the Princess. She had become aware of him when at the Pulteney Hotel whither he had been to wait on his kinswoman the Grand Duchess of Oldenburg. He had encountered the Princess Charlotte there and begged to be allowed to conduct her to her carriage. It was then that he had received the invitation which he hesitated to accept without the Regent's consent.

'And I should hope not!' cried the Regent. 'So he would call on my daughter! And for what purpose do princes call on princesses? Charlotte is a minx and she is trying to elude her responsibilities. Orange must come back and she must be married without delay. As for Master Leopold, he can return whence he came for he is certainly not going to Warwick House.'

He called for writing materials and penned a courteous note to Leopold. He was sure the Prince would understand that he could not give him permission to call on the Princess Charlotte. With clever innuendo he suggested that in view of the fact that Leopold had become involved in a rather embarrassing situation the best way of extricating himself from it would be for him to leave the country. He was sure it could be arranged graciously and he knew that Leopold would agree with him.

That settled Leopold.

The Regent sent a message to the Prince of Holland telling him that it would be wise for him to return to England without delay.

Those matters settled, he next sent a message for Miss Knight telling her that her presence was required at Carlton House.

* * *

Miss Knight came with much apprehension. Charlotte's behaviour has been no credit to her lady companions and because Charlotte ignored the Duchess of Leeds and had made Cornelia her friend, she, Cornelia, would be the one who must take the blame for that indecorous conduct.

The Regent received her as soon as she arrived and his cool manner alarmed her. She who was usually calm and in full possession of her wits very frequently came near to losing them in his presence. He could be so regal and change so quickly; at one moment he made her feel that he regarded her as a wise friend and in the next that he despised her for a bungling fool. It was all done by the lift of an eyebrow, a gesture of the hand, the intonation of that very musical voice. He was a great actor who always played the part he intended to without giving anyone any doubt of his intentions.

'Miss Knight,' (not 'my dear Chevalier' which would have meant he felt kindly towards her), 'I am disturbed.' He looked at her reproachfully to set the scene. She was responsible for his disturbed feelings.

'I am indeed sorry, Sir.'

'Yes, yes. But this will not do. The Princess Charlotte has been placed in your care ... and that of the Duchess; and it grieves me that she should behave in the way she does. This last escapade ... this invitation to a most insignificant member of the Tsar's entourage ... Really, Miss Knight, how could she have come to be so lacking in what is required of her? She meets him on the *stairs* of an hotel ... like ... like a chambermaid. How came she to be on the stairs of an hotel? How could she in the company ... unattended ... of any young men who might care to accost her? It is beyond my understanding. But perhaps, Miss Knight, not beyond yours?'

He paused and she said nervously: 'Sir, she was visiting the Duchess of Oldenburg ...'

He interrupted pettishly: 'There have been too many
visits to the Duchess of Oldenburg. I do not wish these visits
to continue.'

'Does Your Highness wish them to be stopped completely?'

'Not completely. We do not want an incident. You will
agree with that, I hope, Miss Knight. But the visits are too
frequent. I hear that the Princess sees the Duchess every day.
That is most unseemly. They should not meet more than once
a week. Soon our visitors will be leaving us but until they do I
wish that the Princess Charlotte does not spend all her time in
the company of the Duchess of Oldenburg. You will see to
that, Miss Knight.'

'Indeed yes, Sir. And if the Prince of Saxe-Coburg should
call at Warwick House . . . what are your instructions?'

'The Prince of Saxe-Coburg will *not* call at Warwick
House. I have made my wishes clear to him. He had the grace
to write to tell me what had happened. He will be preparing
to leave the country at this very time.'

'I see, Your Highness.'

He began to pace up and down. 'And so, Miss Knight, I ask
you to carry out my wishes and by so doing ensure that I am
not further disturbed by these upheavals which to a father . . .'
he paused as though considering whether a tear was necessary
and decided that a husky note in the voice was more suited to
the occasion . . . 'can be most upsetting. You may go now.'

*   *   *

'Well,' said Charlotte, 'What was that about?'

'Your father is very displeased. He knows that you invited
the Prince of Saxe-Coburg here and he thinks that reprehensible.'

'How did he know? Someone must have told him. I am
spied on. I tell you I won't be spied on!'

'It was Leopold himself who told the Prince.'

'Leopold!'

'Oh, yes, he thought he should ask permission to call before
doing so.'

Hot colour flooded into Charlotte's cheeks.

'He didn't!'

'The Prince Regent told me that he did. He said he had a
letter from him to the effect that he had met you at the Pulteney and handed you into your carriage and that you then
invited him to call at Warwick House.'

'I don't believe it.'

Miss Knight shrugged her shoulders.

'It's not true, is it?' begged Charlotte.

'Why should your father say so if it were not? How should he know of it?'

'I shall ask Leopold when he comes.'

'He won't come. He is leaving the country.'

'No!'

'On the Regent's request. And your visits to the Duchess are to be considerably curtailed.'

'I won't have it,' declared Charlotte. And then: 'So he wrote to my father. He *asked* permission to call. The man's an idiot.'

Miss Knight was smiling complacently and Charlotte could have slapped her. She wanted to burst into tears; she wanted to sob out her misery; but she wasn't going to show Cornelia how deeply she felt.

So she railed against Leopold.

'What a ninny! He asks permission. So he has gone away, has he? He won't come to Warwick House? Well, I'm glad, I tell you. Let him stay away. I never want to see him again.'

The Dismissal of Orange

IT was ridiculous to feel so wretched over a man to whom she had scarcely spoken and who should be so timid that he must ask her father's permission before calling; but she did. She was however not going to allow anyone to know it.

She pretended to be excited about the banquet which her father was giving to the foreign visitors at Carlton House.

'Come,' she said to Louisa, 'make me beautiful—if that's possible.'

'It's the easiest thing in the world,' declared the fond Louisa.

Had he thought her beautiful? Attractive? Evidently not attractive enough to risk her father's displeasure for her sake!

'Feathers, Louisa. Yes, feathers. They are so becoming. And what dignity they give. I need it. I think I am lacking more in dignity than in beauty. Don't deny it, Louisa. And my silver tissue dress ... the one trimmed with silver lace and embroidered in lama. You know the one.'

Louisa knew it and she exclaimed with delight as she dressed her volatile young mistress in it. 'If Your Highness could stand a little more still it would be easier. Feathers take such fixing.'

And the result—enchanting! But Master Leopold would not be there to see it. 'Coward!' murmured Charlotte.

Her father behaved as though there had been no conflict between them. The perfect host, receiving his guests, charming them, accepting their compliments on the exquisite taste of Carlton House and implying that all his efforts in gathering together these artistic treasures was not in vain since it gave them such pleasure. She would never be like him, she thought wistfully.

The Duchess of Oldenburg was present. The Regent could
not exclude her as he would have liked to do; and since the
Tsar had arrived it was necessary for him to be constantly in
her company for where her brother went so did she.

The Duchess approached Charlotte with a handsome man
beside her. Not very young, this one, thought Charlotte. In
his thirties perhaps. Not as handsome as Leopold, but far
more worldly. Not the sort of young man who would run to
her father if she gave him an invitation.

'Dearest Charlotte, may I present Prince Augustus of
Prussia to you.'

His bow was eloquent but not more so than his expression.
He was quite clearly charmed by the vision in silver tissue and
feathers.

'F has seen you on several occasions, haven't you, F? He's
really Friedrich, Wilhelm, Heinrich, Augustus—but F to
me. Ever since he's been badgering me to present him to
you.'

F! thought Charlotte. What delightful familiarity.

'Well,' said Charlotte awkwardly, 'and now you have.'

'It is an ambition realized,' said F.

'I am sure it does not stop there,' laughed the Duchess. 'I do
believe you will find this young man a most entertaining
creature, as I do.'

'I shall hope to do so,' said Charlotte.

'You might begin by allowing him to dance with you.'

With that he took Charlotte's hand and bowing to the
Duchess—and somehow he managed to convey a great deal of
gratitude in that bow—he led Charlotte away.

It was bold, of course. She looked anxiously towards the
mass of people who were circulating about her father. He was
hidden from view and since she could not see him presumably
he could not see her.

They danced. F performed with grace and led her through
the steps so that she felt she had never danced so well. He
treated her as though she were a desirable woman rather than
a princess on whom it was a duty to dance attendance. He
reminded her of Captain Hesse and in a sudden panic she
remembered that those letters were still unreturned ... but
she refused to spoil an occasion like this by thinking of
them.

He told her that his father was Prince Augustus of Prussia
and that he had fought against Napoleon and had been taken
prisoner.

Was he married? Should she be presented to his wife?

He had no wife in actual fact, although he had been married *de la main gauche* as the saying went.

Charlotte's eyes were wide; she giggled with mingled pleasure and confusion. No man had ever spoken to her in this way before.

'For a man of my age and experience,' he said, 'you must admit that it would be surprising if it were not the case.'

Charlotte supposed it was and believed that if her father could hear this conversation he would be far more perturbed than at the prospect of a visit from Leopold.

But F—she was already thinking of him as that—would be the last man to run away for fear of her father's wrath; she had a notion that he might be attracted by it.

He told her about his adventures in the Army and his conversation was racy and amusing. She was very sorry when it was necessary to do her duty to others of her father's guests, but she found an opportunity to talk to F again.

'Don't think,' he said, 'that I shall wait to be presented again. We are friends now. If we don't meet soon I shall write to you. I shall find some means of enjoying your company.'

'My father would not permit you to call. A certain prince was requested to leave the country because he asked that permission.'

'It's sometimes a mistake to ask and the only wise thing to do is to take.'

How bold he was!

'I shall write to you.'

'The letter might be taken straight to my father.'

'Oh ... there must be someone who would help me. It would have to be someone who is in the plot.'

'Plot. You call it a plot!'

'I am determined to see Your Highness even if I have to plot to do so.'

She laughed. She felt happier than she had since Leopold's desertion. At least here was one man who was ready to take risks for the sake of her company.

'Who would carry my letters to you?' he asked.

'Cornelia Knight might do so.'

'She *will* do this. I shall insist. Can you trust her?' How deliciously exciting he made it all seem.

'I would most assuredly trust Cornelia.'

*   *   *

Thus began the intrigue with F. Cornelia was against it at first but Charlotte had been so cold to her lately that she was anxious to win back her confidence and promised to help.

If only Mercer were at hand, thought Cornelia, they could discuss this together; and to ease her conscience Cornelia told herself that since Charlotte was set against the Orange match, F as a Prussian prince might be a suitable husband for her. If this was so, she was justified in helping them to carry on a clandestine correspondence.

Oh dear, she thought, I do hope Charlotte is not being too indiscreet. Had she forgotten the Hesse letters still not retrieved? Hesse was a villain not to send them back; again and again he made excuses and still he retained that correspondence, and Heaven knew how far Charlotte had gone in that.

Yet, she thought, the Orange match is not to Charlotte's liking, and Charlotte is not a princess who can be forced!

That was Cornelia's defence for helping Charlotte to become involved with a worldly prince who was no newcomer to romantic intrigue.

*   *   *

The Princess of Wales was furiously angry because she was not included in the celebrations to welcome the visitors. It was yet another example of her husband's contempt for her, and she assured her lady-in-waiting, Lady Charlotte Campbell, that she was coming near to the end of her endurance.

Cut off from her daughter! Shut out from the celebrations! What could she do? She could only react in the way her character dictated and that was to show them that she did not care. She rode out frequently in her carriage and when she did so she was cheered lustily. Rather different from His Highness the Prince Regent, she commented gleefully. When the people expressed their indignation that she was kept from her daughter she looked sorrowful and let them see her weep.

'Shame!' they cried.

She was going to discountenance the man who was responsible for her position and she thought of a way which would displease him most. He was taking the Tsar to the opera and she would be there too.

She chattered to Lady Charlotte Campbell while she was dressed and even her women who were accustomed to her strange costumes were taken aback by the sight of her that night in her velvet gown cut so low that her bosom was exposed.

'And why not?' she demanded. 'It's the best part of me, so I'm told.'

'Slap it on! Slap it on,' she cried, seizing the rouge pot. 'Paint me and don't be sparing with the white lead. A contrast is so striking.'

She lifted the glittering diamond tiara and placed it on her black curly wig. 'Magnificent,' she cried. 'He'll have to notice me, won't he? Couldn't do much else.'

As if that were not enough she must add enormous black feathers to wave above her head over the tiara.

'Where's Willie? Willikin, my love, come and admire Mamma.'

Willie came, dressed in spangles, and her ladies looked at him in horror.

'Madam,' cried Lady Charlotte, 'you cannot take the boy with you. You would lose all sympathy with the people if you did. It would seem as if . . .'

Caroline looked at Willie; her ladies thought him a stupid child, for he always had his mouth open, but to her he was beautiful. She frowned. They were right. How she would love to take Willie, to flaunt him in the face of the Regent, to make people say: Is he her child or isn't he? But Campbell was right. It would not be wise.

'Come and kiss Mamma before she goes, my love,' she said. 'She'll soon be back with her boy.'

And the ladies were relieved. At least she was not going to commit the fatal error of taking him with her. Her presence there would be bad enough.

When they had got her safely into her carriage—quite a feat considering her bulk and the plumes, she settled down in her seat and thought with pleasant mischief of what was to come.

It was going to be a successful evening. She was aware of that from the beginning, for as soon as she entered the opera house the people rose to cheer her. She stood back in the box because immediately facing her was the Prince Regent with his guests.

'The people are cheering you, Madam,' whispered Lady Charlotte.

But she stood back. 'Punch's wife must take a back seat when Punch is there,' she said with a grin.

This was astonishing, for her ladies had been under the impression that her sole purpose in coming was to make him feel uncomfortable.

And then of course the Regent gave his display of impeccable good manners. Although he loathed the thought of her, although he had not seen her for a very long time, he could not ignore the fact that she was in the opera house. He rose from his seat and gave her that most elegant of bows which, however much they reviled him, never failed to fascinate his people.

There were cheers then for them both; he ground his teeth in chagrin. It was ironical that the only way he could win their approval was by being polite to *her*.

The evening was a great success, she decided, because the Tsar of Russia could not keep his eyes from her box; he actually put up his quizzing glass and quite openly stared.

'What a handsome man!' cooed Caroline. 'Ha, ha, I don't see why he should not visit Punch's wife although Punch has done all in his power to keep him away.'

What an evening. The opera over, the people cheered her in the theatre. She bowed to them several times and hoped the Regent was watching—which of course he was while pretending not to.

And then out to her carriage and the people surrounding it. 'Long live the Princess of Wales. May your daughter be restored to you. Shame on them for parting you. Long life to Caroline and Charlotte and down with their persecutors.'

Oh, very pleasant. 'You good people,' she cried. 'You good, *good* people.'

'Shall we go and burn down Carlton House?' called a voice in the crowd.

It would serve him right. And that they should do that for her!

'No,' she cried. 'Don't do that, good people. Go home to your beds and sleep well. As I shall do. Your goodness to me has made me so happy.'

So back to Connaught House to throw off her plumes and her tiara and step out of the black velvet which was too tight . . . as all her clothes seemed to be.

'A successful evening,' she said to Lady Charlotte. 'And did you see how taken the Tsar was with me? Tomorrow I shall invite him to be my guest.'

*   *   *

She was dressed in one of her most flamboyant gowns; the paint and the white lead had been 'slapped on'; she lay back in her chair, her short legs swinging for they did not reach the floor.

'This will be one of the greatest triumphs of my life,' she

told Lady Charlotte. 'The Tsar is coming to see me. He will be my guest from now. Do you know I saw a twinkle in his eyes for me? He liked what he saw ... and he saw plenty of me. You look shocked, Lady Charlotte. You are easily, my dear. It does not do when you are in the service of the Princess of Wales. Yes, he liked me. I saw it. He will be constantly here. You will see.'

But it seemed that she had miscalculated, for the hour she had fixed for the Tsar's arrival in her invitation to him came and passed and he did not come.

'Delayed on the road,' said Caroline, and asked that a looking glass be brought that she might see that her toilette was as good as it had been an hour before.

Time passed and still he did not come; it was two hours before she would face the fact that he would not come at all.

Then her fury broke loose. 'You know why! *He* has stopped this. He won't have the Tsar visiting me. He's always been afraid of my popularity with the people. Now he's afraid of it with the Tsar. He has told wicked tales of me. He has hinted at his displeasure if my visitor comes. Oh, it is too bad.'

She was like a child who has been denied a promised treat. She tore off her feathers and threw them aside.

'He won't come now. He'll never come. I shall never have any visitors. Even my daughter is kept from me. I won't endure it.'

She kicked her chair as though it were her husband she were kicking; then she shrugged her shoulders and lay back in it, her eyes closed.

They could only guess at the bitterness of her disappointment.

'I saw a gipsy last week. She told my fortune. She insisted. She said great events were hovering about me. She told me that I should lose my husband and go abroad and find another.'

Lady Charlotte shivered. One did not talk of the reigning sovereign's death. It might be treason. But Caroline cared nothing for treason. She was ready to commit it ten times a day if it could add to the Regent's discomfort.

'To go abroad,' she said. 'To travel. It is something I have always longed for. To have adventures in strange countries ... to meet people ... people who will be my friends. Why should I not travel? What is there for me here? To tell the truth, Lady Charlotte, I am heartily sick of this country. I have never known any happiness in it ... except when Charlotte was born. And they soon took her away from me. I never see her. I might as well have no daughter. I reckon I should be happier abroad.'

She talked of foreign countries and Lady Charlotte encouraged her to do so. At least it took her mind off the Tsar's discourtesy.

*　　*　　*

The Prince of Orange had arrived in England. Compared with F with whom Charlotte was now deeply involved by correspondence he looked more unattractive than ever.

'I won't have him,' Charlotte declared to Cornelia, who merely smiled and said she doubted that Charlotte would. For Cornelia—although sometimes she could not understand herself—was completely committed to further the affair with F and had quite made up her mind that he was to be Charlotte's bridegroom.

Charlotte was writing long letters to Mercer and they were full of the perfections of F.

'He is so bold,' she wrote. 'I am sure that if my father got to hear of our friendship and tried to stop it, *he* would find some means of continuing it.'

The Duchess of Oldenburg was amused. She discussed the affair with F, for she was determined that the Orange match should not take place.

'Dearest F,' she said to him one day, 'how would you like to be consort of the Queen of England?'

To her amazement F was not enthusiastic.

'The point is, dear Duchess, that I am scarcely a marrying man.'

'Oh, I know you have had love affairs with every pretty girl in Germany but surely you will settle down one day and where could you find a more gilded settlement?'

'Nowhere. I'm sure of that.'

'And yet you hesitate?'

'Do you think I would be acceptable to your plump friend?'

'Plump the gentleman is, but not my friend. My dear F!' The Duchess laughed with relish. 'Charlotte could be made to see that her wishes are consulted and if she tried she could no doubt get her way. Have you noticed how the people love her—and her vulgar mother; and how they dislike the fat gentleman? I think he will have to act very carefully, and it may be he has the sense to know it. So don't despair.'

He was silent and she said: 'I can't believe it can be so, but it would seem that you are not over eager.'

'Perhaps I've been free too long.'

'Good God, you don't still hanker after Madame Récamier?
That woman's an iceberg. And her only claim to fame is that
she was painted on a sofa.'

The Prince did not wish to discuss the only woman with
whom he could say he had ever been in love, although he had
made love to many.

'I find Charlotte's youth and naïveté attractive,' he admitted.

'And she is even more attracted to you than you to her.
What a pleasant situation for you! Think about it, my dear F.
Don't throw away such a glorious chance . . . just for a whim.
You must admit that it is all very amusing.'

F was ready to agree with that.

*   *   *

The Regent, aware that his daughter was making certain
flighty friendships and that although her visits to the Duchess
of Oldenburg had been curtailed she was still making undesirable acquaintances through that woman, decided to hurry
on the marriage.

The Prince of Orange was now expressing his devotion to
Charlotte; they met frequently and she did not dislike him,
though she found him not in the least exciting. The Duchess
discussing the affair with another of her impecunious princes,
who were only too glad to be members of the Russian entourage, declared that if nothing was done the poor princess
would be hustled into marriage by her overpowering parent.

'Poor child,' she murmured. 'It is the last thing she
wants.'

'Her mother is against it, I hear,' said the Prince.

'Her mother is against everything the Regent desires. Did
ever a child possess such parents? I feel I must do something
for her. Orange is a weakling. He'll never do for her. Someone
should save the poor child from him.'

'Your Imperial Highness for instance?'

'Since no one else will, I must do what I can . . . and you
have always said that you would do anything for me.'

'I am entirely at Your Highness's service, as you know.'

The Duchess laughed and tapped him lightly on the arm.

'Little Orange either drinks a great deal or is unable to
carry what he does take. It came to my ears that he has been
seen once or twice the worse for drink.'

'What gentleman is not?'

'But my little Charlotte happens to find the habit somewhat nauseating. You should have heard her account of a dinner party to which she was invited by her father. The Regent, his brother of York and certain of the guests at their table were unable to stand at the end of the banquet. York actually fell off his chair and cut his head open, and trying to save himself grasped the tablecloth and pulled its contents on top of him. She told me that she was quite disgusted and that she thought that to be the worse for drink was a weakness she would never tolerate in a husband.'

'The Princess is a puritan.'

'About drunkards, yes—and there is this young Billy of Holland who can't carry his drink. Charlotte should know.'

'Surely someone will tell her.'

'Telling is not the same as seeing. It is our duty to let her see him drunk.'

'Our duty, Highness?'

'Our bounden duty,' said the Duchess solemnly. 'So ... accompany him to the races. Let him be merry there and make sure that he rides back ... dead drunk and publicly.'

The Prince bowed. 'At Your Imperial Highness's service,' he said. 'I shall make it my duty to see that the Princess Charlotte is a witness of the inebriate habits of Slender Billy.'

'I knew we could rely on you.'

*   *   *

Charlotte was angry.

'I tell you this, Notte,' she said. 'I will not marry a drunken man. Do you know he drove back from *Ascot* quite *insensible*. And this is the husband they have chosen for me. I will not marry him.'

Cornelia soothed her. 'Your Highness should stand firm. I am sure that if you do you will marry the man of your choice.'

'I am going to write to dear F immediately. I am going to tell him that I will not tolerate Orange's drunkenness. As soon as I have written you will take the letter to your friend and see if there is one for me. Cornelia I am sending him my ruby ring. It is a token of my feelings for I do believe the foolish man believes that I am not serious.'

'And Your Highness?'

'Deadly serious,' said Charlotte.

So in the circumstances, thought Cornelia, surely she was not wrong to act as go-between. The fact was that if she did not Charlotte would be cold towards her; and that was something Cornelia could not endure.

She was relieved when Brougham and Whitbread came to see the Princess. Cornelia conducted them to Charlotte's apartment and asked if it was the Princess's wish that she should remain during the interview.

Charlotte hesitated and the two men decided that Cornelia should stay with them. She could help to advise the Princess, they thought, because there was no doubt that Her Royal Highness needed strong friends.

'The Princess of Wales will most assuredly leave the country if your marriage to the Prince of Holland takes place,' Brougham told her.

'Leave the country!' cried Charlotte.

'Indeed yes, Your Highness. She is declaring that you are the only reason she remains. She has been so ill-treated here, so humiliated that she wishes to leave. But while she feels that you may need her, she will stay. Your marriage to Dutch William would mean that you had placed yourself with her enemies and that would decide her.'

'I would never place myself with her enemies,' cried Charlotte. 'Oh, please assure her of my unwavering affection.'

'I will do so,' said Brougham. 'But the best assurance would be your refusal of the Dutch marriage.'

Charlotte's eyes sparkled. She was not alone. She had her mother to work for her—and her mother's friends.

'Pray tell my mother,' she said, 'that I think of her often. Tell her that I am touched to know that she remains here on my account. If she left me I should feel desolate. Pray tell her that.'

The men left, feeling that their mission had not been without success.

As for Cornelia, she could assure herself that in helping Charlotte to carry on her clandestine affair with F, she was doing the right thing.

*   *   *

Charlotte received a note from the Prince Regent. He saw no reason why the wedding should be delayed and they would fix a date immediately. He was sending her a list of those who would be present at the wedding. If there was any of whom she did not approve would she strike out that name.

She studied the list headed by herself, the bridegroom and the Regent.

There was no mention of her mother! So they were planning a wedding at which the bride's mother was to be excluded!

Boldly, thinking of her friends—her mother, Brougham, Whitbread . . . and thinking too of the ardent F—she took up her pen and struck out the name of William, Hereditary Prince of Orange.

She awaited the Prince's angry repercussions. They did not come.

Perhaps he had not seen the list. Or perhaps he preferred to ignore what he thought was facetious folly.

* * *

But she could not stand idle. Unless she were going to be hustled into marriage she must do something quickly.

William called at Warwick House as he was now making a habit of doing. Every day she saw him and she became more and more convinced that she would not marry him. She kept thinking of him the worse for drink; and sometimes it was quite clear that he was recovering from a drinking bout of the previous night. He came to her once slovenly dressed, and she was sure it was on this account.

She had complained because he had not been lodged at one of the royal palaces or at Carlton House but had merely been given lodgings over a tailor's shop in Clifford Street. Now she was glad. Serve him right, she thought. It was all he deserved; and since Leopold of Saxe-Coburg had had to lodge over a greengrocer's shop, Clifford Street was good enough for Orange. But she had stopped thinking of Leopold, she reminded herself, when she had recognized the superior attractions of her darling F.

She had made up her mind. She was not going to marry Orange, and she could be bold because she had friends and supporters. She had her mother and her mother's friends.

She was in a truculent mood on this day. He was a little astonished for he did not realize that she had steeled herself to this.

'You are in a perverse mood today, Charlotte,' he said.

'I often am,' she replied.

'You are always frank.' He smiled, implying that he liked her frankness.

'I am thinking of my mother. You know that I am not allowed to visit her as I wish. I have to have permission. Do you think that is a reasonable manner in which to treat me?'

She was disconcerting. He wanted to please her, but he did not want to say anything that might be reported to the Regent and annoy that important gentleman. He was in awe of the Regent who was grand, so friendly sometimes yet so imperious. His intended father-in-law could be jocular; with his passion for nicknames he had given William the one of 'Young Frog' which William was not sure that he liked; but there seemed to be a certain amount of affection in it so he accepted it with a good grace. Indeed how could he do otherwise? He had to keep in the Regent's good books until the marriage had taken place. When they were in Holland he could be more free.

'I am sure your father knows what is best,' he said diplomatically.

She gave him a withering look. Chinless William, who had no spirit either. Slender Billy, Young Frog! And this was the mate they had chosen for her when there were princes in the world like F . . . and Leopold.

'When we are married,' she said, 'I shall expect to see my mother when I please.'

'I am sure that then your father will have no objection.'

'We shall receive her in our house whenever she wishes to come. Do you agree to that?'

'I don't think that we can allow her to visit our house.'

'So you will not have my mother in our house?'

'I do not think it would be wise, Charlotte.'

'Then if you cannot accept my mother I cannot accept you as my husband.'

He looked startled. But now she was in a truly militant mood. She had started and she was not going back.

'When we are married, you will expect me to live in Holland, I suppose?'

'For some part of the time, yes. It will be necessary.'

'Then let me tell you at once that I have no intention of leaving England . . . ever. My place is here and here I shall stay.'

'Your place is with your husband.'

'That may be, but since my place is in England I will not marry a man whose place is not there also.'

'Charlotte, what can you mean?'

'I should have thought I had made it very clear. But I see I have not. I shall put it on paper. Yes, that is the best way. I shall write it. Then you will know that I mean what I say.'

A bewildered Prince of Orange drove away from Warwick House. Charlotte was extraordinary. Sometimes he wondered whether she was as mad as her mother was reputed to be.

*   *   *

Her uncle Augustus, the Duke of Sussex, one of her favourite uncles, called to see her.

He had heard that all was not going well between her and Orange.

'The plain fact is,' said Charlotte, 'that I don't like him. We are not of a kind and I have no intention of leaving this country.'

Uncle Augustus applauded her decision. 'Your father wants you out of the country, I fear. That's why he's so eager for the marriage. He doesn't like your popularity and you know that he wants to divorce your mother so that he can get a son.'

She felt hurt and angry. She had begun to think that he had some affection for her, and it was all a pretence to get her married to William so that she would have to go to Holland.

'I won't leave the country,' she said firmly.

'You are right,' he said. 'You must not. Your whole future depends on your staying here. Why, if you went you could lose the Crown. You must stay, but at the same time don't anger your father. I am worried about his health. It is not good, you know.'

How like Uncle Augustus—at one moment he was all for her, then he swayed to his brother. At one time he had married his Augusta and given up everything for her sake; but that did not last and he and Goosey were no longer together. It was their son Augustus d'Este who had gazed longingly at her. He was rather charming and Charlotte was sure he would have liked to marry her. But he was too much like his father and was not the man she would look up to as a husband. She wanted a strong man like F . . . or Leopold. How stupid to think of *him*. He was not strong. He had run away rather than face her father's anger. What she wanted was a prince who would be prepared to live in England and be consort of the Queen; she would choose her own husband and if F offered for her and if it were possible, she would take him. Most willingly, she thought fiercely, and refused to think of that handsome young man who had made such an impression when he had handed her into her carriage at the Pulteney Hotel.

But if she could not take Uncle Augustus very seriously, it was different with Brougham and Whitbread.

They called. They had heard that she wished to break off the Orange match. Then perhaps she would allow them to draft the letter for her.

She had gone so far and there was no turning back. In any case it was what she had decided.

So in his rooms in Clifford Street a bewildered Prince of Orange read a letter from his affianced bride which set down her refusal in such terms which might have been composed by a lawyer—which indeed they had.

Night Flight

CHARLOTTE waited for the storm to break.

There was only one thing to do. She wrote to Mercer begging her to come to Warwick House with all speed. She needed her now as never before.

Mercer arrived and when she came it was to find that the Prince whom Mercer knew through Charlotte's letters as F was with the Princess.

'Alone!' cried Mercer, shocked.

Cornelia admitted that this was so.

'But this is madness,' said Mercer coolly. 'For Heaven's sake go in and put a stop to this.'

'I dare not,' said Cornelia. 'The Princess has changed lately. She would be very angry and she does not listen to me as she used to.'

Mercer looked at Cornelia in surprise. What had happened to the strong-minded woman whom she had grudgingly admired and made her ally?

She herself strode into the room and broke up the *tête-à-tête*.

It was not difficult, for at the sight of her friend Charlotte gave a cry of joy and flung herself into Mercer's arms.

'Thank God you have come, Mercer,' she cried; and for a few moments she even forgot F in the joy of having her friend with her.

* * *

Mercer took charge. Had Charlotte written to her father? Charlotte explained that she had thought William would have done so; but apparently William had not.

'You must write to your father without delay,' said Mercer.

'You must tell him that you have broken the engagement. We will compose the letter immediately and send it to him.'

Charlotte obeyed as always and when the letter was written she felt so frightened that the pain in her knee was almost unbearable and on Mercer's suggestion she went to bed.

The Regent would be reading the letter *now*! she thought. It would only take a very short time to deliver it, as Warwick House was next door to Carlton House and if he were at home it would be in his hands now.

Several days passed during which Charlotte found the suspense intolerable.

The foreign visitors left England. The Duchess of Oldenburg—slyly delighted at the thought of the impending storm which she had helped to raise—took a fond farewell of Charlotte and wished her all happiness in the future.

F was leaving with the Russian party. He came to see Charlotte but Mercer would not allow a private *tête-à-tête*, insisting that Cornelia be present.

F was not entirely sorry to go; he knew that trouble was imminent and he was not sure that the life of a Prince Consort was one which would suit him; he liked to roam the world in search of romance; he could see how stultifying to a man of his temperament marriage—even such a brilliant one—would be. Moreover, Charlotte's naïveté was delightful, up to a point; he preferred the cultured company of Madame Récamier. But he was automatically ardent. Charlotte did not know it but it was a habit of his with the woman of the moment and his great success was due, as he was well aware, to his ability while he was with a woman, to make her feel that she was the only person in the world of any consequence to him. Whereas F, being a realist, admitted to himself that the only person of any consequence in the world to him was F himself.

'You will write to me,' said the young Princess.

'Nothing will prevent me.'

'Cornelia will arrange that your letters reach me and mine reach you.'

Cornelia swore that she would do so; and on that guarantee the lovers parted.

A few days passed. It was Mercer's opinion that the Regent had been waiting for the departure of the visitors, whom he had accompanied to Dover with great pomp and ceremony, before allowing the storm to break. He would not want to have his visitors laughing at his domestic troubles behind his back.

'It'll come now,' said Mercer; and as usual, Mercer was right.

The Prince Regent commanded his daughter Charlotte to come to Carlton House in the company of Miss Knight.

Charlotte, pale and trembling, rose from her bed and immediately collapsed into the arms of Louisa Lewis.

'It's my knee, Louisa. I can't stand.'

Mercer was called. 'You must write at once to your father and tell him that you are too ill to go to him and beg him to come to you.'

The letter was sent and a day of anxiety followed. Charlotte got up and found that she could walk more easily.

It would be better to face him standing up than lying down.

At six o'clock in the evening the Regent arrived accompanied by the Bishop of Salisbury. He ignored everyone and strode into the drawing room. Then he cried in a voice of thunder: 'Pray tell the Princess Charlotte that I command her presence here without delay.'

Cornelia, trembling, turned to Mercer who stood white-faced though calm.

'What can I *do*, Mercer?' implored Charlotte.

'There is only one thing you can do,' said the intrepid Mercer. 'Go down and see him. He commanded you to go in any case, and you must go quickly for his mood will not be improved by delays.'

'Oh, Mercer . . .'

'If you stand by your decision, he cannot force you. Remember that.'

Charlotte turned away and went into the drawing room.

He was standing by the fireplace, his back to it, his arms folded behind as though warming himself although there was no fire on that hot July day. The Bishop of Salisbury stood by, self-righteous, resigned, firm ally of his Regent, prepared to support him in whatever action he decided to take against his recalcitrant daughter.

Charlotte looked imploringly at her father, but his expression was cold and it was clear that at this moment he hated her.

He took first the familiar self-pitying role. 'What have I done to be treated in this way?' he demanded plaintively. 'Have I deserved such an ungrateful child?'

The Bishop gave a sympathetic little cough but Charlotte wanted to shout: Yes, you have. You have never loved me as I wanted to be loved ... as I needed to be loved. If you had, everything would have been different.

But she was silent.

He went on pitying himself for a few moments and then his anger flared up. 'You have broken off this marriage ... without consulting *me*. *You* have decided that a match, to which I and my ministers have given much thought, much consideration ... and all for *your* good, your personal benefit ... is to be broken off in this churlish fashion. I do not understand how a daughter of mine can behave in such a way.'

And on and on. She was not listening to the words; she was watching the expressions fleeting across his face. He is acting, she thought; he always acts. He does not know it but he has been acting all his life. He is listening to his own voice now, admiring it. In a moment he will weep. He will be Lear weeping for a daughter's ingratitude. If only one could explain to him. But how could one? He never saw anyone clearly. He only saw the Prince Regent as he wished to see him and people were good or bad according to their behaviour towards him.

If she remembered this she could be defiant. She could tell herself that she no longer cared for his esteem, that she hated him.

I have my mother, she thought. She loves me. And the thought sustained her.

'You and your household have consistently gone against my wishes,' he was saying. 'I am going to put a stop to that. Your household here is to be dismissed and you are to leave Warwick House.'

'W ... when?' she stammered.

'This very night. You will come tonight to Carlton House and stay there until you move to Cranbourne Lodge.'

'C ... Cranbourne Lodge!'

'Pray do not repeat me in that stuttering fashion. It offends me. I have a new household for you and you will shortly be introduced to them. They will serve you at Cranbourne Lodge.'

Cranbourne Lodge, she thought. In Windsor Park. She would leave London. The Queen and the Old Girls would be at Windsor and she would have to be constantly in their company. And Cornelia ... was Cornelia dismissed? How then was she going to keep up her correspondence with F?

'I must ask you ...'

'You must ask nothing. You must merely obey. Very shortly your new household will be arriving here to meet you. In the

meantime go and tell your women that you are leaving Warwick House for Carlton House tonight—and tell Miss Knight
to come to me here.'

She stumbled out of the room.

She found Cornelia alone in her room in a state of great
apprehension.

'It is terrible,' she cried. 'There is to be a new household.
You are to go to him at once.'

*   *   *

'Miss Knight.' The Regent looked at her with such coldness
that she began to shiver.

'Your Highness.'

'I am sorry, Miss Knight, to put you to inconvenience, but
I'm afraid I must ask you to leave Warwick House without
delay.'

'Tonight, Your Highness?'

'Tonight. Your room will be needed for one of the ladies of
the Princess's new household. I must inform you that the
Princess Charlotte is leaving tonight for Carlton House where
she will spend a few days before travelling down to Cranbourne Lodge in Windsor Park with her new household.'

'New household, Sir, but . . .'

'With her new household,' repeated the Prince, painfully
surprised that Miss Knight should interrupt him. 'I think it
will be better for all concerned if the Princess is not allowed
so much freedom. The Queen will be at Windsor and for a
time I wish her to be the only visitor whom Charlotte will
receive. The Countess of Ilchester will be at the head of the
new household and she will be assisted by Lady Rosslyn and
Mrs. Campbell. Now, Miss Knight, I repeat I am distressed to
have to put a lady to inconvenience but I shall need your
room and no doubt you will have a few preparations to make
before you leave Warwick House this evening.'

'Sir,' cried Miss Knight, 'I beg of you tell me in what way I
have failed?'

'I am making no complaints, Miss Knight,' he replied, 'but
I wish to make changes in my daughter's household. You will
agree that if I so wish it is a matter for me to decide without
explanations. I should blame myself if I allowed the situation
now existing at Warwick House to continue. Now I think
there is no more to be said. If you have nowhere to go tonight,
you may have a room at Carlton House.'

'I fear, sir,' said Miss Knight, 'that that might put you to
some inconvenience. My father served His Majesty the King

for thirty years; he lost a fortune in that service and his health suffered considerably. It would be extraordinary if I could not put myself to a little inconvenience for the sake of my Sovereign.'

'Very well, Miss Knight. You may leave us now.'

She curtsied and left the room.

This is the end, she thought. I have lost Charlotte now.

She would go to her; she would summon Mercer; they would discuss this and make some plan before she left Warwick House.

She ran to Charlotte's room.

'Where is the Princess?' she demanded of a white-faced, scared Louisa.

'I don't know. I saw her rushing out of the room like a mad thing. She put on a bonnet and shawl and sped past me.'

'She can't have left Warwick House.' Cornelia felt as though her knees would not support her. 'Where is Miss Elphinstone? Pray ask her to come to me at once.'

Mercer arrived. 'What has happened? Is Charlotte still with her father?'

'No, and we don't know where she is. She put on a bonnet and shawl and ran out. She can't have gone into the streets.'

'I think I know where she has gone,' said Mercer. 'She has mentioned it often. She has been saying for the last few days that if her father were unkind to her or tried to force her to anything, she would go to her mother.'

'She wouldn't!'

'In her present mood she would do anything.'

Mercer ran down the stairs summoning the servants. Had any of them seen the Princess?

They had seen someone in a bonnet and shawl running out of the house, someone who looked like the Princess Charlotte but clearly could not be.

And where did she go? Out of the house, into the streets!

'Someone,' said Mercer, 'will have to tell the Regent.'

* * *

The Regent was talking to the Bishop when Mercer, with Cornelia, begged leave to enter. It was graciously given.

'Your Highness,' said Mercer, 'I fear the Princess has left the house.'

'Left?' said the Regent. 'Where can she have gone?'

'I fear to her mother, Sir.'

The Regent smiled. 'Then, of course, the world will know

the type of person she is. No one will marry her now. She has
ruined her reputation.'

There were tears in Mercer's eyes. 'I trust Your Highness
does not blame me for this.'

His manners would not allow him to be unmoved by a
lady's tears so he said gently: 'I am making no complaints, as
I told Miss Knight. I have merely decided to act.'

The Bishop said: 'Is it Your Highness's wish that I and
Miss Elphinstone should follow the Princess?'

'It might be a wise thing to do.'

'Perhaps Miss Knight would accompany us,' suggested
Mercer.

Miss Knight, fearing that she was at any moment going to
disgrace herself by bursting into tears, could only think of
placating the Regent. 'I could not bear to enter that house,
she said with a shudder.

The Prince Regent was looking a trifle bored. He said:
'You must do what you will. I am due at a card party at the
Duke of York's.'

With that he left them. They stood bemused, listening to
the sound of his carriage wheels as they faded into silence.

* * *

When Charlotte snatched up her shawl and bonnet there
was one thought in her mind: she must go to her mother.
There she would find refuge. She would wait to consult no
one ... not even Mercer. She must delay not one second for if
she did it might be too late. Only her mother could save her
from ... prison, for that was what it would be. Cranbourne
Lodge would be far worse than anything that had happened
before. She had defied her father and she was sure that he
would never allow that to happen again, if he could help it.
But her mother would protect her. She ought to have gone to
her long before.

She ran out into the street where she had never been alone
before. What did people do when they wanted to get from one
place to another? They took a hackney coach and there was
one coming towards her now.

'Stop!' she cried. 'Stop!'

The whip was held up to denote that the coach was free and
a whiskered face was close to hers.

'Hop in, lady, and where do you want to go?'

'To Connaught House. Do you know the way?'

'Connaught House. That's the Princess of Wales's place,
that is. That's where you want to go, is it?'

'Oh, yes, please, and quickly. Can you hurry?'

'Anything to please a lady.'

Up the Haymarket and on to Oxford Street. Charlotte looked out on the passing scene. What was happening now at Warwick House? What was her father saying? Had he discovered her flight? There would be storms. But never mind, she would be with her mother and she would not leave her. They would live together and have the people on their side.

'Connaught House, lady.'

And praise to God, there she was.

What did one do? Pay the man? She had no money.

'Wait a moment,' she cried imperiously. One of the doormen was gaping at her.

'Your Royal Highness . . .'

'Blimey!' said Mr. Higgins the hackney coachman.

'Pray give this man three guineas,' said the Princess. 'He has driven me here and deserves it.'

What an adventure! thought Mr. Higgins. He would talk of this night for the rest of his life. And three guineas! She was a real princess, this one.

Charlotte went into Connaught House. 'Pray take me to the Princess of Wales at once,' she said.

'Your Highness, the Princess left an hour ago for Blackheath.'

'Then let someone ride there immediately and tell her that I am here. It is a matter of the utmost importance.'

A messenger was hastily despatched.

Mr. Higgins was not the only one who believed this was going to be a night to remember.

*   *   *

The groom who had been despatched to Blackheath caught up with the Princess of Wales in her carriage, accompanied by Lady Charlotte Lindsay on the way to Blackheath.

She put her head out of the window and asked what brought him.

'Madam,' she was told, 'the Princess Charlotte has run away from Warwick House and is at Connaught House. She has come to you for protection, she says. She sent me off immediately to tell you so and to beg you to return.'

The Princess of Wales chuckled.

'Well, this will cause a bit of excitement in some quarters, I know,' she said to Lady Charlotte. 'Turn the horses,' she commanded. 'We're galloping back to London with all speed.'

On the way she said: 'We'd better have Brougham and

Whitbread. Oh yes, we'd better have this done in the right manner. I'll swear *he's* champing with rage. So she has run away from him to me! It's the best thing that's happened for a long time.'

'Call at Mr. Brougham's house,' she shouted, 'and after that at Mr. Whitbread's.'

She was laughing softly as she lay back against the upholstery.

*   *   *

Mercer was the first to arrive at Connaught House. When Charlotte saw her she went to her and embraced her.

'My dearest Mercer, I knew you'd come. I won't go back. I am going to live with my mother from now on. I should have done it years ago. She loves me. She wants me. *He* never did.'

'The Bishop is downstairs,' said Mercer. 'We came together. It was not very wise of you to run out like that.'

'It was the only thing I could think to do. I feared that if I stayed it would be too late. He was there ... with the old Bishop ready to carry me off to prison. I would never have been allowed to come to my mother.'

'Where is your mother?'

'She had left for Blackheath. She will soon be with me for she was not very far on the road and I sent a groom galloping after her. I am sure she will be here soon.'

'She may feel embarrassed because you have run to her.'

Charlotte laughed a little hysterically. 'My mother never feels embarrassed.'

'We must wait and see what she has to say ... when she comes ... if she comes,' said Mercer.

'If she comes! Of course she will come. She would never desert me. I can't think why I didn't see it before. I should have run away long ago.'

Mercer looked dubious and for once Charlotte did not believe her friend was entirely with her.

'You saw my father?' she asked.

'Yes.'

'And he is very angry. Mercer, you are not on *his* side?'

'Sides?' said Mercer. 'Why should it be a matter of taking sides? While I think you were right to refuse Orange, I do not think you should have run away.'

Charlotte was crestfallen. Could it possibly be that Mercer was afraid of offending the Regent?

There was the sound of carriage wheels below. Charlotte had run to her window. The guttural penetrating tones of the Princess of Wales could be heard below.

Charlotte turned to Mercer triumphantly. 'She's come. She turned back immediately. I knew she would.'

She ran to the door. The Princess of Wales was coming up the stairs.

'Where is Charlotte? Where is my daughter?'

'Here, Mamma.'

The Princess Caroline opened her arms with a dramatic gesture and Charlotte threw herself into them.

'So my angel came to her Mamma! Bless you, my precious daughter. And what is *he* going to do about this, eh?'

The embrace was suffocating; but it was what Charlotte needed. Reassurance. Security. At last she had come home.

'Travelling makes me hungry. It's dinner time. We'd better eat, my love. I've an idea we may have company to-night. Now, Lindsay, love, give the orders. Tell them that I'm back ... if they don't know it. Tell them that I've got a very important guest and I can't let her starve.'

Charlotte began to laugh. 'Oh, Mamma, it is so good to be with you.'

All this time, she thought, I have tried to love him when she was waiting to love me. It had had to be a matter of taking sides and now she had taken hers.

*   *   *

Dinner was served in the dining room. Caroline was in good spirits; she kept bursting into laughter, imagining the scenes that must be going on around the Regent.

She laughed hilariously and Charlotte, in a state of near hysteria, joined in. Mercer was cool and seemed remote. She was not so happy with the situation as Charlotte was.

When they were half way through dinner the carriages began to arrive. The Duke of Sussex was the first to come. He had not seen Caroline since the Delicate Investigation in which he had played a part, but they greeted each other affectionately. Charlotte was immediately aware of his dismay.

'You shouldn't have run away,' he said. 'It wasn't wise.'

'Should I have stayed to be a prisoner?'

'You should have stayed,' he told her.

'I hope,' said Charlotte, 'that some of you are going to be on my side.'

'We are on your side,' he assured her.

'Yes,' she said bluntly, 'and on my father's at the same time.'

But there was her mother. She could rely on her.

Lord Eldon arrived. That coal heaver! thought Charlotte.

Trust him to come. He would do all in his power to humiliate her.

Dinner was over and no one seemed to be quite so merry as they had before. People kept arriving and each one whispered to Charlotte that he wanted to help her but he feared she had acted rashly. The best thing was to return to Carlton House and then try to come to some agreement with her father.

To all this she replied: 'No. I shall stay with my mother.'

Caroline whispered to her: 'Brougham and Whitbread will be here soon. I called at their houses on my way but they weren't at home. I left messages for them to come at once. They'll be here soon.'

She was right. They arrived in due course and they both looked grave. Surely they were not going to tell her that she ought not to have come!

Miss Knight arrived—unlike herself and tearful. What had happened to Cornelia? Charlotte had thought she would be calm and precise in any circumstances, but it seemed that the Regent had the power to change people; he had certainly changed Cornelia.

'I have brought Louisa Lewis with Your Highness's night things,' she said.

The Duke of York, who had since arrived, not very pleased to have been called from his card party, but kind and gentle with his niece as always, retorted: 'Night things! Charlotte cannot stay here. My dear niece, you must not spend a night other than under your own roof or that of your father.'

'I am happy to be under that of my mother,' retorted Charlotte.

So many people had now come to Connaught House that it was like the gathering before a conference. It was growing late, being past midnight, and they went on talking together and coming to her one by one and telling her that she must either go back to Warwick House or to Carlton House.

'Mercer,' she whispered, '*you* understand.'

'Yes,' said Mercer, 'I understand, but they are right. You should never have come.'

'Why not? My mother wants me. Why should a daughter not be with her mother? Because *he* hates her that does not mean that I must. Where is Brougham? He is the only one who is not afraid of my father.'

Hearing his name he was at her side.

'Mr. Brougham,' she said, 'tell these people that I must stay here.'

He shook his head. Even he! She wanted to burst into tears.

'Your Highness should not spend a night anywhere but under your own roof.'

'But this is my mother's house.'

'You should not stay here.'

'So you are against me, too?'

'It is precisely because I am *for* you that I say this.'

'Please, listen to me.' She began to cry weakly. She was tired; she was frightened, too. At dinner it had seemed so different; with her mother laughing beside her she had believed that she had escaped and that they were going to be together from then on. But her mother was not beside her now. She was yawning in a corner, her wig awry, her paint beginning to run.

Charlotte felt frightened and alone but she clung to her resolution. 'I won't go. I will stay here. My place is with my mother.'

Brougham said: 'Come to the window. It's nearly two o'clock. It'll be dawn soon.'

'And this fearful night will be over.'

'Your Highness, soon the streets and the Park will be full of people. They will learn that you are here, that you have run away from your father to come to your mother.'

'Do you think they will be surprised? And why shouldn't they know the truth?'

'It could mean riots, bloodshed. They would attack Carlton House. It needs only a little thing like this to ignite the bonfire. Are you going to be the one to do this? You would never forgive yourself if you brought about such conflict.'

She was silent, looking out on the darkness of the streets and the Park.

'If you return to Carlton House now, this need go no further.'

'It means I . . . I accept what he has planned for me.'

'You can refuse Orange.'

'He will make me his prisoner and you will then tell me that I must take Orange or there will be bloodshed.'

'I will never tell you that. In fact you can sign a statement now to the effect that if you ever marry Orange it will be against your will. If I have that paper in my possession to show the people, you may rest assured that they will never allow you to be forced into marriage. You have nothing to lose now by going back. You have escaped Orange. The victory is yours and believe me that is the only one which is of importance.'

'I want to live with my mother.'

'You cannot do that.'

'Why not? She wants me to be with her and I with her. She is my mother. Why should we be parted?'

Brougham hesitated. Then he said: 'Your mother would not want you to live with her now. It would mean cancelling her plans to go abroad.'

'Cancelling her plans . . .'

'You did not know that she is leaving this country shortly? The Regent has given his permission; he has increased her allowance. Nothing would change her mind now, I am sure.'

'But this will change her mind. *I* will change her mind.'

'Speak to her,' said Brougham. 'Speak to her now.'

Charlotte went to her mother.

'Mamma,' she said, 'there is something I must say to you. Brougham has just told me that you are planning to leave England.'

'Yes, my love.'

'But now that I am going to live with you . . .'

Caroline's eyes were evasive. How could Charlotte live with her . . . abroad.

'Now, Mamma,' Charlotte pleaded, 'you will not go, of course.'

'It is all arranged, my pet. We will write to each other . . . every day. Perhaps we can arrange a visit for you . . .'

Oh God, thought Charlotte, she doesn't *care*.

Brougham was at her side.

'It will soon be light,' he said. 'I think Your Highness should delay no longer.'

She stood up; her eyes were very bright. 'Yes,' she said, 'I will go now. But I insist on travelling in one of my father's carriages. To do otherwise might be harmful to my reputation.'

'Your Highness shows great wisdom,' said Brougham. He kissed her hand. 'It shall be my pleasure and my duty to serve you with all my heart now and in the future.'

Charlotte felt limp and listless. She would go back to prison. She saw now that it had been a mistake to leave it.

The strange adventure was over.

The Reconciliation

'THIS is the saddest and most desolate time of my life,' said Charlotte to Louisa Lewis, one of the few who had been left to her, presumably because she was too insignificant to be considered of any importance.

'It'll pass,' Louisa comforted her.

So it might, but she would never be quite the same again. She could not forget that her mother did not want her, that all those protestations of affection in the past had meant little. Hadn't Charlotte always known that she preferred Willie Austin? More important than Charlotte's welfare was her desire to leave the country.

'She will stay there, I suppose,' she mused. 'I have a feeling that I shall never see her again.'

Louisa tried to interest her in a new dress. As if she could be interested in dresses now! She had defied her father to go to her mother because she had wanted him to know that someone loved her if he did not; and she had been shown so clearly that her mother did not care that she was lonely and desolate and desperately in need of her.

'So here I am, a prisoner,' she said.

Her great comfort was in thinking of Queen Elizabeth who had been a prisoner so many times. Why, she comforted herself, look what humiliations she had to suffer! Yet she became a great queen. So shall it be with Charlotte.

It could not last. Every month that passed was a month behind her. She must endure this imprisonment in Cranbourne Lodge because it could not last.

She had not seen *him* since he came to Warwick House on that fateful night. His carriage had taken her back to Carlton

House where she had stayed for a few days before the journey with her band of old ladies.

'Ugh!' she said aloud, considering them. Lady Ilchester! Well, give her her due. She tried to be pleasant. As for Lady Rosslyn, she could not endure her. She was so thin that you imagined you could hear her bones rattling. 'Old Famine', Charlotte secretly called her. And then Mrs. Campbell who had been in her household long ago. She had liked her well enough then, but the fact was she deplored the change and was not prepared to like any of them now.

She thought often of her father who at least had cared enough to make rules for her and to be shocked by her behaviour. Her mother had laughed with her, consoled her, comforted her and deserted her.

It was fortunate perhaps that she felt too listless to care. Her head ached and there was this persistent pain in her knee. She was content to spend long hours in her room reading. She liked reading about great queens of the past, Elizabeth naturally being her favourite of them all; she imagined her imprisoned in the Tower in fear of her life. At least, she thought, they can't *kill* me. And when she came to the throne she hoped she would be as great as Elizabeth. She dreamed of herself being crowned in the Abbey. 'Long live the Queen!' She could hear the echoes of peers' voices. To achieve greatness one must reckon to suffer first.

She would endure it—all the petty humiliations. She was not even allowed to have a bedroom to herself for it was her father's order that one of her ladies should sleep in her room. She had insisted that the woman sleep in the next room with the communicating door open and this wish had been granted her. She wondered whether her father had had a debate with his ministers over the matter, and she laughed, which showed she was no longer so miserable.

Every letter she wrote must be censored by Lady Ilchester or by Old Famine; every letter which arrived for her was first read by them. How could she receive the letters which might be coming to Cornelia from F? And Cornelia herself was completely cut off from her.

It'll pass, she told herself, every week that goes by is a step towards something better.

Her optimism was rewarded when one day Lady Ilchester told her that she had a visitor who came to see her with the Regent's permission.

She could not believe her eyes when the door opened.

'Mercer!' she cried.

'Yes, I am here,' said Mercer. 'His Highness thinks that my friendship does you no harm.'

Charlotte began to laugh and hug Mercer at the same time and so fiercely did she laugh that she was almost in tears.

Mercer was shocked by Charlotte's appearance and decided that she would find some means of letting the Regent know that this treatment was harming his daughter's health. But the very sight of her beloved friend brought a sparkle into Charlotte's eyes.

Mercer set out to cheer her with the news. The Regent had given a wonderful fête at Carlton House in honour of Wellington and there had been two thousand five hundred people there. The dresses! The costumes! Mercer described them in detail. People had lined the Mall to see the carriage pass along and there had been no dissenting cries at all. Everyone had been delighted with the celebrations.

'Your father has such original ideas,' said Mercer, and Charlotte nodded proudly.

A pity you couldn't have seen the Jubilee in the parks. You know how fascinated your father is with everything Oriental. Well, a Chinese bridge was put over the canal in St. James's Park and a pagoda was built on it. This was for the firework displays and alas, it was burned down during one of them. A temple was put up in Green Park, and a battle was staged on the Serpentine which was supposed to be a sea fight between the English and Americans. Guess who won.'

'The English,' giggled Charlotte.

'Right first time. Then of course there was the balloon ascent. The Regent is determined that no one shall forget this is victory year. There's a fair in Hyde Park which has been going on for weeks.'

'Oh, Mercer, it's wonderful to see you. It's like being alive again.'

*　　*　　*

'His Highness has given his permission for you to go to Connaught House to say goodbye to Her Highness the Princess of Wales before she leaves on her travels.'

Lady Ilchester was smiling for she thought the news would please Charlotte. She really tried very hard to make life more bearable and Charlotte reproached herself for disliking her. But it was not really Lady Ilchester whom she disliked; it was the fact that she had been appointed jailer under the odious name of governess.

'Thank you,' said Charlotte. 'When am I to be released?'

Lady Ilchester did not look shocked as she would have done a short time ago. They had all grown accustomed to Charlotte's frankness.

'We can go tomorrow if you so wish.'

'Very well,' said Charlotte. 'Tomorrow let it be.'

So she would see her mother for the first time since that night when she had realized that she was of no great importance to her. She was not quite sure what her feelings would be. All the same it was pleasant to leave Cranbourne Lodge, like leaving prison and coming out into the world again.

No one recognized her carriage for which she was pleased. She did wonder how the people would act, for they would have heard some version—probably garbled—of that night's adventure. They would be on her side, she knew that, because they hated her father so much; and she did not want them to take sides against her.

The Princess Caroline was in a state of great excitement. Her voluminous velvet gown was almost slipping off her shoulders, her voice shrill with excitement.

'My precious Charlotte!' she screamed. 'So he has allowed you to come and say goodbye to your mother.'

The embrace was suffocating and Charlotte wanted to escape from it.

'So you are going on your odyssey, Mamma,' she said.

'Far away from this country and glad of it ... except of course for leaving my darling daughter.'

'You will have Willie to console you,' said Charlotte with a touch of asperity.

'Dear Willie, deprived of my Charlotte as I am, he is a great solace. The *Jason* will soon be sailing. Imagine it. I always wanted to see the world. Oh, Charlotte, you would be surprised if you could hear my plans.'

'Nothing you did would surprise me, Mamma,' said Charlotte.

'How solemn you are, dearest!'

'Is it not a solemn occasion?'

'Why, of course it is, and a sad one, for we are to be parted.'

She looks anything but sad, thought Charlotte.

She was glad when the final goodbyes had been said and she was on the way to Cranbourne Lodge. She was seeing her mother through her father's eyes. A vulgar, unstable woman, one on whom a daughter could place no reliance.

*   *   *

Mercer had intimated to the Regent, with the assistance of

Sir Henry Halford, that the Princess Charlotte's health was
not as good as it should be. Her knee was troubling her, she
suffered from mysterious pains, and her low spirits did not
help to improve her condition. Sir Henry thought that sea air
had always been beneficial to the Princess and that a few
weeks at Weymouth before the summer was over would be of
great benefit.

The Regent declared that his daughter should go to Weymouth.

Charlotte was delighted with the news, which Mercer came
to impart to her. Mercer thought this might be a good time to
tell her that there had been no communication from F in case
she had been thinking that Cornelia had been unable to
smuggle his letters to her.

'I think,' said the practical Mercer, 'that you should consider
that affair over.'

Charlotte was desolate. Was she to be deserted by her lover
as well as her mother?

'You know,' said Mercer, 'it was really never serious. Could
you imagine a match being arranged between you?'

'Why not? He was a prince.'

'I don't think he would have had the approval of your
father or the Parliament.'

'They are obsessed by Orange.'

'Hush,' warned Mercer. 'Don't mention him. Let us forget
there was ever an Orange. Now, you must be looking forward
to the sea breezes.'

She was, but she felt sad. Why was it that everything
went wrong? Even F could not remain faithful—for she was
sure he was not. And Leopold had not had the courage to
remain.

It was time she stopped thinking of Leopold; and it would
be good to be free again, because she was always more so at the
sea. They could not keep her imprisoned there when she was
going for the sole enjoyment of the fresh air.

She had Mercer; she was going to Weymouth; life was
improving a little.

*   *   *

What pleasure to arrive at beautiful Weymouth. The
people knew she was coming and were waiting to welcome her
as though she were already their Sovereign. When she reached
Gloucester Lodge she saw them all gathered on the esplanade
and they kept shouting 'Long live Princess Charlotte' and
'God Bless her' and lots of other comforting words.

How different from being incarcerated in Cranbourne
Lodge!

She felt better already.

The Mayor and his Aldermen called on her and delivered a
long loyal address—boring but comforting. She felt like
Queen Elizabeth receiving them.

Every morning she rode out into the fresh and beautiful
country, whipping up her horse, escaping when she could
from her attendants. How she loved the hills and valleys but
most of all the sea. Often she drove into the village of Up-
way—one of her favourite spots.

'Hallelujah!' she would cry to whoever was with her. 'This
is different from Windsor.' She was better already.

Her great pleasure was to meet the people. She would stop
her carriage and have a word or two with old men and women,
and children above all delighted her; she loved their quaint
sayings and their absence of awe because they did not know
they were speaking to one who might one day be their queen.

On one occasion she went across to Portland Island. How
she enjoyed being on the sea! She climbed the rock and stood
at a high point looking back at the mainland.

'How beautiful it is!' And that was England . . . her England . . . the England of which she would be queen. Why had
she thought that life was dreary when she was to be the Queen
of this beautiful country?

'Take care, Your Highness. You are too near the edge,' said
Lady Ilchester.

'I hope everyone standing on the brink of destruction will
be able to retrace their steps as easily as I can,' she said with a
laugh.

Oh, yes, she felt alive again.

*   *   *

The Countess of Ilchester suggested that she might care to
visit Abbotsbury Castle where her mother-in-law, the Dowager
Countess, would be delighted to receive her. Charlotte said
she would be pleased to visit the Ilchester's ancestral home
and accordingly she and her party set out for the castle.

The Dowager Countess received her as though she were
already queen and after that nothing would satisfy her but to
visit Lulworth Castle which was the home of Thomas Weld.
Lulworth particularly delighted her when she learned that
Mrs. Fitzherbert had been married to a Mr. Weld, the previous owner of the castle, and that she had actually been the
chatelaine for the short duration of her marriage.

'How I should like to see Mrs. Fitzherbert again!' sighed Charlotte.

And after Lulworth the magnificent ruins of Corfe Castle.

These trips, the fresh air, her pleasure in the beautiful country of Dorset greatly restored the Princess's spirits and with them, her health.

There was no doubt that the visit to Weymouth had been an unqualified success, and with the coming of November, with its mists and cold winds, it was decided that the time had come for her to return to Cranbourne Lodge.

* * *

Shortly after her return to Cranbourne the Regent came to see her.

When she knew that he was the house she was thrown into a flutter of excitement; she tried to calm herself; she prayed for courage. She was terrified that he would express his disappointment in her.

She found him looking younger than he had looked for some years. It was due to a nut-brown wig, discreetly curled and unpowdered. His face looked less ruddy beneath it and this gave him a look of better health. His dazzling white neckcloth took care of his chins, and not having seen him for so long she had forgotten how beautifully his clothes seemed to have been moulded on to his body; and his buckskin breeches fitted so neatly that they too seemed like part of him; his calves really were magnificent and surely the diamond star on his dark-blue coat glittered more brilliantly than ever.

She lifted her eyes to his almost appealingly and was immediately taken into his scented embrace.

'My dear Charlotte, I rejoice to see you in such healthy looks.'

'Why, Papa . . . you . . . you look more handsome than ever.'

She had spoken spontaneously and for once she had chosen the right words.

He laughed. 'I hear the Weymouth expedition was a great success. I am glad. You are like me. We do appreciate the sea air. You must come and inspect my new improvements at the Pavilion. You will see changes.'

So they were not going to refer to what he had called her 'elopement'; that was done with; they were going on from there. A sense of wild happiness seized her. Perhaps now everything was going to be different.

He took her arm and they walked around the room. He liked sauntering about rooms, although Cranbourne Lodge could not offer him the pleasure he derived from the Pavilion and Carlton House.

She would soon be of age, he said, and they must be seen more together. For the moment she must stay at Windsor but he had plans for her ... plans. The year had been one of the most glorious in English history. He wanted everyone to realize this. That was why all honour must be paid to the great Wellington. They were fighting a sea war, as she no doubt knew, with America and this was something which grieved him, for here were Englishmen fighting against Englishmen. Very different she would understand from fighting that fellow Napoleon. But he had great hopes that in a few weeks she would hear that peace had been declared between the English and Americans; and she would be as delighted as he was.

She listened nodding, agreeing because she was happy to walk with him thus, up and down, to the windows looking out, through to the next room and back again, and all the time his arm through hers, as though he were interested in talking to her.

He had never been quite like this before.

'It is a relief to me,' he said at length, 'that your mother is out of the country. You must understand these matters now. You are no longer a child, Charlotte. We must be watchful of that boy of hers. While I am alive no harm can be done, but I sometimes think of what will happen to you, my dear, *after* my death.'

'Oh, Papa,' she said quickly, 'do not speak of it.'

He pressed her hand and took out his handkerchief to wipe a tear which was not there. But again she had pleased him— and without guile too.

'Alas,' he said, 'we must speak of unhappy things sometimes. I shall not be content—and I think of you, my daughter—until I have proved to the world the immorality of that woman. Perhaps you understand now, my child, why I have acted as I have in the past.'

'Oh, Papa, dearest Papa!'

It was wonderful. They were in accord. He loved her after all. But she knew in her heart, of course, that he was only acting the part of devoted parent. But it served ... for the moment. He cared enough to act for her as he had acted for others in the past.

She was weeping and as he never could resist giving an example of how that affecting habit could be best performed, he wept with her.

It was forgiveness. They were no longer enemies.

Life at Cranbourne Lodge changed. It was not now necessary for her to be continually watched; no longer need one of her women sleep in the next room with the door open; she could receive and write letters that were not submitted to rigid censorship.

She was in favour with her father.

*   *   *

Mercer came to see her, and they talked of Hesse, who had not returned her letters.

'Mercer, what can I do?'

'We did tell him that if he did not return the letters you would make a full confession to your father. Perhaps that is what you should do.'

Charlotte turned pale.

'My dear Charlotte,' said Mercer, 'he has been in a similar scrape himself and now that he is trying to cultivate your affection is the time to confess.'

Charlotte thought about it. She was fully aware that something would have to be done about the Hesse affair; and she was beginning to wish she had not written such impassioned letters to F. How foolish she had been in the past. She was already beginning to forget F, for quite clearly he had not been serious. It seems very difficult, she thought, for a Princess to find people who really love her.

One day during one of her father's visits he mentioned the name of Hesse and before she realized it she had started to confess.

'Papa. I have something to tell you. I need your help.'

He smiled warmly. He liked the new relationship with his daughter. It had all come about because that dreadful woman was no longer in England. He wanted Charlotte to understand this and he was constantly mentioning some vulgarity of Caroline's; and Charlotte had lost that irritating habit of rushing to her defence.

'Proceed,' he said. 'My help is yours as you know before you begin.'

So it was easy to tell him and she described it all: the first meeting with Hesse; her loneliness; his charm; and how Lady de Clifford had scolded her for being as she said too free with him; and how her mother had overheard the scolding and reprimanded Lady de Clifford. If her daughter wished for friendship with a handsome young man she should have it, said Caroline.

'And Papa, she used to arrange that he should be there when I called; and she helped us to exchange letters.'

The Prince's expression was grave. 'My poor, poor child,' he said, 'in the hands of such a monster!'

Realizing how much easier it was to confess than she had dared hope, she told him of the occasion when her mother had locked them in the bedroom.

He covered his eyes with his hand.

Then he turned and embraced her. 'My poor, poor child, what can I say? I did not think even she could be capable of such conduct.'

'But I do not wish you to be angry with Captain Hesse, Father. He always treated me with the greatest respect, but God knows what would have happened to me if he had not.'

'My dear child, it is Providence alone that has saved you.'

He then went on to talk about her mother—her eccentricities, her madness, her unsuitability to be the Princess of Wales.

'Can you wonder my child that she revolts me?'

And Charlotte could say with sincerity: 'No, Papa. I cannot.'

'She is the most vulgar woman it has ever been my misfortune to meet . . . and think of my fate, child! They married her to me!'

'Oh, my dearest Papa.'

So he embraced her. She was his child now. She agreed with him. She would learn to hate her mother as he did; and that was what he wanted.

In a way, she thought, it is the price he asks for his love.

But the Hesse affair could be settled now. An intimation from the Prince Regent's secretary that he expected the return of his daughter's letters brought an alarmed reply from the Captain that he had no such letters, that he had destroyed at the time of receiving them all those which were not already returned. He was informed that the Duke of York's favour would be withdrawn from him if there was ever a hint of trouble on this score.

'So the Hesse letters,' said Mercer, who managed to get all such information through her various friends in high places, 'need worry us no more. He couldn't return what he hadn't got and didn't want to admit that he had destroyed them at the time of receiving them, which was not a very lover-like action.'

'I begin to believe that men are not the romantic sex,' said Charlotte, and she was thinking of Leopold.

*   *   *

Even the Queen's manner had changed towards Charlotte now; she no longer treated her as a child but gave her a kind of sour and reluctant affection. The Old Girls were positively gushing; and it was quite clear that the period of penance was over.

The Regent told Charlotte that in view of the Hesse affair he thought it was time she was married and he wondered whether she would think again about Orange.

'Papa,' she said, 'I would do anything you ask of me except marry Orange. That is something which I can never do. Pray do not press me.'

And he had the grace to be silent.

Then everything else was forgotten for Napoleon had escaped from Elba. News came that he had reached the Tuileries, that thousands of men were rallying to him with cries of '*Vive l'Empereur*', that Louis XVIII had left Paris and set up his court in Ghent, and the war was about to start again.

The Regent could think of nothing else. He had long conferences with Wellington. Excitement was in the air. Had last year's celebrations been premature?

Then came the famous battle of Waterloo and the defeat of Napoleon who flattered the Regent by an appeal to him: 'I ask for the hospitality of the British nation,' he wrote. 'I place myself under the protection of their laws which I claim from Your Royal Highness as the most powerful, the most constant and the most generous of my enemies.'

The Regent ignored the appeal and Napoleon was exiled to St. Helena.

There was rejoicing throughout the country and the Regent believed, as he did at such times, that the people did not hate him quite so much as they had before.

Charlotte in Love

WHEN the excitement was over the Regent began to think
once more of his daughter. She must be married soon and he
continued to hope for the Orange Alliance. It would be ideal
he reasoned with himself; a Protestant union, alliance with
Holland, and the Princess necessarily spending some time in
her husband's country. If she were not here might not his
subjects forget a little of their animosity towards him because
however much he was seen with his daughter in affectionate
companionship they would persist in believing that he treated
her badly.

'My love,' he said to her, 'I think often of that most infamous business with Captain Hesse and how necessary it is
for you to have a husband. I think it is something that should
not be neglected.'

'But how, Papa,' she asked, 'could my marriage affect it?'

'If it became public knowledge there would be scandals
about you. Only marriage could prevent those scandals. I
know one who would marry you at once. You know you did
listen to slander about him.'

'Not Orange, Papa.'

'They poisoned your mind against him, you know.'

She was stubborn as he remembered her from the past.

'Never, never will I marry Orange,' she declared.

He sighed and patted her hand. In his new rôle it was
necessary to be the indulgent parent.

* * *

He summoned Mercer to Carlton House and hoped that
the flattery of a private *tête-à-tête* would influence her.

'Come and sit beside me, my dear. How beautiful you are looking! I want to tell you how grateful I am to you for being such a good friend to Charlotte.'

Mercer blushed with pleasure; she remarked that Charlotte's friendship was what she valued most in her life.

'It is so comforting for a father to know,' he said. 'Your word carries great weight with her. That infamous affair with Hesse. I shudder to recall it and what might have happened but for the intervention of Providence.'

Mercer agreed solemnly.

'It is necessary for Charlotte to marry to put an end to any gossip which might arise.'

Mercer looked puzzled.

'Yes,' he said firmly. 'Marriage is necessary and I should like to see her affianced to Orange again.'

'Your Highness, she would never agree.'

'Why should she not be persuaded, eh?'

He smiled at her knowing how flattering it must be to be invited into a conspiracy with the Regent. But Mercer had her principles; she was not going to attempt to persuade Charlotte to something with which she did not agree, even at the risk of displeasing the Regent. Moreover she knew it was hopeless.

'I am sure, Sir,' she said, 'that nothing I or anyone could say could possibly make the Princess change her mind. I knew her to be adamant on this point.'

The Prince coolly began to talk of other things. He no longer seemed to find Mercer attractive.

* * *

Charlotte could not understand the change in the Queen. She seemed less harsh, but perhaps she was ill. She still went on in her dreary routine; she was still highly critical, but her manner had seemed to soften in some way. It was almost as though she were sorry for Charlotte. She criticized her manners which were decidedly not royal; she lectured her; but on one occasion she said: 'Your father is eager for the Orange match.' And as Charlotte shrank from her she went on: 'Do not be persuaded, my child, to marry a man you do not like.'

Charlotte was startled.

'One grows old,' said the Queen as though talking to herself. 'One learns lessons. One looks back and sees perhaps more clearly. Don't marry anyone you don't like. You could ask my help.'

Charlotte could not believe that she had heard correctly. But she was elated. The old Begum was with her in this; and if she was, so would her daughters be.

*   *   *

It was pleasant to visit Oatlands again. The Duchess's menagerie had grown since Charlotte had last seen it. She had to become once more accustomed to the smell of animals and not be surprised to find a monkey perching on her shoulder.

She visited the pets' cemetery and saw the new graves; she listened to the Duchess's account of the ailments of this one and the death of that.

Then one day when the Duchess sat in her chair a large cat lying against her feet and a dog on her lap, she said to Charlotte: 'The Duke tells me that a certain young Prince wants to ask your father for your hand in marriage.'

'A certain young Prince?' asked Charlotte alert. 'What . . . who!'

'I thought I would sound you and tell the Duke how you felt. I believe you met him once.'

'Please tell me who he is.'

'He came over here with the Russians. It's Leopold of Saxe-Coburg.'

The Duchess, stroking the dog fondly said: 'I see that the suggestion is not repulsive to you. May I tell the Duke?'

*   *   *

His Serene Highness, Prince Leopold of Saxe-Coburg, feeling cold and ill, left the boat at Dover and stepped into the waiting carriage. Ever since he had received the summons to come to England to 'woo' the Princess Charlotte he had been fighting his wretched physical condition. He remembered her so well. A bouncing exuberant young woman of great charm and some good looks which might be converted into real beauty with grace, poise and decorum. She had attracted him apart from the glittering prospects she could offer a prince whose future hopes without a grand marriage were scarcely promising.

Heiress to the throne of England and more than that—a girl who had excited him from the moment he had first seen her when the Duchess of Oldenburg had hinted that his attentions might be welcomed. How wise he had been to retire from the field when he had done so! Had he stayed he would most certainly, while perhaps making some headway with the Princess, have ruined his chances of being accepted by her father.

Leopold always paused to think before he acted for he had at an early age learned that this was a wise way of life.

And now he was invited to England and such an invitation would never have been made if his success was not almost certain. He had, naturally, to win the regard of Charlotte herself and she was a young woman of some spirit for had she not sent Orange packing, although it was a match on which her father had set his heart!

He wished he did not feel so ill; the pain in his head— 'rheumatism' the doctors called it—made him dizzy; but when it was warmer he would feel better. This February east wind seemed to cut right into his bones. He must remember that he had acquired these ailments on the battlefield and a life of peace and comfort would soon banish them. He was, after all, a young man.

Lord Castlereagh who had come to meet him advised him to bury his face in his fur collar and make sure his travelling coat was wrapped about his legs. They were going to London where His Serene Highness could rest for a day and after that the Prince Regent would receive him at Brighton.

*　　*　　*

Charlotte sat bolt upright in the carriage which was taking her to Brighton. There was the faintest colour in her cheeks, a sign of intense excitement. Ever since she had heard that Leopold was coming to England she had had to restrain her emotion; she did not want everyone to know how elated she was. Leopold! Now she could think of him freely; she did not have to attempt to banish him when he came into her mind. How glad she was that F had not offered for her; what tragedy if she had taken him!

Leopold! The most handsome man she had ever seen. Or he had been. Was he still? That was something she would know in a very short time. She could scarcely wait.

She looked from Lady Ilchester seated beside her—so calm, so unaffected by this great occasion—to Old Famine opposite, bony hands on her lap looking more like a skeleton than ever.

I'm glad, thought Charlotte, that I am not thin, but that would be very unlikely for a member of our family. But does he like thin women? Surely not. Everyone must like a certain amount of plumpness. Was she too plump? In some places perhaps. But Louisa always said she had beautiful arms because they were rounded and white and well-covered. Did he like tall women? Well, she was not tall, and she was not short,

either. And her complexion really was very good—if pale—
for this smooth white skin *was* attractive. F had commented
on it; so had Hesse. But she did not want to think of them.

The Pavilion glittered in the early spring sunshine like an
oriental vision. She hoped her father would be kind to Leopold. He would be openly so because good manners would
demand it, but if she heard that cold note in his voice she
would know that there was going to be trouble.

Oh, dearest Papa, she thought, *please* like Leopold.

And then she laughed at herself. She didn't even know
whether she herself liked him yet. After all he *had* run away
when he had thought there was going to be trouble.

She would remind him of that.

Her father, seated in a chair on wheels which he could
operate himself, was waiting in the Chinese drawing room.
His gout was bad, he told her, and he could not, without great
pain, put his foot to the ground.

She expressed her concern which pleased him; and she *was*
concerned to see him look so old. Even his impeccable clothes
seemed for once to do little for him. She thought he looked as
fat and ugly as old Louis XVIII. But perhaps that was because
she was dreaming of a Prince Charming and with that image
in her mind everyone else looked ugly.

'Well, Charlotte,' said the Regent a little sadly, still thinking of Orange perhaps, 'very shortly this young man will be
here.'

'Yes, Papa.'

'We shall see. We shall see.'

'I am hoping that we are both going to like him,' she said.

'H'm,' said the Regent, inclined to be predisposed not to
like Saxe-Coburg when it should have been Holland

He glanced at Charlotte. He had rarely seen her look so
attractive and she was not uncomely this daughter of his.
Lately she had improved.

Charlotte intercepted his glance and knew what it meant.
She wondered what he would have said if he knew that the
night before she had left Cranbourne Lodge she had put on
an officer's uniform and ridden out into the forest. It was a
daring thing to have done but she had felt the desire to do it.
She had passed through villages and people had glanced casu-
ally at her—an officer from the Guards at Windsor. What
would they have said if they had known that it was the
Princess Charlotte!

A mad thing to do, Mercer would say when told. It was the
sort of thing her mother would have done. But she had had to

do it; she had to curb the wild exultation. And now she wondered why.

Mercer was a little preoccupied with her own affairs, for she had met a fascinating French Count, and Charlotte believed that her friend was very serious about this young man. The last time they had met she had talked of little else. The Comte de Flahault had been an aide-de-camp to Napoleon and had come to England when the Bourbons were restored to the throne. He was very romantic and according to Mercer, madly in love with her.

She will talk of the Comte de Flahault, thought Charlotte, and I of Leopold.

Leopold!

Her heart began to flutter for they were announcing him now.

'His Serene Highness, the Prince Leopold of Saxe-Coburg.' And there he was being presented to her father, every bit as handsome as she remembered him. A little pale, but that made him all the more fascinating.

'Welcome,' said the Regent extending an elegant glittering hand to be kissed. 'I hear you have had a wretched journey.'

Leopold replied in rather halting English (How endearing! thought Charlotte) that the crossing had been bad and the weather inclement.

'I must present you to my daughter, Her Royal Highness, the Princess Charlotte.'

They stood and looked at each other and smiled.

It was, said Charlotte, afterwards to Mercer, love at first sight—or rather a renewal of it because I *knew*—although I tried to delude myself that it was not so—that he was the Only One from the moment I first met him in the Pulteney Hotel.

The formal pleasantries over she was allowed to withdraw with him to a corner of the room that they might exchange a few words while the Regent was in conversation with Lord Castlereagh.

'It gives me great ... how do you say ... to be here?' said Leopold.

'Well, it depends on what you want to say. It could be pleasure, sorrow, happiness or misery. There's a whole choice. The point is are you *glad*?'

'Glad?' His eyes were beautiful, the most beautiful in the world—and serious. She liked his seriousness. F and Hesse had been such *frivolous* men ... and look how they had behaved— Hesse refusing to return her letters and F skulking off and letting everything peter out. Leopold would never refuse to return her letters, not that there would be any need to. They would be together so there would be no necessity to write at all; but if they did he would keep them forever ... his dearest possessions.

'It means you are *pleased*,' she said. 'Are you? Shall we speak in French? That's better. I shall have to teach you English, I can see.'

He told her in French how happy he was to be here, how he had thought of her ever since their last meeting.

'And yet you went away. I asked you to come to Warwick House and you refused my invitation.'

'How I wanted to come! But I looked ahead. I thought there would come a day such as this and I was ready to deny myself the pleasure then that this greater and more lasting happiness might come.'

She clasped her hands together. It was the answer she needed. It explained everything.

She was never one to hide her feelings. 'I am very happy that you have come,' she told him.

Leopold thought her charming; he was feeling better already. She was too impetuous, of course; she flouted etiquette and her manners were boisterous, but a tender restraining hand would remedy that. And she was warm in the affection which she already had for him.

She thought him wonderful, a hero out of a tale of chivalry. She needed so much that love which she had missed all her life. Her mother had failed her and she knew in her heart that she would never have from her father what she longed for; even Mercer now had the Comte de Flahault. And here he was—the perfect knight, the deliverer, the most handsome, delightful and desirable man in the world. Leopold!

The Prince Regent, less enchanted, was murmuring to Castlereagh: 'He's too thin. Wants fattening up and I don't much care for the fellow.'

* * *

But Charlotte cared—how she cared! She bloomed; she looked almost beautiful and in good health. She rode out with Prince Leopold and the people gathered around the carriage to cheer them. Two handsome young people and a wedding soon to take place with the promise of elaborate celebrations and rejoicing.

'Long live Charlotte and Leopold!' they cried.

He was devoted; she was adoring.

'For the first time in my life,' she told Louisa, 'I am truly happy.'

Everyone was delighted except the Regent who could not forget Orange nor really like his daughter's future husband. Leopold was too solemn; he did not laugh easily. 'No humour,' said the Regent. 'Dull fellow.' Leopold was abstemious. He looked on with disapproval at the Regent's drinking habits. 'I never did believe that the consumption of large quantities of wine was good for the body or the mind,' he told Charlotte. 'How I agree with you!' she cried, and told him about Orange coming home from Ascot decidedly drunk. She shivered when she thought how near she had come to marrying Orange. The idea of being denied all this happiness!

She wanted only to please Leopold. She wanted to know his thoughts on everything. She admired so much his industry because he worked hard every day studying English. He was such a paragon of virtue; she had not dreamed there could have been such a person in the world.

He did not like to see her riding horseback. He thought it somewhat unladylike.

She laughed, remembering that ride in military costume. Better not tell him about that.

'Well, my dearest,' she said, 'I shall never ride on horseback again. Why should I when I have my carriage?'

'You are very charming,' said Leopold; and she would have given up all the horses in the world to hear him say that.

She wrote to Mercer. She was the happiest girl on Earth. Nothing else mattered now that she had Leopold. Did Mercer understand her feelings? Did she feel the same for her Comte? Mercer must come at once. She would not be content until her dearest Mercer met her adored Leopold. 'You two must love each other.'

She talked often of Mercer to Leopold.

'She is a little domineering, this lady?' he asked.

'Domineering! Mercer! Oh, Mercer is *always* right . . . and so naturally she says so. She has been my *dearest* friend for years and years. You are going to love her.'

Leopold smiled fondly. Was that an order? he wanted to know.

Yes, it was, declared Charlotte. It was going to be one of those orders which he would not be able to disobey even if he wished.

He was everything that she had hoped for. He was calm and gentle—how calm and how gentle! He never insisted on having his way but he did, because naturally she wished to please him and she already believed that everything Leopold did must be right.

When Louisa told her that it had been said that he was the handsomest Prince in Europe, she replied she was surprised that Louisa should mention something so obvious in that tone of wonder.

Charlotte was happy as never before. Everyone was aware of it, for she could not keep such a secret. Even the Queen smiled rather indulgently; as for the Princesses, they were torn between their delight and their envy. The Regent was glad that Charlotte was not being recalcitrant and that the people were pleased with the match; but he did wish it could have been Young Frog whom he much preferred from every point of view.

The first little check to Charlotte's happiness came with the meeting between Mercer and Leopold. It was incomprehensible. They did not like each other. Mercer who had dared stand up to the Regent was not going to be overawed by a mere Prince of Saxe-Coburg; and to see Charlotte, who had once been so wholeheartedly devoted to herself, so besotted about this young man was mildly irritating.

'You two will love each other.' Such an introduction was almost certain to have the opposite effect.

They measured each other: Prudish, calculating, determined to be the master, thought Mercer. Domineering wanting to take charge of Charlotte, wanting to run the household. We'll have to be rid of her, thought Leopold.

They were coolly polite and Charlotte, to make things easier, asked Mercer how the Comte de Flahault was and when she was going to bring him to see her.

Leopold stiffened and Mercer, sensing this, replied that the Comte was very well and no doubt in due course she would be in a position to present him.

Mercer left earlier than Charlotte had anticipated and as soon as she had gone she cried: 'Is she not the most attractive woman you have ever seen!'

'Certainly not,' replied Leopold. 'Have I not met you?'

Charlotte giggled delightedly. Giggling was a habit, Leopold decided, of which she must be cured. 'But next to me, eh, Leopold . . . next to me, my dear Mercer is the most attractive woman you have ever met?'

'I cannot say that.'

'Oh, Leopold, you are not going to say that you don't think Mercer is beautiful! That lovely red hair!'

'I like best the flaxen.'

'Darling Leopold! But you must love Mercer. I insist.'

'A man cannot love to order even when commanded to do so by one whose all other wishes are law.'

'But why not this wish, eh, Leopold? Answer that!'

He shook his head. 'Alas, it cannot be. I can love one woman only. She is Charlotte.'

Charlotte embraced him fiercely. Her darling, darling Leopold!

'*Doucement, chérie,*' he whispered, '*doucement.*'

She laughed aloud. It was a phrase he used often when attempting to restrain her.

'Now, my dearest Doucement,' she said, 'I am going to make you change your mind. When Mercer brings Flahault . . .'

His expression hardened. 'Such a man cannot be presented to *you.* He was Napoleon's aide. I do not like what I hear of him. I could not consent to such a man approaching my dearest Princess.'

'Leopold! But Mercer *loves* him.'

'So recently an enemy.'

'But that's all over.'

'We have fought cruel battles against this man and his followers who sought to dominate Europe. I cannot receive Flahault. If you wish to . . .'

'Oh, Leopold. It would grieve you very much if I did?'

He nodded sadly.

'I would never grieve you, Leopold. Never. *Never.*'

And she thought: Not even to please Mercer.

Leopold was very tender. He had been warned: 'You should start as you intend to go on. She is one who will try for her own way.'

She was, and he understood his Charlotte well; but he would control her through gentleness, through love.

He was not now seriously concerned about the friendship with Mercer. It should gradually fade away.

*　*　*

Louisa controlled the sewing women who were working as long as the daylight lasted. Charlotte stood in the room while the dresses were fitted—a tiring necessity, but she scarcely noticed it. Her wedding dress would be made of silver lama over silver tissue. She would look beautiful. Her trousseau was the most magnificent collection she had ever seen. There was gold lama over white satin richly embroidered, a glorious white figured tissue, an embroidered gold muslin and many, many more. Her father had presented her with the priceless jewellery which was the property of the Queens of England; she tried them on and gloated over them and thought all the time of Leopold. Her most precious piece of jewellery was the diamond bracelet which he himself had given her. She kissed it a hundred times a day, and told Leopold that it meant more to her than all the rest of the jewels put together.

He nodded gravely, well pleased. 'Dearest Doucement!' she called him.

The government was quibbling over what her allowance should be and where she should live. They decided on Camelford House as a temporary residence, and the Duke and Duchess of York had offered the couple Oatlands for the honeymoon.

Charlotte listened as though in a dream. Nothing mattered; even the fact that she had not seen Mercer did not matter.

It was April; the grass had never been so green in the parks; the birds had never sung so joyously; it was as though the whole world knew that the Princess Charlotte was in love and during this glorious month of April was to marry the husband of her choice.

Married Bliss

I<small>T</small> was the second of May—the great day itself. Crowds had been assembling in the Mall all through the day. Charlotte was at Buckingham House with the Queen; Leopold was at Clarence House; they would meet at Carlton House where the ceremony was to take place.

Charlotte studied her reflection while her women fussed round her.

That radiant image was herself—Princess Charlotte on her wedding day! She looked taller than usual—in fact she scarcely recognized herself; the very faint flush in her usually pale cheeks was very becoming and she was beautiful.

It's my dress, said Charlotte to herself; and indeed she had never possessed such a dress. The silver lama shimmered over the silver tissue slip trimmed with the finest Brussels point lace. Her mantua was held at her throat with a large diamond brooch and on her head she wore an arrangement of roses and diamonds.

Louisa stood beside her, starry-eyed. 'How I wish dear Mrs. Gagarin could have lived to see this day!' Then she wished she had not spoken for she wanted no sad thought to mar the perfection of Charlotte's happiness.

The Queen was to drive with Charlotte to Carlton House and Louisa whispered that it was almost time for them to leave, and how strange it was to see the old Begum looking almost handsome in her magnificent gown of gold tissue with its flounces of silver net and gold lama.

Stepping into the carriage Charlotte felt almost fond of her grandmother. The two eldest Old Girls Augusta and Elizabeth rode with them in the carriage—four scintillating figures of silver and gold.

As soon as their carriage came into sight a great shout went up from thousands of spectators.

'Bless me!' cried Charlotte and the Queen had to put out a hand to restrain her. 'What a multitude! The Park is crowded.'

Charlotte bowed and waved to the people who cheered all the more. Every single cheer was for her although the Queen acknowledged them graciously.

At Carlton House the Regent greeted them; and immediately Charlotte felt less grand for although this was her wedding he must be the most striking figure on the stage. He was wearing the Order of the Garter over the uniform of a Field Marshal—scarlet coat embroidered with gold.

Charlotte was moved as she looked at him and thought how wonderful he was because although he did not in his heart wish for this marriage he gave no sign of it. He was the beneficent god; he was going to give his daughter to Leopold, and he would do so she knew with perfect grace.

'Oh, dearest Papa!' she murmured; and although the Queen might frown at such a departure from etiquette, he did not. He responded immediately with tears in his eyes; 'My precious child, God bless you.'

In the crimson saloon the altar had been set up; the setting was magnificent but Charlotte only saw Leopold, for there he was beside her in the uniform of a British General (her father had recently bestowed this rank on him). His belt glittered with diamonds and on his chest shone the orders which he had won on the field of battle.

The Archbishop of Canterbury performed the ceremony and Charlotte's high young voice as she made her marriage vows was firm and resonant.

'I will!' she cried fervently.

The ceremony was over. She was Leopold's wife.

The Regent held out his arms and embraced her. Their tears mingled.

The Queen was waiting. Charlotte kissed her hand; then she kissed all the Princesses and went among the company receiving their congratulations.

This, she told herself, is the happiest day of my life.

And when they were on their way to Oatlands for the honeymoon she told Leopold so.

*　　*　　*

It was just before midnight when the newly married pair reached Oatlands. Charlotte was so excited that she was chattering all the time. She told him about the eccentric Duchess and that he must not be surprised if he found a troupe of monkeys invading the nuptial chamber. At this she laughed heartily and Leopold permitted himself an indulgent smile.

'*Doucement, my chérie, doucement,*' he murmured.

'Of course I will be *douce* if you wish it, dearest Doucement,' she cried; and she lay against him, silent as they drove up to the house.

*　　*　　*

It was pleasant to wander through the park at Oatlands, to visit the little graves in the animal cemetery, to romp with the dogs, although Leopold pointed out that romping was scarcely correct now that she was a married woman.

'Who cares about being correct. I'm happy, dearest Leo.'

'I'm delighted, my darling,' replied Leopold, 'but in your position, alas, you must be correct as well as happy. And, dearest, do you think you should call me Leo in front of the servants?'

'What should I call you? My dearest one? My darling *Doucement*?'

'You are incorrigible.'

'Who would not be, married to the most handsome man in the world.'

He was delighted with her. Her exuberance was so spontaneous; but it must be curbed of course, for it was so unsuitable.

'My love,' he said, 'in spite of being the most delightful Princess in the world you are also one of the greatest heiresses. Should you not remember this?'

'I want to remember nothing but that I am my darling Leo's wife. Leo, Leo, Leo!' she laughed at him mockingly. 'But not in front of the servants. What, my dearest, do you wish me to call you in front of the servants?'

'In their presence and on all public occasions I think you should refer to me as Coburg.'

She laughed hilariously. 'Coburg indeed. My dearest Coburg! Coburg! The way in which I will say it it will sound even more affectionate than Leo.'

'But you will say it, my love . . . to please me.'

'Dearest Leo Coburg, I would *die* to please you.'

*　　*　　*

The Prince Regent rode over to Oatlands to see how the honeymoon was progressing. For the first time in her life Charlotte would have preferred him not to bestow a mark of affection.

He could not come without a certain amount of pomp and he broke up the honeymoon intimacy of Oatlands.

He held out his arms and embraced her.

'I see that I have intruded into paradise,' he said with a Jove-like smile.

'Dearest Papa, it is so good of you to come.'

'My only child I have been thinking of you.'

He wrinkled his nose. The smell of animals offended him. One of the Duchess's dogs came to sniff at those highly polished boots.

Charlotte whistled to the dog and the Regent winced; he noticed that Leopold was not always pleased at Charlotte's stable-boy manners. The fellow had some dignity, he thought —perhaps too much for an insignificant princeling but now he was basking in the reflected glory of a future Queen of England. He couldn't like him, however. Whenever he saw him he thought of all the trouble over Orange and how much he would have preferred a Dutch match.

Charlotte slipped her arm through her father's and his good humour was restored; he liked outward displays of affection; and it was good for people to see them after all the scandal there had been over family quarrels.

'Being a wife becomes you.'

'And, er . . . er . . . Coburg?'

So it was Coburg! thought the Prince. Quite formal. Good God, has Leopold been schooling her already?

They sat in the drawing room while refreshment was brought and he noticed how little Leopold drank. It was almost a reproach to the Regent, but he was determined to remain in good humour. He said that Leopold had looked well in her General's uniform and had he been aware of the uniforms of the guard? He then went on to discuss these uniforms in detail which set Charlotte yawning and longing for his departure, while Leopold listened intently and feigned an interest.

'Camelford House is not really suitable,' said the Regent. 'You must go out and look at that place at Esher. I think it would be an ideal spot. You will probably wish to make changes there and if you need any advice I shall be pleased to give it.'

He was off on another of his favourite topics, the additions to Carlton House and the Pavilion. He gave Leopold an account of the Pavilion's history, how it was a near-derelict old farmhouse when his major-domo Weltje had discovered it.

The visit seemed to last a long time.

When he left the Regent said playfully to Leopold, 'Be careful or she will govern you. You should begin as you intend to go on.'

'Dearest Papa,' replied Charlotte, 'there is no question of one governing another. I shall do as Coburg wishes because it is my deepest pleasure to do so.'

'Spoken like a loving bride,' declared the Regent; and he added cynically to himself: In the first week of her honeymoon.

But he was sad when he left them, thinking of those days of ecstasy which had followed a certain ceremony in Maria Fitzherbert's house in Park Street.

He said then as he had said thousands of times before: I should never have left Maria.

*   *   *

'When you are happy there is nothing to write about,' said Charlotte to Louisa.

She was thinking of Mercer, who had once meant so much to her. It was an excuse perhaps for not writing, but Mercer was surely not showing her usual good sense for she had written of her intentions to marry the Comte de Flahault, a man of whom Leopold could not approve. Perhaps it was because she had never met anyone of Leopold's profound good sense that she had been so impressed by Mercer's. At least Mercer would be so busy with her own affairs and perhaps she would not notice the absence of Charlotte's letters. In the past the correspondence had been so regular. But how different it was when one was married!

It was only natural in this most perfect of unions that the most desired event should occur almost immediately. Charlotte was pregnant.

'We will not mention it,' said cautious Leopold, 'until we are absolutely certain.'

Darling Doucement, he knew his Charlotte's weaknesses. She would have announced to the entire household and in no time there would have been cartoons and lampoons circulating throughout the country. It was a matter, in any case, said Leopold, that he would not care to be the subject for crudities.

How she agreed with him! And though bubbling over with excitement she managed to suppress it.

It was not easy, particularly as, at Camelford House, which was on the corner of Oxford Street and Park Lane, they were in London and it was necessary for them to show themselves frequently. When they went to see Mr. Kean perform in *Bertram* the ovation was the biggest she had ever heard. How proud she had been of Leopold-Coburg for the occasion—in his General's uniform and all the decorations which proclaimed his bravery displayed on his chest.

But when she and Leopold were to see Mrs. Siddons in the role of Lady Macbeth, for which she was famous, Charlotte had felt suddenly unwell; and it had been necessary to cancel the arrangement.

The first shadow then touched the ideal marriage. Charlotte had a miscarriage. She was not very ill for the young life had scarcely begun, but her doctors ordered her to rest and the papers discovered the reason. The people were sorry and they loved her more than ever.

Leopold consoled her. It was but a slight misfortune, and they were both so young.

*   *   *

Charlotte hoped she would recover in time to attend the marriage of the Princess Mary to the Duke of Gloucester. She was delighted that this was at last to take place for she had felt many an uneasy qualm at the trick she had played on Mary when she had pretended that she had wanted Silly Billy for herself.

But when the day came her doctors advised her that it would be unwise for her to attend.

She was petulant. 'But this,' she said, 'is the marriage of my dear old aunt. I must go.'

The doctors shook their heads..

'I *shall* go!' she declared.

Leopold, who was present, quietly signed to the doctors to leave.

'My dearest,' he said when they were alone, 'you should obey the doctors.'

'I feel very well and I must go to Mary's wedding ... if I don't she will think it is because I still have a fancy for Silly Billy.' That made her laugh that loud laugh which always made Leopold wince a little.

Then she told him, with much laughter, of how when they

had been trying to force her on Orange she had pretended she
would have Gloucester instead.

'So you see, dearest Leo, I must go to this wedding.'

'I do not see that it is necessary.'

'Oh, my darling sober old Doucement, you must allow me
to know best about my own family.'

'But, dearest Charlotte, I do not accept that you know the
state of your health better than the doctors.'

'A lot of old women! I am going in any case. Poor Mary,
she has waited years and years for this. When she came yesterday she described her wedding dress to me. It's very fine ... as
fine as mine and very like it, too. Silver tissues and scalloped
lama and Brussels point lace. Her headdress is diamonds, too.
She will look quite lovely, in spite of her age. Poor old girl!
And I am sure Silly Billy will be proud of her.'

Leopold coughed lightly—a sign of disapproval. 'Charlotte,
you should not talk of our royal kinsmen in this way.'

'Oh, but I do, Leo darling, and as you have discovered I do
a great deal that I should not. I always have.'

'There is no reason why you should continue to perform
these not very admirable acts.'

'Leo, darling, I love the way you talk ... as though you are
addressing the House of Commons instead of your adoring
wife.'

'I am not sure that she does adore me.'

'Leo, how can you utter such perfidy!'

'She does not please me.'

'How can you say that? Ah, I know what it is. You have
another woman. Did I see you glancing admiringly at Wellington's sister-in-law?'

'You are being foolish now. She is an old woman nearly
twenty years older than I.'

'That's no reason why you shouldn't admire her. Papa
always likes mature women. Perhaps princes do. Oh, Leopold,
am I too *young* for you?'

'Sometimes I think this inconsequential behaviour may be
due to youth.'

She was angry suddenly. Was it true that he had liked
Wellington's sister-in-law? Oh, she couldn't bear it! And she
must go to Mary's wedding. How could she possibly not see
her poor old aunt, after waiting all these years, married to
solemn old Silly Billy! She could imagine herself in Mary's
place for although she had not been serious, some people had
thought she was.

'I am going to Mary's wedding,' she said coldly.

Leopold stood up, clicked his heels, bowed and departed.

* * *

The first quarrel. She could not endure it. Leopold was displeased with her. He had never before looked at her so coldly.

Yet if I wish to go, I'll go, she told herself. He must remember that even though he is my husband *I* shall be the Queen of England and he merely my Consort.

What should she wear for the wedding? A very special dress. Gold lama—no longer silver because now she was a married woman.

But there was no comfort in thinking of her dress, no comfort in making Leopold realize that she would have her own way. In fact, she did not want her own way. In her heart she knew that she only wished to please Leopold.

Yet, I must remember that one day I shall be Queen and he must remember it too.

What a miserable day! He avoided her; and when she saw him in the presence of others he seemed aloof.

He was right, of course. The doctors had said she should not go. How foolish she was and how disappointed Leopold must be in her.

She called to one of her women: 'Go and tell ... go and *ask* the Prince of Saxe-Coburg if he will come to me here ... as soon as he finds it convenient to do so.'

He was with her almost immediately.

'Charlotte.'

'Oh, Leo ... dearest Doucement, how stupid I am! How right you were to let me know it. What can I say? I shall not go to Mary's wedding. It would be such folly. Oh, Leopold, can you forgive me for my stupid ways?'

Leopold could and did.

He was grave and tender. He loved his dearest Charlotte more than ever; he admired her courage in admitting that she was wrong. He was so proud of her.

'Then it is as it was ... before? Oh, Leopold, that makes me so happy. I was thinking this ... this difference between us was going on and on and that nothing would ever be the same again.'

'We must never allow differences to go on and on.'

'We must never allow differences, dearest Leopold.'

He smiled his grave judicious smile. 'They might occur, but let us make a vow now that we will never let the sun set on any misunderstanding ... however small.'

'Oh, do let us do that,' she said, and they took their solemn vow.

So Charlotte did not attend the Princess Mary's wedding to the Duke of Gloucester.

*   *   *

Claremont was the perfect setting for her idyllic marriage. Charlotte decided. Here she and Leopold could shut themselves away from the world and live as she called it, like simple folk.

She wanted to live quietly, in a domestic fashion, she told Leopold. She wanted to know what went on in her household—like any housewife. He smiled indulgently. She was becoming more docile every day.

They had both loved Claremont from the moment they had seen it. The situation in the beautiful vale of Esher was perfect. The Earl of Clare had bought the estate from Sir John Vanbrugh and built this house on it giving it his name. When Charlotte had first seen it she had run excitedly up the thirteen steps of the entrance. She had fondly touched the Corinthian pillars which held up the pediment, and she had known, she told Leopold in her impulsive way, that she had come home.

There were eight very large rooms on the ground floor and she had run through them delightedly. She felt like an ordinary housewife, she told her husband, choosing the home in which she was to bring up her family.

Leopold had restrained her in his usual tender way. She should be happy in her home of course, but it was not wise for the future Queen of England to think too frequently of herself as an ordinary housewife.

'Nor an important prince as an ordinary husband,' she went on. 'And indeed you are not that. You are the best husband in the world.'

Then she was throwing her arms about him, kissing him there in the drawing room of Claremont where anyone could have seen.

She laughed at him indulgently. How she enjoyed teasing him!

Claremont, she thought, is the most lovely house in the world because no one has ever been as happy as I am going to be in it.

She loved the half mile drive and the first sight of the house on a slight incline, she loved the island on the lake immediately inside the drive; she loved the old woman who lived in the lodge and who had been so terrified when she knew the Princess was coming to Claremont because she feared that she would be turned out. Charlotte had gone in person to reassure her, and when she discovered that she took pupils to help to keep herself and her blind husband, Charlotte's heart was touched.

'You will find me your friend,' she declared, 'and you shall remain here as long as you wish. It pleases me to see you so devoted to your afflicted husband.'

They were the happiest days of her life, she declared; even happier than those of the honeymoon. *Then* she had had to learn so much. Now she promised herself, she had learned.

*   *   *

She and Leopold were happy at Claremont. They lived as simply as possible. Charlotte drove about the countryside, interested herself in the people and was delighted when it was possible to bring some comfort to her poor neighbours. She even went to the kitchens and concerned herself with the buying and cooking of food.

Most of all she enjoyed looking after Leopold. He was amused by her fussing. She insisted on airing his linen. 'How otherwise do I know it is properly aired?' she demanded. 'And do not forget when you first arrived you had that dreadful rheumatism!' She herself would test the hot water which was brought for his bath, and very often when he went out shooting with the members of his household she would prepare the food he would have on his return. She took a great delight in combing his hair.

One could not of course live the simple life all the time. There were visitors from London including the Regent himself.

'But,' said Charlotte, 'having had our ceremonies it makes me return all the more gleefully to the simple life.'

And soon she was happier still; for she discovered that she was to have a child.

'This time,' said Leopold, 'we must make sure that nothing goes wrong.'

He lifted a warning finger, which she seized and bit—just to shock him a little and to amuse him too. For however he tried to change her, she reminded him, she would remain Charlotte, the impulsive hoyden.

He pretended to sigh and murmured: 'I suppose it is so.'

She could not resist writing to Mercer now and then, for

after all it was a habit of years; and Leopold had not said it would displease him if she wrote.

Poor Mercer, who was married to that dreadful Comte de Flahault, could not enjoy this bliss.

'This marriage makes my whole happiness,' she wrote, and happily she signed herself Charlotte Coburg.

The End

ALL was in readiness. Soon, thought Charlotte, my baby will be born. She hoped for a son . . . a son for England. But did she really care? This would be the ultimate happiness, her own child; she, the young Princess to be a mother.

'I can scarcely wait for the day,' she told Leopold.

'Patience!' he warned, and that made her laugh aloud.

'Really, how *can* one be patient at such a time?'

'One not only can but one must,' was the answer.

Dearest Leopold! Right as usual!

The baby's layette was folded and lay in readiness in the drawers, delicately scented; she took out the little garments and folded them again. Sir Richard Croft the well-known *accoucheur* was to be in attendance with Dr. Baillie, one of the most important doctors in England.

Leopold said that he was going to have his own physician, Dr. Stockmar, at hand in case he should be needed. Leopold had great faith in Stockmar and Charlotte liked him; she had had many a conversation with him during the preceding months and she had been amused at first because she sensed his disapproval of her boisterous ways. His stern Germanic ideals, so like Leopold's, made him look for more modesty in a woman, even though she was a princess. But in time dear Stocky as she called him had succumbed to her charms and was now one of her ardent admirers.

'He can look after *you*, dearest Doucement,' she announced. 'For I do declare that from the fluster you are sometimes in over this affair it would seem that it is your ordeal rather than mine.'

In addition to the doctors there was to be Mrs. Griffiths—an excellent nurse recommended by the doctors.

'And so,' sighed Charlotte, 'all we can do now is wait, patiently if possible and if not . . . well, as you so rightly point out, my dearest, wait in any case.'

*   *   *

The Queen called at Claremont. She said she wished to assure herself that all was well with her dearest granddaughter.

Charlotte sat with her in the drawing room overlooking the Park and the Queen talked of confinements of which Charlotte conceded, she must be very knowledgeable, having given birth to fifteen children.

'You have the best possible doctors,' said the Queen, 'and Griffiths is excellent. I have made absolutely sure that you are in good hands.'

'I feel very cherished, Your Majesty.'

'It is a very important occasion. The child you are to bear will one day be a King or Queen of England.'

'It's a sobering thought, Grandmamma.'

'I am glad,' commented the Queen, with a touch of asperity, 'to see you serious.'

'I have changed. Grandmamma.'

'I am glad to hear it. I shall go to Bath very relieved.'

'And I shall pray that the waters have the desired effect and you will come back in much better health.'

'If the great event should occur I shall return immediately. We have taken three houses at Sydney Place near the Parade. Elizabeth is coming with me and will be such a comfort. But I am going to insist that Sir Richard Croft moves in to Claremont House without delay. Griffiths too.'

'We could get them here in a very short time, Grandmamma.'

'No doubt. No doubt. But I prefer them to *be* here and I have given orders that it shall be. They will arrive tomorrow.'

The autocratic old Begum! thought Charlotte almost tenderly.

Becoming a mother made one see other people in a different light. Or perhaps she did not care any more that she was treated like a child, who could not make her own decisions.

All she cared about was Leopold and the child that was soon to be born.

*   *   *

She was glad that Mrs. Griffiths had come for she took an immediate liking to her. The nurse was respectful yet firm and she cared passionately for babies and would talk about them by the hour.

She told Charlotte what to expect when the pains started, and trusted that the labour would be over quickly.

'Don't worry,' laughed Charlotte. 'I promise not to bawl or shriek.'

Mrs. Griffiths said: 'Your Highness will have the very best of doctors and that is a mighty relief.'

And every day they waited for the pains to start; in the stables the horses were ready and the grooms were on the alert so that the news that the birth was imminent could be carried round to those who should be present on this important occasion.

The days began to pass. Charlotte grew larger but there was no sign of the birth.

* * *

At last on a misty November day the pains began.

The message went to the grooms in the stables who sped off in various directions that the privy councillors and the Archbishop of Canterbury might be present at the birth. The latter had been staying with the Bishop of London at Fulham, this palace being nearer than the Archbishop's own residence at Canterbury.

Very soon the carriages of the Archbishop, the Lord Chancellor and other ministers were on the road to Claremont.

They expected on arrival to hear that the child was born but the Princess's ordeal was slow and laborious.

* * *

In the library which adjoined the Princess's bedroom the eminent assembly waited for the cry of a child and the inevitable summons.

They went on waiting.

'It's slow,' said Lord Eldon.

The Archbishop commented that he had been afraid he would not arrive in time but it seemed there was time to spare.

'Sir Richard has told us that all is going as well as we could possibly wish,' replied Eldon.

The waiting continued.

The day was well advanced when Sir Richard Croft, looking less confident than previously, announced that he and Dr. Baillie had decided to call in Dr. Sims, the well-known *accoucheur*.

Dr. Sims arrived at three o'clock the following morning while the birth of the child was still awaited.

* * *

All through the day Charlotte's labour persisted. Everything was not as it should be. No one could shut their eyes to that now. The doctors were giving out reassuring bulletins but in the streets the people stood in little crowds, silent and solemn.

Poor Princess, what an ordeal for her. But it must soon be over now.

At nine o'clock the child was delivered—a boy, perfectly formed but dead.

* * *

Leopold was at her bedside. She smiled at him.

'So I have failed you,' she said.

He shook his head, tears in his eyes. 'My darling, you were so brave. Only one thing matters, you are here with me. I feared . . . how much I feared.'

'Well, then I find I am not so unhappy. It will be as it was before and next time there will be a living boy.'

'My dearest . . . don't speak of it.'

'I believe you suffered more than I.'

Mrs. Griffiths came to the bedside with some chicken broth. 'How smart you are looking, Griffiths,' said Charlotte. 'I see you have changed your dress. Why didn't you put on the silk one? You know it is my favourite.'

'I will wear it, Your Highness, on the day you leave your bed.'

'I shall keep you to that. When shall I be able to comb Leopold's hair again?'

'When you have drunk this nice chicken broth and grown strong again.'

'Griffiths treats me as though I'm a child,' she said with a grimace.

It was the old Charlotte. Leopold was deeply moved she saw and she asked him why.

'Because I feared so much . . .'

'Dear Leopold, so you truly love me?'

He could not speak—he, the calm, the precise one, found that words choked him.

She was happy to lie there holding his hand, dreaming of the future. They would have children. Perhaps she had not taken enough care. Next time it would be different. She would make him understand this when she was stronger.

Now she would have him put his head on the pillow beside her. 'I feel happier that way,' she said.

And they stayed like this for some minutes when suddenly she cried out.

'It's a pain, Leopold . . . such a pain . . .'

Leopold ran from the room to call the doctors.

*   *   *

The doctors were round the bed. The Princess's body was as cold as ice and they could not bring warmth back to it. They gave her hot wine and brandy; they applied hot flannels and bottles of hot water, to no effect.

Leopold stood by the bed gazing at her in an agony of distress. Charlotte's eyes never left him and now and then she made as though to stretch out her hand to him.

She said to Sir Richard Croft: 'Am I in danger?'

'If you lie still and remain calm there will be none.'

She smiled wanly. 'I think I know what you mean,' she said, and she thought: This is the end then. This is where it all stops. My divided love for my parents, my destiny . . . I will never be like Queen Elizabeth now. All the time Fate was mocking me. I was learning to be a queen who never would be. And Leopold . . . who made me happy at last, my dearest Leopold will be all alone.

She wanted him to know what he had done for her, how he had brought her that security of love for which she had striven all her life . . . twenty-one years of living. Leopold, she thought, I am leaving you now.

She stretched out her hand. He took it and murmured her name.

But she could scarcely see him now.

Leopold, gazing at her, saw the glazed expression in her eyes, heard the death rattle in her throat.

Time was playing strange tricks. He was in the Pulteney Hotel; he was handing her into a carriage, she was laughing at him, teasing her Doucement. Hundreds of pictures of Charlotte, anything to shut out the Charlotte he was seeing now.

Sir Richard Croft laid his hand on his shoulder.

'Your Highness,' he said, 'it is over.'

And Leopold threw himself on to his knees, frantically kissing her hands as though by so doing he could bring her back to life.

BIBLIOGRAPHY

Letters of the Princess Charlotte — Edited by Arthur Aspinall

A Biographical Memoir of Princess Charlotte of Wales and Saxe-Coburg (1817)

The Life of the Late Princess Charlotte (1818)

National and Domestic History of England — William Hickman Smith Aubrey

The Years of Endurance — Sir Arthur Bryant

George III—His Court and Family — Henry Colburn

The Reign of Beau Brummell — Willard Connely

The Life and Times of George IV — The Rev. George Croly

The Good Queen Charlotte — Percy Fitzgerald

The Life of George IV — Percy Fitzgerald

George IV — Roger Fulford

Memoirs of Her Late Royal Highness Princess Charlotte of Wales and Saxe-Coburg — Thomas Green

Unsuccessful Ladies — Jane-Eliza Hasted

Memoirs of Charlotte Augusta, Princess of Wales — Robert Huish

The Princess Charlotte of Wales — Mrs. Herbert Jones

The Great Corinthian — Doris Leslie

George IV — Shane Leslie

The Loves of Florizel — Philip Lindsay

The First Gentleman of Europe — Lewis Melville

An Injured Queen Caroline of Brunswick — Lewis Melville

Queen Caroline — Sir Edward Parry

The Beloved Princess — Charles E. Pearce

The Four Georges — Sir Charles Petrie

The House of Hanover — Alvin Redman

*The Ill-fated Princess
Life of Charlotte, Daughter of the Prince Regent* — G. J. Renier

Caroline, the Unhappy Queen — Lord Russell of Liverpool

George, Prince and Regent — Philip W. Sergeant

The Dictionary of National Biography — Edited by Leslie Stephen and Sir Sidney Lee

Daughter of England — D. M. Stuart

Portrait of the Prince Regent — D. M. Stuart

The Four Georges — W. M. Thackeray

British History — John Wade

A Brief Memoir of the Princess Charlotte of Wales — The Lady Rose Weigall

Mrs. Fitzherbert and George IV — W. H. Wilkins